SEEDS

Virginia Andrews [illegible] studied art at college and during the Sixties worked as a fashion illustrator, commercial artist, and later a portrait painter.

Flowers in the Attic was based on a true story and become an immediate bestseller on publication in 1979, receiving tremendous acclaim on both sides of the Atlantic and being adapted for the big screen. It was followed by more books about the Dollanganger family, *Petals on the Wind*, *If There be Thorns*, *Seeds of Yesterday*, and a prequel to *Flowers in the Attic*, *Garden of Shadows*. In addition to these novels, she is also the author of *My Sweet Audrina* and the Casteel family saga: *Heaven*, *Dark Angel*, *Fallen Hearts*, *Gates of Paradise* and *Web of Dreams*, all set in Virginia Andrews' home state, West Virginia, and in Boston.

Virginia Andrews died in 1986, and left a considerable amount of unpublished material.

By the same author

Flowers in the Attic
If There Be Thorns
Petals on the Wind
My Sweet Audrina
Seeds of Yesterday
Heaven
Fallen Hearts
Garden of Shadows
Gates of Paradise
Web of Dreams

VIRGINIA ANDREWS

Seeds of Yesterday

HARPER

This novel is entirely a work of fiction.
The names, characters and incidents portrayed in it are the work of the author's imagination. Any resemblance to actual persons, living or dead, events or localities is entirely coincidental.

Harper
An imprint of HarperCollins*Publishers*
77–85 Fulham Palace Road,
Hammersmith, London W6 8JB

www.harpercollins.co.uk

This paperback edition 2008
1

First published in Great Britain by
Fontana 1984

ISBN 978-0-00-783868-4

Set in Sabon

Printed and bound in Great Britain by
Clays Ltd, St Ives plc

BOOK ONE

FOXWORTH HALL

And so it came to pass the summer when I was fifty-two and Chris was fifty-four that our mother's promise of riches, made long ago when I was twelve and Chris was fourteen, was at last realized.

We both stood and stared at that huge, intimidating house I'd never expected to see again. Even though it was not an exact duplicate of the original Foxworth Hall, still I quivered inside. What a price both Chris and I had paid to stand where we were now, temporary rulers over this mammoth house that should have been left in charred ruins. Once, long ago, I'd believed he and I would live in this house like a princess and prince, and between us we'd have the golden touch of King Midas, only with more control.

I no longer believed in fairy tales.

As vividly as if it had happened only yesterday, I remembered that chill summer night full of mystical moonlight and magical stars in a black velvet sky when we'd first approached this place, expecting only the best to happen. We had found only the worst.

At that time Chris and I had been so young, innocent and trusting, believing in our mother, loving her, believing as she led us and our five-year-old twin brother and sister through the dark and somehow scary night, to that huge house called Foxworth Hall, that all our future days would be coloured green for wealth and yellow for happiness.

What blind faith we'd had when we tagged along behind.

Locked away in that dim and dreary upstairs room, playing in that dusty, musty attic, we'd sustained ourselves by our belief in our mother's promises that someday Foxworth

Hall and all its fabulous riches would be ours. However, despite all her promises, a cruel and heartless old grandfather's bad but tenacious heart refused to stop beating in order to let four young and hopeful hearts live, and so we'd waited, and waited, until more than three long-long years passed, and Momma failed to keep her promise.

And not until the day she died – and her will was read – did Foxworth Hall fall under our control. She had left the mansion to Bart, her favourite grandson, my child by her own second husband, but until he was twenty-five, the estate was held in trust by Chris.

Foxworth Hall had been ordered reconstructed before she moved to California to find us, but it wasn't until after her death that the final touches were completed on the new Foxworth Hall.

For fifteen years the house stood empty, overseen by caretakers, legally supervised by a staff of attorneys who had either written or called Chris long distance to discuss with him the problems that arose. A waiting mansion, grieving, perhaps, waiting for the day when Bart decided he'd go there to live, as we'd always presumed one day he'd do. Now he was offering this house to us for a short while, to be our own until he arrived and took over.

There was always a catch in every lure offered, whispered my ever-suspicious mind. I felt the lure now, reaching out to ensnare us again. Had Chris and I travelled such a long road only to come full circle, back to the beginning?

What would be the catch this time?

No, no, I kept telling myself, my suspicious, ever-doubting nature was getting the better of me. We had the gold without the tarnish . . . we did! We did have to realize our just rewards some day. The night was over – our day had finally come, and we were now standing in the full sunlight of dreams come true.

To actually be here, planning to live in that restored home, put sudden familiar gall in my mouth. All my pleasure vanished. I was actually realizing a nightmare that wouldn't vanish when I opened my eyes.

I threw off the feeling, smiled at Chris, squeezed his

fingers and stared at the restored Foxworth Hall, risen from the ashes of the old, to confront and confound us again with its majesty, its formidable size, its sense of abiding evil, its myriad windows with their black shutters like heavy lids over stony dark eyes. It loomed high and wide, spreading over several acres in magnificent but intimidating grandeur. It was larger than most hotels, formed in the shape of a giant T, only crossed on each end to give it an enormous centre section, with wings jutting off north and south, east and west.

It was constructed of rosy pink bricks. The many black shutters matched the roof of slate. Four impressive white Corinthian columns supported a gracious front portico. A sunburst of stained glass was over the black double front doors. Huge brass escutcheon plates decorated the doors and made what could have been plain rather elegant and less somber.

This might have cheered me if the sun hadn't suddenly taken a fugitive position behind a passing dark cloud. I glanced upward at a sky turned stormy and foreboding, heralding rain and wind. The trees in the surrounding forest began to sway so that birds took alarmed flight and screeched as they flew for cover. The green lawns so immaculately kept were quickly littered with broken twigs and falling leaves, and the blooming flowers in geometrically laid-out beds were lashed to the ground unmercifully.

I trembled and thought: *Tell me again, Christopher Doll, that it's going to work out fine. Tell me again, for I don't really believe now that the sun has gone and the storm is drawing nearer.*

He glanced upward, too, sensing my growing anxiety, my unwillingness to go through with this, despite my promise to Bart, my second son. Seven years ago his psychiatrists had told us their treatment was successful and that Bart was quite normal and could live out his life without needing therapy on a regular basis.

To give me comfort Chris's arm lifted to encircle my shoulders. His lips lowered to brush my cheek. 'It's going to work out for all of us. I know it will. We're no longer the Dresden dolls trapped in an upstairs room, dependent on our elders to do the right thing. Now we're the adults, in control of our lives. Until Bart reaches the stated age of inheritance, you and I are the owners. Dr and Mrs Christopher Sheffield from Marin County, California, and no one will know us as brother and sister. They won't suspect that we are truly descendants of the Foxworths. We have left all troubles behind us. Cathy, this is our chance. Here, in this house, we can undo all the harm done to us and to our children, especially Bart. We'll rule not with steel wills and iron fists, as was Malcolm's way, but with love, compassion and understanding.'

Because Chris had his arm about me, holding me tight against his side, I gained strength enough to look at the house in a new light. It was beautiful. For Bart's sake we'd stay until his twenty-fifth birthday, and then Chris and I would take Cindy with us and fly to Hawaii, where we'd always wanted to live out our lives, near the sea and white beaches. Yes, that's the way it was supposed to be. The way it had to be. Smiling, I turned to Chris. 'You're right. I am not afraid of this house, or any house.' He chuckled and lowered his arm to my waist, pressuring me forward.

Soon after finishing high school, my first son Jory had flown to New York City to join his grandmother, Madame Marisha. There, in her ballet company, he'd soon been noticed by the critics and was given leading roles. His childhood sweetheart, Melodie, had flown east to join Jory.

At the age of twenty, my Jory had married Melodie, who was only a year younger. The pair of them had struggled and worked to reach the top. They were now the most notable ballet team in the country, a team of perfect, beautiful co-ordination, as if they could read each other's mind and signal with a flash of their eyes. For five years they'd been riding the crest of success. Every performance brought rave reviews from the critics and from the public. Television exposure had given them a larger audience than they could ever have gained by personal appearances alone.

Madame Marisha had died in her sleep two years ago, though we could console ourselves by knowing she'd lived to be eighty-seven and had worked up until the very day she passed away.

Around the age of seventeen, my second son Bart had transformed almost magically from a backward student into the most brilliant one in his school. By that time Jory had flown on to New York. I had thought at the time that Jory's absence had brought Bart out of his shell and made him interested in learning. Just two days ago, he had graduated from Harvard Law School, the valedictorian of his class.

Chris and I had joined Melodie and Jory in Boston, and in the huge auditorium of Harvard Law School we'd watched Bart receive his law degree. Only Cindy, our adopted daughter, was not there. She was at her best friend's house in South Carolina. It had given me new pain to know that Bart could not let go of his envy of a girl who'd done her best to win his approval – especially when he'd done nothing to win hers. It gave me additional pain to know that Cindy couldn't let go of her dislike of Bart long enough to help him celebrate.

'No!' she'd shouted over the telephone, 'I don't care if he did send me an invitation! It's just his way of showing off. He can put ten degrees behind his name and I still won't admire or like him – not after all he did to me. Explain to Jory and Melodie why, so their feelings won't be hurt. But you won't have to explain to Bart. He'll know.'

I'd sat between Chris and Jory and stared, amazed that a son who was so reticent at home, so moody and unwilling to communicate, could rise to the top of his class and be named valedictorian. His impassioned words created a mesmerizing spell. I glanced at Chris, who looked proud enough to burst before he grinned at me.

'Wow, who would have guessed? He's terrific, Cathy. Aren't you proud? I know I am.'

Yes, yes, of course, I was very proud to see Bart up there. Still, I knew the Bart behind the podium was not the Bart we all knew at home. Maybe he was safe now. Completely normal – his doctors had said so.

To my way of thinking, there were many small indications that Bart had not changed as dramatically as his doctors thought. He'd said just before we parted, 'You must be there, Mother, when I come into my own.' Not a word about Chris being there with me. 'It's important to me that you be there.'

Always he had to force himself to speak Chris's name. 'We'll invite Jory and his wife down, too, and, of course, Cindy.' He'd grimaced just to say her name. It was beyond me how anyone could dislike a girl as pretty and sweet as our beloved adopted daughter. I couldn't have loved Cindy more if she'd been flesh of my flesh, and blood of my Christopher Doll. In a way, since she'd come to us at the age of two, she was our child, the only one we could claim as truly belonging to both of us.

Cindy was sixteen now, and much more voluptuous than I'd been at her age. But Cindy hadn't been as deprived as I. Her vitamins had come from fresh air and sunshine, both of which had been denied four imprisoned children. Good food and exercise . . . she'd had the best. We'd had the worst.

Chris asked if we were going to stay out here all day and wait for pelting rain to drench us both before we went inside. He tugged me forward, urging me on with his cheerful confidence.

Gradually, step by slow step, as the thunder began to crash and swiftly come closer, with the swollen, heavy sky zigzagging with frightening electrical bolts, we approached the grand portico of Foxworth Hall.

I began to notice details I'd missed before. The portico floor was made of mosaic tiles in three shades of red intricately laid to form a sunburst pattern that matched the glass sunburst over the double front doors. I looked at those sunburst windows and rejoiced. They hadn't been here before. Perhaps it was just as Chris had predicted. It wouldn't be the same, just as no two snowflakes were the same.

Then I was frowning, for to all intents and purposes, who every saw the differences in falling snowflakes?

'Stop looking for something to steal the pleasure from this day, Catherine. I see it on your face, in your eyes. I vow on my word of honour that we will leave this house as soon as Bart has his party and fly on to Hawaii. If a hurricane comes and blows a tidal wave over our home once we're there, it will be because you expect that to happen.'

He made me laugh. 'Don't forget the volcano,' I said with a small giggle. 'It could hurl hot lava at us.' He grinned and playfully spanked my bottom.

'Quit! Please, please. August tenth will see us on our plane – but a hundred to one you'll worry about Jory, about Bart, and wonder what he's doing all alone in this house.'

That's when I remembered something forgotten until now. Waiting inside Foxworth Hall was the surprise Bart had promised would be there. How strangely he'd looked when he'd said that.

'Mother, it will blow your mind when you see – ' He'd paused, smiled and looked uneasy. 'I've flown down there each summer just to check things over and see that the house wasn't being neglected and left to mould and decay. I gave orders to interior decorators to make it look exactly as it used to, except for my office. I want that modern, with all the electronic conveniences I'll need. But . . . if you want, you can do a few things to make it cosy.'

Cosy? How could a house such as this ever be cosy? I knew what it felt like to be enclosed inside, swallowed, trapped forever. I shivered as I heard the click of my high heels beside the dull thuds of Chris's shoes as we neared the black doors with their escutcheons made decorative with heraldic shields. I wondered if Bart had looked up the Foxworth ancestry and found the titles of aristocracy and the coats of arms he desperately wanted and seemed to need. On each black door were heavy brass knockers, and in between the doors a small, almost unnoticeable button to ring a bell somewhere inside.

'I'm sure this house is full of modern gadgets that would shock genuine historical Virginia homes,' whispered Chris.

No doubt Chris was right.

Bart was in love with the past, but even more infatuated with the future. Not an electronic gadget came out that he didn't buy.

Chris reached into his pocket for the door key Bart had given to me just before we flew from Boston. Chris smiled my way before he inserted the large brass key. Before he could complete the turning action, the door swung silently open.

Startled, I took a step backward.

Chris pulled me forward again, speaking politely to the old man who invitingly gestured us inside.

'Come in,' he said in a weak but raspy voice as he quickly looked us over. 'Your son called and told me to expect you. I'm the hired help – so to speak.'

I stared at the lean old man who was bent forward so that his head projected unbecomingly, making him seem to be climbing hills even while standing on a flat surface. His hair was faded, not grey and not blond. His eyes were a watery pale blue, his cheeks gaunt, his eyes hollowed out, as if he'd suffered greatly for many, many years. There was something about him . . . something familiar.

My leaden legs didn't want to move. The fierce wind whipped my white, full-skirted summer dress high enough to show my thighs as I put one foot inside the grand entrance foyer of the Phoenix called Foxworth Hall.

Chris stayed close at my side. He released my hand to put his arm around my shoulders. 'Dr and Mrs Christopher Sheffield,' he introduced us in his kindly way, 'and you?'

The wizened old man seemed reluctant to put out his right hand and shake Chris's strong, tanned one. His thin old lips wore a cynical, crooked smile that duplicated the cock of one bushy eyebrow. 'My pleasure to meet you, Dr Sheffield.'

I couldn't take my eyes off that bent old man with his watery blue eyes. Something about his smile, his thinning hair with broad streaks of silver, those eyes with startling dark lashes. Daddy!

He looked as our father might have looked if he'd lived to be as old as this man before us – and had suffered through every torment known to mankind.

My daddy, my beloved handsome father who'd been the joy of my youth. How I'd prayed to see him again some day.

The stringy old hand was grasped firmly by Chris, and only then did the old man tell us who he was. 'Your long lost uncle who was, ostensibly, lost in the Swiss Alps fifty-seven years ago.'

JOEL FOXWORTH

Quickly Chris said all the right words to cover the shock that obviously showed on both our faces. 'You've startled my wife,' he politely explained. 'You see, her maiden name was Foxworth . . . and she has believed until now that all her maternal family was dead.'

Several small, crooked smiles fleeted like shadows on 'Uncle Joel's' face before he pasted on the benign, pious look of the sublimely pure in heart. 'I understand,' said the old man in his whispery voice that sounded like a faint wind rustling unpleasantly in dead, fallen leaves.

Deep in Joel's watery cerulean eyes lingered shadows, dark, troubled shadows. I knew without speaking that Chris would tell me my imagination was working overtime again.

No shadows, no shadows, no shadows . . . but those I created myself.

To lift myself above my suspicions of this old man who claimed to be one of my mother's two older and dead brothers, I gazed with interest around the foyer that had often been used as a ballroom. I heard the wind pick up velocity as the thunderclaps drew ever closer and closer together, indicating the storm was almost directly overhead.

Oh, sigh for the day when I'd been twelve and stared out at the rain, wanting to dance in this ballroom with the man who was my mother's second husband and would later be the father of my second son, Bart.

Sigh for all that I'd been then, so young and full of faith, so hopeful that the world was a beautiful and benign place.

What had seemed to me impressive as a child should have shrunk in comparison to all I'd seen, since Chris and I had travelled all over Europe and had been to Asia, Egypt and India. Even so, this foyer seemed to me twice as elegant and impressive as it had when I was twelve.

Oh, the pity of that, to still be overwhelmed! I gazed with

reluctant awe, a strange aching beginning in my heart, making it thud louder, making my blood race fast and hot. I stared at the three chandeliers of crystal and gold that held real candles. Each was fully fifteen feet in diameter, with seven tiers of candles. How many tiers had there been before? Five? Three? I couldn't remember. I stared at the huge mirrors with gold frames that lined the foyer, reflecting the elegant Louis IV furniture where those who didn't dance could sit and watch and converse.

It wasn't supposed to be this way! Things remembered never lived up to expectations – why was this second Foxworth Hall overwhelming me even more than the original?

Then I saw something else – something I didn't expect to see.

Those dual curving staircases, one on the right, the other on the left of the vast expanse of red and white checkered marble. Weren't they the same stairs? Refurbished, but the same? Hadn't I watched the fire that had burned Foxworth Hall until it was only red embers and smoke? All eight of the chimneys had stood; so had the marble staircases. The intricately designed banisters and rosewood railing must have burned and been replaced. I swallowed over the hard lump that came to choke in my throat. I'd wanted the house to be new, all new . . . nothing left of the old.

Joel was watching me, telling me my face revealed more than Chris's. When our eyes locked, he quickly looked away before he gestured that we were to follow him. Joel showed us through all the beautiful first-floor rooms as I remained numb and speechless, and Chris asked all the questions, before at last we settled down in one of the salons and Joel began telling his own story.

Along the way he'd paused in the enormous kitchen long enough to put together a snack for our lunch. Refusing Chris's offer to help, he had carried in a tray with tea and dainty sandwiches. My appetite was small, but as was to be expected, Chris was ravenous and in a few minutes had dispatched six of the tiny sandwiches and was reaching for another as Joel poured him a second cup of tea. I ate but one of the miniature tasteless sandwiches and sipped twice from the tea, which was steaming hot and very strong, expectantly anticipating the tale Joel would tell.

His voice was frail, with those gritty undertones that made it seem he had a cold and speaking was difficult. Yet soon I forgot the unpleasant sound of his voice as he began to relate so much of what I'd always wanted to know about our grandparents and our mother when she was a child. In no time at all it became clear that he'd hated his father very much, and only then could I begin to warm up to him.

'You called your father by his Christian name?' My first question since he'd begun his story, my voice an intimidated whisper, as if Malcolm himself might be hovering somewhere within hearing.

His thin lips moved to twist into a grotesque mockery of a smile. 'Of course. My brother Mel was four years older than I, and we'd always referred to our father by his given name, but never in his presence. We didn't have that kind of nerve. Calling him Daddy seemed ridiculous. We couldn't call him Father because he wasn't a real father. "Dad" would have indicated a warm relationship, which we didn't have and didn't want. When we had to, we called him Father. In fact, we both tried not to be seen or heard by him. We'd disappear when he was due home. He had an office in town from which he conducted most of his business and another office here. He was always working, seated behind a massive desk that was to us a barrier. Even when he was home, he managed to keep himself remote, untouchable. He was never idle, always jumping up to take long distance calls in his office so we couldn't overhear his business transactions. He seldom talked to our mother. She didn't seem to mind. On rare occasions we'd seen him holding our baby sister on his lap, and we'd hide and watch, with strange yearnings in our chests.

'We'd talk about it afterwards, wondering why we'd feel jealous of Corrine, when Corrine was often just as severely punished as we were. But always our father was sorry when he punished *her*. To make up for some humiliation, some beating, or being locked in the attic, which was one of his favourite ways to punish us, he'd bring Corrine a costly piece of jewellery, or an expensive doll or toy. She had everything any little girl could desire – but if she did one wrong thing, he took from her what she loved most and gave it to the church he patronized. She'd cry and try to win back his affection, but he could turn against her as easily as he could turn towards her.

'When Mel and I tried to win gifts of consolation from him, he'd turn his back and tell us to act like men, not children. Mel and I used to think your mother knew how to work our father very well to get what she wanted. We didn't know how to act sweet, or how to be beguiling, or demure.'

Behind my eyes I could see my mother as a child, running through this beautiful but sinister home, growing accustomed to having everything lavish and expensive, so that later on when she married Daddy, who had earned a modest salary, she still didn't think about how much she paid for anything.

I sat there with wide eyes as Joel went on. 'Corrine and our mother didn't like each other. As we grew up, we recognized the fact that our mother was jealous of her own daughter's beauty, and the many charms that enabled her to twist any man around her fingers. Corrine was exceptionally beautiful. Even as her brothers we could sense the power she would be able to wield one day.' Joel spread his thin, pale hands on his legs. His hands were gnarled and knotted, but somehow they still maintained a remnant of elegance, perhaps because he used them gracefully, or perhaps because they were so pale. 'Look around at all this grandeur and beauty – and picture a household of tormented people, all struggling to be free of the chains Malcolm put on us. Even our mother, who'd inherited a fortune from her own parents, was kept under stringent control.

'Mel escaped the banking business, which he hated and had been forced into by Malcolm, by jumping on to his motorcycle and racing away into the mountains, where he'd stay in a log cabin he and I had constructed together. We would invite our girlfriends there, and we did everything we knew our father would disapprove of deliberately, out of defiance for his absolute authority.

'One terrible summer day Mel went over a precipice; they had to dig his body out of the ravine. He was only twenty-one. I was seventeen. I felt half dead myself, so empty and alone with my brother gone. My father came to me after Mel's funeral and said I'd have to take the place of my older brother and work in one of his banks to learn about the financial world. He might as well have told me I'd have to cut off my hands and feet. I ran away that very night.'

All about us the huge house seemed to wait, very quiet, too quiet. The storm outside seemed to hold its breath as well, although I could glimpse the leaden grey sky growing more and more swollen and turgid. I moved slightly closer to Chris on the elegant sofa. Across from us in a wing-back chair, Joel sat silently, as if caught in melancholy memories, and Chris and I no longer existed for him.

'Where did you go?' asked Chris, putting down his teacup and leaning back before he crossed his legs. His hand reached for mine. 'It must have been difficult for a boy of seventeen on his own . . .'

Joel jerked back to the present, seeming startled to find himself back in his hated childhood home. 'It wasn't easy. I didn't know how to do anything practical, but at music I was very talented. I caught a freight steamer and worked as a deckhand to pay my way over to France. For the first time in my life I had calluses on my hands. Once I was in France, I found a job in a nightclub and earned a few francs a week. Soon I grew tired of the long hours and moved on to Switzerland, thinking I'd see all the world and never return home. I found another job as a nightclub musician in a small Swiss inn near the Italian border and soon was joining skiing parties into the Alps. I'd spend most of my free time skiing, and in the summer, hiking or bicycling. One day good friends asked me to join them on a rather risky trip, to downhill ski from a very high peak. I was about nineteen then, and the four others ahead were laughing and yelling at each other and didn't notice when I lost control and went tumbling headlong into a deep ice crevice. I broke my leg in the fall. I lay down there a day and a half, partly in shock, when two monks travelling on donkeys heard my weak cries for help. They knew how to get me out – but I don't remember much about that, for I was weak with hunger and half out of my mind from pain. When I came to, I was in their monastery, and smooth, bland faces were smiling at me. Their monastery was on the Italian side of the Alps, and I didn't know a word of Italian. They taught me their Latin as my broken leg healed, and then they used my slight artistic talent to help them paint wall murals and decorate handwritten scripts with religious illustrations. Sometimes I played their organ. By the time my leg was healed so I could walk, I found I liked their quiet life, the artwork they gave me to do, the music I played at dawn and sunset, the silent routine of their uneventful days of prayers and work and self-denial. I stayed on and eventually became one of them. In that monastery, high in the mountains, I finally found peace.'

His story was over. He sat looking at Chris, then turned his pale but burning eyes on me.

Startled by his penetrating gaze, I tried not to shrink away and show the revulsion I couldn't help feeling. I didn't like him, even though he faintly resembled the father I'd loved so well, and certainly I had no reason to dislike him. I suspected it was my own anxiety and fear that he'd know that Chris was really my brother and not my husband. Had Bart told him our story? Did he see how Chris resembled the Foxworths? I couldn't really tell. He was smiling at me, using his own kind of failing charm to win me over. Already he was wise enough to know it wouldn't be Chris he had to convince . . .

'Why did you come back?' asked Chris.

Again Joel tried to smile. 'One day an American journalist came to the monastery to write a feature story about what it was like to be a monk in today's modern world. Since I was the only one there who spoke English, they used me to represent all of them. I casually asked if he'd ever heard of the Foxworths of Virginia. He had, since Malcolm had made a huge fortune and was often involved in politics, and only then did I learn of his death, and that of my mother. Once the journalist had gone, I couldn't stop thinking about this house and my sister. Years can easily blend one into the other when all days are alike, and calendars weren't kept in sight. Finally came a day when I resolved that I wanted to go home again and talk to my sister and get to know her. The journalist hadn't mentioned if she had married. It wasn't until after I came to the village, almost a year ago, and settled into a motel that I heard how the original house had burned one Christmas night and my sister had been put away in a mental rest home, and all that tremendous fortune had been left to her. It wasn't until Bart came that summer that I learned the rest – how my sister died, how he inherited.'

His eyes lowered modestly. 'Bart is a very remarkable young man; I enjoy his company. Before he came, I used to spend a lot of my time up here, talking to the caretaker. He told me about Bart and his many visits to talk to the builders and decorators, how he had expressed his desire to make this new house look exactly like the old one. I made it my business to be here when Bart came the next time. We met, I told him who I was, and he seemed overjoyed . . . and that's the whole of it.'

Really? I stared at him hard. Had he come back thinking he'd have his share of the fortune Malcolm had left? Could he break my mother's will and take away a good portion for himself? If he could, I wondered why Bart wasn't very upset to know he was still alive.

I didn't put any of my thoughts into words, just sat on, as Joel fell into a long, moody silence. Chris stood up. 'It's been a full day for us, Joel, and my wife is very tired. Could you show us to the rooms we are to use so we can rest and refresh ourselves?'

Instantly Joel was on his feet, apologizing for being a poor host, and then he was leading the way to the stairs.

'I will be happy to see Bart again. He was very generous to offer me a room in this house. However, all these rooms remind me too much of my parents. My room is over the garage, near the servants' quarters.'

Just then the telephone rang. Joel handed me the telephone. 'It's your older son calling from New York,' he said in that stiff, gritty voice. 'You can use the phone in the first salon if both of you want to talk to him.'

Chris hurried to pick up another phone as I greeted Jory. His happy voice disspelled some of the gloom and depression I was already feeling. 'Mom, Dad, I've managed to cancel a few commitments, and Mel and I are free to fly down and be with you. We're both tired and need a vacation. Besides, we'd like to get a look at that house we've heard so much about. Is it really like the original?'

Oh, yes, only too much so. I was filled with joy that Jory and Melodie were coming to join us, and when Cindy and Bart arrived, too, we'd be a complete family again, all living under the same roof – something I hadn't known in a long time.

'No, of course I don't mind giving up performing for a while,' he said cheerfully in answer to my question. 'I'm tired. Even my bones feel weak with fatigue. We both need a good rest . . . and we have some news for you.'

He'd say nothing more.

We hung up, and Chris and I smiled at each other. Joel had retreated to give us privacy, and now he reappeared, tottering uncertainly around a jutting French table with a huge marble urn filled with a dried flower arrangement, speaking of the suite of rooms Bart had planned for my use. He glanced at me, then at Chris before he added, 'And for you as well, Dr Sheffield.'

Joel swivelled his watery eyes to study my expression, seeming to find something there that pleased him.

Linking my arm with Chris's, I bravely faced the stairs that would take us up, up, and back to that second floor where it had all begun, this wonderful, sinful love that Chris and I had found in the dusty, decaying attic gloom, in a dark place full of junk and old furniture, with paper flowers on the wall and broken promises at our feet.

MEMORIES

Midway up the stairs I paused to look down, wanting to see everything that might have slipped my notice before. Even as Joel had told us his story, and we'd eaten our sparse lunch, I'd stared at everything I'd seen but twice before, and never had I seen enough. From the room where we'd been, I could easily look into the foyer with its myriad mirrors and fine French furniture placed stiffly in small groupings that tried unsuccessfully to be intimate. The marble floor gleamed like glass from many polishings. I felt the overwhelming desire to dance, dance, and pirouette until I blindly fell . . .

Chris grew impatient as I lingered and tugged me upwards until at last we were in the grand rotunda and again I was staring down into the ballroom-foyer.

'Cathy, are you lost in memories?' whispered Chris, somewhat crossly. 'Isn't it time we both forget the past and move on? Come, I know you must be very tired.'

Memories . . . they came at me fast and furious. Cory, Carrie, Bartholomew Winslow – I sensed them all around me, whispering, whispering. I glanced again at Joel, who'd told us he didn't want us to call him Uncle Joel. He was saving that distinguished title for my children.

He must look as Malcolm did, only his eyes were softer, less piercing than those we'd seen in that huge, lifesize portrait of him in the 'trophy' room. I told myself that not all blue eyes were cruel and heartless. Certainly I should know that better than anyone.

Openly studying the aged face before me, I could still see the remnants of the younger man he'd once been. A man who must have had flaxen blond hair and a face very much like my father's – and his son's. Because of this I relaxed and forced myself to step forward and embrace him. 'Welcome home, Joel.'

His frail old body in my arms felt brittle and cold. His cheek was dry as my lips barely managed a kiss there. He shrank from me as if contaminated by my touch, or perhaps he was afraid of women. I jerked away, regretting now that I'd made an attempt to be warm and friendly. Touching was something no Foxworth was supposed to do unless there was a marriage certificate first. Nervously my eyes fled to meet Chris's. Calm down, his eyes were saying, it's going to be all right.

'My wife is very tired,' reminded Chris softly. 'We've had a very busy schedule what with seeing our youngest son graduate, and all the parties, and then this trip . . .'

Joel finally broke the long, stiff silence that kept us standing uncomfortably in the dim upstairs rotunda and mentioned that Bart would be hiring servants. Already he'd called an employment agency, and, in fact, had even said we could screen people for him. He mumbled so inaudibly that I didn't catch half of what he said, especially when my mind was so busy with speculations as I stared off towards the northern wing and that isolated end room where we'd been locked up. Would it still be the same? Had Bart ordered two double beds put in there, with all that clutter of dark, massive, antique furniture? I hoped and prayed not.

Suddenly from Joel came words I wasn't prepared for. 'You look like your mother, Catherine.'

I stared at him blankly, resenting what he must have considered a compliment.

He kept standing there, as if waiting for some silent summons, looking from me to Chris, and then back to me before he nodded and turned to lead the way to our room. The sun that had shone so brilliantly for our arrival was a forgotten memory as the rain began to pelt down with the hard, steady drive of bullets on the slate roof. The thunder rolled and crashed overhead, and lightning split the sky, crackling every few seconds, sending me into Chris's arms as I cringed back from what seemed to me the wrath of God.

Rivulets of water ran on the windowpanes, sluiced down from the roof into drains that soon would flood the gardens and erase all that was alive and beautiful. I sighed and felt miserable to be back here where I felt young and terribly vulnerable again.

'Yes, yes,' Joel muttered as if to himself, 'just like Corrine.' His eyes scanned me critically once more, and then he was bowing his head and reflecting so long five minutes could have passed. Or five seconds.

'We have to unpack,' Chris said more forcefully. 'My wife is exhausted. She needs a bath, then a nap, for travelling always makes her feel tired and dirty.' I wondered why he bothered to explain.

Instantly Joel pulled himself back from where he'd been. Maybe monks often just stood with bowed heads and prayed, and lost themselves in silent worship, and that was all it meant. I didn't know anything at all about monasteries and the kind of lives monks lived.

Slow, shuffling feet were at last leading us down a long hall. He made another turn, and to my distress and dismay he headed towards the southern wing where once our mother had lived in sumptuous rooms. I'd longed to sleep in her glorious swan bed, sit at her long, long dressing table, bathe in her black marble sunken tub with mirrors overhead and all around.

Joel paused before the double doors above two wide, carpeted steps that curved outward in half-moons. He smiled in a slow, peculiar way. 'Your mother's wing,' he said shortly.

I paused and shivered outside those too familiar double doors. Helplessly I looked back at Chris. The rain had calmed to a steady staccato drumming. Joel opened one side of the doors and stepped into the bedroom, giving Chris the chance to whisper to me, 'To him we are only husband and wife, Cathy – that's all he knows.'

Tears were in my eyes as I stepped into that bedroom – and then I was staring bug-eyed at what I'd thought burned in the fire. The bed! The swan bed with the fancy rosy bedcurtains held back gracefully by the tips of wing feathers made into curling fingers. That graceful swan head had the same twist of its neck, the same kind of watchful but sleepy red ruby eye half open to guard the occupants of the bed.

I stared disbelievingly. Sleep in that bed? The bed where my mother had been held in the arms of Bartholomew Winslow – her second husband? The same man I'd stolen from her to father my son Bart? The man who still haunted my dreams and filled me with guilt. No! I couldn't sleep in that bed! Not ever.

Once I'd longed to sleep in that swan bed with Bartholomew Winslow. How young and foolish I'd been then, thinking material things really did bring happiness, and having him for my own would be all I'd ever want.

'Isn't that bed a marvel?' asked Joel from behind me. 'Bart went to a great deal of trouble to find artisans who'd handcarve the headboard in the form of a swan. They looked at him, so he said, as if he were crazy. But he found some old men who were delighted to be doing something they found uniquely creative, and financially rewarding. It seems Bart has detailed descriptions of how the swan should have its head turned. One sleepy eye set with a ruby. Fingertip feathers to hold back filmy bed curtains. Oh, the flurry he made when they didn't do it right the first time. And then the little swan bed at the foot, he wanted that, too. For you, Catherine, for you.'

Chris spoke, his voice hard. 'Joel, just what has Bart told you?' He stepped beside me and encircled my shoulders with the comfort of his arm, protecting me from Joel, from everything. With him I'd live in a thatched hut, a tent, a cave. He gave me strength.

The old man's smile was faint and sardonic as he took notice of Chris's protective attitude. 'Bart confided all his family history to me. You see, he's always needed an older man to talk to.'

He paused meaningfully, glancing at Chris, who couldn't fail to catch the implication. Despite his control I saw him wince. Joel seemed satisfied enough to continue. 'Bart told me about how his mother and her brothers and a sister were locked away for more than three years. He told me that his mother took her sister, Carrie, the twin left alive, and ran off to South Carolina, and you, Catherine, took years and years to find just the right husband to suit your needs best –

and that's why you are now married to . . . Dr Christopher Sheffield.'

There were so many innuendoes in his words, so much he left unsaid. Enough to make me shiver with sudden cold.

Joel finally left the room and closed the door softly behind him. Only then could Chris give me the reassurance I had to have if I was to stay here for even one night. He kissed me, held me, stroked my back, my hair, soothed me until I could turn around and look at everything Bart had done to make this suite of rooms just as luxurious as they'd been before. 'It's only a bed, a reproduction of the original,' Chris said softly, his eyes warm and understanding. 'Our mother has not lain on this bed, darling. Bart read your scripts, remember that. What's here is here because you constructed the pattern for him to follow. You described that swan bed in such exquisite detail that he must have believed you wanted rooms just like our mother used to have. Maybe unconsciously you still do, and he knows that. Forgive us both for misunderstanding if I'm wrong. Think only that he wanted to please you and went to a great deal of trouble and expense to decorate this room as it used to be.'

Numbly I shook my head, denying I'd ever wanted what she had. He didn't believe me. 'Your wishes, Catherine! Your desire to have everything she did! I know it. Your sons know it. So don't blame any of us for being able to interpret your desires even when you cover them with clever subterfuges.'

I wanted to hate him for knowing me so well. Yet my arms went around him. My face pressed against his shirtfront as I trembled and tried to hide the truth, even from myself. 'Chris, don't be harsh with me,' I sobbed. 'It came as such a surprise to see these rooms, almost as they used to be when we came here to steal from her . . . and her husband . . .'

He held me hard against him. 'What do you really feel about Joel?' I asked.

Considering thoughtfully before he answered, Chris spoke. 'I like him, Cathy. He seems sincere and overjoyed that we're willing to let him stay on here.'

'You told him he could stay?' I whispered.

'Sure, why not? We'll be leaving soon after Bart has that twenty-fifth birthday when he "comes into his own". And just think of the wonderful opportunity we'll have to learn more about the Foxworths. Joel can tell us more about our mother when she was young, and what life was like for all of them, and perhaps when we know the details, we will be able to understand how she could betray us, and why the grandfather wanted us dead. There has to be an awful truth hidden back in the past to warp Malcolm's brain so he could override our mother's natural instincts to keep her own children alive.'

In my opinion Joel had said enough downstairs. I didn't want to know more. Malcolm Foxworth had been one of those strange humans born without conscience, unable to feel remorse for any wrong thing he did. There was no explaining him, and no way to understand.

Appealingly Chris gazed into my eyes, making his heart and soul vulnerable for my scorn to injure. 'I'd like to hear about our mother's youth, Cathy, so I can understand what made her the way she turned out to be. She wounded us so deeply I feel neither one of us will ever recover until we do understand. I have forgiven her, but I can't forget. I want to understand so I can help *you* to forgive her . . .'

'Will that help?' I asked sarcastically. 'It's too late for understanding or forgiving our mother, and, to be honest, I don't want to find understanding – for if I do, I might have to forgive her.'

His arms dropped stiffly to his sides. Turning, he strode away from me. 'I'm going out for our luggage now. Take a bath, and by the time you're finished I'll have everything unpacked.' At the doorway he paused, not turning to look my way. 'Try, really try, to use this as an opportunity to make peace with Bart. He's not beyond restoration, Cathy. You heard him behind the podium. That young man has a remarkable ability for oratory. His words make good sense. He's a leader now, Cathy, when he used to be so shy and introverted. We can count it a blessing that at last Bart has come out of his shell.'

Humbly I bowed my head. 'Yes, I'll do what I can. Forgive me, Chris, for being unreasonably strong-willed – again.'

He smiled and left.

In 'her' bath that joined a magnificent dressing room, I slowly disrobed while the black marble sunken tub filled. All about me were gold-framed mirrors to reflect back my nudity. I was proud of my figure, still slim and firm, and my breasts that didn't sag. Stripped of everything, I lifted my arms to take out the few hairpins still left. *Déjà vu*-like, I saw my mother as she must have stood, doing this same thing while she thought of her second and younger husband. Had she wondered where he was on the nights he spent with me? Had she known just who Bart's mistress was before my revelations at the Christmas party? Oh, I hoped she had!

An unremarkable dinner came and went.

Two hours later I was in the swan bed that had given me many daydreams, watching Chris undress. True to his word, he'd unpacked everything, hung my clothes as well as his own and stowed our underwear in the bureau. Now he looked tired, slightly unhappy. 'Joel told me there will be servants coming for interviews tomorrow. I hope you feel up to that.'

Startled, I sat up. 'But I thought Bart would do his own hiring.'

'No, he's leaving that up to you.'

'Oh.'

Chris hung his suit on the brass valet, again making me think of how much that valet seemed the same one Bart's father had used when he lived here – or in that other Foxworth Hall. Haunted, that's what I was. Stark naked, Chris headed for the 'his' bath. 'I'll take a quick shower and join you shortly. Don't fall asleep until I'm through.'

I lay in the semi-darkness and stared around me, feeling strangely out of myself. In and out of my mother I flitted, sensing four children in a locked room overhead in the attic. Feeling the panic and guilt that surely must have been hers while that mean old father below lived on and on, threatening even when he was out of sight. Born bad, wicked, evil. It seemed I heard a whispery voice saying this over and over again. I closed my eyes and tried to stop this craziness. I didn't hear any voices. I didn't hear ballet music playing, I didn't. I couldn't smell the dry, musty scent of the attic. I couldn't. I was fifty-two years old, not twelve, thirteen, fourteen or fifteen.

All the old odours were gone. I smelled only new paint, new wood, freshly applied wallpaper and fabric. New carpets, new scatter rugs, new furniture. Everything new but for the fancy antiques on the first floor. Not the real Foxworth Hall, only an imitation. Yet, why had Joel come back if he liked being a monk so much? Certainly he couldn't want all that money when he'd grown accustomed to monastery austerity. There must be some good reason he was here other than just wanting to see what remained of his family. When the villagers must have told him our mother was dead, still he'd stayed. Waiting his chance to meet Bart? What had he found in Bart that kept him staying on? Even allowing Bart to put him to use as a butler until we had a real one. Then I sighed. Why was I making such a mystery of this when a fortune was involved. Always it seemed money was the reason for doing anything and everything.

Fatigue closed my eyes. I fought off sleep. I needed this time to think of tomorrow, of this uncle come from nowhere. Had we finally gained all that Momma had promised, only to lose it to Joel? If he didn't try to break Momma's will, and we managed to keep what we had, would it carry a price?

In the morning Chris and I descended the right side of the dual staircase, feeling we had at long last come into 'our own' and we were finally in control of our lives. He caught my hand and squeezed it, sensing from my expression that this house no longer intimidated me.

We found Joel in the kitchen busily preparing breakfast. He wore a long white apron and cocked on his head was a tall chef's cap. Somehow it looked ludicrous on such a frail, tall, old man. Only fat men should be chefs, I thought, even as I felt grateful to have him take on a chore I'd never really liked.

'I hope you like Eggs Benedict,' said Joel without glancing our way. To my surprise, his Eggs Benedict were wonderful. Chris had two servings. Then Joel was showing us rooms not yet decorated. He smiled at me crookedly. 'Bart told me you like informal rooms with comfortable furniture, and he wants you to make these empty rooms cosy, in your own inimitable style.'

Was he mocking me? He knew Chris and I were here only for a visit. Then I realized perhaps Bart might want me to help with the decorating and was ruluctant to say so himself.

When I asked Chris if Joel could break our mother's will and take from Bart the money he felt so necessary for his self-esteem, Chris shook his head, admitting he really didn't know all the ins and outs of legal ramifications when a 'dead' heir came back to life.

'Bart could give Joel enough money to see him through the few years he has left,' I said, wracking my brain to remember every word of my mother's last will and testament. No mention of her older brothers, whom she'd believed dead.

When I came back from my thoughts, Joel was in the kitchen again, having found what he wanted in the pantry stocked with enough to feed a hotel. He spoke in reply to a question Chris had asked and I hadn't heard. His voice was sombre. 'Of course, the house isn't exactly the same, for no one uses wooden pegs for nails anymore. I put all the old furniture in my quarters. I don't *really* belong, so I'm going to stay in the servants' quarters over the garage.'

'I've already said you shouldn't do that,' said Chris with a frown. 'It just wouldn't be right to let a family member live in such frugal style.' Already we'd seen the huge garage, and the servants' quarters above could hardly be called frugal, just small.

Let him! I wanted to shout, but I said nothing.

Before I knew what was happening, Chris had Joel established on the second floor in the western wing. I sighed, somehow regretful that Joel would be under the same roof with us. But it would be all right; as soon as our curiosity was satisfied and Bart celebrated his birthday, we'd leave with Cindy for Hawaii.

In the library around two in the afternoon, Chris and I settled down to interview the man and woman who came with excellent references. There wasn't any fault I could find, except something furtive in both pairs of eyes. Uneasily I fidgeted from the way they looked so knowingly at both of us. 'Sorry,' said Chris, catching the slight negative gesture I made, 'but we've already decided on another couple.'

Husband and wife stood up to go. The woman turned in the doorway to give me a long, meaningful look. 'I live in the village, Mrs Sheffield,' she said coldly. 'Been there only five years, but we've heard a great deal about the Foxworths who live on the hill.'

What she said made me turn my head away.

'Yes, I'm sure you have,' said Chris dryly.

The woman snorted before she slammed the door behind them.

Next came a tall, aristocratic man with upright military bearing, immaculately dressed down to the slightest detail. He strode in and politely waited until Chris asked him to sit down.

'My name is Trevor Mainstream Majors,' he said in his brisk British style. 'I was born in Liverpool fifty-nine years ago. I was married in London when I was twenty-six, and my wife passed away three years ago, and my two sons live in North Carolina . . . so I am here hoping I can work in Virginia and visit my sons on my days off.'

'Where did you work after you left the Johnstons?' asked Chris, looking down at the man's resume. 'You seem to have excellent references until one year ago.'

By this time Chris had invited the Englishman to seat himself. Trevor Majors shifted his long legs and adjusted his tie before he replied politely, 'I worked for the Millersons, who moved away from the Hill about six months ago.'

Silence. I'd heard my mother mention the Millersons many times. My heart began to beat more rapidly. 'How long did you work for the Millersons?' asked Chris in a friendly way, as if he had no fears, even after having caught my look of anxiety.

'Not long, sir. They had five of their own children there, and nephews and nieces were always showing up, plus friends who stayed over for visits. I was their only servant. I did the cooking, the housework, the laundry, the chauffeuring, and it's an Englishman's pride and joy to do the gardening. What with chauffeuring the five children back and forth to school, dancing classes, sporting events, flicks and such, I spent so much time on the road I seldom had the chance to prepare a decent meal. One day Mister Millerson complained I'd failed to mow the lawn and hadn't weeded the garden, and he hadn't eaten a good meal at home in two weeks. He snapped at me harshly because his dinner was late. Sir, that was rather much, when his wife had ordered me out on the road, kept me waiting while she shopped, sent me to pick up the children from the movies . . . and then I was supposed to have dinner on time. I told Mister Millerson I wasn't a robot able to do everything, and all at once – and I quit. He was so angry he threatened he'd never give me a good reference. But if you wait a few days, he may cool down enough to realize I did the best I could under difficult circumstances.'

I sighed, looked at Chris and made a furtive signal. This man was perfect. Chris didn't even look my way. 'I think you will work out fine, Mister Majors. We'll hire you for a trial period of one month, and if at that time we find you unsatisfactory, we will terminate our employment agreement.'

Chris looked at me. 'That is, if my wife agrees . . .'

Silently I stood and nodded. We did need servants. I didn't intend to spend my vacation dusting and cleaning a huge house.

'Sir, my lady, if you will, just call me Trevor. It will be my honour and pleasure to serve in this grand house.' He'd jumped to his feet the moment I stood, and then, as Chris rose, he and Chris shook hands. 'My pleasure indeed,' he said as he smiled at us both approvingly.

In three days we hired three servants. It was easy enough when Bart was highly overpaying them.

The evening of our fifth full day here, I stood beside Chris on the balcony, staring at the mountains all around us, gazing up at that same old moon that used to look down on us as we lay on the roof of the old Foxworth Hall. That single great eye of God I'd believed when I was fifteen. Other places had given me romantic moons, beautiful moonlight to take away my fears and guilts. Here I felt the moon was a harsh investigator, ready to condemn us again, and then again and again.

'It's a beautiful night, isn't it?' asked Chris with his arm about my waist. 'I like this balcony that Bart added to our suite of rooms. It doesn't distract from the outside appearance since it's on the side, and just look at the view it gives us of the mountains.'

The blue-misted mountains had always represented to me a jagged fence to keep us forever trapped as prisoners of hope. Even now I saw their soft rounded tops as a barrier between me and freedom. *God, if you're up there, help me through the next few weeks.*

Near noon the next day, Chris and I, with Joel, stood on the front portico, watching the low-slung red Jaguar speeding up the steeply spiralling road that led to Foxworth Hall.

Bart drove with reckless, daredevil speed, as if challenging death to take him. I grew weak just watching the way he whipped around the dangerous curves.

'God knows he should have better sense,' Chris grumbled. 'He's always been accident prone – and look at the way he drives, as if he's got a hold on immortality.'

'There are some who do,' said Joel enigmatically.

I threw him a wondering glance, then looked again at that small red car that had cost a small fortune. Every year Bart bought a new car, never any colour but red; he'd tried all the luxury cars to find which he liked best. This one was his favourite so far, he'd informed us in a brief letter.

Squealing to a stop, he burned rubber and spoiled the perfection of the curving drive with long black streaks. Waving first, Bart threw off his sunglasses, shook his head to bring his dark tumbled locks back into order, ignored the door and jumped from his convertible, pulling off driving gloves and tossing them carelessly on to the seat. Racing up the steps, he seized me up in his strong arms and planted several kisses on my cheeks. I was stunned with the warmth of his greeting. Eagerly I responded. The moment my lips touched his cheek he put me down and shoved me away as if he tired of me very rapidly.

He stood in full sunlight, six feet three, brilliant intelligence and strength in his dark brown eyes, his shoulders broad, his well-muscled body tapering down to slim hips and long legs. He was so handsome in his casual white sports outfit. 'You're looking great, Mother, just great.' His dark eyes swept over me from heels to hair. 'Thanks for wearing that red dress . . . it's my favourite colour.'

I reached for Chris's hand. 'Thank you, Bart, I wore this dress just for you.' Now he could say something nice to Chris, I hoped. I waited for that. Instead, Bart ignored Chris and turned to Joel.

'Hi, Uncle Joel. Isn't my mother just as beautiful as I said?'

Chris's hand clenched mine so hard it hurt. Always Bart found a way to insult the only father he could remember.

'Yes, Bart, your mother is very beautiful,' said Joel in that whispery, raspy voice. 'In fact, she's exactly the way I would imagine my sister Corrine looked at her age.'

'Bart, say hello to your – ' and here I faltered. I wanted to say *Father* but I knew Bart would deny that rudely. So I said *Chris*. Turning his dark and sometimes savage eyes briefly to stare at Chris, Bart bit out a harsh hello. 'You don't ever age either, do you?' he said in an accusatory tone.

'I'm sorry about that, Bart,' answered Chris evenly. 'But time will do its job eventually.'

'Let's hope so.'

I could have slapped Bart.

Turning around, Bart ignored both Chris and I and

surveyed the lawns, the house, the luxurious flower beds, the lush shrubbery, the garden paths, the birdbaths and other statuary, and smiled with an owner's pride. 'It's grand, really grand. Just as I hoped it would be. I've looked the world over and no mansion can compare with Foxworth Hall.'

His dark eyes moved to clash with mine. 'I know what you're thinking, Mother, I know this isn't truly the best house yet, but one day it will be. I intend to build, and add new wings, and one day this house will outshine every palace in Europe. I'm going to concentrate my energies on making Foxworth Hall truly an historic landmark.'

'Who will you impress when you accomplish that?' asked Chris. 'The world no longer tolerates great houses and great wealth, or respects those who gain it by inheritance.'

Oh, damn it! Chris so seldom said anything tactless or rude. Why had he said what he did? Bart's face flamed beneath his deep bronze tan. 'I intend to increase my fortune with my own efforts!' Bart flared, stepping closer to Chris. Because he was so lean, and Chris had put on weight, especially in the chest, he appeared to tower over Chris. I watched the man I thought of as my husband stare challengingly into my son's eyes.

'I've been doing that for you,' said Chris.

To my surprise, Bart seemed pleased. 'You mean as trustee you have increased my share of the inheritance?'

'Yes, it was easy enough,' said Chris laconically. 'Money makes money, and the investments I made for you have paid off handsomely.'

'Ten to one I could have done better.'

Chris smiled ironically. 'I could have predicted you'd thank me like that.'

From one to the other I looked, feeling sorry for both of them. Chris was a mature man who knew who and what he was, and he could ride along on that confidence with ease, while Bart was still struggling to find himself and his place in the world.

My son, my son, when will you learn humility, gratitude? Many a night I'd seen Chris working over figures, trying to decide on the best investments, as if he knew that sooner or later Bart would accuse him of poor financial judgment.

'You'll have your chance to prove yourself soon enough,' Chris responded. He turned to me. 'Let's take a walk, Cathy, down to the lake.'

'Wait a minute,' called Bart, appearing furious that we'd leave when he'd just come home. I was torn between wanting to escape with Chris and the desire to please my son. 'Where's Cindy?'

'She'll be coming soon,' I called back. 'Right now Cindy is visiting a girlfriend's home. You might be interested to learn that Jory is going to bring Melodie here for a vacation.'

Bart just stood there staring at me, perhaps appalled with the idea, and then came that strange excitement to replace all other emotions on his handsome, tanned face. 'Bart,' I said, resisting Chris's desire to hurry me away from a known source of trouble, 'the house is truly beautiful. All that you've done to change it has been a wonderful improvement.'

Again he appeared surprised. 'Mother, you mean it's not exactly the same? I thought it was . . .'

Oh, no, Bart. The balcony outside our suite of rooms wasn't there before.'

Bart whirled on his greatuncle. 'You told me it was!' he shouted.

Smiling sardonically, Joel stepped forward. 'Bart, my son, I didn't lie. I never lie. The original Hall did have that balcony. My father's mother ordered it put there. And by using that balcony, she was able to sneak in her lover without the servants seeing. Later she ran off with that lover without waking her husband, who kept their bedroom door locked and the key hidden. Malcolm ordered the balcony torn down when he was the owner . . . but it does add a certain kind of charm to that side of the house.'

Satisfied, Bart turned again to Chris and me. 'See, Mother, you don't know anything at all about this house. Uncle Joel is the expert. He's described to me in great detail all the furniture, the paintings, and, in the end, I'll have not only the same, but better than the original.'

Bart hadn't changed. He was still obsessed, still wanting to be a carbon copy of Malcolm Foxworth, if not in looks, in personality and in determination to be the richest man in the world, no matter what he did to gain that title.

MY SECOND SON

Not long after Bart arrived home, he began making elaborate plans for his upcoming birthday party. Apparently, to my surprise and delight, he'd made many friends in Virginia during the summer vacations he'd spent here. It used to hurt that he spent such a few of his vacation days with us in California, where I had considered he belonged. But now it seemed he knew people we'd never heard of, and had met young men and women in college that he intended to invite down to help him celebrate.

I'd only spent a few days at Foxworth Hall and already the monotony of days with nothing to do but eat, sleep, read, look at TV, and roam the gardens and woods had me on edge and eager to escape as soon as possible. The deep silence of the mountainside gripped me in its spell of isolation and despair. The silence wore on my nerves. I wanted to hear voices, many voices, hear the telephone ring, have people drop in and say hello, and nobody did. There was a group of local society members that had known the Foxworths well, and this was the very group Chris and I had to avoid. There were old friends in New York and California that I wanted to call and invite to Bart's party, but I didn't dare without Bart's approval. Restlessly I prowled the grand rooms alone, and sometimes with Chris. He and I walked the gardens, strolled through the woods, quiet sometimes, garrulous others.

He had his old hobby of watercolouring to begin again, and that kept him busy, but I wasn't supposed to dance anymore. Nevertheless I did my ballet exercises every day of my life just to keep myself slim and supple, and willingly enough I'd pose when he asked me to do that. Joel came upon me once as I held on to a chair in our sitting room, exercising in red leotards. I heard his gasp from the open doorway and turned to find him staring at me as if I were naked. 'What's wrong?' I asked worriedly. 'Has something terrible happened?'

He threw his thin, long, pale hands wide, his face expressive as he scanned over my body with contempt.

'Aren't you a little old to try to be seductive?'

'Have you ever heard of exercise, Joel?' I asked impatiently. 'You don't have to enter this wing. Just stay away from our rooms and your eyes won't be so scandalized.'

'You are disrespectful to someone older and wiser,' he said sharply.

'If I am, I apologize. But your words and your expression offend me. If there is to be peace in this house during our visit, stay away from me, Joel, while I am in my own wing. This huge house has more than enough space to give us all privacy without closing the doors.'

He stiffly turned away, but not before I'd seen the indignation in his eyes. I hurried to stare after him, wondering if I could be mistaken, and he was only a harmless old man who couldn't mind his own business. But I didn't call out to apologize. Instead I took off my leotards, put on shorts and a top, and with thoughts of Jory and his wife coming soon comforting me, I went to find Chris. I hesitated outside Bart's office door and listened to him talking to the caterer, planning for a minimum of two hundred guests. Just listening to him made me feel numb inside. *Oh, Bart, you don't realize some won't come, and if they do, Lord help us all.*

As I continued to stand there, I heard him name several of his invited guests, and they were not all from this country. Many were notables from Europe that he'd met on his tours. Throughout his college days he'd been tireless in his efforts to see the world and to meet important people, people who ruled and dominated either with political power, brains, or financial wizardry. I thought his restlessness was due to his inability to be happy in one place, and he was always longing for the next greener, farther field.

'They'll all come,' he said to the party on the other end of the line. 'When they read my invitation, they won't be able to decline.'

He hung up, then swung his chair about to face me. 'Mother! Are you eavesdropping?'

'It's a habit I caught from you, my darling.'

He scowled.

'Bart, why don't you just make your party a family affair? Or invite just your best friends. The villagers around here won't want to come. According to the tales my mother used to tell us, they have always disliked the Foxworths, who had too much when they had too little. The Foxworths came and went while the villagers had to stay. And please don't include the local society, even if Joel has told you they are his friends, and therefore yours and ours.'

'Afraid that your sins will be found out, Mother?' he asked without mercy. I was accustomed to this, but nevertheless I recoiled inwardly. Was it so terrible that Chris and I lived together as man and wife? Weren't the newspapers full of much worse crimes than ours?

'Oh, come, Mother, don't look like that. Let's be happy for a change.' His bronzed face took on a cheerful, exciting look, as if nothing I said would daunt his excitement. 'Mother, be excited for me, please. I'm ordering the best of everything. When the word spreads around, and it will because my caterer is the best in Virginia, and he loves to boast, no one will be able to resist coming to my party. They'll hear I'm sending to New York and to Hollywood for entertainers, and what's more, I'm sure everyone will want to see Jory and Melodie dance.'

Surprise and happiness filled me. 'Have you asked them?'

'No, but how can my own brother and sister-in-law refuse? You see, Mother, I'm planning to hold my party outdoors in the garden, in the moonlight. The lawns will be all lit up with golden globes. I'm having fountains put everywhere, and coloured lights will play upon the sprinkling water. There'll be imported champagne by the crates, and every other liquor you can name. The food will be the best. I'm having a theatre constructed in the midst of a wonderworld of fantasy where tables will be covered with beautiful cloths of every colour. Colour upon colour. Flowers will be banked all over. I'll show the world just what a Foxworth can do.'

On and on he enthused.

When I left his office and found Chris talking to one of the gardeners, I felt happy, reassured. Perhaps this was going to be the summer when Bart found himself, at last.

It would be as Chris had always predicted: Bart would not only inherit a fortune, he would inherit his sense of pride and worth and find himself . . . and pray God he found the right self.

Two days later I was in his office again, seated in one of his luxurious, deep, leather chairs, amazed to see how much he'd accomplished in his short time home. Apparently all this special extra office equipment had been ready and waiting to be installed the moment he was here to direct the placement. The small bedroom beyond the library he used for his office, where our detested grandfather had lived until he died, had been converted into a room of filing cabinets. The room where our grandfather's nurses had stayed became an office for Bart's secretary when or if he ever found one who met his stiff requirements. A computer dominated one long, curving desk, with its two printers that typed out different letters even as Bart and I conversed. It had surprised me to see him typing faster than I could. The drumming of the printers was muffled by heavy plexiglass covers.

Proudly he showed me how he could keep in touch with the world while staying at home, just by pushing buttons and joining up with a programme called 'The Source.' Only then did I learn that one summer he'd taken two months of computer programming. 'And, Mother, I can execute my buy and sell orders and avail myself of expert technical and fundamental data just by using this computer. I'll occupy my time that way until I open my own law firm.' For a moment he looked reflective, even doubtful. I still believed that he'd gone to Harvard just because his father had. Law held no real interest for him at all; he was only interested in making money, and then more money.

'Don't you have sufficient money already, Bart? What is it you can't buy?'

Something boyishly wistful and sweet visited his dark eyes. 'Respect, Mother. I don't have any talent, like you, like Jory. I can't dance. I can't draw a decent representation of a flower, much less draw the human form.' He was referring indirectly to Chris and his painting hobby. 'When I visit an art museum, I'm baffled by everyone's awe. I don't see anything wonderful about the "Mona Lisa". I see only a bland-faced, rather plain-looking woman who couldn't have been exciting. I don't appreciate classical music, any kind of music . . . and I've been told I have a rather good singing voice. I used to try and sing when I was a kid. Goofy kind of kid, wasn't I? Must have given you a million laughs.' He grinned appealingly, then spread his arms supplicatingly. 'I have no artistic talents, and so I fall back upon the kind of figures I can readily understand, those representing dollars and cents. I look around in museums, and the only things I see to admire are jewels.'

Sparkle came to his dark eyes. 'The glitter and sparkle of diamonds, rubies, emeralds, pearls . . . all that I can apprecitate. Gold, mountains of gold – that I can understand. I see the beauty in gold, silver, copper and oil. Do you know I visited Washington just to watch gold minted into coins? I felt a certain kind of elation, as if one day all that gold would be mine.'

Admiration faded and pity for him flooded me. 'What about women, Bart? What about love? A family? Good friends? Children? Don't you hope to fall in love and marry?'

He stared at me blankly for a moment or so, drumming his strong, square-nailed fingertips on his desktop before he got up to stand before a wide wall of windows, staring out at the gardens and beyond them the blue-misted mountains. 'I've experienced sex, Mother. I didn't expect to enjoy it, but I did. I felt my body betrayed my will. But I've never been in love. I can't imagine how it would be to devote myself to one woman when so many are beautiful and only too willing. I see a beautiful girl walk by, I turn and stare, only to find her turning and staring back at me. It's so easy to get them into my bed. No challenge at all.' He paused and turned his head to look at me. 'I use women, Mother, and sometimes I'm ashamed of myself. I take them, discard them, and even pretend I don't know them when I meet them again. They all end up hating me.'

He met my wide eyes with watchful challenge. 'Aren't you shocked?' he asked pleasantly. 'Or am I just the churlish type you always expected?'

I swallowed, hoping this time I could say the right thing. In the past it seemed I'd never said anything right. I doubted anyone could say words that would change Bart from what he was, and what he wanted to be . . . if he even knew. 'I suspect you are a product of your times,' I began in a soft voice, without recriminations. 'I almost pity your generation for missing out on the most beautiful aspect of falling in love. Where is the romance in your kind of taking, Bart? What do you give to the women you go to bed with? Don't you know it takes time to build a loving, lasting relationship? It doesn't happen overnight. One-night stands don't form commitments. You can look at a beautiful body and desire that body, but that's not love.'

His burning eyes showed such intensity and interest I was encouraged to go on, especially when he asked, 'How do you explain love?'

It was a trap he baited, knowing the loves of my life had all been ill-fated. Still I answered, hoping to save him from all the mistakes he was sure to make. 'I don't explain love, Bart. I don't think anyone can. It grows from day to day from having contact with that other person who understands your needs, and you understand theirs. It starts with a faltering flutter that touches your heart and makes you vulnerable to everything beautiful. You see beauty where before you'd seen ugliness. You feel glowing inside, so happy without knowing why. You appreciate what before you'd ignored. Your eyes meet with the eyes of the one you love, and you see reflected in them your own feelings, your own hopes and desires, and you're happy just to be with that person. Even when you don't touch, you still feel the warmth of being with that one person who fills all your thoughts. Then one day you do touch. Perhaps his hand, or her hand, and it feels good. It doesn't even have to be an intimate touch. An excitement begins to grow, so you want to be with that person, not to have sex . . . just to be with them and gradually grow towards one another. You share your life in words before you share your body. Only then do you start seriously thinking about having sex with that person. You begin to dream about it. Still you put it off, waiting, waiting for the right moment. You want this love to stay, to never end. So you go slowly, slowly towards the ultimate experience of your life. Day by day, minute by minute, second by second, and from moment to moment you anticipate that one person, knowing you won't be disappointed, knowing that person will be faithful, dependable . . . even when she's out of sight, or you're out of sight. There's trust, contentment, peace, happiness when you have genuine love. To be in love is like turning on a light in a dark room. All of a sudden everything becomes bright and visible. You're never alone because she loves you, and you love her.'

I paused for breath, saw his continued interest that gave me the courage to go on. 'I want that for you, Bart. More than all the billions of tons of gold in the world, more than all the jewels in vaults, I want you to find a wonderful girl to love. Forget money. You have enough. Look around, open your eyes and discover the joys of living, and forget your pursuit of money.'

Musingly, he said, 'So that's the way women feel about love and sex. I always wondered. It's not a man's kind of feeling, I do know that . . . still, what you said is interesting.'

He turned away before he went on. 'Truthfully, I don't know just what I want out of life but more money. They tell me I'll make an excellent attorney because I know how to debate. Yet I can't decide what branch of law I want. I don't want to be a criminal lawyer like my father was, for I'd often have to defend those I know were guilty. I couldn't to that. I think corporate law would be a bore. I've thought about politics, and this is the area I find most exciting, but I've got my damned psychological background to mar my record . . . so how can I go into politics?'

Rising from behind his desk, he stepped close enough to catch my hand in his. 'I like what you're telling me. Tell me more about your loves, about which man you loved best. Was it Julian, your first husband? Or was it that wonderful doctor named Paul? I think I would have loved him if I could remember him. He married you to give me his name. I wish I could see him in my memory, like Jory can, but I can't. Jory remembers him well. He even remembers seeing my father.' His manner turned very intense as he leaned to lock his eyes with mine. 'Tell me that you loved my father best. Say *he* was the one and only man who really seized your heart. Don't tell me you only used him for your revenge against your mother! Don't tell me that you used his love to escape from the love of your own brother.'

I couldn't speak.

His brooding, morose, dark eyes studied me. 'Don't you realize yet that you and your brother have always managed with your incestuous relationship to ruin and contaminate my life? I used to hope and pray someday you'd leave him, but it never happens. I've adjusted to the fact that the two of you are obsessed with one another and perhaps enjoy your relationship more because it is against the will of God.'

Snared again! I rose to my feet, knowing he'd used his sweet voice to beguile me into his trap.

'Yes, I loved your father, Bart, don't you ever doubt that. I admit I wanted revenge for all that our mother had done to us, so I went after my stepfather. Then, when I had him, and I knew I loved him, and he loved me, I felt I'd trapped myself as well as him. He couldn't marry me. He loved me in one way – and my mother in another way. He was torn between us. I decided to end his indecision by becoming pregnant. Even then he was undecided. Only on the night when he believed my story of being imprisoned by his own wife did he turn against her and say he'd marry me. I thought her money would bind him to her forever, but he would have married me.'

I rose to leave. Not a word did Bart say to give me a hint as to his thoughts. At the door I turned to look back at him. He was seated again in his desk chair, his elbows on the blotter, his hands cradling his bowed head. 'Do you think anyone will ever love me for myself and not for my money, Mother?'

My heart skipped a beat.

'Yes, Bart. But you won't find a girl around here who doesn't know you're very wealthy. Why don't you go away? Settle in the Northeast or in the West. Then when you find a girl she won't know you are rich, especially if you work as an ordinary lawyer . . .'

He looked up then. 'I've already had my surname changed legally, Mother.'

Dread filled me, and I didn't really need to ask, 'What is your last name now?'

'Foxworth,' he said, confirming my suspicion. 'After all, I can't be a Winslow when my father was not your husband. And to keep Sheffield is deceitful. Paul wasn't my father, nor was your brother, thank God.'

I shivered and turned icy with apprehension. This was the first step . . . turning himself into another Malcolm, what I'd feared most. 'I wish you'd chosen Winslow for your surname, Bart. That would have pleased your dead father.'

'Yes, I'm sure,' he said dryly. 'And I did consider that seriously. But in choosing Winslow, I would forfeit my legitimate right to the Foxworth name. It's a good name, Mother, a name respected by everyone except those villagers, who don't count anyway. I feel Foxworth Hall truly belongs to me without contamination, without guilt.' His eyes took on a brilliant, happy glow. 'You see, and Uncle Joel agrees, not everyone hates me and thinks I am less than Jory.' He paused to watch my reaction. I tried to show nothing. He seemed disappointed. 'Leave, Mother. I've got a long day of work ahead of me.'

I risked his anger by lingering long enough to say, 'While you're shut away in this office, Bart, I want you to keep remembering your family loves you very much, and all of us want what's best for you. If more money will make you feel better about yourself, then make yourself the richest man in the world. Just find happiness, that's all we want for you.

Find your niche, just where you fit, that's the most important thing.'

Closing his office door behind me, I was headed for the stairs when I almost bumped into Joel. A guilty look flashed momentarily through the blue of his watery eyes. I guessed he'd been listening to Bart and me. But hadn't I done the same thing inadvertantly? 'I'm sorry I didn't see you in the shadows, Joel.'

'I didn't mean to eavesdrop,' he said with a peculiar look. 'Those who expect to hear evil will not be disappointed,' and away he scurried like an old church mouse, lean from lack of enough fuel to feed his appetite for making trouble. He made me feel guilty, ashamed. Suspicious, always so damned suspicious of anyone named Foxworth.

Not that I didn't have just cause.

MY FIRST SON

Six days before the party, Jory and Melodie flew into a local airport. Chris and I were there to meet them with the kind of enthusiasm you saved for those you hadn't seen for years, and we'd parted less than ten days ago. Jory was immediately chagrined because Bart hadn't come along to welcome them to his fabulous new home.

'He's busy in the gardens, Jory, Melodie, and asked us to give you his apologies' (although he hadn't). Both looked at me as if they knew differently. Quickly I went into details of how Bart was supervising hordes of workmen come to change our lawns into paradise, or something as near that as possible.

Jory smiled to hear of such an ostentatious party; he preferred small, intimate parties where everyone knew each other. He said pleasantly enough, 'Nothing new under the sun. Bart's always too busy when it comes to me and my wife.'

I stared up into his face so like that of my adolescent first husband, Julian, who had also been my dancing partner. The husband whose memory still hurt and filled me with that same old tormenting guilt. Guilt that I tried to erase by loving his son best. 'Every time I see you you look more like your father.'

We were seated side by side, as Melodie sat beside Chris, and occasionally said a few words to him. Jory laughed and put his arms about me, inclining his dark, handsome head to brush my cheek with his warm lips. 'Mom . . . you say that each and every time you see me. When am I going to reach the zenith of being my father?'

Laughing, too, I released him and settled back to cross my legs and stare out at the beautiful countryside. The rolling hills, the misty mountains with the tops hidden in the clouds. Near Heaven, I kept thinking. I had to force my attention back to Jory, who had so many virtues Julian had never possessed, could never have possessed. Jory was more like Chris in personality than like Julian, although that, too, filled me with guilt, with shame, for it could have been different between Julian and I – but for Chris.

At the age of twenty-nine, Jory was a wonderfully handsome man, with long, strong, beautiful legs and firm, round buttocks that made all the women stare when he danced on to stage wearing tights. His thick hair was blue-black and curly, but not frizzy; his lips exceptionally red and sensuously shaped, his nose a perfect slope with nostrils that could flare wide with anger or passion. He had a hot temper he'd learned to control a long time ago, mostly because of all the control it took for him to tolerate Bart. Jory's inner beauty radiated from him with an electric force, a *joie de vivre*. His beauty was more than mere handsomeness; he had the added strength of a certain spiritual quality and was like Chris in his cheerful optimism, his faith that all that happened in his life had to be for the best.

Jory wore his success with grace, with touching humility and dignity, displaying none of the arrogance that had been Julian's even when he had performed poorly.

So far Melodie had said very little, as if she contained volumes of secrets she was dying to spill out, but for some reason was holding back, awaiting her opportunity to be centre stage. Customarily my daughter-in-law and I were very good friends. Countless times she twisted around in the front seat to smile back at me happily. 'Stop teasing,' I admonished. 'What's this good news you have to tell us?'

Again came that taut look on her face as she flicked her eyes to Jory, making her appear a locked gold purse about to burst if she didn't tell us soon. 'Is Cindy there yet?' she asked.

When I said no, Melodie turned again to face the windshield. Jory winked. 'We're going to keep you in suspense a while longer, so everyone can enjoy our surprise to its full extent. Besides, right now Dad's so intent on seeing we reach that house safely that he couldn't give our secret the appreciation it needs.'

After an hour's ride we were turning on to our private road, which spiralled up the mountain, with deep ravines or precipices always on one side, forcing Chris to drive even more carefully.

Once we were in the house and I'd shown them around downstairs, and they had exclaimed and oh'ed and ah'ed, Melodie came flying into my arms, ducking her head shyly down on my shoulder, for she was inches taller than I. 'Go on, darling,' encouraged Jory softly.

Quickly she released me and threw a proud smile at Jory, who smiled back at her reassuringly. Then she was spilling out the contents of that bulging gold purse.

'Cathy, I wanted to wait for Cindy and tell you all at once, but I'm so happy I'm bursting. I'm pregnant! You just don't know how thrilled I am when I've been wanting this baby ever since the first year Jory and I married. I'm a little over two months along. Our baby is due in early January.'

Stunned, I could only stare at her before I glanced at Jory, who had told me many times he didn't want to begin a family until he'd had ten years at the top. Still, he stood there smiling and looking as proud as any man would at this instant, as if he were accepting this unexpected and unplanned child very well.

That was enough to make me overjoyed. 'Oh, Melodie, Jory, I'm so thrilled for you both. A baby! I'm going to be a grandmother.' Then I sobered. Did I want to be a grandmother? Chris was slapping Jory on the back as if he were the first man ever to impregnate his wife; then he was embracing Melodie and asking questions about how she felt and if she was experiencing morning sickness – just like the doctor he was.

Because he was seeing something I wasn't, I looked at her more closely. She had shadows beneath hollowed eyes, and was much too thin to be pregnant. However, there was nothing that could steal from Melodie her classical type of cool blonde beauty. She moved with grace, appearing regal even when she just picked up a magazine and flipped through it – as she was doing now. I was baffled. 'What's wrong, Melodie?'

'Nothing,' she said, gone stiff for no apparent reason, telling me instead that everything was wrong.

My eyes met briefly with Jory's. He nodded, indicating he'd tell me later what was bothering Melodie.

All the way back to Foxworth Hall I'd been dreading the meeting between Bart and his older brother, fearing there would be an ugly scene to start everything out wrong. I strode to a window overlooking a side lawn and saw that Bart was on the racket ball court, playing by himself with the same kind of intensity to win, as though he had a partner to batter down to defeat. 'Bart!' I called, opening a French door, 'your brother and his wife are here.'

'Be there in a sec,' he called back, and continued to play.

'Where are all the workers?' asked Jory, looking around at the spacious gardens empty now of anyone but Bart. I explained most left about four, wanting to drive home before they were caught in the late evening traffic.

Finally Bart threw down his racket and sauntered our way, a broad, welcoming smile on his face. We all stepped on to a side terrace covered with multicoloured flagstones and decorated with many live plants and pretty patio furniture with colourful umbrellas to shield us from the sun. Melodie seemed to pull in her breath and straighten her spine as she moved closer to Jory. She didn't need his protection this time. Bart's steps picked up until eventually he was running, and Jory was speeding to greet him. My heart could have burst . . . brothers, at last! Like they had been when both were very young. They pounded each other on the back, ruffled each other's hair, and then Bart was pumping Jory's hand up and down, slapping him on the shoulder again, the way men often do. He turned to look Melodie over.

All his enthusiasm died. 'Hi, Melodie,' he said briefly, then went on to congratulate Jory for their successes on stage and the adulation they received. 'Proud of you both,' he said with a strange smile.

'We've got news for you, brother,' said Jory. 'You are now looking at the happiest husband and wife in the world, for we're going to be parents come January.'

Bart gazed at Melodie, who avoided meeting his eyes. She half turned towards Jory, with the sun behind her turning her honey-blond hair fiery red near her scalp, making a golden haze of the outer strands, so it almost seemed she was sporting a golden halo. Madonna pure she stood in profile as if poised for flight. The grace of her long neck, the gentle slope of her small nose, the fullness of her pouting rosy lips gave her the kind of ethereal beauty that had helped to make her one of the most beautiful and admired ballerinas in America.

'Pregnancy becomes you, Melodie,' Bart said softly, ignoring what Jory was telling him about cancelling one year of bookings so he could be with Melodie throughout her pregnancy and help after the baby was born in all kinds of husbandly ways.

Bart stared towards the French door where Joel stood silently watching our family reunion. I resented his being there; then, ashamed, I gestured him forward even as Bart called out, 'Come, let me introduce you to my brother and his wife.'

Advancing slowly, Joel shuffled along the flagstones, making each step whisper. Gravely he greeted Jory and Melodie after Bart's introduction, not extending his hand to be shaken. 'I hear that you are a dancer,' he said to Jory.

'Yes . . . I've worked all my life to be called that.'

Joel turned and left without another word to anyone.

'Just who is that weird old man?' asked Jory. 'Mom, I thought you told us that both your maternal uncles died in accidents when they were very young.'

I shrugged and let Bart explain.

In no time at all, we had Jory and his wife established in a very rich-looking suite with heavy red velvet draperies, red carpet and dark panelled walls that made the suite exceedingly masculine. Melodie took a look around, wrinkling her nose a bit in distaste. 'Rich . . . nice . . . really,' she said with heavy effort.

Jory laughed. 'Honey, we can't always expect white walls with blue carpet, can we? I like this room, Bart. It looks like your kind of bedroom – classy.'

Bart wasn't listening to Jory. He still had his eyes glued on Melodie, who glided from one piece of furniture to another, running her long, graceful fingers over the slick, polished tops before she glanced into the adjacent sitting room and then went on into the magnificent bath with an old-fashioned walnut tub lined with pewter. She laughed to see the tub. 'Oh, I'm going to enjoy that. Look at the depth – water right up to your chin if you want it that way.'

'Fair women look so dramatic in dark settings,' said Bart almost without realizing he'd spoken. No one said a word, not even Jory, who gave him a hard look.

In that bath was also a walk-in shower and a lovely dressing table of the same walnut with a three-winged gold-framed mirror, so the occupant seated on the velvet-covered stool could see herself from every angle.

We dined early and sat outside on a terrace in the twilight hours. Joel didn't join us, and for that I was grateful. Bart had little to say, but he couldn't keep his eyes off Melodie in her frail blue dress that moulded to every delicate curve of thigh, hip, waist and bust. I felt a sinking sensation to see him studying her so closely, with desire written clearly in those dark, blistering eyes.

At the breakfast table on the terrace outside the dining room, the daisies were yellow. We had hope now. We could look at yellow and not fear we'd never see sunlight again.

Chris was laughing at something funny Jory had just reported, while Bart only smiled, still keeping his eyes on Melodie, who picked at her breakfast without appetite. 'Everything I eat comes up sooner or later,' she explained with a small look of embarrassment. 'It's not the food, it's me. I'm supposed to eat slowly and not think about losing the meal . . . but that's all I'm thinking of.' Just beyond her shoulder, in the shadows of a giant live palm planted in a huge clay pot, Joel had his gaze riveted also on Melodie, studying her profile. Then he was looking at Jory, narrowing his eyes again.

'Joel,' I called, 'step forward and join us for breakfast.'

He advanced reluctantly, cautiously, whispering his soft-soled shoes over the flagstones, holding his arms crosswise over his chest, as if he wore an invisible coarse, brown, homespun monk's habit, and his hands were tucked neatly out of sight up the wide sleeves. He seemed a judge sent to weigh us in for Heaven's pearly gates. His voice was slight and polite as he greeted Jory and Melodie, nodding in answer to their questions that plied him for information on what it was like to live as a monk. 'I couldn't bear life without women,' said Jory, 'without music and lots of different types of people all around. I get a little from this person, something else from another. It takes hundreds of friends to keep me happy. Already I'm missing those in our ballet company.'

'It takes all kinds to make the world go round,' said Joel, 'and the Lord giveth before he taketh away.' Then he ambled off, his head bowed low, as if he whispered prayers and fingered a rosary. 'The Lord must have known what he was doing when he made each of us so different,' I heard him murmur.

Jory swivelled about in his chair to stare after Joel. 'So that's our greatuncle, who we presumed died in a skiing accident. Mom, wouldn't it be odd if the other brother turned up as well?'

Jumping to his feet, Bart's face flamed furious. 'Don't be ridiculous! Malcolm's eldest son died when his motorcycle went over a precipice, and they found his body and buried it. It's in the family cemetery that I've visited often. According to Uncle Joel, his father sent detectives looking for his lost second son, and that's one reason my uncle had to stay hidden in that monastery, until eventually he grew used to it and began to fear life on the outside.' He flicked his eyes at me, as if to recognize the fact that we, too, as children, had grown accustomed to our imprisoned life, fearing the outside.

'He says when you are isolated for long periods, you begin to see people as they really are – as if distance gives you better perspective.'

Chris and I met eyes. Yes, we knew about isolation.

Standing, Chris gestured to Jory and offered to show him around. 'Bart's planning horse stables, so he can have fox hunts like Malcolm used to have. Perhaps one day we may even want to join in that kind of sport.

'Sport?' queried Melodie, rising gracefully and hurrying to catch up with Jory. 'I don't call a pack of hungry hounds chasing a cute little harmless fox a true sport – it's barbaric, that's what!'

'That's the trouble with those in the ballet – too sensitive for the real world,' Bart retorted before he stalked off in a different direction.

Later on in the afternoon, I found Chris in the foyer watching Jory work out before the mirrors, using a chair for a barre. The two men shared the kind of relationship I hoped would develop one day between Chris and Bart. Father and son, both admiring and respecting the other. My arms crossed over my breasts to hug myself. I was so happy to have all my family together, or at least it would be when Cindy arrived. And the expected baby would be more cement to bind us together . . .

Jory had warmed up enough and began to dance to *The Firebird* music. Whirling so fast he was a dazzling blur, whipping his legs, leaping into the air, bounding to land as light as a feather so you didn't hear his feet hit the floor. His muscles rippled as he jetéd again and again, spreading his legs so his outstretched arms allowed his fingertips to touch his toes. I filled with excitement, watching him perform, knowing he was showing off for our benefit.

'Would you look at those jetés?' said Chris when he caught sight of me. 'Why, he clears the floor by twelve feet or more. I don't believe what I'm seeing!'

'Ten feet, not twelve,' corrected Jory as he whirled by, spinning, spinning, covering the immense space of the foyer in mere seconds. Then he fell breathlessly down on a quilted floor mat put there so he'd have a place to rest without his body sweat fading the delicate and fancy chair coverings. 'Damned hard floor if I fall . . .' he gasped as he lay back and rested on his elbows.

'And the spread of his legs when he leaps, it's unbelievable he can be so supple at his age.'

'Dad, I'm only twenty-nine, not thirty-nine!' protested Jory, who had a thing about growing older and losing the spotlight to a younger *danseur*. 'I've got at least eleven good years ahead before I begin to slide.'

I knew exactly what he was thinking as he sprawled there on the mat, looking so much like Julian. It was as if I were twenty or so again. The muscles of all male dancers approaching forty began to harden and become brittle so that their once magnificent bodies weren't as attractive to the audience any longer. Off with the old, on with the new . . . the fear of all performers, although ballerinas with their layer of fat under their skin could hold on longer. Falling on the mat beside Jory, I sat cross-legged in my pink slacks.

'Jory, you are going to last longer than most *danseurs*, so stop worrying. It's a long and glamorous road you have to travel to reach forty, and who knows, maybe you'll be fifty before you retire.'

'Yeah, sure,' he said, tucking his hands behind his curly head and staring up at the distant ceiling. 'Fourteenth in a long line of dancers has to be the lucky number, doesn't it?'

How many times had I heard him say he couldn't live without dancing? Since he was a small boy of two, I'd put his feet on the road to where he was now.

Down the stairs Melodie glided, looking beautiful and fresh from a recent bath and shampoo, seeming a fragile spring flower in her blue leotards. 'Jory, my doctor said I could keep on with light practice, and I want to dance as long as possible to keep my muscles supple and long . . . so dance with me, lover. Dance and dance, and then let's dance some more.'

Instantly Jory bounded to his feet and whirled to the foot of the stairs, where he fell upon one knee in the romantic position of a prince seeing the princess of his dreams. 'My pleasure, my lady . . .' and swinging her off her feet, he whirled with her in his arms before he put her down with the skilled practice and grace that made her seem to have the weight of a feather. They whirled around, always dancing for the other, as once Julian and I had danced for the sure delight of being young, alive and able. Tears came to my eyes as I stood beside Chris and watched them.

Sensing my thoughts, Chris put his arm about my shoulder and drew me closer. 'They're beautiful together, aren't they? Made for each other, I would say. If I squint my eyes and see them hazily, I see you dancing with Julian . . . only you were far prettier, Catherine, far prettier . . .'

Behind us Bart snorted.

Whipping around, I saw Joel had trailed behind Bart like a well-trained puppy and at his heel he stopped, his head low, his hands still tucked up those invisible brown homespun sleeves. 'The Lord giveth, and the Lord taketh away,' mumbled Joel again.

Why the devil did he keep saying that?

Uneasily I looked from Joel to Bart and found his admiring gaze again riveted on Melodie, who was in arabesque position, waiting for Jory to sweep her up in his arms. I didn't like what I saw in Bart's dark, envious look, the desire that burned hotter by the hour. The world was full of unmarried women – he didn't need Melodie, his brother's wife!

Wildly Bart applauded as their dance ended and both were gazing transfixed at each other, forgetting we were there. 'You've got to dance like that at my birthday party! Jory, say that you and Melodie will.'

Reluctantly Jory turned his head to smile at Bart. 'Why, if you want me, of course, but not Mel. Her doctor will allow a little mild dancing and practicing, like we just did, but not that strenuous kind needed for a professional performance, and I know you'll want only the best.'

'But I want Melodie, too,' protested Bart. He smiled charmingly at his brother's wife. 'Please, for my birthday, Melodie, just this one time . . . and you're not so far along anyone will notice your condition.'

Appearing uncertain, Melodie stared at Bart. 'I don't think I should,' she said lamely. 'I want our baby to be healthy. I can't risk losing it.'

Bart tried to persuade her, and might have, but Jory put a brisk end to the debate. 'Now, listen, Bart, I told our agent Mel's doctor didn't want her to perform, and if she does, he might get wind of it and we could be sued. Besides, she's very fatigued. The kind of easy fun dancing you just witnessed is not the kind we do when we're serious. A professional performance demands hours and hours of warm-ups and practice and rehearsal. Don't plead, it's embarrassing. When Cindy comes she can dance with me.'

'No!' Bart snarled, frowning now and losing all his charm. 'She can't dance like Melodie.'

No, she couldn't. Cindy wasn't a professional, but she did well enough when she wanted to. Jory and I had trained her since she was two.

Several feet behind Bart, like a skinny dark shadow, Joel's hands came out of wide sleeves and templed beneath his bowed head. He had his eyes closed, as if again in prayer. How irritating to have him around all the time.

Deliberately I turned my thoughts from him to Cindy. I couldn't wait to see her again. Couldn't wait to hear her breathless girlish chatter that told of proms and dates and the boys she knew. All the things that brought back to me my own youth, and my own desires to have what Cindy was experiencing.

In the rosy glow of the evening sunset, I stood unobserved in the shadows of a great arch overhead and watched Jory again dancing with Melodie in the huge foyer. Again in leotards, this time violet ones, with the filmy tunic to flutter enticingly, Melodie had bound violet satin ribbons under her small, firm breasts. She appeared a princess dancing with her lover. Oh, the passion Jory and Melodie had between them stirred a wistful longing in my own loins. To be young again like them . . . to have the chance to do it all over . . . do it right the second time around . . .

Suddenly I was aware that Bart was in another alcove, as if he'd waited to spy . . . or, more generously, watch as I watched. And he was the one who didn't like ballet and didn't care for beautiful music. He leaned casually against a door frame, his arms folded over his chest. But the burning dark eyes that followed Melodie weren't casual. They were full of the desire I'd seen before. My heart skipped.

When had Bart ever not wanted what belonged to Jory?

The music soared. Jory and Melodie had forgotten they might be observed and became so involved in what they were doing that they danced on and on, wildly passionate, entranced with each other, until Melodie ran to leap into his outstretched arms. Even as she did her lips pressed down on his. Parting lips that met again and again. Hands that roamed to seek out all the secret places. I was as much caught up in their lovemaking as Bart, unable to back away. Their kisses seemed to devour one another. In the heat of kindled desire, they fell to the floor and rolled on to the mat. Even as I strode towards Bart, I heard their heavy breathing, growing louder.

'Come, Bart, it's not right to stand and watch when the dancing is over.'

He jumped as if my touch on his arm burned. The yearning in his eyes both hurt and frightened me.

'They should learn to control themselves when they're guests in my home,' he said in a gruff voice, not taking his eyes off the forgetful pair rolling about on the mat, arms and legs entwined, sweaty hair wet and clinging as they kissed.

I yanked Bart into the music room and softly closed the door behind us. This was not a room I favoured. It had been decorated to please Bart's very masculine taste. There was a grand piano that no one every played, although I'd seen Joel finger it once or twice, then snatch his hands away as if the ivory keys singed him with sin. But the piano lured him so often he just stood staring at it, his fingers flexing and unflexing.

Bart strode towards a cabinet that opened to reveal a lighted bar. He reached for a crystal decanter to pour himself a stiff scotch. No water or ice. In one gulp he downed it. Then he was looking at me in a guilty fashion. 'Nine years of marriage. Still they aren't tired of one another. What is it that you and Chris have that Jory has captured and I haven't?'

I flushed before my head bowed low. 'I didn't know you drank alone.'

'There's a lot you don't know about me, dear Mother.' He poured a second scotch, I heard the slow gurgle of the fluid without looking up. 'Even Malcolm had a drink once in a while.'

Curiosity filled me. 'Do you still think about Malcolm?'

He fell into a chair, crossed his legs by placing one ankle on the opposite knee. I looked away, thinking that once my second son had the most irritating ways of putting his feet on anything available, ruining many a good chair with his muddy boots, and bedspreads suffered early deaths. Then my eyes went back to his shoes. How did he keep the soles so clean, so they appeared never to have walked on anything but velvet?

Bit by bit Bart had lost all his messy ways on the way towards manhood. 'Why do you stare at my shoes, Mother?'

'They're very handsome.'

'Do you really think so?' He gazed down at them indifferently. 'They cost six hundred bucks, and I paid another hundred to have the soles treated so they'll never show scuff marks or dirt. It's the "in" thing to do, you know. Wear shoes with clean soles.'

I frowned. What psychological message did that impart? 'The tops will wear out before the soles do.'

'So what?'

I had to agree. What did money mean to any of us now? We had more than we could possibly spend. 'When the tops wear, I'll throw them out and buy a new pair.'

'Then why bother to have the soles treated?'

'Mother, really,' he said crossly. 'I like everything to keep its new appearance until I'm ready to discard it – I'm going to hate looking at Melodie when she's bulging in the middle like some breeding cow . . .'

'I'll be happy the day she shows, then perhaps you can move your eyes away from her.'

He lit a cigarette, met my eyes calmly. 'I bet I could easily take her away from Jory.'

'How dare you say such a thing?' I cried angrily.

'She never looks at me, have you noticed? I don't think she wants to see that I'm better looking than Jory now, and taller, and smarter, and a hundred times richer.'

Our eye contact held. I swallowed nervously, plucked invisible lint from my clothes. 'Cindy's coming tomorrow.'

He shut his eyes briefly, gripped the arms of his chair harder, but otherwise showed no expression. 'I disapprove of that girl,' he finally managed.

'I hope you won't be unkind to her while she's here. Can't you remember the way she used to tag around, adoring you? She loved you before you turned her against you. She'd still adore you if you'd stopped teasing her so unmercifully. Bart . . . aren't you sorry for all the ugly things you said and did to your sister?'

'She's *not* my sister.'

'She is, Bart, she is!'

'Oh, God, Mother, I'll never think of Cindy as my sister. She's adopted, not truly one of us. I've read a few of those letters she writes to you. Can't you see what she is? Or do you only read what she says, and not what she means? How can any girl be that popular and not be giving out?'

I jumped to my feet. 'What's wrong with you, Bart?' I yelled. 'You deny Chris as your father, Cindy as your sister, Jory as your brother. Don't you need to have anyone but yourself – and that hateful old man who trails you about?'

'I've got a little of you, don't I, Mother?' he said, narrowing his eyes to sinister slots. 'And I've got my Uncle Joel, who is a very interesting man, who is, of this moment, praying for all our souls.'

A red flag waved in my face. I flamed with instant anger. 'You're an idiot if you prefer that creepy old man to the only father you've ever had!' I tried to keep my emotions under control but failed, as I'd always failed when it came to Bart and control. 'Have you forgotten all the many kind deeds Chris has done for you? Is still doing for you?'

Bart leaned forward, piercing me with his diamond-hard glare. 'But for Chris I would have had a happy life. With you married to my real father, I could have been the perfect son! Far more perfect than Jory. Maybe I'm like *you*, Mother. Maybe I need *my* revenge more than I need anything else.'

'Why do *you* need revenge?' Surprise was in my voice, a certain kind of hopelessness. 'No one has done to you what was done to me.'

He leaned forward, very intense as he bit out, 'You think because you gave me all the necessary things, all the clothes I needed, all the food I could eat, and a house to shelter me, you made yourself believe that was enough, but it wasn't. I knew you saved the best of your love for Jory. Then, after Cindy came, you gave your second best to her. You had nothing left to give me but pity – and I hate you for pitying me!'

Sudden nausea almost made me gag. I was glad I had the chair beneath me. 'Bart,' I began, struggling not to cry and show the very kind of weakness he'd despise, 'perhaps once I did pity you for being clumsy, for being unconfident. Most of all, I was sorry you hurt youself so often. But how can I pity you now? You're very handsome, intelligent, and when you want to be, extremely charming as well. What reason do I have now for pitying you?'

'That's what bothers me,' he said in a low voice. 'You make me look at myself in the mirror, wondering what it is you see. I've come to the conclusion that you just don't like me. 'You don't trust me, don't believe in me. I see in your eyes right now that you don't believe I'm completely sane.' Suddenly his eyes, which had half-closed, opened wide. He stared penetratingly into my eyes, which had always been easy to read. He laughed short and hard. 'It's there, dear Mother, that suspicion, that same fear. I can read your mind, don't think I can't. You think someday I'll do something to betray you and your brother, when I've had chances enough to do exactly that and I've done nothing. I've kept your sins to myself.

'Why not be honest and say now you didn't love your mother's second husband. Say truthfully you only used him as the instrument of your revenge. You went after him, got him, conceived me, then he was dead. True to the kind of woman you are, you then headed straight back to that poor doctor in South Carolina, who no doubt believed in you and loved you beyond reason. Did he realize you married him just as a means to give your bastard child a name? Did he know you used him to escape Chris? See how much thought I've given to your motivations? And now I've come to another conclusion: you see a lot of Chris in Jory – and that's what you love! You look at me and see Malcolm, and although my face and physique may resemble that of my true father, you ignore that and see what you want to in my eyes. In my eyes you think you see the soul of Malcolm. Now tell me that I've presumed wrongly! Go on, tell me I'm not speaking the truth.'

My lips parted to deny every word, but nothing came out.

I panicked inside, wanting to run to him and pull his head against my breast, as I so often comforted Jory, but I couldn't make my feet move in Bart's direction. I truthfully did fear him. As he was now, fiercely intense and cold and hard, I was afraid of him, and fear made my love turn to dislike.

He waited for me to speak, to deny his charges, and in the end, I did the worst thing possible – I ran from the room.

On my bed I threw myself down and cried. Every word he'd said was true! I hadn't known Bart could read me like an open book. Now I was terrified of what he might do someday to destroy not only Chris and me, but Cindy, Jory and Melodie.

CINDY

Around eleven the next day, Cindy arrived in a taxi, running into the house like a fresh, invigorating, spring breeze. She hurled herself into my arms, reeking of some exotic perfume I thought too sophisticated for a girl of sixteen, an opinion I knew I'd better keep to myself.

'Oh, Momma,' she cried, kissing and hugging me repeatedly, 'it's so good to see you again!' Her lavishings of affection left me quite breathless as I eagerly responded. All the while, even as we embraced, she managed to stare around at the grand rooms with all their elegant furnishings. Holding to my hand, she pulled me from one room to another, gasping and exclaiming at the beauty of everything so fine and rich.

'Where's Dad?' she asked. I explained that Chris had driven into Charlottesville to turn in his rented car for a more luxurious model.

'Darling, he hoped to be back before you reached here. Something must have slowed him down. Be patient, and in a second or two he'll stroll in the door and welcome you.'

Satisfied, she again exclaimed, 'Momma, wow-wow! What a house! You didn't tell me it would be like this. You made me think the new Foxworth Hall would be just as ugly and scary as the first.'

To me, Foxworth Hall would always be ugly and scary, yet it was thrilling to watch Cindy's excitement flow over. She was taller than I, her young breasts ripe and full, her waist very slender so it emphasized the gentle swell of her beautifully formed hips with the flat belly, while her buttocks rounded out her short skirt delightfully. Looking at her figure sideways, I had to compare her to a burgeoning flower, so tender, so frail appearing, and yet she had exceptional endurance.

Her full and heavy long golden hair was casually styled. It blew wild in the wind as we went out to watch Jory and Bart fighting it out on the new tennis courts. 'Oh, gosh, Momma, you do have two beautiful sons,' she whispered as she stared at their bronzed, strong bodies. 'I never thought Bart would grow up to be just as handsome as Jory, not when he was such an ugly little brute.'

Amazed, I stared at her. Bart had been too thin, always with scabs and scars on his legs, and his dark hair had never been tidy, but he'd been a good-looking little boy, certainly not ugly looking – only ugly acting. And once upon a time, Cindy had worshipped Bart. A knife twisted in my heart as I realized so much of what Bart had said last night was true. I *had* put Cindy ahead of him. I had thought she was perfect and incapable of doing wrong, and still did.

'Do try to be kind and thoughtful to Bart,' I whispered, seeing Joel coming our way.

'Who's that funny-looking old man?' asked Cindy, turning to stare at Joel as he bent stiffly to pull up a few weeds. 'Don't tell me Bart has hired somebody like him for a gardener – why, he can hardly straighten up once he's crooked.'

Before I could answer, Joel was upon us, smiling as broadly as his false teeth would allow. 'Why, you must be Cindy, the one Bart talks about all the time,' he said with some faint leftover charm, taking Cindy's reluctantly offered hand and putting it to his thin, crooked lips.

I could tell she wanted to yank her hand away, yet she tolerated the touch of his lips. The sun through Joel's almost white hair still streaked with Foxworth gold made it seem terribly thin. Suddenly I realized I hadn't told Cindy about Joel and hastened to introduce them. She seemed fascinated once she knew who he was. 'You really mean you knew that hateful old Grandfather Malcolm? You are really his son? Why, you must be really ancient . . .'

'Cindy, that's not tactful . . .'

'I'm sorry, Uncle Joel. It's just when I hear my mom and dad talk of their youth, it seems a million years ago.' She laughed charmingly, smiling apologetically at Joel. 'You know something, you look a lot like my dad in some ways. When he's really old, no doubt he'll grow to look like you.'

Joel turned his eyes towards Chris, who'd just driven up and was even now stepping out of a beautiful new blue Cadillac with his arms full of packages. He'd picked up gifts I'd had engraved for Bart's birthday. For his birthday, I'd gone all out and given him only the best, as he would expect: an attaché case of the finest leather, with combination locks, for Chris to give him. Eighteen-carat gold cufflinks with his initials in diamonds and a matching gold cigarette case, also monogramed in diamonds – the gem Bart respected most, from me. His father had carried such a cigarette case, given to him by my mother.

Dropping the packages on to a lawn chair, Chris held his arms open. Cindy hurled herself into his welcoming embrace. She covered his face with a rain of small kisses, leaving her lip marks all over his face. Staring up into his face, she pleaded. 'This is going to be the best summer of my life. Daddy, can't we stay here until school starts in the fall, so I can know what it's like to live in a real mansion, with all those beautiful rooms and fancy bathrooms. I already know which one I want, the one with all those pink and white and gold girlish things. He knows I just adore pink, really love pink, and already I adore and love this house! Just love it, love it!'

A shadow flickered through Chris's eyes as he released her and turned to look at me. 'We'll have to talk that over, Cindy. As you know, your mother and I are here just to help Bart celebrate his twenty-fifth birthday.'

I looked over towards where Bart smashed the tennis ball with such force it's a wonder it didn't burst. Running like a streak of white light, Jory slammed the yellow ball back to Bart, who ran just as fast to swoop and cleverly whack it back with just as much force. Both were hot and sweaty, their faces reddening from the exercise and the hot sun. 'Jory, Bart,' I called, 'Cindy's here. Come to say hello.'

Instantly Jory turned his head to smile, causing him to miss the next yellow ball that came hurtling his way. He failed to return it, and Bart whooped for joy. He jumped up and down, hurled down his expensive racket, shouting, 'I win!'

'You win by default,' said Jory, throwing down his racket as well. He ran our way, his face all smiles. He threw back at Bart, 'Default winning doesn't count.'

'It does so count!' bellowed Bart. 'What the hell do we care whether or not Cindy's here? You just used that to quit before my score topped yours.'

'Have it your way,' answered Jory. In a moment he was swinging Cindy off her feet, whirling her around and around, making her blue skirt fly and reveal skimpy bikini panties. It amused me to see that Cindy still dressed from the skin out in one colour.

Melodie rose from a marble garden seat where she'd been watching the tennis game, until now half hidden by high shrubbery. I saw her lips tighten as she observed Cindy's too affectionate greeting.

'Like mother like daughter,' mumbled Bart from behind me.

Cindy approached Bart warily, with so much decorum she didn't seem like the same girl who had kissed Jory. 'Hello, brother Bart. You're looking very fit.'

Bart stared at her as if he'd never seen her before. It had been two years, and at fourteen, Cindy had still worn her hair in pigtails, or ponytails, and she had braces on her teeth. Now her gleaming white teeth were perfectly spaced. Her hair was a loose-flowing mass of molten gold. There wasn't a girl in the skin magazines that had a better figure or more perfect complexion, and only too unhappily I realized that Cindy knew she looked sensational in her tight blue and white tennis dress.

Bart's dark eyes lingered on her ripe, unfettered breasts that jiggled when she walked, their peaks jutting out clearly. His eyes measured her hand-span waist before he stared at her pelvic area; then he lowered his eyes to take in very pretty long legs that ended in white sandals. Her toenails were painted bright red to match her fingernails and lipstick.

She was breathtakingly lovely in a sweet, fresh and innocent way that strove unsuccessfully to appear sophisticated. I didn't believe for a moment that that long, intense look she gave Bart meant what apparently he took it to mean.

'You're not my type,' he said scornfully, turning away. When he did, he stared long and meaningfully at Melodie. Then again he turned to Cindy. 'You have a certain cheap quality, despite all your expensive clothes – you don't possess nobility.'

It hurt to hear him deliberately try and squelch Cindy's youthful pride. Her radiant expression faded. Like a tender flower without the admiration of rain to nourish her faith in herself, she wilted before me as she turned into Chris's waiting arms.

'Apologize, Bart,' ordered Chris. I cringed, knowing Bart would never apologize.

Bart curled his lips, his scorn so apparent, even as he acted indignant and angry. His lips parted to insult Chris as he'd done so many times, but then he glanced at Melodie, who'd turned to look at him in a detached, curious way. A deep flush heated Bart's face. 'I'll apologize when she learns how to dress and act like a lady.'

'Apologize now, Bart,' ordered Chris.

'Don't make demands, Christopher,' said Bart, looking Chris meaningfully in the eyes. 'You're in a very vulnerable position. You and my mother. You're not a Sheffield, not a Foxworth – or at least you can't let it be known you're a Foxworth. So just what are you that counts? The world is full of doctors, too many doctors – and younger and more knowledgeable ones than you are.'

Chris stood taller. 'My ignorance about medicine has saved your life more than once, Bart. And the lives of many others. Perhaps one day you'll recognize that fact. You've never said thank you for anything I've done for you. I'm waiting for that day.'

Bart paled, I suspected not so much from what Chris had just said. I thought he was embarrassed because Melodie was watching and listening. 'Thank you, *Uncle* Chris,' he said sarcastically.

How mocking and insincere his words and his tone of voice. I watched the two men in silent challenge, seeing Chris wince from the way Bart put stress on 'Uncle'. Then, for no reason at all, I glanced at Joel.

He'd moved closer to pause just behind Melodie, and on his face was the kindest, most benign smile. But in his eyes lurked something darker. I moved to stand beside Chris, just as Jory lined up with him on the other side.

My lips parted to add a long list of things Bart should thank Chris for, when suddenly Bart was striding towards Melodie, ignoring Cindy. 'Have I told you the theme of my party? The dance I've chosen for you and Jory? It's going to cause a sensation.'

Melodie stood up. She stared Bart straight in his eyes with open contempt. 'I'm not going to dance for your birthday guests. I think Jory has explained to you more than once that I'm doing everything I can to see I have a healthy baby – and that doesn't include dancing for your amusement and that of people I don't even know.'

Her voice was cold. Dislike for Bart glared from her dark blue eyes.

She left, taking Jory with her, leaving the rest of us to follow. Joel tagged along at the very end like a tail that didn't know how to wag.

Quick to recover from all wounds, as always she'd rebounded from Bart's rebuffs, Cindy gushed happily about the expected baby that would make her an aunt. 'How wonderful! I can hardly wait. It's going to be one beautiful baby, I know, when it has parents like Jory and Melodie, and grandparents like you and Dad.'

Cindy's delightful presence made up for so much of Bart's hatefulness. I hugged her close and she snuggled down on the loveseat in my private sitting room and began to spill out all the details of her life. I listened eagerly, fascinated by a daughter who was making up for all the excitement Carrie and I had missed out on.

Each morning Chris and I were up early to enjoy the beauty of the cool mountain mornings, with the perfume of roses and other flowers drifting to delight our nostrils. Cardinals scarlet as flames flew everywhere while bluejays shrieked and purple martins searched the grass for insects. It surprised me to see dozens of birdhouses to accommodate wrens, martins and other species, and fabulous birdbaths and rock garden pools where the birds had a merry time taking quick, fluttery baths. We ate on one terrace or another to enjoy different views, talking often of all this that had been denied us when we were young and would have been appreciated even more than it was now. Sad, so sad to think of our little twins and how they had cried to go outside, outside, and the only playground they had was the attic garden we made for them out of paper and cardboard. And this had been there then, unused, unenjoyed, when two little five-year-olds would have been in seventh heaven to have had just a little of what we could enjoy daily now.

Cindy liked to sleep late, as did Jory and especially Melodie, who complained a great deal about nausea and fatigue. As early as seven-thirty Chris and I watched workmen and party decorators drive up. Caterers came to prepare for the party, and interior designers arrived to complete the appointments in some of the unfinished rooms, but not one neighbour dropped in to welcome us. Bart's private phone rang often, but the telephones on other lines hardly rang at all. We sat at the top of the world, or so it seemed, all by ourselves, and in some ways it was nice, in other ways it was a little frightening.

In the distance, faint and hazy, we could faintly see two church steeples. When the nights were still and without wind, we could faintly hear them chime away the hours. I knew one had been patronized by Malcolm when he lived, and about a mile away was the cemetery where he and our grandmother were buried side by side, with elaborate headstones and guardian angels put there by our mother.

I filled my days with playing tennis with Chris, with Jory, sometimes with Bart, and that's when he really seemed to like me most. 'You surprise me, Mother!' he yelled over the net, slamming that yellow ball so hard it almost went through my racket. Somehow I managed to race to hit it back, and then my troublesome knee started hurting and I had to quit. Bart complained I was using that knee as an excuse to abandon play with him.

'You find any reason to stay away from me,' he yelled as if Chris's words meant nothing. 'Your knee doesn't hurt . . . or you'd be limping.'

I did limp as I climbed the stairs, but Bart wasn't around to notice this. I soaked in a tub of hot water for an hour to take away the pain. Chris came in to tell me I was doing it wrong again. 'Ice, Catherine, ice! You only inflame your knee more when you sit in hot water. Now get out while I fill a bag with crushed ice, and keep it on your knee for twenty minutes.' He kissed me to take the sting from his words. 'See you later,' he said, hurrying back to the tennis courts to take on Jory, while Bart left with Joel in tow. All this I could see from our bedroom balcony while I sat with that ice bag held to my knee, and soon enough the cold worked, chasing away the throbbing hot pain.

I was beginning a layette for Jory's expected baby. This demanded many shopping sprees for yarns, needles, crochet hooks, for visiting adorable baby shops. Often we drove into Charlottesville with Cindy and Chris to shop, and twice we made the longer drive to Richmond and shopped there, went to the movies and stayed overnight. Sometimes Jory and Melodie went with us, but not as often as I would have liked. Already Foxworth Hall's charm was palling.

But if it palled for me, for Jory and Melodie, it worked its charm on Cindy, who adored her room, her fancy French furniture, her ultra-feminine bath with its pink decor enhanced with gold and mossy pale green. Hugging herself, she danced around. 'So he doesn't like me,' she laughed, spinning around before the many mirrors, 'and yet he decorates a room exactly the way I'd want. Oh, Momma, how can either of us understand Bart?'

Who could answer that?

PREPARATIONS

As Bart's twenty-fifth birthday approached, a kind of feverish insanity descended on the Hall. Different kinds of decorators came to measure our lawns, our patios, our terraces. In groups they whispered, made lists, sketches, tried different colours for the tablecloths, talked in huddles to Bart, discussed the theme of the dance and made their secret plans. Bart still refused to reveal the theme – at least to the members of his family. Secrets didn't sit well with anyone but Bart. The rest of us became a close-knit family that Bart didn't want to join.

Workmen with wood and paint and other construction materials began to build what appeared to be a stage and platforms for the orchestra. I heard Bart brag to one of his entourage that he was hiring opera stars, very famous ones.

Whenever I was outdoors, and I stayed outside as much as possible, I stared at the blue-misted mountains all around us and wondered if they remembered two of the attic mice shut upstairs for almost four years. I wondered if ever again they'd transform an ordinary little girl into someone full of fanciful dreams she had to make come true. And I had made a few come true, even if I'd failed more than once to keep husbands alive. I wiped away two tears and met Chris's still-loving gaze and felt that old familiar sadness wash over me. How sane Bart could have been if only Chris hadn't loved me – and I hadn't loved him.

Blame the wind or stars of fate – but I still blamed my mother.

Despite our dire anticipations of what lay ahead, I couldn't help but feel happier than I'd felt in some time, just watching all the excitement in the gardens that gradually turned into something straight from a movie set. I gasped to see what Bart wanted done.

It was a biblical scene!

'*Samson and Delilah*,' Bart said flatly when I asked, all his enthusiasm squelched because Melodie kept refusing to dance the role he wanted. 'Often I've heard Jory say he loved the chance to produce his own productions, and he does love that role most of all.'

Pivoting about, Melodie headed for the house without answering, her face pale with anger.

Again, I should have known. What other theme would capture Bart's fancy as much?

Cindy ran to throw her arms about Jory. 'Jory, let me dance the role of Delilah, I can! I just know I can.'

'I don't want your amateurish attempts!' shouted Bart.

Ignoring him, Cindy tugged pleadingly on both of Jory's hands. 'Please, please, Jory. I'd love to do it. I've kept up my ballet classes, so I won't be stiff and awkward and make you look unskilled, and between now and then you can help me gain better timing. I'll rehearse morning, night and noon!'

'There's not enough time to rehearse when the performance is two days away,' complained Jory, throwing Bart a hard, angry look. 'Good lord, Bart, why didn't you tell me before? Do you think just because I choreographed that particular ballet that I can remember all the difficult routines? A role like that needs weeks of rehearsing, and you wait until the last moment! Why?'

'Cindy's lying,' said Bart, looking longingly at the door through which Melodie had disappeared. 'She was too lazy to keep up her classes before, so why should she when Mother's not there to force her?'

'I have! I have!' cried Cindy with great excitement and pride, when I knew she hated violent exercises. Before the age of six, she'd loved the pretty tutus, the cute little satin slippers, the little sparkling tiaras of fake jewels, and the fantasy of the fanciful productions had put her in a spell of beauty I'd once believed she'd never abandon. But Bart had ridiculed her performances just one too many times, and she'd let him convince her she was hopelessly inadequate. She'd been about twelve when he stole her pleasure in the ballet. From then on she'd never gone to classes. Therefore

I was doubly amazed to hear she'd never really given up on the dance, only on allowing Bart see her perform.

She turned to me, as if pleading for her life. 'Really, I am telling the truth! Once I was in the private girl's school, and Bart wasn't around to ridicule me, I started again and ever since have kept up my ballet classes, and I tap dance as well.'

'Well,' said Jory, apparently impressed, giving Bart another hard look, 'we can devote what time we have left to practising, but you were extremely unthinking to believe we wouldn't need to practise for weeks, Bart. I don't expect to have much difficulty myself since it's a familiar role – but Cindy, you've not even seen that particular ballet.'

Rudely interrupting, Bart asked with great excitement, 'Do you have the lenses, the white lenses? Can you really see through them? I saw you and Melodie in New York about a year ago, and from the orchestra you really did look blind.'

Frowning at his unexpected question, Jory studied Bart seriously. 'Yes . . . I have the contacts with me,' he said slowly. 'Everywhere I go someone asks me to dance the role of Samson, so I take the lenses. I didn't know you appreciated ballet so much.'

Laughing, Bart slapped Jory on the back as if they'd never had a disagreement. Jory staggered from the strength of that blow. 'Most ballets are stupid bores, but this particular one catches my fancy. Samson was a great hero and I admire him. And you, my brother, perform extraordinarily well as Samson. Why, you even look just as powerful. I guess that's the only ballet that has ever thrilled me.'

I wasn't listening to Bart. I was staring at Joel, who leaned forward. Muscles near his thin lips worked almost spasmodically, hovering near a smirk or a laugh, I couldn't tell which. All of a sudden I didn't want Jory and Cindy to dance in that particular ballet, which included very brutal scenes. And it had been Bart's idea years and years ago . . . hadn't he been the one to suggest that the opera would provide the music for what he considered would make the most sensational ballet of all?

All through the night I thought and I thought of how to stop Bart from wanting that particular production.

He'd never been easy to stop as a boy.

As a man . . . I didn't know if I had a chance. But I was going to give it a try.

The very next morning I was up early and running out into the yard to catch Bart before he drove off. He listened to me with impatience, refusing to change the theme of his party. 'I can't now, even if I wanted to. I've had the costumes designed and they are almost finished, as are the sets and flats. If I cancel anything if will be too late to plan another ballet. Besides, Jory doesn't mind, why should you?'

How could I tell him that some small, intuitive voice was warning me not to let this particular ballet be performed near the place of our confinement – with Malcolm and his wife in the ground not so far away the music wouldn't fill their dead ears.

Jory and Cindy practised and rehearsed night and day, both catching a certain excitement as they worked together and Jory found out that Cindy was good; certainly she wouldn't perform as well as Melodie would have, but she'd dance more than adequately, and she was so lovely with her hair bound up in classical ballerina style.

The morning of Bart's birthday dawned bright and clear, heralding a perfect summer day without rain or clouds.

I was up early with Chris, strolling in the gardens before breakfast, enjoying the perfume of roses that seemed to herald a beautiful, perfect birthday for Bart. He'd always wanted birthday parties, like the ones we threw for Jory and Cindy, yet when they came round, he somehow managed to antagonize every guest so that many left early, and usually in a huff.

He was a man now, I kept telling myself, and this time it would be different. Chris was saying that to me, as if we had some sort of telepathy, both with the same thoughts.

'He's coming into his own,' I said. 'Isn't it odd how he's hung on to that childish expression, Chris? Will the attorneys read the will again after the party?'

Smiling and happy looking, Chris shook his head. 'No, darling, we'll all be too tired. The reading is set for the next day.' A shadow came to darken his expression. 'I can't remember anything in that will that would spoil Bart's birthday, can you?'

No, I couldn't, but at the time of our mother's will reading, I'd been too upset, crying, half hearing, not really caring if none of us inherited the Foxworth fortune that seemed to come with its own curse.

'There's something Bart's attorneys aren't telling me, Cathy . . . something they say I must not have clearly understood at the time when our mother's will was read shortly after her death. Now they don't want to speak of it because Bart has demanded that I not be included in any legal discussions. They look at him as if he scares or intimidates them. It surprises me to see middle-aged men with years of experience yield under his pressure, as if they want to keep his good will, and mine be damned. It annoys me, and then I ask myself, what the hell do I care? Soon we'll be leaving and making a new home for ourselves, and Bart can take his fortune and rule with it . . .'

My arms went about him, angry because Bart refused to give him the credit he deserved for handling that vast fortune for so many years, and doing a darn good job of it, too, despite his medical practice that stole so much of his time.

'How many millions will he inherit?' I asked. 'Twenty, fifty, more? One billion, two, three – more?'

Chris laughed. 'Oh, Catherine, you never grow up. You always exaggerate. To be honest, it's difficult to calculate the net worth of all those holdings when they are scattered into so many areas of investments. However, he should be pleased when his attorneys give a rough estimate . . . it's more than enough for ten greedy young men.'

In the foyer we paused to watch Jory rehearsing with Cindy, both hot and sweaty from all their efforts. Other dancers who'd be in the ballet were with them, standing around idly, either watching Jory and Cindy or staring around at what they could see of the fabulous house. Cindy was doing exceptionally well, and that truly surprised me;

imagine keeping up her ballet classes and not telling me. She must have used some of her allowance meant for clothes and cosmetics and other trivial things she was always needing.

One of the older dancers strolled over to me, smiling as she spoke of seeing me dance a few times in New York. 'Your son is very much like his father,' she went on, glancing back at Jory, who was whipping himself up into such a passion I wondered if he'd have any energy left for tonight's performance. 'Maybe I shouldn't say this, but he's ten times better. I was only about twelve when you and Julian Marquet danced in *The Sleeping Beauty*, but it was the inspiration that gave me the desire to become a dancer myself. Thank you for giving us another wonderful dancer like Jory Marquet.'

What she said filled me with happiness. My marriage to Julian hadn't been a total failure when it had produced Jory. Now I had to believe Bartholomew Winslow's son would eventually fill me with just as much pride as I felt right now.

The rehearsal over, Cindy came to me, quite out of breath. 'Mom, how did I do, okay?' Her eager face waited for my approval.

'You did beautifully, Cindy, really you did. Now, if you just remember to feel the music . . . keep the timing, you will turn in a remarkable performance for a novice.'

She grinned at me. 'Always the instructor, huh, Mom? I suspect I'm not nearly as good as you want me to believe, but I'm going to give this performance my everything, and if I fail, it won't be because I didn't try.'

Jory was surrounded by admirers, while Melodie sat quietly on a love seat beside Bart. They didn't appear to be conversing, nor did they seem friendly. Yet, seeing them on that lovely small seat for two, I felt somehow uneasy. Tugging Chris forward, we moved closer to the pair on the love seat. 'Happy birthday, Bart,' I said cheerfully. He looked up and smiled with genuine charm.

'I told you it was going to be a great day, with sun and no rain.'

'Yes, you told us.'

'Can we all eat now?' he asked, standing and reaching for Melodie's hand. She ignored him and stood without assistance. 'I'm starving!' Bart went on, looking only a little crestfallen from another of her rebuffs. 'Those little Continental morning snacks just don't satisfy me.'

We made a happy assembly at the luncheon table, all but Joel, who sat at his own small, round table on the terrace, apart from the rest of us. It was his claim that we were too rowdy and ate too much, insulting his monkish tastes, which dictated a serious attitude towards food and long prayers before and after eating. Even Bart grew annoyed with Joel when he became too pious, and especially on this day his impatience showed. 'Uncle Joel, do you have to sit there all by yourself? Come, join the family group and wish me a happy birthday.'

Joel shook his head. 'The Lord scorns ostentatious displays of wealth and vanity. I disapprove of this party. You could show your gratitude to be alive in a better way, by contributing to charities.'

'What have charities done for me? This is my time to shine, Uncle, and even if dear old dead Malcolm flips over in his grave, I'm having the time of my life tonight!'

I was flooded with delight. Quickly I leaned to kiss him. 'I love to see you like this, Bart. This is your day . . . and the gifts we have for you are going to open your eyes wide.'

'Hope so,' he said, all smiles. 'I see they're heaping up on the gift table. We'll open them soon after the guests are here, so we can get on to the entertainment.'

Across from where I sat, Jory was staring into Melodie's eyes with concern. 'Honey, are you feeling all right?'

'Yes,' she whispered, 'except I'd like to be dancing the role of Delilah. It feels strange watching you dance with someone else.'

'After the baby comes, we'll dance together again,' he said before he kissed her. Her eyes clung worshipfully to him as he got up to practise again with Cindy.

That's when Bart lost his happy expression.

* * *

Delivery men were constantly at the door bringing Bart more gifts. Many of his fraternity brothers from Harvard were coming with their girlfriends or wives. Those who couldn't make it were sending presents. Bart came and went, almost on the run, checking on every aspect of the party. Bouquets of flowers arrived by the dozens. The caterers filled the kitchen, so I felt an intruder when I wanted to prepare my own kind of midday snack. Then Bart had me by the arm and was pulling me through all the rooms that were overflowing with flowers. 'Do you think my friends will be impressed?' he asked worriedly. 'You know, I think I might have done a bit too much bragging when I was in school. They'll expect a mansion beyond compare.'

I took another look around. There was something about a house ready for a party that made it especially beautiful, and Foxworth Hall was not only festive but spectacular with all its fresh flowers to give it warmth and grace, as well as beauty. All the crystal sparkled, the silver gleamed, the copper glowed . . . oh, yes, this house could rival the very best.

'Darling, stop fretting. You can't out-best everyone in the world. This is a truly beautiful house, and your decorators have done a marvellous job. Your friends will be impressed, don't you doubt that for one second. The caretakers did keep it well over the years, and gave all the gardens a chance to become well established.'

He wasn't listening, just staring beyond me, frowning slightly. 'You know, Mother,' he said in a low voice, 'I'm going to rattle around here after you and your brother go, and Melodie and Jory leave. It's a good thing I've got my Uncle Joel, who will stay on until he dies.'

I heard this with a sinking heart.

Cindy's name wasn't mentioned, for obviously he'd never miss her. 'Do you really like Joel that much, Bart? This morning he seemed to irk you with his monkish ways.'

Clouds shadowed his already dark eyes, made grave his handsome face. 'My uncle is helping me find myself, Mother, and if sometimes he annoys me, it's because I'm still so uncertain about my future. He can't help his habits formed over all those years living with monks who weren't allowed to speak, only pray out loud and sing at services. He's told me a bit about how it was, and it must have been very grim and lonely . . . yet he says he found peace there, and belief in God and everlasting life.'

My arm dropped from his waist. He could have turned to Chris and found everything he needed – peace, security, and the faith that had sustained Chris throughout life. Bart had blind eyes when it came to seeing the goodness in a man who'd tried so hard to make a son out of Bart.

But my relationship with my brother condemned him, blinded Bart to anything but that.

Sadly I left Bart and climbed the stairs to find Chris on the balcony staring down at the workers in the yard. I joined him there, feeling the sun hot on my head. Silently we watched all that bustle of activity, while I prayed this house was finally going to give us something other than misery.

We napped for two hours, then ate a small dinner before all of us hurried back up to dress for the party. I went again out on to the balcony that gave Chris and I so much pleasure. Below me spread the birthday fairyland. The colours of the fading day filled the heavens with deep rose and violet, streaked it with magenta and orange, and sleepy birds flew like dark tears towards their nests. Cardinals were making their little beeping sounds, not chirps or cheeps but more like electronic, metallic bleeps. When Chris stepped up beside me, damp and fresh from his shower, we didn't speak or feel the need to; we just embraced, looking downward, before we finally turned away and went inside.

Bart, the child of my revenge, was coming into his own. I held fast to my hopes – wanting a party that turned out well and gave him the assurance he needed that he had friends and was well liked. I held off my fears and told myself over and over again that it was Bart's just due, and ours, too.

Maybe Bart would be satisfied tomorrow when the will was reread. Maybe, just maybe . . . I wanted the best for him, wanted fate to make up for so many things.

Behind me Chris moved in our dressing room, stepping into his tux trousers, stuffing in his shirt-tails, tying his own bow tie, then asking me to do it all over again. 'Make the ends even.' Gladly I retied it for him. He brushed his beautiful blond hair that was just a bit darker at the back than it had been when he was forty. Each decade both darkened the blond and brought a touch more of silver in both our heads of hair. Easily I could keep mine coloured, but Chris refused to do that. Fair hair had a lot to do with the way I thought about myself. My face was still pretty. I was both mature and young looking.

Chris's reflection moved closer to my dressing table, hovering over my shoulders. His hands, so familiar to me now, moved to slip inside my bodice and cup my breasts before his lips pressed on my neck. 'I love you. God knows what I would do if I didn't have you.'

Why was he always saying that?

As if he expected one day I'd leave or die before he did. 'Darling, you'd live, that's what. You're important to society, I'm not.'

'You're the one who keeps me going,' he whispered in a hoarse voice. 'Without you I wouldn't know how to continue on – but without me, you'd go on and probably marry again.'

I saw his eyes, his blue eyes wistfully waiting.

'I've had three husbands and one lover, and that's enough for any one woman. If I am so unlucky as to lose you first, I'll sit day by day before a window, staring out and remembering how it used to be with you.'

His eyes turned softer, meeting and locking with mine as I went on. 'You look so beautiful, Chris. You'll make your sons envious.'

'Beautiful? Isn't that an adjective used to describe females?'

'No. There's a difference between handsome and beautiful. Some men can look handsome, but not radiate inner beauty – like you do. You, my love, are beautiful – inside and out.'

Again his blue eyes lit up. 'Thank you very much. And may I say that I find you ten times as beautiful as you find me.'

'My sons will be jealous when they behold the beauty of my Christopher Doll.'

'Yes, of course,' he answered with a wry grin. '*Your* sons see much to envy in me.'

'Chris, you know Jory loves you. Someday Bart's going to find out he loves you, too.'

'Someday my ship will come . . .' he sang lightly.

'It's his ship, too, Chris. Bart is at last coming into his own. And with that fortune in his control, rather than yours, he'll relax, find himself and turn to you as the best father he could have had.'

Reflectively he smiled, a small smile of sadness. 'To be honest, darling, I'll be happy when Bart has his money and I'm out of the picture. It's no easy chore handling all that money, though I could have hired a money manager to do it for me. As trustee, I guess I wanted to prove myself to Bart, that I'm more than just a doctor, since that never seemed enough for him.'

What could I say? Nothing Chris did seemed to change the way Bart felt about him. Because of that one thing he couldn't change – he was my brother – Bart would never accept him as his father.

'What are you thinking, my love, that's ugly, and making you frown?'

'Nothing much,' I answered, then I stood. The silky white of my clinging Grecian-styled dress felt whispery and sensuous against my bare skin. My hair had a single long curl to drape over my shoulder, the rest of it piled high on the crown of my head. Holding it in place was a diamond hair clip, the only jewellery I wore but for my wedding rings.

In the middle of the bedroom we shared, Chris and I reached for each other. There we stood, wrapped in each other's arms, holding fast to the only security we ever had that lasted: each other. All about us the house felt so quiet. We could have been lost and alone in eternity.

'All right, spill it out,' said Chris after long minutes passed. 'I can always tell when you're worried.'

'I wish things could be different between you and Bart, that's all,' I replied in an offhand way, not wanting to spoil this evening.

'I feel my relationship with Jory and Cindy more than makes up for Bart's antagonism. And, more importantly, I genuinely sense Bart does not hate me. There are times when I feel he wants to reach out to me, but there's that shame, that knowledge of our true relationship that holds him as if bound by chains of steel. He wants guidance but is ashamed to ask for it. He wants a father, a real father. His psychiatrists have always told us that. He looks at me, finds me sadly lacking . . . so he looks elsewhere. First it was Malcolm, his great-grandfather, already dead in his grave. Then it was John Amos, and John failed him, too. Now he turns to Joel, fearfully suspecting that he, too, may have his flaws. Yes, I can tell at times he doesn't really trust his great-uncle. And because he can think like this, Bart is not beyond saving, Cathy. We still have time to reach him – for we're alive and he's alive.'

'Yes, yes! I know, I know. While there's life there's always hope. Say it again, and then again. And if you say it often enough, maybe the day will come when Bart says to you, "Yes, I love you. Yes, you've done your best. Yes, you are the father I've been looking for all my life" – and wouldn't that be wonderful?'

His head bowed into my hair. 'Don't sound so bitter. That day will come, Cathy. As surely as you and I love each other – and our three children – that day will come.'

I knew I'd do anything that was necessary to see that one day Bart would speak genuine words of love to his father! I'd live forever to see the day when Bart not only accepted Chris and said he loved him and admired him and thanked him, I'd also live to see him a real brother to Jory again . . . and a brother to Cindy.

Minutes later we were at the head of the stairs, starting to descend and join Jory and Melodie, whom we could see near the newel post at the bottom. Melodie wore a simple black gown that draped from black shoestring straps. Her only jewellery was a string of gleaming pearls.

Upon hearing the clatter of my high-heeled silver slippers on the marble, Bart stepped into view wearing his custom-tailored tux. My breath caught. He could have been his father when I'd seen him the first time.

His moustache – that small amount of fuzz first seen seven days ago – had grown thicker. He looked happy, and that was enough to make him look even more handsome. His dark eyes were full of admiration as he saw my dress, my hair, smelled my perfume. 'Mother!' he cried, 'you look stunning! You bought that lovely white dress especially for my party, didn't you?' Laughing, I said yes, of course, I couldn't wear anything old to a party such as this.

We all had compliments for each other, except Bart didn't say anything at all to Chris, although I saw him surreptitiously glancing at him, as if Chris's steadfast good looks kept taking him by surprise. Melodie and Jory, Chris and I, with Bart and Joel, formed a circle at the bottom of the stairs, all of us but Joel trying to talk at the same time. Then . . .

'Momma, Daddy!' called Cindy, running down the stairs towards us and holding up her long flame-red dress so she wouldn't trip. I turned to stare at her disbelievingly.

I didn't know where Cindy had found the shocking red dress she wore. It seemed the kind a hooker would wear to display her charms. I filled with such sickening dread of Bart's reaction that all my former happiness flowed like stale wine down into my slippers and disappeared through the floor. The thing she wore clung like a coat of scarlet paint, the neckline plunged almost to her waist, and obviously she wore nothing underneath. The peaks of her jutting breasts were too obvious; and when she moved she jiggled embarrassingly. The clinging satin sheath was cut on the bias, and clung . . . oh, it did cling. There wasn't a bulge or a ripple to betray an ounce of fat, only a superb young body she wanted to display.

'Cindy, go back to your room,' I whispered, 'and put on that blue dress you promised to wear. You're sixteen, not thirty.'

'Oh, Momma, don't be so stodgy. Times have changed. Nudity is in, Momma, IN. And compared to some I could have chosen, this dress is modest, absolutely prudish.'

Just one glance at Bart told me he didn't think Cindy's gown was modest. He stood as if dumbstruck until this very moment, with his face flame red, his dark eyes bulging as he stared at her mincing around, because the skirt was so tight she could hardly move her legs.

Bart stared at us, looked again at Cindy. Bart's rage was so furious he couldn't speak. In those few seconds I had to think quickly of how to appease him. 'Cindy, please, run back and change into something decent.'

Cindy had her eyes fixed on Bart. Obviously she was challenging him to do something to stop her. She seemed to be enjoying his reaction, his bulging eyes, his gaping lips that showed his indignation and shock. She made more of a show of herself by sashaying around like a prancing pony in heat, swishing those hips in an undulating, provocative way. Joel moved next to Bart, his watery blue eyes cold and scornful as he looked Cindy up and down, and then his eyes lifted to meet mine. *See, see what you have raised,* he said mutely.

'Cindy, do you hear your mother?' Chris bellowed. 'Do as she says! Immediately!'

Appearing shocked, Cindy froze, staring at him with defiance as she flushed and stood her ground.

'Please, Cindy,' I added, 'do as your father says. The other dress is very pretty and appropriate. What you have on is vulgar.'

'I am old enough to choose what I want to wear,' she said in a quivery voice, refusing to move. 'Bart likes red, so I wear red!'

Melodie stared at Cindy, glanced helplessly up at me and tried to smile. Jory appeared amused, as if this were all a joke.

Cindy had by this time finished her burlesque performance. She looked somewhat crestfallen as she paused before Jory, staring up at him expectantly. 'You look absolutely divine, Jory – and you, too, Melodie.'

Obviously Jory didn't know what to say or where to look, so he looked away, then looked back. A slow blush rose from the neckline of his tucked formal shirt. 'And you look like . . . Marilyn Monroe . . .'

Bart's dark head snapped around. His fiery gaze raked over Cindy again. His face flamed even redder so it seemed he might go up in smoke. He exploded, all control vanished. 'You go straight back to your room and put on something decent! Instantly! Move before you get what you deserve! I won't have anyone in my home dressing like a whore!'

'Get lost, you creep!' she snapped back.

'WHAT DID YOU SAY?' he yelled.

'I said, Get lost, creep! I will wear exactly what I have on!' I saw her tremble. But for once Bart was right.

'Cindy, why? You know that dress is wrong, and everyone is right to be shocked. Now, do what's expected, go upstairs and change. Don't create more distress than you already have – for you do look like a street prostitute, and certainly you must know that. Usually you have very good taste. Why did you select that thing?'

'Momma!' she wailed, 'you're making me feel bad!'

Bart stepped towards her, his expression very threatening. Instantly Melodie moved between them, spreading her slender white arms before she turned pleadingly to Bart. 'Can't you see she's only doing this to annoy you? Stay calm, or else you will give Cindy exactly the satisfaction she wants.'

Turning, she said to Cindy in a cool but authoritative voice, 'Cindy, you have achieved the shock effects you wanted. So why don't you go back upstairs and put on that pretty blue dress you started to wear in the first place?'

Bart ignored both Chris and me as he strode to seize Cindy, but she pranced away out of his reach, turning to teasingly mock him for being slow and not as agile as she was, even hobbled as she was in that slim, straight, tight skirt. I could have slapped Cindy when I heard her say silkily, 'Bart, darling, I was so sure you'd love this scarlet gown . . . since you think I'm a cheap, trashy thing, anyway, I'm just living up to your expectations – and playing the role you wrote for me.'

In one flashing bound he reached her. His open palm slammed against her cheek.

The pain in his hard slap rocked Cindy backward so that she sat down very hard on the second stair step. I heard the skirt of her red gown rip down the midback seam. Moving quickly, I hurried to help her up. Tears came to Cindy's eyes.

Hurriedly standing, Cindy backed up the stairs, struggling to maintain dignity. 'You are a creep, brother Bart. A weird pervert who doesn't know what the real world is about. I bet you're a virgin, or else gay!'

The rage on Bart's face sent her scurrying up the stairs in a hurry. I moved to prevent Bart from following Cindy, but he was too quick.

Ruthlessly he shoved me aside, so I, too, almost fell. Crying like a chastised child, Cindy disappeared with Bart close at her heels.

In a distant hall, I faintly heard Bart shout, 'How dare you try to embarrass me? You're the trashy one I've had to protect from all the dirty stories I hear about you. I used to think they lied. Now you've proved yourself exactly what they said you were! As soon as this party is over, I don't ever want to see you again!'

'AS IF I WANT TO SEE YOU!' she screamed. 'I HATE YOU, BART! HATE YOU!'

I heard her scream, the wailing cries . . . I started to head up the stairs while Chris tried to restrain me. Tugging free, I had climbed five steps when Bart appeared with a satisfied smirk on his handsome but momentarily evil face. He whispered as he passed, 'I just gave her what you never did – a thorough spanking. If she can sit for a week comfortably, she's got an ass made of iron.'

I glanced backwards in time to see Joel scowl at the use of that word.

Ignoring Joel for a change, smiling like the perfect host, Bart arranged us into a receiving line, and soon guests began to arrive. Bart introduced all of us to people I hadn't known he knew. I was amazed at the style he showed, the poise, the ease with which he handled everyone and made them welcome. His college chums came flocking in, as if to see all that he'd told them about. If Cindy hadn't put on that horrible dress, I could have really felt proud of Bart. As it was, I was baffled, believing Bart could be anything that suited his purpose.

Right now he was set on charming everyone. And he succeeded, even more than Jory, who obviously and wisely intended to take a back seat and allow Bart to shine. Melodie stayed close at her husband's side, clinging to his hand, his arm, looking pale, unhappy. I was so absorbed in watching Bart perform that I was startled when someone tugged on my arm. It was Cindy, wearing the modest little blue silk sheath I'd chosen for her. She looked sweet-sixteen-and-never-been-kissed. I scolded, 'Really, Cindy, you can't blame Bart. This time you deserved a spanking.'

She choked out, 'Damn him to hell! I'll show him! I'll dance ten times better than Melodie has ever danced! I'll make every man at this party want me tonight, despite this deadly mousey gown you chose.'

'You don't mean that, Cindy.'

Softening, she fell into my arms. 'No, Momma, I don't mean that.'

Bart saw Cindy with me, raked his eyes over her girlish gown, smiled sarcastically and then came our way.

Cindy stood taller.

'Now, listen, Cindy. You'll put on your costume when the time comes and forget anything happened between us. You'll perform your part to perfection – okay?'

Playfully he pinched her cheek. So playfully his pinch left a deep red indentation on her face. She squealed and kicked out. Her high heel dug into his shin. He yelped and slapped her.

'Bart!' I hissed, 'stop! Don't you hurt her again! You've done enough for one night!'

Chris yanked Bart away from Cindy. 'Now, I've had enough of this idiocy,' he said angrily, and Chris seldom angered. 'You've invited to this party some of the most important people in Virginia – now show them you know how to behave.'

Pulling roughly away from Chris, Bart glared at him, then strode away, very fast, without a comment. I smiled at Chris, and with him beside me, we headed for the gardens. Jory and Melodie took Cindy and began introducing her to some of the young people who'd come with their parents. There were many there that Bart had met through Jory and Melodie, who had hordes of friends and fans.

I could only hope for the best.

SAMSON AND DELILAH

Golden globes everywhere lit up the night, and the moon rode high in a cloudless, starry sky. Out on the lawn were dozens of buffet tables butted together to form a huge U. On these tables food was placed in huge silver dishes. A fountain sprayed imported champagne into the air, then trickled it into layered pools that ran into tiny spigots. On the middle table was a huge ice sculpture of Foxworth Hall.

Besides the main tables ladened with all that money could buy were dozens of small round and square individual tables covered with brilliant cloths – green over rose, turquoise over violet, yellow over orange and other striking combinations. The tablecloths were kept from blowing by heavy garlands of flowers festooned around them.

Although Chris and I had been introduced in the receiving line, it seemed to me most of Bart's guests made it a point not to talk to us. I looked at Chris just as he looked at me. 'What's going on?' he asked in a low whisper.

'The older guests are not talking to Bart, either,' I answered. 'Look, Chris, they've come just to drink, eat and enjoy themselves, and they don't give a damn about Bart, or any of us. They are just here so he can dine and wine them.'

'I wouldn't say that,' Chris replied. 'Everyone makes it a point to speak to Jory and Melodie. Some are even talking to Joel. Doesn't he look a fine and elegant gentleman tonight?'

Never would it cease to amaze me the way Chris could find something to admire in everyone.

Joel looked like a funeral director as he moved solemnly from one group to another. He didn't carry a glass like everyone else. He didn't partake of the refreshments that piled the buffet tables in such a breathtaking array. I nibbled daintily on a cracker spread with goose liver pâté and looked around for Cindy. She was in the centre of five young men, very much the belle of the ball. Even her demure blue dress didn't keep her from looking very seductive – now that she'd shoved the shoulder ruffle down to bare the top half of her bosom.

'She looks like you used to,' said Chris, also watching Cindy. 'Except you had a more ethereal quality, as if your two feet were never firmly on the ground, and never would you stop believing miracles could happen.' He paused and looked at me in that special way that kept my love for him always alive and thriving. 'Yes, love,' he whispered, 'miracles can happen, even here.'

Every wife or husband seemed to be trying to score with any member of the opposite sex besides their spouses. Only Chris and I stuck together. Jory had disappeared, and now Melodie was standing with Bart. He was saying something to her that had her eyes blazing hot. She turned to hurry away, but he seized hold of her arm and yanked her back. She snatched her arm away, only to have him seize it again, and ruthlessly he pulled her into his embrace. They began to dance, with Melodie determinedly keeping him from crushing her against him.

I started to go to them, but Chris caught my arm to restrain me. 'Let Melodie handle him. You'd only make him furious.'

Sighing, I watched the small conflict between Bart and his brother's wife and saw to my amazement that he won, for she relaxed and finally seemed to enjoy the dance that soon ended. Then he was leading her from group to group, as if she were his wife and not Jory's.

I'd tasted only a little of this and that when a very beautiful woman stepped forward, smiling first at Chris, then at me. 'Aren't you Corrine Foxworth's daughter, the one who came to that Christmas night party and – '

Abruptly I cut her short. 'If you'll excuse me, I have a few duties to perform,' I said, hurrying away and keeping fast hold of Christopher. The woman ran behind us. 'But Mrs Sheffield . . .'

I was spared the need to answer by the blast of many trumpets. The entertainment began as Bart's guests seated themselves with plates of food and drinks. Bart and Melodie came to join us, while Cindy and Jory ran to warm up in practice outfits before they changed into elaborate costumes.

Soon the professional entertainers had me laughing along with everyone else.

What a wonderful party! I glanced often at Chris, at Bart and Melodie, who sat near us. The summer night was perfect. The mountains all around enclosed us in a friendly romantic ring, and I was again amazed that I could see them as anything but formidable barriers to keep freedom forever out of reach. I was happy to see Melodie laughing and, most of all, happy to see Bart really having a good time. He shifted his chair closer to mine. 'Would you say my party is a success, Mother?'

'Yes, oh, indeed, yes, Bart, you've outdone anything I've ever attended. It's a marvellous party. The evening is breathtakingly beautiful, with the stars and moon overhead, and all your coloured lights. When does the ballet begin?'

He smiled and put his arm lovingly about my shoulders. His voice was tender with understanding when he asked, 'Nothing for you equals the ballet, does it? And you won't be disappointed. You just wait to see if New York or London can equal my production of *Samson and Delilah*.'

Jory had danced the role only three times before, but each time his performances had brought such acclaim it was no wonder Bart was fascinated with the role. The musicians in black sat down, reached for new music sheets and started tuning their instruments.

A few yards away, Joel stood stiffly, a hateful, disapproving look on his face, as if he reflected all that his father's ghost might be feeling to see this extravagant waste of good money.

'Bart, you're twenty-five today, happy birthday! I remember clearly when a nurse laid you in my arms the first time. I had a terrible time giving birth to you, and the doctors kept coming to say I had to make a choice, your life or mine. I chose yours. But I made it, and was blessed with a second son . . . the very image of his father. You were crying, your small hands balled into fists as you flailed the air. Your feet kicked free of the blanket, but the minute you felt my body heat against yours, held close to my heart, you stopped crying. Your eyes, closed until then, parted into slits. You seemed to see me before you fell asleep.'

'I'm sure you thought Jory was a prettier baby,' he said with sarcasm, but his eyes were tender, as if he liked hearing of himself as a baby.

Melodie was regarding me with the strangest expression. I wished she weren't so near. 'You had your own kind of beauty, Bart, your own personality, right from the start. You wanted me with you night and day. I'd put you in your crib, you'd cry. I'd pick you up, you'd stop crying.'

'In other words I was a great big nuisance.'

'I never thought that, Bart. I loved you from the day I conceived you. I loved you more when you smiled. Yours was such a faltering first smile, as if it hurt your face.'

It seemed for a moment I'd touched him. His hand reached for mine, and mine reached for his. But at that moment the overture to *Samson and Delilah* began, and this moment of sweetness between my second son and I was lost in the excited murmur of surprise as Bart's guests looked at the programme and saw that Jory Janus Marquet was going to dance his most famous role, and his sister, Cynthia Sheffield, would play the role of Delilah. Many people looked at Melodie with curiosity, wondering why she wasn't dancing Delilah.

As always, when a ballet began, I was lost to the real world, drifting somewhere on a cloud and feeling so much it was painful, beautiful, and I was transported to another world.

The curtain lifted to show the inside of a colourful silken tent set against a backdrop representing a starry night in the desert. Stuffed but real-looking camels were there, palm trees swayed gently. On stage was Cindy, dressed in a diaphanous costume that clearly showed her slender but ripe figure. She wore a dark wig, cleverly bound around her head with jewelled bands. She began a seductive, undulating dance, enticing Samson, who lingered just off stage. When Jory came on, the birthday guests stood and gave him a resounding ovation.

He stood waiting until the applause ended, then began his dance. He wore nothing but a lion skin loincloth held up by a strap that crossed his well-muscled broad chest. His skin, well tanned, appeared oiled. His hair was long and black and perfectly straight; muscles rippled as he whirled, jetéd, duplicating Delilah's steps only more violently, as if he mocked her womanly weakness and delighted in his own agile, masculine strength. The power it took to portray Samson made my spine shiver. He looked so right for the role, danced so well, I shivered again, not from cold but from the pure beauty of seeing my son up there, dancing as if God had gifted him with superhuman style and grace.

Then, as it inevitably had to be, Delilah's beguiling dance of seduction wore down his resistance, and Samson succumbed to the loveliness of Delilah, who let down her dark tresses and slowly began to undress . . . veil by veil she let fall before Samson fell upon her and bore her back on to the pile of animal skins . . . and the stage darkened just before the curtain dropped.

Applause thundered as the curtain came down. I noticed a certain look on Melodie's pale face – was that envy? Was she wishing now she'd danced Delilah?

'You would have made the best Delilah,' whispered Bart softly, his lips brushing the wisps of hair that curled above her pearl-studded ear. 'Cindy can't compare . . .'

'You do her an injustice, Bart,' waspishly answered Melodie. 'When you consider her lack of rehearsal time, she's performed beautifully. Jory told me he was surprised how good she is.' Melodie leaned forward to address me. 'Cathy, I'm sure Cindy has put in hours and hours of general practice, or else she wouldn't dance as well as she is.'

Since the first act of the ballet had gone so well, I leaned back against Chris, who had his arm about me, and relaxed. 'I feel so proud, Chris. Bart is behaving beautifully. Jory is the most accomplished *danseur* I've ever seen. I'm amazed how well Cindy is doing.'

'Jory was born to dance,' said Chris. 'If *he'd* been raised by monks, still he would have danced. But I do remember a rebellious little girl who hated to stretch her muscles and make them hurt.'

We laughed in the way long-married couples do, intimate laughter, expressing more than what we said.

The curtain rose again.

While Samson slept on the colourful couch he and Delilah had shared, she cautiously eased off, drew on a lovely garment of frail silk, then stole quietly to the opening of the tent and beckoned inside a group of six warriors previously hidden. All bore shields and swords. Already Delilah had shorn Samson's head of his long dark hair. She held it up triumphantly, giving the timid soldiers confidence.

Startled awake, Samson jumped from the bed, jetéd high into the air and tried to lift his weapon. What was left of his long hair was short and stubby. His sword seemed too heavy. He screamed silently on finding all his strength gone. His despair was made visual as he whirled in frustration, beating his brow with brutal fists for believing in love and Delilah; then he fell to writhe on the ground, twisting about, glaring at Delilah, who tormented him with her wild laughter. He rushed for her, but the six soldiers sprang upon Samson and brought him down. They bound him with chains and ropes as he struggled mightily to free himself.

And all the time, off stage, the most famous tenor from the Metropolitan sang his pleading song of love to Delilah, asking why she had betrayed him. Tears flowed down my face to see my son lashed and whipped before he was hauled to his feet and the soldiers began their dance of torture while Delilah watched.

Even knowing all this horror was feigned, I cringed against Chris when the branding iron, heated white hot, was moved ever closer to Samson's bulging eyes. The set darkened. Only the white-hot iron lit up the stage – and the ghostly shine on Samson's near nude body. The last sound was Samson's scream of agony.

The second act curtain lowered. Again, there was wild applause, and cheers of 'Bravo! Bravo!'

Between acts people chatted, got up for more drinks, to fill their plates again, but I sat beside Chris almost frozen with dread that I couldn't explain.

Beside Bart, Melodie sat as tense as I, her eyes closed and waiting.

Third act time.

Bart shifted his chair closer to Melodie. 'I hate this ballet,' she murmured. 'It always frightens me, the brutality of it. The blood seems so real, too real. The wounds make me feel sick. Fairy tales suit me better.'

'Everything will be fine,' soothed Bart, putting his arm over her shoulders. Immediately Melodie jumped to her feet, and from then on she refused to sit.

The crimson curtain rose. Now we were staring at the representation of a heathen temple. Huge thick columns made of papier-mâché jabbed at his strong legs with small swords, tiny lances. (The dwarfs were really children, costumed to look grotesque.) Jory hefted his fake chains, making them seem very heavy, making himself seem weary enough to drop. His wrists also wore what seemed to be iron manacles.

As he stumbled around the arena, turning in blind circles, trying to feel his way along, the lilting, heartrending music played. Off stage, in her own small blue spotlight, the opera star began to sing that most famous aria of all from *Samson and Delilah*:

'My heart at thy sweet voice . . .'

Blind and tormented from whip lashings weeping blood, Jory began a slow, mesmerizing dance of torment and loss of faith in love, his renewed credence in God restored, using the fake iron chains as part of his action. I'd never seen such a heartbreaking performance.

Blindly, agonizingly, Samson's ordeal of searching for Delilah while she dodged just out of his reach tore at my heart, as if this entire thing was real and not just a performance, so real every person in the audience forgot to eat, to drink, to whisper to a partner.

Delilah wore an even more revealing costume of green. The jewels sparkled as if they were real diamonds and emeralds, and when I peered through opera glasses, I saw to my dismay that they were part of the Foxworth legacy, glittering and shining enough to lend Delilah the appearance of wearing more than she actually did. And just a few hours ago Bart had blasted Cindy with his anger for wearing more than she did now.

Flitting around the temple, Delilah hid herself behind a fake marble column. Samson's outstretched hands pleaded for her help, even as the tenor screamed out his agony of betrayal. I quickly glanced at Bart. He was leaning forward, watching with such intensity it seemed nothing in the world interested him more than this play of agony he'd wanted between brother and sister.

Again I was filled with apprehension. The air seemed fraught with danger.

Higher and higher rose the pitch of the soprano. Samson began to shamble blindly towards his goal – the twin columns he meant to shove apart and bring down the heathen temple.

Overhead the giant obscene god grinned maliciously.

And that song of love made it a thousand times more painful.

As Samson was making his way up the shallow steps, on the temple floor Delilah writhed in apparent regret and agony to see her lover so cruelly treated. Several guards headed to capture her, and no doubt they would treat her as they had Samson. Even so, she began to crawl towards Samson, keeping her body low to the floor and just beneath the chains he lashed about so furiously. Now she grabbed his ankle, looking up at him pleadingly. It seemed he would beat her with his chains, but he hesitated, staring blindly downward before his manacled hand reached tenderly to stroke her long dark hair, to listen to words she mouthed but we couldn't hear.

With calculated thought for drama, with renewed faith in his love and his God, Jory lifted his arms, bulging his biceps, and broke his chains!

The audience gasped at the passion Jory put into the act. He spun around wildly, lashing the separated chains that dangled from his wrist manacles, trying blindly to strike, apparently, anyone. Delilah jumped up to dodge the brutal chains that felled two guards and one dwarf. She made her attempts to get away a dance of such excitement everyone at the party was held in thrall, totally quiet as bit by bit, Delilah cleverly led her blind lover to the exact position he needed, between the two huge columns that supported the temple's god. Dodging, provoking Samson more and more with taunting, silent gestures even as the voice off stage declared her undying love for him. All meant to deceive the priests and the blood-thirsty crowd that wanted to see Samson dead.

All around the arena people were leaning forward, straining to see the grace and beauty of one of the world's most famous *premier danseurs*.

Jory was performing astonishing jetés, lashing himself up into a terrible frenzy before he finally put one hand on a fake marble pillar; and then with more dramatic import, he had the other braced, too.

On the floor, Delilah kissed his feet before she mocked him, tormented him with words she couldn't speak. Tricking the heathen crowd, while he knew she truly loved him and had betrayed him out of jealous spite and greed. With heaving, impressive motions Samson began to labour to bring down the entire temple by pushing against the columns! The tenor's voice off stage called upon God to help him shove down the blasphemous god.

Again the soprano sang, tenderly seducing Samson into believing he couldn't do the impossible.

The last beseeching note died as with a mighty heave, perspiration streaming down his face, dripping on to his oiled body already streaked with red, he glistened in a ghastly way. His blind white eyes shown.

Delilah screamed.

The cue.

With a mighty and terrifying effort, Jory raised his hands again and began with greater effort to shove against the 'stone' columns. My heart was in my throat as I watched those papier mâché columns begin to bulge. As God restored Samson's strength, down would crash the temple, killing everyone!

Stage hands had cleverly arranged a large amount of cardboard backed by clanging junk to clatter down and make frightful noises. They faked thunder by rippling long rectangles of thin metal, as if God would wreak his vengeance in a personal way. Strangely enough, as the lights turned red, and the records of people screaming began to sound, Cindy was to tell me later, she thought she felt something hard brush her shoulder.

Just before the curtain lowered, I saw Jory fall from a huge false boulder that struck him on his back and head.

He sprawled face down on the floor, blood spurting from his cuts! Horrified to realize that sand didn't pour harmlessly out of the broken and tumbled columns, I jumped to my feet and began to scream. Instantly Chris was up and running towards the stage.

My knees buckled beneath me. I sank to the grass, still seeing the terrible vision of Jory flat on his face with the column smashed down on his lower back.

A second column crashed down on his legs.

The curtain was down now.

Applause thundered. I tried to rise and reach Jory, but my leg wouldn't hold me. Someone caught my elbow and half lifted me. I glanced and saw that it was Bart. Soon I was on the stage, staring down at the broken body of my first son.

I couldn't believe what I saw. Not my Jory, my dancing Jory. Not the little boy who'd asked when he was three, '*Am I dancing, Momma?*'

'*Yes, Jory, you are dancing.*'

'*Am I good, Momma?*'

'*No, Jory . . . you are wonderful!*'

Not my Jory, who'd excelled at everything physical, beautiful and heartfelt. Not my Jory . . . my Julian's son.

'Jory, Jory,' I cried, falling upon my knees by his side, seeing Cindy through my tears, crying, too. He should be rising by this time. He lay sprawled . . . and bloody. The 'fake' blood I felt was sticky, warm. It smelled like real blood. 'Jory . . . you're not really hurt . . . Jory . . .?'

Nothing. Not a sound, not a movement.

In my peripheral vision I saw Melodie as through the wrong end of a telescope, hurrying our way, her face so pale she and her black gown seemed darker than the night. 'He's hurt. Really hurt.' Somebody said that. Me?

'No! Don't move him. Call for an ambulance.'

'Someone already has – his father, I think.'

'Jory, Jory . . . you can't be hurt.' Melodie's cry as she ran forward. Bart tried to hold her back. She began to scream when she saw the blood. 'Jory, don't die, please don't die!' she sobbed over and over again.

I knew how she felt. As soon as the curtain was down, every dancer after 'dying' on stage jumped up immediately . . . and Jory wasn't doing that.

Cries came from everywhere. The scent of blood was all around us. And I was staring at Bart, who had wanted this particular opera to be made into a ballet. Why this role for Jory? Why, Bart, why? Had he planned for the accident weeks ago?

How had Bart staged it? I picked up a handful of sand and found it wet. I glared at Bart, who stared down at Jory's sprawled body, wet from sweat, sticky from blood, gritty from sand. Bart had eyes only for Jory as two attendants from the ambulance lifted him carefully upon a stretcher and placed him in the back of the white ambulance.

Running forward, I shoved my way to where I could look inside the ambulance. 'Will he live?' I asked the young doctor who was feeling Jory's pulse. Chris was nowhere in sight.

The doctor smiled. 'Yes, he'll live. He's young and he's strong, but it's my calculated guess it will be a long time before he dances again.'

And Jory had said ten million times that he couldn't live without dancing.

WHEN THE PARTY IS OVER

I crowded into the ambulance beside Jory, and soon Chris was at my side, both of us crouching over Jory's still form strapped to the stretcher. He was unconscious, one side of his face very badly bruised and battered, and blood ran from many small wounds. I couldn't bear to look at his injuries, which overwhelmed me, much less concentrate on those horrible marks I'd seen on his back . . .

Closing my eyes, I turned my head to see the bright lights of Foxworth Hall like fireflies on the mountain. Later I was to hear from Cindy that at first all the guests had been appalled, not knowing what to do or how to act, but Bart had rushed in to tell them Jory was only slightly injured and would be fully recovered in a few days.

Up front, seated with the driver and an attendant, was Melodie in her black formal, glancing back from time to time and asking if Jory had come around yet. 'Chris, will he live?' she asked in a voice thin with anxiety.

'Of course he'll live,' said Chris, feverishly working over Jory, ruining his new tux with the blood. 'He's not bleeding now, I've stopped that.' He turned to the intern and asked for more dressings.

The screaming of the siren rattled my nerves, made me afraid soon all of us would be dead. How could I have deceived myself into believing Foxworth Hall would ever offer us anything but grief? I began to pray, closing my eyes and saying the same words over and over again. *Don't let Jory die, God, please don't take him. He's too young, he hasn't lived long enough. His unborn child needs him.* Only after I'd kept this up for several miles did I remember that I'd said almost the same prayers for Julian – and Julian had died.

By this time Melodie was hysterical. The intern started to inject her with some drug, but quickly I stopped him. 'No! She's pregnant and that would harm her child.' I leaned forward and hissed at Melodie, 'Stop screaming! You're not helping Jory, or your baby.' She screamed louder, turning to beat at me with small but strong fists.

'I wish we'd never come . . . I told him it was a mistake, coming to that house, the worst mistake of our lives, and now he's paying, paying, paying . . .' On and on saying that until finally her voice went, and Jory was opening his eyes and grinning at us.

'Hi,' he said weakly. 'Seems Samson didn't die after all.'

I sobbed in relief. Chris smiled and bathed Jory's head cuts with some solution. 'You're going to be fine, son, just fine. Just hold on to that.'

Jory closed his eyes before he murmured in a weak way, 'Was the performance good?'

'Cathy, you tell him what you think,' Chris suggested in the calmest voice.

'You were incredible, darling,' I said, leaning to kiss his pale face smeared with makeup.

'Tell Mel not to worry,' he whispered as if he heard her crying; then he drifted into sleep from the sedative Chris injected into his arm.

We paced the hospital waiting room outside of the operating theatre. Melodie was by this time a limp rag, sagging from fear, her eyes wide and staring. 'Same as his father . . . same as his father,' repeating the same words over so much I thought she was drilling that notion into her head – and into mine. I, too, could have screamed from the agony of believing Jory might die. More to keep her quiet than anything else, I took her into my arms and smothered her face against my breasts, soothing her with motherly words of assurance when I didn't feel confident about anything. We were, again, caught in the merciless clutches of Foxworths. How could I have been so happy earlier in the day? Where had my intuition fled? Bart had come into his own, and in so doing he had taken from Jory what belonged to him, the most valuable possession he had – his good health and his strong, agile body.

Hours later, five surgeons wearing green brought out my firstborn son from the operating theatre. Jory was covered to his chin with blankets. All his summer tan had disappeared, leaving him as pale as his father had liked to keep his complexion. His dark curly hair seemed wet. Bruises were under his closed eyes.

'He'll be all right now, won't he?' asked Melodie, jumping up to hurry after the stretcher rolling fast towards an elevator. 'He will recover and be as good as new, won't he?'

Desperation made her voice high and shrill.

No one said a word.

They lifted Jory off the stretcher by using the sheet, carefully deposited him on his bed, then chased all of us out but Chris. In the hall outside I held Melodie and waited, waited.

Melodie and I went back to Foxworth Hall towards dawn, when Jory's condition seemed stable enough for me to relax a little. Chris stayed on, sleeping in some little room used by the interns on duty.

I had wanted to stay as well, but Melodie grew ever more hysterical, hating the way Jory slept, hating the medicinal smell of the hospital corridors; hating the nurses who scurried in and out of his room with trays of instruments and bottles; hating the doctors who wouldn't give her, or me, a straight answer.

A taxi drove us both back to the Hall, where a light had been left burning near the front doors. The sun was just peeking over the horizon, flushing the sky with frail pink. Little birds woke up and fluttered tentative fledgling wings, while their parents sang or chirped their territorial rights before they flew away to find food. I supported Melodie up the stairs and into the house. She was by this time so deeply detached from reality that she staggered and seemed drunk.

Up one side of the dual staircase carefully, slowly, with my arm about her waist, thinking every second of the baby she was carrying and the effect this night might have on him or her. In the bedroom she shared with Jory she couldn't manage to undress, her hands trembled so badly. I helped, then slipped a nightgown over her head, tucked her into the bed and turned out the light. 'I'll stay if you want,' I said, as she lay there bleak and hopeless looking. She wanted me to stay, wanted to talk about Jory and the doctors who wouldn't give us any encouragement. 'Why do they do that?' she cried.

How could I tell her how doctors protected themselves with silence until they were sure of their facts? I covered for all Jory's doctors, telling Melodie that Jory had to be all right or they would have wanted her to stay on.

Finally she drifted into restless sleep, fretting and tossing, calling Jory's name, waking up often to jerk back to awareness and cry all over again. Her anguish was painful to see and hear, and I was left feeling wrung out like a rag.

An hour later, much to my relief, she sank into deep sleep, as if even she knew she had to escape that way.

I had a few minutes of sleep myself before Cindy barged into my room and perched anxiously on my bed, waiting for me to wake up. The very sinking of the mattress when she sat opened my eyes. I saw her face, opened my arms and held her while she cried. 'He is going to be all right, Momma?'

'Darling, your father is there with him. Jory had to have immediate surgery. He's in a private room now, asleep and resting comfortably. Chris will be there when he wakes up. I'm going to eat a quick breakfast and then drive to the city to be there, too. I want you to stay here with Melodie – '

Already I'd decided that Melodie was much too hysterical to go to the hospital with me.

Instantly Cindy protested, saying she wanted to go and see Jory herself. I shook my head, insisting she stay. 'Melodie is his wife, darling, and she is taking this very hard, and in her condition she shouldn't go back to the hospital until we know the truth about Jory. I've never seen a woman carry on so much about being in a hospital. She seems to think they are as bad as funeral homes. Now stay, and say anything to keep her calm, wait on her, see that she eats and drinks. Give her the peace she is seeking desperately now . . . and I'll telephone when I know something.'

Melodie, when I peeked in a few minutes later, was so deeply asleep I knew I'd made the right decision. Explain to her why I didn't wait for her to wake up, Cindy, lest she think I'm taking her place . . .'

I drove very fast towards the hospital.

Because Chris was a doctor, I'd spent a great deal of my life going to and from hospitals, letting him off, picking him up, visiting friends, meeting a few patients he particularly favoured. We'd taken Jory to the best hospital in our area. The corridors were broad to allow the passing and turning of stretchers, the windows were wide, with plants hanging. Every modern diagnostic aid was there, despite the expense. But the room where Jory slept on and on in was tiny, so tiny, as were all the rooms. The single window was so recessed it was difficult to look outside, and when I did, I saw nothing but the entranceway to the hospital and, farther away, another wing.

Chris was still sleeping, though a nurse told me he'd been in to check on Jory five times during the night. 'He's really a devoted father, Mrs Sheffield.'

I turned to stare down at Jory, who now wore a heavy cast on his body with a window through which his incision could be viewed and treated, if necessary. I kept staring at his legs, wondering why they didn't twitch, bend, move – they weren't enclosed in the cast.

Suddenly an arm slipped around my waist and warm lips brushed the nape of my neck.

'Didn't I order you not to come back until I called?'

Relief immediately flooded me. Chris was here. 'Chris, how can I stay away? I've got to know what's wrong, or I can't sleep. Tell me the truth, now that Melodie isn't here to scream and faint.'

He sighed and bowed his head. Only then did I see how exhausted he looked, still wearing his rumpled and soiled tux. 'It's not good news, Cathy. I'd rather not go into details until I've talked again with his physicians and surgeon.'

'Don't you pull that old trick on me! I want to know! I'm not one of your patients who thinks doctors are gods on pedestals and I can't ask questions. Is Jory's back broken?

Was his spinal cord injured? Will he walk again? Why doesn't he move his legs?'

First he pulled me out into the hall, in case Jory was awake but had his eyes closed. Softly he closed the door behind him and then led me into a tiny cubicle where only doctors were allowed. He sat me down, standing to tower above me, and made me realize I was about to hear very serious news. Only then did he speak. 'Jory's spine was broken, Cathy. You guessed correctly. It's a lower lumbar fracture, so we can be grateful his injury wasn't higher. He will have full use of his arms and will eventually gain control over his bladder and intestinal functions, but right now they are in shock, so to speak, and tubes and bags will function until he regains the feeling of when he has to go.'

He paused, but I wasn't letting him off that easily. 'The spinal cord? Tell me that it wasn't crushed.'

'No, not crushed, but damaged,' he said reluctantly. 'It is bruised severely enough to keep his legs paralysed.'

I froze. Oh, no! Not Jory! I cried out, with no more control than Melodie. 'He'll never walk again?' I whispered, feeling myself go pale and weak and slightly light-headed. When next I opened my eyes, Chris was on his knees by my side, gripping both my hands hard.

'Hold on . . . he's alive, and that's what counts. He won't die – but he'll never walk again.'

Sinking, I was drowning, drowning, going under again in that same old familiar pool of hopeless despair. The same little sparkling swanhead fish rushed to nibble on my brain, taking bits out of my soul. 'And that means he'll never dance again . . . never walk, never dance . . . Chris, what will this do to him?'

He drew me into his embrace and bowed his head into my hair, his breath stirring it as he spoke in a choked way. 'He'll survive, darling. Isn't that what all of us do when tragedy comes into our lives? We take it, grin and bear it and make the best of what we have left. We forget what we had yesterday and concentrate on what we have today, and when we can teach Jory how to accept what has happened, we will have our son back again – disabled, but alive, intelligent, organically healthy.'

I was jerking with sobs as he talked on. His hands ran up and down my back, his lips brushed over my eyes, my lips, finding ways to calm me.

'We've got to be strong for him, darling. Cry all you want now, for you can't cry when he opens his eyes and sees you. You can't show pity. You can't be too sympathetic. When he wakes up, he's going to look into your eyes, and he's going to read your mind. Whatever fears or pity that you show on your face or in your eyes is going to determine how he looks and feels about his handicap. He's going to be devastated, we both know that. He'll want to die. He'll think about his father and how Julian escaped his plight, we have to keep that in mind as well. We'll have to talk to Cindy and Bart and explain to them the roles they'll play in his recovery. We have to form a strong family unit to see him through this ordeal, for its going to be rough, Cathy, very rough.'

I nodded, trying to control my flow of tears, feeling I was inside Jory, knowing every tormented moment he had ahead was going to tear me apart, too.

Chris went on while he kept his arms about me for support. 'Jory's constructed his entire life around dancing, and he will never dance again. No, don't look at me with that hope. Never again! There is some possibility someday he'll have enough strength to get up on his feet and pull himself around on crutches . . . but he'll never walk normally. Accept that, Cathy.

'We have to convince him that his handicap doesn't matter, that he's the same person he was before. And, most importantly, we have to convince ourselves that he's just as manly, just as human . . . for many families change when a member becomes disabled. They either become too sympathetic, or they become alienated, as if the handicap changes the person they used to love and know. We have to keep to middle ground and help Jory find the strength to see this through.'

I heard a little of what he said.

Crippled! My Jory was crippled. A paraplegic. I shook my head, disbelieving that fate would keep him that way. Tears fell like rain upon Chris's soiled, ruffled, dress shirt. How would Jory live when he found out he was going to spend the rest of his life confined to a wheelchair?

The sun was noon high and still Jory hadn't opened his eyes. Chris decided we both needed a hearty meal, and hospital food was always seasonless sawdust or shoe leather. 'Try to nap while I'm gone, and hold on to your control. If he awakens, try not to panic, keep your cool and smile, smile, smile. He'll be fuzzy-minded and won't be fully cognizant. I'll try to hurry back . . .'

I'd never sleep; I was too busy planning on how to act when Jory eventually woke up long enough to start asking questions. Chris had no sooner closed the door behind him than Jory stirred, turned his head and weakly smiled at me. 'Hey, you been there all night? Or two nights? When was it?'

'Last night,' I whispered hoarsely, hoping he wouldn't notice my throaty voice. 'You've been sleeping for hours and hours.'

'You look exhausted,' he said weakly, touchingly showing more concern for me than for himself. 'Why don't you go back to the Hall and sleep? I'm okay. I've fallen before, and, like before, in a few days I'll be whirling all over that house again. Where's my wife?'

Why wasn't he noticing the cast that bulged out his chest? Then I saw his eyes were unfocused and he hadn't fully pulled out of the sedatives given him to ease the pain. Good . . . if only he wouldn't start asking questions I wanted Chris to answer.

Sleepily he closed his eyes and dozed off, but ten minutes later he was again awake and asking questions. 'Mom, I feel strange. Never felt like this before. Can't say I like the way I feel. Why this cast? Did I break something?'

'The temple papier-mâché columns fell,' I weakly explained. 'Knocked you out. What a way to end the ballet – too real.'

'Did I bring down the house – or the sky?' he quipped, his eyes opening and brightening as the sedative I'd hoped would keep him hazy wore off. 'Cindy was great, wasn't she? You know, each time I see her, she's more beautiful. And she's really a very good dancer. She's like you, Mom, improving with age.'

I sat on my hands to keep them from twisting in the betraying way my mother used to use her hands. I smiled, got up to pour a glass of water. 'Doctor's orders. You've got to drink a lot.'

He sipped as I supported his head. It was so strange to see him helpless, when he'd never been bedridden. His colds had come and gone in a matter of days, and not once had he missed a day in school or ballet class, except in order to visit Bart in the hospital after one of his many accidents that never left him permanently damaged. Jory had sprained his ankles dozens of times, torn ligaments, fallen, got up, but he'd never had a serious unjury until now. All dancers spent some time tending small injuries, and sometimes even larger ones, but a broken back, a damaged spinal cord – it was every dancer's most dreaded nightmare.

Again he dozed off, but before long he had his eyes open and was asking questions about himself. Perched on the side of his bed, I rattled on and on nonsensically, praying that Chris would come back. A pretty nurse came in with Jory's lunch tray, all liquids. That gave me something to do. I fiddled with a half-pint milk carton, opened yogurt, poured milk and orange juice, tucked a napkin under his chin and began with the strawberry yogurt. Immediately he gagged and made a face. He shoved my hands away, saying he could feed himself, but he didn't have an appetite.

Once I had the tray out of the way, I hoped he'd fall asleep. Instead he lay there staring at me, his eyes lucid. 'Can you tell me now why I feel so weak? Why I can't eat? Why I can't move my legs?'

'Your father has gone out to bring in food for the two of us, snack food that's not good for you, but it will be tastier than what we can eat in the cafeteria downstairs. Let him tell you. He knows all the technical terms that I don't.'

'Mom, I wouldn't understand technical terms. Tell me in your own layman's words – why can't I feel or move my legs?'

His dark sapphire eyes riveted on me. 'Mom, I'm not a coward. I can take whatever you have to say. Now spill it out, or else I'm going to presume my back is broken and my legs are paralysed and I'm never going to walk again.'

My heart quickened as my head lowered. He'd said all this in a jocular way, as if none of it could possibly be true . . . and he'd stated his condition exactly.

Desperation came to his eyes as I faltered, trying to find just the right words, and even the right ones would rip out his heart. Just then Chris strode in the door, carrying a paper bag with cheeseburgers. 'Well,' he said brightly, throwing Jory a pleased smile, 'look who's awake and talking.' He took out a burger and handed it to me. 'Sorry, Jory, you can't have anything solid for a few days due to your operation. Cathy, eat that thing while it's still hot,' he ordered, sitting down himself and immediately unwrapping his burger. I saw he'd bought two super ones for himself. He bit into it with relish before he brought out the cola drinks. 'Didn't have the lime you wanted, Cathy. It's Pepsie.'

'It's cold, with lots of ice, that's all I want.'

Jory watched us narrowly as we ate. I forced down the cheeseburger, knowing he was suspicious. Chris did an admirable job of eating two burgers and one cardboard dish of French fries while I managed to eat only half of my burger, and didn't touch the greasy potatoes. Chris balled up his napkin and tossed it in a can, along with our other trash.

By this time Jory's lids were growing heavy. He was struggling hard to stay awake. 'Dad . . . are you going to tell me now?'

'Yes, anything you want to know.' Chris moved to sit on Jory's bed and placed his strong hand on top of Jory's. Jory blinked back sleep.

'Dad, I'm not feeling anything below my waist. All the time you and Mom ate, I was trying to wiggle my toes and I couldn't. If I've broken my back, and that's why I'm in this cast, I want to know the truth, all of it.'

'I intend to tell you all the truth,' said Chris staunchly.

'Is my spine broken?'

'Yes.'

'Are my legs paralysed?'

'Yes.'

Jory blinked, looked stunned, gathered his strength for one last question. 'Will I dance again?'

'No.'

Jory closed his eyes, tightened his lips into a thin line and lay perfectly still.

I stepped closer to lean above him, and tenderly I brushed back the dark curls fallen over his brow. 'Darling, I know you're devastated. It wasn't easy for your father to tell you the truth, but you have to know. You're not alone in this. We're all involved. We're here to see you through, to do everything we can. You'll adjust. Time will heal your body so you won't feel pain, and eventually you'll accept what can't be helped. We love you. Melodie loves you. And you'll be a father come this very January. You reached the top of your profession and have been there five years . . . that's more than most people accomplish in a lifetime.'

Briefly he met my eyes. His were full of bitterness, anger, frustration, a rage so terrible I had to turn away. It was all over him, his fierce anger at having been cheated and stolen from before he'd had enough.

When I looked again, his eyes were closed. Chris had his fingers on his pulse. 'Jory, I know you're not sleeping. I'm going to give you another sedative so you can really sleep, and when you wake up, you are going to think about how important you are to a great many people. You're not going to feel sorry for yourself and allow yourself to wallow in bitterness. There are people walking the streets today who will never experience what you've already had. They haven't travelled the world over and heard the thundering applause and cries of 'bravo, bravo!' They'll never know the heights that were yours and can be yours again in some other field of artistic endeavour. Your world has not stopped, son, you've only stumbled. The road to achievement is still ahead and wide open, only you'll have to roll along that road instead of run or dance; but you'll achieve again, for it's in you to always win. You will just find another craft, another career, and with your family you will find happiness. Isn't that what life is all about when you come down to the basics? We want someone to love us, to need us, to share our lives . . . and you have all of that.'

My son didn't open his eyes, didn't respond. He only lay there as still as if death had already claimed him.

Inside I was screaming, for Julian had reacted in the very same way! Jory was closing us out, locking himself in the narrow, tight cage of his mind that refused life without walking and dancing.

Silently Chris readied a hypodermic needle before he swabbed at Jory's arm, then released the fluid steadily into his arm. 'Sleep, my son. When you wake up, your wife will be here. You'll have to be brave for her sake.'

I thought I saw Jory shudder.

We left him deeply asleep, in the care of a private-duty nurse instructed to never leave him alone. Chris drove us back to Foxworth Hall so he could shower and shave, take a nap, put on fresh clothes before he drove back to be with Jory. We expected Melodie to return with us.

Her blue eyes went terror stricken and stark when Chris told her as kindly as possible Jory's condition.

She uttered a small cry and clutched at her abdomen. 'You mean . . . never dance? Never walk?' she whispered, as if her voice were failing her. 'There must be something you can do to help him.'

Chris soon dashed that hope. 'No, Melodie. When the spinal cord is injured, it prevents the legs from receiving the messages from the brain. Jory can will his legs to move, but they won't receive the message. You have to accept him as he is now, and do everything you can to help him survive what is probably the most traumatic event he will ever have to face.'

She jumped to her feet, crying out pitifully, 'But he won't be the same! You just said he's refusing to talk – I can't go there and pretend it doesn't matter when it does! What will he do? What will *I* do? Where will we go, and how will he survive without walking and dancing? What kind of father will he make now that he has to spend the rest of his life in a wheelchair?'

Standing, Chris spoke firmly. 'Melodie, this is no time for you to panic and throw hysterical tantrums. You have to be strong, not weak. I realise you are suffering, too, but you have to show him a bright, smiling face that will give him the assurance that he hasn't lost the wife he loves. You don't marry just for the good times, but for the bad times as well. You'll bathe, dress, put on your makeup, style your hair and go to him and hold him in your arms as best you can, and kiss him and make him believe he has a future worth staying alive for.'

'But he doesn't!' she yelled. 'He doesn't!'

Then, breaking, she was crying bitter tears. 'I didn't mean that . . . I love him, I do . . . but don't make me go and see him lying like that so still and quiet. I can't stand to see him until he's smiling and accepting, and then maybe I can face up to what he's become . . . maybe I can . . .'

I disliked her for showing such spineless hysteria and failing Jory when he needed her most. Stepping to Chris's side, I linked my arm through his. 'Melodie, do you think for one moment that you are the first wife and expectant mother to suddenly find the world crashing down on your head? You're not. I was expecting Jory when his father was in a fatal auto accident. Just be grateful Jory is alive.'

She sank in a crumpled heap on a chair and bowed her head into her hands and cried for long minutes before she looked up, her eyes darker and more bleak than before. 'Perhaps death is what he'd prefer – have you thought of that?'

It was the thought that tormented my hours, that Jory would do something to end his life, as Julian had done.

I wouldn't let it happen. Not again. 'Then stay here and cry,' I said with unintentional hardness. 'But I'm not going to leave my son alone to fight this out by himself. I'm going to stay with him night and day to see that he doesn't give up hope. But you keep this in mind, Melodie: you are carrying his child, and that makes you the most important person in his life – and important in mine, too. He needs you and your support. I'm sorry if I sound harsh, but I have to think first of him . . . why can't you?'

Speechless, she stared up at me, her lovely face stricken, tears streaking her cheeks. 'Tell him I'll come soon . . . tell him that,' she whispered hoarsely.

We told him that.

He kept his eyes closed, his lips glued together. There were ways of telling he wasn't asleep, only shutting us out.

Jory refused to eat until tubes were put in his arms to feed him intravenously. Summer days came and went; long days that were full and mostly sad. Some hours gave me faint pleasures when I was with Chris and Cindy, but few gave me hope.

If only, if only were the words that started off my mornings, as they finished off my nights. If only I could live my life all over again, then, perhaps, I could save Jory, Chris, Cindy, Melodie, myself – and even Bart. If only.

If only he hadn't danced that role –

I tried everything, as Chris and Cindy did, to pull Jory back from that terrible lonely place where he'd taken himself. For the first time in my life I couldn't reach him, couldn't ease his sorrow.

He'd lost what mattered most to him, the use of his dancing legs. With his legs he'd soon lose his wonderfully powerful and skilled body. I couldn't look at those beautifully shaped strong legs lying so still beneath the sheet, so damned useless.

Had the grandmother been right when she said we were cursed, born for failure and pain? Had she programmed us for tragedy to steal the fruit of our successes?

Had Chris and I achieved anything of real value when our son lay as if dead, and our second son refused to visit Jory but once?

Bart had stood and stared down at Jory lying helpless and still with his eyes closed, his arms straight down at his sides. 'Oh, my God,' he'd whispered before he hurried from the tiny room.

Never could I convince him to visit again. 'Mother, he

doesn't know I'm there, so what's the good? I can't bear to see him like that. I'm sorry, really sorry . . . but I can't help.'

I stared at him, wondering if I had wanted to help *him* so much I'd risked the life of my beloved Jory.

That's when I began to tell myself that I wasn't going to believe he'd never walk, never dance again. This was a nightmare to be endured, but eventually we'd awaken and Jory would be whole again, just as he'd been.

I told Chris my plan to convince Jory he could and he would walk again, even if he never danced.

'Cathy, you can't give him false hope,' warned Chris, looking terribly distressed. 'All you can do now is help him accept what can't be changed. Give him your kind of strength. Help him – but don't lead him down false trails that will bring him only disappointment. I know it will be difficult. I'm in hell, too, just as much as you are. But remember, our hell is nothing compared to his. We can sympathize and feel dreadfully sorry, but we're not inside his skin. We're not suffering his loss – he's all alone in that. Facing up to agony you and I can't even begin to understand. All we can do is be here when he decides to pull out of his protective shell. Be here to give him the confidence he needs to go on . . . for damned if Melodie is giving him anything!'

That was something almost as awful as Jory's injury . . . that his own wife would shun him now as if he were a leper. Both Chris and I pleaded with her to come with us, even if she said nothing but hello, I love you, she had to come.

'What can I say that you haven't already said?' she screamed. 'He doesn't want me to come and see him like that! I know him better than either of you do. If he wanted to see me, he'd say he did. Besides, I'm afraid to go, afraid I'll cry and say all the wrong things, and even if I stay quiet, he might open his eyes and see something on my face that would make him feel worse, and I don't want to be responsible for what might happen then. Stop insisting! Wait until he wants me to visit . . . and then, maybe, I can find the courage I need.'

She flew away from Chris and I as if we carried with us some plague that might contaminate her dream that this nightmare would end happily.

Standing in the hall outside our rooms was Bart, staring after Melodie with his heart in his eyes. He turned to glare at me.

'Why don't you leave her alone? I've been to see him, and it tore me all apart. Certainly in her condition she needs to find some security, even if its only in her dreams. She sleeps a great deal, you know. While you stay with him, she cries, walks as if in a dream, with her eyes unfocused. She half eats. I have to plead with her to swallow, to drink. She stares at me, and obeys like a child. Sometimes I have to spoon the food into her mouth, hold the glass for her to sip. Mother, Melodie is in shock – and all you think about is your precious Jory, not caring what you do to her!'

Sorry now, I hurried to her side and held her in my arms. 'It's all right. I understand now. Bart has explained how you can't accept this yet . . . but try, Melodie, please try. Even if he doesn't open his eyes and speak, he's aware of what's going on, and who comes to see him and who doesn't.'

Her head was on my shoulder. 'Cathy . . . I am trying. Just give me time.'

The next morning Cindy came into our bedroom without knocking, causing Chris to frown. She should have known better. But I had to forgive her after seeing her pale face and frightened expression. 'Momma . . . Daddy, I've just got to tell you something, and yet I don't know if I should. Or if it really means anything.'

I was distracted from her words by the outfit she wore: a white bikini so brief it was barely there. The swimming pool Bart had ordered was now complete and this was the first day it was ready. Jory's tragic accident was not going to inhibit Bart's style of living.

'Cindy, I wish you would wear those beach coverups at the poolside. And that suit is much too skimpy.'

She appeared startled, crestfallen and hurt because I criticized her suit. Glancing down at herself briefly, she shrugged indifferently. 'Holy Christ, Momma! Some friends of mine wear string bikinis – you should see those if you think this one is immodest. Some of my friends wear nothing at all . . .' Her large blue eyes studied mine seriously.

Chris tossed her a towel, which she wrapped around herself. 'Momma, I've got to say I don't like the way you make me feel, somehow dirty, like Bart makes me feel – when I came to tell you something I overheard Bart talking about.'

'Go on, Cindy,' urged Chris.

'Bart was on the telephone. He'd left his door ajar. I heard him talking to an insurance agency.' She paused, sat down on our unmade bed and lowered her head before she spoke again. Her soft, silky hair hid her expression. 'Mom, Dad, it seems Bart took out some kind of special "party" insurance in case any of his guests were injured.'

'Why, that's not at all unusual,' said Chris. 'The house is covered by homeowner's insurance . . . but with two hundred guests, he needed plenty of extra insurance that night.'

Cindy's head jerked upward. She stared at her father, then at me. A sigh escaped her lips. 'I guess it's okay then. I just thought maybe . . . maybe . . .'

'Maybe what?' I asked sharply.

'Momma, you picked up a handful of that sand that spilled from the columns when they broke. Wasn't the sand supposed to be dry? It wasn't dry. Someone made it wet – and that made it heavier. The sand didn't come pouring out like it was supposed to. It made those columns stand upright – and the sand clumped down on Jory like cement. Otherwise Jory wouldn't have been hurt so severely.'

'I knew about the insurance,' said Chris dully, refusing to meet my eyes. 'I didn't know about the wet sand.'

Neither Chris nor I could find words to defend Bart. Still, surely, surely he wouldn't want to injure Jory – or kill him? At some point in our lives, we had to believe in Bart, give him the benefit of doubt.

Chris paced our bedroom, his brow deeply wrinkled as he explained one of the stage crew could have put water on the sand, hoping to make the columns steadier. It didn't have to be Bart's orders he was following.

All three of us descended the stairs solemnly, finding Bart outside on the morning terrace with Melodie. With the mountains in the distance, the woods before them, the gardens lush with blooming flowers, the setting was beautifully romantic. Sunlight filtered through the lacy leaves of the fruit trees, slipped under the brightly striped umbrella that was supposed to shield the occupants seated at the white wrought-iron table.

Melodie, to my surprise, was smiling as her eyes lingered on the strong lines of Bart's face. 'Bart, your parents don't understand why I can't bring myself to go and see Jory in the hospital. I see your mother looking at me resentfully. I'm disappointing her, disappointing myself. I'm a coward about illnesses. Always have been. But I know what's going on. I know Jory lies on that bed, staring up at the ceiling, refusing to talk. I know what he's thinking. He's lost not only the use of his legs, but all the goals he's set for himself. He's thinking of his father and the way he died. He's trying to withdraw from the world by making himself into a nothing thing that we won't miss when one day he kills himself just like his father did.'

Bart quickly looked at her disapprovingly. 'Melodie, you don't know my brother. Jory would never kill himself. Maybe he does feel lost now, but he'll come around.'

'How can he?' she wailed. 'He's lost the most important thing in his life. Our marriage was based not only on our love for each other, but on our mutual careers. Each day I tell myself that I can go to him, and smile, and give him what he needs. Then I pause, flounder, and wonder what can I say. I'm not good with words like your mother. I can't smile and be optimistic like his father – '

'Chris is not Jory's father,' stated Bart flatly.

'Oh, to Jory Chris is his father. At least the one who counts most. He loves Chris, Bart, respects and admires him, and forgives him for what you call his sins.' She went on while we three hung back, waiting to hear more of why she was acting as she was.

And all we heard was a concluding statement. 'I'm ashamed to say it, but I can't go and see him like he is.'

'Then what are you going to do?' asked Bart in a cynical way. He sipped his coffee while staring directly into her eyes. If he'd turn his head just a little, he'd see the three of us watching and listening, and learning so much.

Her answer was an anguished wail. 'I don't know! I'm coming apart inside! I hate waking up and knowing that Jory will never be a real husband to me again. If you don't mind, I'm going to move into the room across the hall that doesn't hold so many painful memories of what we used to share. Your mother doesn't realize that I'm just as lost as he is, and I'm having his baby!'

Her sobs started then. Bowing her head, she put it down on the arms she folded on the table. 'Someone has to think of me, help me . . . someone . . .'

'I'll help,' said Bart softly, laying his tanned hand on her shoulder. His right hand set the coffee aside and lightly he brushed that hand over her spill of flowing hair. 'Whenever you need me, if only for a shoulder to cry on, I'll be there, anytime.'

If I'd heard Bart speak as compassionately before to anyone but Melodie, my heart would have jumped for joy. As it was, it plunged. Jory needed his wife – not Bart!

I stepped forward into the sunlight and took my place at the breakfast table. Bart snatched his hands away from Melodie, staring at me as if I'd interrupted something that was very important to him. Then Chris and Cindy joined us. Silence came that I had to break.

'Melodie, I want to have a long talk with you as soon as we finish breakfast. You're not going to run away this time, or turn deaf ears, and shut out my voice with your blank stare.'

'Mother!' flared Bart. 'Can't you see her viewpoint? Maybe someday Jory will be able to drag himself around on crutches, if he wears a heavy back brace and a harness . . . can you imagine Jory like that? I can't. Even I don't want to see him like that.'

Melodie let out a shrieking cry, jumping to her feet. Bart followed suit, to hold her protectively in his arms.

'Don't cry, Melodie,' he soothed in a tender, caring voice. Melodie uttered another small cry of distress, then fled the terrace. The three of us sat quietly staring after her. When she was out of sight, our eyes fixed on Bart, who sat down to finish his breakfast as if we weren't there.

'Bart,' said Chris in this opportune moment before Joel joined us, 'what do you know about the wet sand in the papier-mâché columns?'

'I don't understand,' said Bart smoothly, appearing very distracted as he stared at the door through which Melodie had disappeared.

'Then I'll explain more carefully,' went on Chris. 'It was understood the sand would be dry so it would spill out easily and not harm anyone. Who wet the sand?'

Narrowing his eyes first, Bart answered sharply, 'So now I'm going to be accused of causing Jory's accident – and deliberately ruining the best time I've had until he was hurt. Why, it's just like it used to be when I was nine and ten. My fault, everything was always my fault. When Clover died, you both presumed I was the one to wrap the wire about his neck, never giving me the benefit of a doubt. When Apple was killed, again you thought it was me, when you knew I loved both Clover and Apple. I've never killed anything. Even when you found out later it was John Amos, you put me through hell before you said you were sorry. Well, say you're sorry now, for damned if I'll take the blame for Jory's broken back!'

I wanted to believe him so much tears came to my eyes. 'But who wet the sand, Bart?' I asked, leaning forward and reaching for his hand. 'Somebody did.'

His dark eyes went bleak. 'Several of the workhands disliked me for being too bossy . . . but I don't really think they would do anything to hurt Jory. After all, it wasn't me up there.'

For some reason I believed him. He didn't know anything about the wet sand, and when I met Chris's eyes, I knew he was convinced as well. But in asking, we'd alienated Bart . . . again.

He sat silently now, not smiling as he finished his meal. In the garden I glimpsed Joel in the shadows of dense shrubbery as if he'd been eavesdropping on our conversation while pretending to admire the flowers in bloom.

'Forgive us if we hurt you, Bart. Please, do what you can to help us find out who did wet the sand. But for that, Jory would have the use of his legs.'

Wisely Cindy had kept very quiet during all of this.

Bart started to reply, but at that moment Trevor stepped from the house and began serving us. Quickly I swallowed a light breakfast, then rose to go. I had to do something to bring back Melodie's sense of responsibility. 'Excuse me, Chris, Cindy. Take your time and finish your breakfast. I'll join you later.'

Joel slipped out of the shadows of the dense shrubbery and seated himself beside Bart. As I turned to glance back over my shoulder, I saw Joel lean towards Bart, whispering something I couldn't make out.

Feeling heavy of heart, I headed for the room that Melodie now used.

Face down on the bed she and Jory had shared, Melodie was crying. I perched on the side of her bed, thinking about all the right words to say – but where were the right words? 'He's alive, Melodie, and that counts, doesn't it? He's still with us. With you. You can reach out and touch him, talk to him, say all the things I wish I'd said to his father. Go to the hospital. Every day you stay away, he dies a bit more. If you don't go, if you just stay here and feel sorry for yourself, you'll live to regret it. Jory can still hear you, Melodie. Don't leave him now. He needs you now more than he's ever needed you before.'

Wild and hysterical, she turned to beat at me with small fists. I caught her wrists to keep from being injured.

'But I can't face him, Cathy! I've known he lies there, silent and alone where I can't reach him. He doesn't answer when *you* speak, so why would he respond to me? If I kissed him and he said or did nothing, I'd die inside. Besides, you don't really know him, not like I do. You're his mother, not his wife. You don't realize just how important his sexual life is to him. Now he won't have any. Do you have any idea of what that one thing is doing to him? To say nothing of losing the use of his legs, and giving up his career. He so wanted to prove himself for his father's sake – his real father's sake. And you kid yourself to think he's alive. He isn't. He's already left you, Cathy. Left me, too. He doesn't have to die. He's already dead while he's still alive.'

How her impassioned words stung me. Maybe because they were all too true.

I panicked inside, realizing that Jory could very well do as Julian had done – find a way to end his life. I tried to console myself. Jory was not like his father, he was like Chris. Eventually Jory would come around and make the best of what he had left.

I sat on that bed, staring at my daughter-in-law, and realized I didn't know her. Didn't know the girl I'd seen off and on since she was eleven. I'd seen the facade of a pretty, graceful girl who'd always seemed to adore Jory. 'What kind of woman are you, Melodie? Just what kind?'

She flipped over on her back and glared angrily at me.

'Not your kind, Cathy!' she almost screamed. 'You're made of special rugged stuff. I'm not. I was spoiled like you spoil your dear little Cindy. I was an only child and was given everything I wanted. I found out when I was small that life isn't all pretty picture book fables. And I didn't want it that way. When I was old enough, I ran to hide in the ballet. I told myself only in the world of fantasy could I find happiness. When I met Jory he seemed the prince I needed. Princes don't fall and injure their spinal cords, Cathy. They are never crippled. How can I live with Jory when I don't see him as a prince anymore? How, Cathy? Tell me how I can blind my eyes, and numb my senses, so I won't feel revulsion when he touches me.'

I stood up.

I stared down at her reddened eyes, her face made puffy from so much crying and felt all my admiration for her fade away. Weak, that's what she was. What a fool to believe that Jory wasn't made of the same flesh and blood as any other man. 'Suppose the injury had been yours, Melodie. Would you want Jory to desert you?'

She met my eyes squarely. 'Yes, I would.'

I left Melodie still crying on her bed.

Chris was waiting for me downstairs. 'I thought if you went this morning, I'd visit him this afternoon, and Melodie can go to him tonight with Cindy. I'm sure you convinced her to go.'

'Yes, she'll go, but not today,' I said without meeting his eyes. 'She wants to wait until he opens his eyes and speaks – so that's my plan, to somehow reach him and make him respond.'

'If anyone can do that, it will be you,' Chris murmured in my hair.

Jory lay supine on his hospital bed. The fracture was so low on his back that one fine day in the far future he might even gain back his potency. There were certain exercises he could do later on.

I'd bought two huge long boxes of mixed bouquets that I'd put into tall vases.

'Good morning, darling,' I said brightly as I entered his small, sterile room.

Jory didn't turn his head to look my way. He lay as I'd seen him last, staring straight up at the ceiling. Kissing his faintly chilled face, I began to arrange the flowers.

'You'll be happy to know Melodie is no longer suffering from morning sickness. But she's tired most of the time. I remember I was tired, too, when I was pregnant with you.'

I bit down on my tongue, for I'd lost Julian not long after I knew I was with child. 'It's a strange kind of summer, Jory. I can't say I really care for Joel. He seems very fond of Bart, but he does nothing but criticize Cindy. She can do nothing right in Joel's eyes, or in Bart's. I'm thinking it would be a good idea to send Cindy off to a summer camp until school starts in the fall. You don't think Cindy is misbehaving, do you?'

No answer.

I tried not to sigh, or look at him with impatience. I drew a chair close to Jory's bed and caught hold of his limp hand. No response. It was like holding a dead fish. 'Jory, they're going to keep on feeding you intravenously,' I warned. 'And if you still refuse to eat, they will put tubes in other veins, and use other methods to keep you alive, even if we have to eventually put you on every machine that will keep you going until you stop acting stubborn and come back to us.'

He didn't blink, or speak.

'All right, Jory. I've been easy on you up until now – but I've had enough!' My tone turned harsh. 'I love you too much to see you lie there and will yourself to die. So you don't care about anything anymore, do you?

'So you're crippled and you'll have to sit in a wheelchair until you can manage crutches, if you ever have that much ambition. So you're feeling sorry for yourself, and wondering how you can go on. Others have done it. Others have made lives for themselves, and been in worse condition than you are. So you tell yourself what others do doesn't count when it's your body, and your life – and maybe you're right. It doesn't matter what others do, if you want to think selfishly.

'Tell me that the future holds nothing for you now. I thought that, too, at first. I don't like to see you lying there so still, Jory. It breaks my heart, your father's heart, and Cindy is beside herself with worry. Bart is so concerned he can't bear to come and see you lying there so withdrawn. And what do you think you're doing to Melodie? She's carrying your child, Jory. She's crying all day long. She's changing into a different person because she hears us talking about your lack of response and your stubborn inability to accept what can't be changed. We're sorry, terribly sorry you've lost the use of your legs – but what can any of us do but make the best out of a miserable situation? Jory, come back to us. We need you with us. We're not willing to stand back and watch you kill yourself. We love you. We don't give a damn if you can't dance and can't walk, we just want you alive, where we can see you, talk to you. Speak to us, Jory. Say something, anything. Speak to Melodie when she comes. Respond when she touches you . . . or you'll lose Melodie and your child. She loves you, you know that. But no woman can live on love when the object of her love turns away and rejects her. She doesn't come because she can't face the rejection that she knows you give us.'

During this long, impassioned speech, I'd kept my eyes on his face, hoping for some slight change of expression. I was rewarded by seeing a muscle near his tight lips twitch.

Encouraged, I went on. 'Melodie's parents have called and suggested that she return to them to have the baby. Do you want Melodie to go, thinking she can't do anything more for you? Jory, please, please, don't do this to all of us, to yourself. You have so much you can give the world. You're more than just a dancer, don't you know that? When you have talent it's only one branch on a tree full of many limbs. Why, you've never begun to explore the other branches. Who knows just what you might discover? Remember, I, too, made dancing my life, and when I couldn't dance, I didn't know what to do with myself. I'd hear the music playing, and you'd be dancing with Melodie in our family room. I'd stiffen inside and try to shut out the music that made my legs want to dance. My soul went soaring . . . and then I'd crash to earth and cry. But when I started writing, I stopped thinking about dancing. Jory, you'll find something of interest to replace dancing, I know you will.'

For the first time since he'd known he would never walk or dance again, Jory turned his head. That alone filled me with breathless joy.

He met my eyes briefly. I saw the tears there, unshed but shining. 'Mel is thinking about going to her parents?' he asked in a hoarse voice.

Hope struggled to survive within me. I didn't know what Melodie would do now, even if he did come back to being himself. Yet I had to say everything right, and so seldom was I adequate. I'd failed with Julian, failed with Carrie. *Please, God, don't let me fail with Jory.*

'She'd never leave you if you'd come back to her. She needs you, wants you. You turn away from us, proving to her that you'll turn from her as well. Your prolonged silence and unwillingness to eat say so much, Jory, so much to keep Melodie afraid. She's not like me. She doesn't bounce back, spring forth and kick and yell. She cries all the time. She only half eats . . . and she's pregnant, Jory. Pregnant with your baby. You think about how you felt when you heard what your father did and consider the effects your death will have on your child. Think long and hard about that before you continue with what you've got your mind set on. Think about yourself, and how much you wanted to have your own natural father. Jory, don't be like your father and leave a fatherless child behind you. Don't destroy us, when you destroy yourself!'

'But, Mom!' he cried in great distress. 'What am I going to do? I don't want to sit in a wheelchair the rest of my life! I'm angry, so damned angry I want to strike out and hurt everyone! What have I done to deserve this kind of punishment? I've been a good son, a faithful husband. But I can't be a husband now. There's no excitement down there anymore. I feel nothing below my waist. I'd be better off dead than like this!'

My head lowered to press my cheek against his inert hand. 'Maybe you would be, Jory. So go on and starve yourself, and will yourself to die, and never sit in a wheelchair – and don't think about any of us. Forget the grief you'll bring into our lives when you're gone. Forget about all those Chris and I have lost before. We can adjust, we're used to losing those we love most. We'll just add you to our long list of those to feel guilty about . . . for we will feel guilty. We'll search and search until we find something we failed to do right, and we'll enlarge that and make it grow, until it shuts out the sun and all happiness, and we'll go into our graves blaming ourselves for yet another life gone.'

'Mom! Stop! I can't stand to hear you talk like that!'

'I can't stand what you're doing to us! Jory! Don't give up. It's not like you to even think of surrendering. Fight back. Tell yourself you're going to lick this and turn out a better, stronger person because you've faced up to adversities others can't even imagine.'

He was listening. 'I don't know if I want to fight back. I've lain here since that night and thought about what I could do. Don't tell me I don't have to do anything because you're rich, and I've got money, too. Life is nothing without a goal, you know that.'

'Your child . . . make your child your goal. Making Melodie happy, another goal. Stay, Jory, stay . . . I can't bear to lose another, I can't, can't . . .' and then I was crying.

And I'd determined not to show weakness and cry. I sobbed brokenly without looking at him. 'After your father died, I made my baby the most important thing in my life. Maybe I did that to ease a guilty conscience, I don't know. But when you came along on Valentine's Night and they laid you on my stomach so I could see you, my heart almost burst with pride. You were so strong looking, and your blue eyes were so bright. You grasped by finger and didn't want to let go. Paul was there, and Chris, too. They both adored you right from the beginning. You were such a happy, well-behaved baby. I think we all spoiled you, and you never had to cry to get what you wanted. Jory, now I know you are incapable of being spoiled. You've got an inner strength that will see you through. Eventually you'll be glad you hung on to see that child of yours. I know you'll be glad.'

During all of this, I'd sobbed my words almost incoherently. I think Jory felt sorry for me. His hand moved so he could wipe away my tears with the edge of his white sheet.

'Got any ideas about what I could do in a wheelchair?' he asked in a small, mocking voice.

'A thousand ideas, Jory. Why, this day isn't long enough to list them. You can learn to play the piano, study art, learn to write. Or you can become a ballet instructor. You don't have to strut around to do that – all you need is a good vocabulary and an untiring tongue. Or you can do something more mundane, like become a CPA, study law and give Bart some competition. In fact, there is very little you can't do. We're all handicapped in one way or another. You should know that. Bart's got his invisible handicap, worse than any you'll ever have. Think back to all his problems while you were dancing and having the time of your life. He was tormented by psychiatrists probing painfully into his deepest self.'

His eyes were brighter now, filling with vague hope that tried to find a mooring.

'And think about the swimming pool Bart put in the yard. Your doctors say your arms are very strong, and after some physical therapy you can swim again. What's more, there's a whole new world of electronics out there that might interest you.'

'What do *you* want me to do, Mom?' His voice was soft, gentle as his hand moved over my hair, and his gaze was tender.

'Live, Jory, that's all.'

His eyes were soft now, full of tears that didn't fall. 'What about you, Dad and Cindy? Weren't you planning to move to Hawaii?'

For weeks I hadn't thought of Hawaii. I stared blankly before me. How could we leave now that Jory was injured and Melodie was in such distress? We couldn't leave.

Foxworth Hall had trapped us again.

BOOK TWO

THE RELUCTANT WIFE

Regretfully Chris and I neglected Cindy as we spent most of our time in the hospital with Jory. Cindy grew restless and bored in a hostile house with Joel, who gave her only disapproval, with Bart, who gave her only scorn, with Melodie, who had nothing to give to anyone.

'Momma,' she wailed. 'I'm not having a good time! It's been a terrible summer, the worst. I'm sorry Jory's in the hospital and he won't ever walk or dance again, and I want to do what I can for him, but what about me? They only allow him to have two visitors at a time and you and Daddy are always with him. Even when I do see him, half the time I don't know what to say, or what to do. And I don't know what to do with myself when I'm here, either. This house is so isolated from the rest of the world it's like living on the moon – boring, boring. You tell me not to go into the village, not to have dates unless you know about them, and you're never here to ask when someone invites me. You tell me not to swim when Bart and Joel are around. You tell me not to do so many things . . . what is it that I *can* do?'

'Tell me what you want to do,' I said with sympathy. She was sixteen and had expected this vacation to give her great pleasure. Now the mansion she'd admired so much in the beginning was proving, in some ways, to be as much a prison for her as the old one had been for us.

She came to sit cross-legged on the floor near my feet. 'I don't want to hurt Jory's feelings by leaving, but I'm going crazy here. Melodie stays in her room all the time with her door locked and refuses to let me in. Joel dries me up with his mean old eyes. Bart pretends he doesn't see me. Today a letter came from my friend Bary Boswell, and she's going to this marvellous summer camp just a few miles north of Boston, where there is a summer stock theatre nearby. And there's swimming in the lake nearby, and sailing, and dances every Saturday, plus they teach all kinds of crafts. I like being with girls my own age, and I think that's just the kind of camp I'd enjoy. You can check into it and see that it has a good reputation, but let me go, please, before I go batty.'

I'd so wanted all of us to have a close getting-to-know-you-all-over-again kind of summer, and here she was, wanting to leave, and I hadn't spent nearly enough time with her. Still, I easily understood. 'I'll talk to your father about it tonight,' I promised. 'We want you to be happy, Cindy, you know that. I'm sorry if we've neglected you while we care for Jory. Let's talk now about you. What about boys you met at Bart's party, Cindy? What's going on between you and them?'

'Bart and Joel hide the keys to the cars so I can't drive off. And that's exactly what I would do, permission or not. I want to slip out of a window, but they're all so high above the ground, and I'm afraid to jump and fall and hurt myself. But I think about boys all the time, that's what. I miss being with them, having dates and going to dances. I know what you're thinking, because Joel is always muttering about me being without morals . . . I'm trying hard to hang on to them, really I am. Yet I don't know how long I can keep myself a virgin. I tell myself that I'm going to be old-fashioned and hold out until I'm married, but I plan not to marry until I'm at least thirty. Then, when I'm out with a boy I really like, and he begins to apply pressure, I want to surrender. I like the sensations I feel leaping up and making my heart beat faster. My body wants it to happen. Momma, why can't I find the kind of strength you have? How do I find the real me? I'm caught in a world that doesn't really know what it wants, you tell me that all the time. So if the world doesn't know, how can I? I want to be what you want me to be, sweet and pure, while I want to be sexy. The two contradict each other. I want you and Daddy to always love me, so I try to be as sweet as you think I am – but I'm not that innocent, Momma. I want all the good-looking boys to be in love with me – but someday I'm not going to be able to hold back.'

I smiled to see her troubled expression, her fearful glance to see if I'd be shocked. I guessed, too, that she was afraid she'd just ruined her chances to escape this house. My arms went around her. 'Hang on to morality, Cindy. You're much too talented and too beautiful to give yourself away like a bit of worthless trash. Think highly of yourself, and others will as well.'

'But Momma – how do I say no, and still keep the boys liking me?'

'There are a lot of boys who won't expect you to "give out", Cindy, and that's the kind you want. Those who demand sex for one reason or another are more than likely to dump you quickly after they get what they want. There's something about men that makes them want to conquer every woman, especially an exceptional beauty like you. Remember, too, they talk amongst themselves and report on the most intimate details when they don't really love you.'

'Momma! You make me feel that being a woman is a trap! I don't want them to trap me – I want to trap them! But I have to confess, I'm not good about resisting. Bart's made me feel so insecure about myself that I keep wanting the boys to convince me differently. But every time from this day forward, when some jerk gets me on the backseat and says he'll fall ill if I don't satisfy his lust, I won't feel sorry for him. I'll just think of you and Daddy and bash in his head – or give him the knee where it hurts worse.'

She made me laugh, when I hadn't laughed in weeks. 'All right, darling, I know in the end you'll do the right thing. So let's talk more about that summer camp so I can give your father all the details.'

'You mean I haven't spoiled my chances?' she asked in a delighted way.

'Of course not. I think Chris will agree that you need a break from all this tragedy here.'

Chris did agree, thinking as I did that a sixteen-year-old girl needed this special summer for fun. The moment Cindy knew, she had to visit Jory and spill it all out to him. 'Now, just because I'm leaving doesn't mean I don't care, but I'm so damned bored, Jory. I'm going to write often and send you little gifts.' She embraced him, kissed him, her tears falling to put beads on his clean-shaven face. 'Nothing can take away what you are, Jory – that wonderful thing that makes you so special, and it doesn't live in your legs. I'd want you for my own if you weren't my brother.'

'Sure you would,' he said with some irony. 'But thanks anyway.'

Chris and I left Jory alone with his nurse long enough to drive Cindy to the nearest airport, where we kissed her goodbye and he handed her some 'pin' money. She was delighted with the amount and had to kiss him again and again before she backed off, waving vigorously. 'I'll write real letters,' she promised, 'not just postcards, and I'll send pictures. Thanks for everything, and don't forget to write often and tell me what's going on. In a way, living in Foxworth Hall is like being caught up in some deep, dark, mysterious novel, only it's too frightening when you're actually living the story.'

On the way to the hospital to stay with Jory again, Chris told me of his plans. We couldn't move to Hawaii now and abandon Jory to the frail mercies of Bart and Joel, and Melodie wasn't able to care for herself, much less a husband in a back cast, even if she did hire a nurse. And neither Jory nor Melodie would be in any condition to make the long plane trip to Hawaii for many months.

'I won't know what to do with myself when Jory goes back to the Hall and has his own attendants, any more than Cindy knew how to keep herself occupied and happy. Jory won't need me every hour. I'm going to feel useless unless I do something meaningful, Cathy. I'm not an old man. I still have many good years ahead of me.'

Sadly I turned my head to watch him as he kept his eyes on the traffic. He went on without turning to meet my eyes. 'Medicine has always played a very important part in my life.That doesn't mean I'm breaking my promise to share more time with you and my family than I do professionally. Just remember what losing a career means to Jory . . .'

Sliding closer on the seat, I lowered my head to his shoulder, telling him in a choked voice to go ahead and do what he felt was right. '. . . but keep in mind a physician has to have an impeccable record, and someday there may be gossip about us.'

He nodded, saying he'd already considered that fact. This time he was going into the research side of medicine. He wouldn't be meeting the public, who might recognize him as a Foxworth. He'd already thought enough on the subject. Already he was bored with staying home and contributing nothing. He had to do something important or lose the identity he felt he needed. I put on a bright smile even if my heart was sinking, for his dream of living in Hawaii had also been my dream..

With arms about each other, we entered the huge house that waited with its gaping jaws wide.

Melodie had sequestered herself in her room, Joel was in that little room without furniture, down on his knees praying while a single candle burned in the gloom. 'Where is Bart?' asked Chris, looking around as if astonished that anyone would want to spend so many hours in such a dismal place.

Joel frowned, then faintly smiled, as if he had to remember to appear friendly. 'Bart is off in some bar drinking himself under the table, as he put it.'

I'd never known Bart to do such a thing. Regret for setting up the performance that ruined his brother's legs, and cost him his career? Regret for driving Cindy away? Did Bart know how to feel regret? I didn't know. I stared blankly at Joel as he paced the floor, seeming terribly upset, when what difference did Bart's behaviour make to him?

The old man followed us as usually he followed Bart. 'He should know better,' muttered Joel. 'Whores and harlots hang out in bars, though I've warned him about them.'

His words intrigued me. 'What's the difference between a whore and a harlot, Joel?'

His smeary eyes turned my way. As if light blinded him, he shaded those eyes with his knarled hand.

'Are you mocking me, niece? The Bible mentions both nouns, so there must be some difference.'

'Perhaps a whore is worse than a harlot, or vice versa? Is that what you mean?'

He glared at me, telling me with his glittering, faded eyes that I was tormenting him with my silly questions.

'Then there's a strumpet, Joel, and today we have hookers, call girls and prostitutes – do they come between harlots and whores, or are they the same?'

His eyes hardened to rivet on me with the piercing glare of a virgin saint. 'You don't like me, Catherine. Why don't you like me? What have I done to make you distrust me? I stay to save Bart from the worst in himself, or I'd leave today because of your attitude, and I am more Foxworth than you are.' Then his expression changed, and his lips quirked. 'No, I take that back. You are twice the Foxworth I am.'

How I hated him for reminding me! Still, he did manage to make me feel ashamed, as if I'd misconstrued the silent messages he sent out. I didn't defend myself, or protest to convince him otherwise. Nor did Chris say a word to prevent this confrontation he'd already sensed would come sooner or later.

'I don't know why I distrust you, Joel,' I said in a kinder voice than I customarily used with him. 'Perhaps you protest too much about your father, making me doubt you are one whit better or different.'

Without another word, but with a sad look that I think he feigned, he turned and shuffled off, his hands again tucked up those invisible brown monk sleeves.

That very evening, when Melodie insisted on dining in her room alone again, I made up my mind. Even if she didn't want to go, and fought against me, I was driving Melodie to see Jory!

I stalked into her room and removed her almost untouched dinner tray without saying a word. She wore the same shabby robe that she'd worn for days. I pulled her best-looking summer outfit from her closet and tossed it on the bed. 'Shower, Melodie, and shampoo your hair. Then get dressed – you are going to visit Jory tonight, whether or not you want to.'

Instantly she jumped up and protested, acting hysterical as she said she couldn't go yet, wasn't ready yet, and I couldn't make her do anything she didn't want to do. I overrode everything she said, shouting back it seemed she'd never be ready, and I didn't care what excuses she offered, she was going.

'You can't make me do one damned thing!' she yelled, very pale as she backed away. Then, sobbing, she pleaded for me to give her more time to become adjusted to the idea of Jory being crippled. I said she'd had enough time. I'd adjusted, Chris had, Cindy had . . . and she could pretend; after all, she was supposed to be a professional used to playing roles.

I had to literally drag Melodie to the shower and shove her inside when she wanted the tub. But I knew about Melodie in a bathtub. There she'd sit until her skin puckered, and visiting hours would be over. Waiting outside the shower door, I urged her to hurry. She stepped out, swathed in a towel, still sobbing as her blue eyes pleaded for mercy.

'Stop crying!' I ordered, shoving her down on the dressing room stool. 'I'm going to blow-dry your hair while you put on your makeup – and do a good job of concealing that red puffiness around your eyes, for Jory will be very perceptive. You've got to convince him that your love for him hasn't changed.'

On and on I talked to convince her that she would find the right words to say, the right expressions to wear, as I dried her pretty honey-blond hair.

Her hair had marvellous sheen, more depth to the colour than mine had. No red in mine at all. The texture was stronger than my frail, fine hair of flaxen colour. When I had Melodie dressed, I sprayed her lightly with the perfume Jory loved most, as she stood as if in a trance of not knowing what to do next. I hugged her before I pulled her to the door.

'Come now, Melodie, it's not going to be that bad. He loves and needs you. Once you're there and he looks at you, you'll forget his legs are paralysed. You'll instinctively do and say the right things. I know you will because you love him.'

Pale beneath the makeup, her large eyes stared at me bleakly, as if she had her doubts and knew better than to bring them up again.

By this time Bart had come home from whatever bar had served him enough to make his legs limp and his eyes unfocused. He slouched in a deep chair, legs sprawled forward, and behind him in the shadows, Joel sagged limp as a dying palm. 'Where yuh goin'?' Bart asked in a slurred voice, as I tried to slip Melodie down the hall to the garage without him noticing us.

'To the hospital,' I said, pulling Melodie towards the huge garage. 'And I think it's time you went to visit your brother again, Bart. Not tonight, but tomorrow. Buy him a gift that will entertain him . . . he's going mad in there from doing nothing.'

'Melodie, you don't have to go if you don't want to,' Bart said, rising unsteadily to his feet. 'Don't let my dominating mother push you around.'

She was trembling, hanging back to plead mutely with him. Ruthlessly I pulled her on and forced her into the car.

Bart came staggering into the garage, calling out to Melodie that he would save her . . . and then he lost his drunken balance and fell to the floor. I pushed the electric button to open one of the huge garage doors and backed out of the garage.

All the way into Charlottesville, until I was parking in the hospital lot, Melodie trembled, sobbed and tried to convince me she'd harm Jory more than she'd help him. And all the way, I'd tried to give her confidence that she could handle the situation.

'Please, Melodie, walk into that room with a smile. Put on your nobility, that regal princess air that you used to wear all the time. Then when you're near his bed, take him in your arms and kiss him.'

Numbly she nodded, as a terrified child would.

I shoved the roses I'd purchased into her arms, and other gifts I'd wrapped prettily, one she'd chosen to give him after Bart's party. 'Now, tell him you haven't been before because you've been feeling weak, sleepy and sick. Tell him all your other concerns if you want to. But don't you dare even hint that you can't feel towards him like a wife anymore.'

Like a blind, automated robot she nodded stiffly, forcing herself to keep pace with me.

We ran into Chris coming down the hall as we left the elevator on the sixth floor. He beamed happily to see Melodie with me. 'How wonderful, Melodie,' he said, giving her a quick hug before he turned to me. 'I went out and bought Jory his dinner, and enough for me as well. He's in a fairly good mood. He drank all his milk and ate two bites of the pecan pie. And usually he adores pecan pie. Melodie, if you can, try to see that he eats more of that pie. He's losing weight rapidly, and I'd like to see him gain some back.'

Still speechless, her eyes wide and blank. Melodie nodded, looking towards the door numbered 606 as if she faced the electric chair. Chris gave her a friendly, understanding pat on her back, kissed me, then strode off. 'I'm going to talk to his doctors. I will join you later on and follow you home in my car.'

For the life of me I couldn't feel confident as I ushered Melodie towards Jory's closed door. He had a privacy fetish about keeping his door closed at all times so no one could see a former *premier danseur* lying helpless on his bed. I rapped once, then twice, our signal. 'Jory, it's only I, your mother.'

'Come in, Mom,' he called with more welcome than he'd used before. 'Dad told me you'd be showing up any second. I hope you brought me a good book to read. I've finished – '

He broke off and stared as I shoved Melodie into his room first.

Because I'd called Chris to tell him my plans, Chris had helped Jory out of his hospital garment, and he was now wearing a blue silk pyjama top. His hair was neatly brushed, his face was clean shaven and he'd had his first haircut since his accident. He looked better than he had since that horrible night.

He tried to smile. Hope flared in his eyes, so glad to see her again.

She stood where I'd pushed her and didn't take another step towards his bed. This caused his tentative smile to freeze on his face as he tried to hide his hunger . . . his faltering flame of hope as his eyes tried to meet with hers. She refused to meet his eyes. Quickly the smile vanished as the flame in his eyes sputtered, flickered, then went out. Dead eyes now. He turned his face towards the wall.

Instantly I stepped up behind Melodie, pushing her towards his bed, before I moved to see what she was revealing on her face. She stood there with her arms full of red roses and gifts, rooted to the floor and trembling like an aspen tree in a high wind. I gave her a sharp nudge. 'Say something,' I whispered.

'Hi, Jory,' she said in a quivery, small voice, her eyes desperate. I shoved her closer to him. 'I've brought you roses . . .' she added.

Still he kept his face to the wall.

Again I nudged her, thinking I should get out and leave them alone; yet I feared the minute I did she'd whirl about and run.

'I'm sorry I haven't visited before,' she said in a stumbling way, inching bit by bit closer to his bed. 'I've also brought you gifts . . . a few things your mother said you needed.'

He whipped his head about, his dark blue eyes full of smouldering rage and resentment. 'And my mother forced you to come, right? Well, you don't have to stay. You've delivered your roses and your gifts – now get out!'

Melodie broke, dropping the roses on to his bed, her gifts to the floor. She cried out as she tried to take his hand, a hand he quickly snatched away. 'I love you, Jory . . . and I'm sorry, so sorry . . .'

'I don't doubt for a minute you are sorry!' he shouted. 'So sorry to see all the glamour disappear in a flashing moment, and now you're stuck with a crippled husband! Well, you're not stuck, Melodie! You can file for divorce tomorrow and leave!'

Backing towards the door, I was filled with pity for him – and for her. Gently I eased out but left the door ajar just enough to hear and see what went on. I was so afraid Melodie would take this chance to leave, or else she'd do something to kill his desire to live . . . and if I could, I would do anything to stop her.

One by one Melodie picked up the fallen roses. She threw old, dying flowers into the trash basket, filled the vase with water in the small adjacent bath, then carefully arranged the red roses, so carefully, taking so long, as if just by doing something she could hold off destroying him. When she'd done that, she turned again to the bed and picked up the three gifts. 'Don't you want to open them?' she asked weakly.

'I don't need anything,' he said flatly, again staring at the wall so she saw only the back of his curly head.

From somewhere she drew courage. 'I think you'll like what's inside. I've heard you say many a time what you wanted . . .'

'All I ever wanted was to dance until I was forty,' he choked out. 'Now that is over, and I don't need a wife or a dance partner, I don't need or want anything.'

She put the gifts on the bed and stood there wringing her pale, thin hands, her silent tears beginning to fall. 'I love you, Jory,' she choked. 'I want to do everything right, but I'm not brave like your mother and father, and that's why I didn't visit before. Your mother wanted me to say I was sick, unable to come, but I could have come. I stayed in that house and cried, hoping I could find the strength I needed to smile when I did eventually come. I'm coming apart with shame for being weak, for not doing all I should for you when you need me . . . and the longer I stayed away, the harder it became for me to show up. I feared you wouldn't talk to me, wouldn't look at me, and I'd do something stupid to make you hate me. I don't want a divorce, Jory. I'm still your wife. Chris took me to an obstetrician yesterday, and our baby is progressing normally.'

Pausing, she tentatively reached to touch his arm. He jerked spasmodically, as if her hand burned, but he didn't snatch his arm away – she snatched hers.

From where I stood in the hallway, I could see enough of Jory's face to know he was crying and trying hard not to let Melodie know that. Tears were in my eyes, too, as I cringed there, feeling a sneaky intruder who had no right to watch and listen. Even so I couldn't move away, when I'd moved from Julian's side only to find him dead the next time I looked. Like father, like son, like father like son beat the unhappy tattoo of the drums of fear in my head.

Again she reached to touch him, this time his hair. 'Don't turn your face away, Jory. Look at me. Let me see that you don't hate me for failing you when you needed me most. Shout at me, hit me, but don't stop communicating. I'm tied up in knots. I can't sleep at nights, feeling I should have done something to keep you from dancing that role. I've always hated that particular ballet and didn't want to tell you when you choreographed it and made it your signature.' She wiped at her tears, then sank to her knees by his bed and bowed her head on to his hand, which she'd managed to seize.

Her low voice barely reached my ears. 'We can make a life together. You can teach me how. Wherever you lead, Jory, I'll follow . . . just tell me that you want me to stay.'

Maybe because she was hiding her face now, with her tears wetting his hand beneath her cheek, he turned his head and looked at her with such tormented, tragic eyes. He cleared his throat before he spoke and dried his tears with the edge of the sheet.

'I don't want you to stay if living with me is going to be a burden. You can always go back to New York and dance with other partners. Because I'm crippled doesn't mean you have to be crippled, too. You have your career, and all those years of dedicated work. So go, Mel, with my blessings . . . I don't need you now.'

My heart cried out, knowing differently.

She looked up, her makeup ruined from so many tears. 'How could I live with myself, Jory? I'll stay. I'll do my best to make you a good wife.' She paused while I thought her timing was so wrong, so damned wrong. She gave him time to think that he didn't need a wife, only a nurse and companion, and a substitute mother for his child.

I closed my eyes and began to pray. *God, let her find the right words.* Why isn't she telling him the ballet meant nothing without him? Why didn't she say his happiness counted more than anything else? Melodie, Melodie, say something to make him believe his handicap doesn't matter, it's the man he'll always be that you love. But she said nothing like this.

She only opened his gifts for him, showed them to him, while he studied her face with bleaker and bleaker eyes.

He thanked her for the best-selling novel she'd brought (chosen by me); thanked her for the travelling shaving kit with the sterling silver razors – straight edged, electric and a third kind, dual edged – with a silver-handled lathering brush and a round mirror that could be attached to anything with a suction cup guaranteed to work. There was also a fancy silver mug with soap, cologne and after shave lotion. Then finally she was opening the best gift, a huge mahogany box full of watercolours, a hobby that Chris enjoyed. He planned to teach Jory the technique of using watercolours as soon as he came home. Jory stared at the paintbox for the longest time without interest before he looked away. 'You have good taste, Mel.'

Bowing her head, she nodded. 'Is there anything else you need?'

'No. Just leave. I'm sleepy. It's nice to see you again, but I'm tired.'

She backed off hesitatingly, while my heart cried for them both. So much in love before his accident, and all that passion had been washed away in the deluge of her shock and his humiliation.

I stepped into the room.

'I hope I'm not interrupting anything, but I think Jory is tired, Melodie.' I smiled at both brightly. 'You just wait until you see what we're planning for your return home. If painting doesn't interest you now, it will later on. At home we've got other treasures waiting for you. You're going to be thrilled, but I can't tell you anything. It's all supposed to be a huge welcome-back surprise.' I hurried to embrace him, which wasn't easy to do when his body was so bulky and hard with the cast. I kissed his cheek, ruffled his hair and squeezed his fingers. 'It's going to be all right, darling,' I whispered. 'She has to learn to accept just like you do. She's trying hard, and if she doesn't say the words you want to hear, it's because she's too much in shock to think straight.'

Ironically he smiled. 'Sure, Mom, sure. She loves me just as much as she did when I could walk and dance. Nothing has changed. Nothing important.'

Melodie was already out of his room and standing in the hall waiting, so she didn't hear any of this. Over and over again she repeated on our way home, with Chris following in his car, 'Oh, my God, my God . . . oh, my God . . . what are we going to do?'

'You did fine, Melodie, just fine. The next time you'll do even better,' said I, brightly.

A week passed and Melodie did do better on her second visit, and even better on her third. Now she didn't resist when I told her where she had to go. She knew it wouldn't do her any good to resist.

Another day I sat in my dressing room before the long mirror, carefully applying mascara. Chris stepped into view with a look of pleasure on his face.

'I've got something great to tell you,' he started. 'Last week I went to visit the university scientific staff and filled out an application for their cancer research team. They realize there, of course, that I've only been an amateur biochemist in my spare time. Nevertheless, for some reason, some of my answers seemed to please them, and they have asked me to join their staff of scientists. Cathy, I'm thrilled to have something to do. Bart has agreed to allow us to stay on here as long as we like, or until he marries. I've talked to Jory, and he wants to be near us. His apartment in New York is so small. Here he'll have wide halls and large rooms that will accommodate his wheelchair.

Right now he says he'll never use one, but he will change his mind when that cast comes off.'

Chris's enthusiasm for the new job was contagious. I wanted to see him happy, with something to do to take his mind off Jory's problems. I stood to head for the closet, but he pulled me down on his lap to polish off his story. Some of what he said I didn't understand, for every so often he'd forgetfully slip into medical jargon, which was still Greek to me.

'Will you be happy, Chris? It's important for you to do what you want with your life. Jory's happiness is important as well, but I don't want you staying on here if Bart is going to be insufferable. Be honest . . . can you tolerate Bart just to give Jory a wonderful place to live?'

'Catherine, my love, as long as you are here, then of course I'll be happy. As for Bart, I've put up with him all these years, and I can take it for as long as need be. I know who is seeing Jory through this traumatic period. I may help a little, but it's you who brings more sunshine with your gossipy chatter, your lilting manner, your armloads of gifts and your consistent reassurances that Melodie will change. He considers every word you say as if it comes straight from God.'

'But you'll be coming and going, and we won't see much of you,' I moaned.

'Hey, take that look off your face. I'll drive home every night and try to reach here before dark.' He went on to explain that he didn't have to reach the university lab until ten, and that would give us plenty of time to breakfast together. There wouldn't be emergency calls to take him away at night; he'd have every weekend off, a month off with pay, not that money mattered to us. We'd take trips to conventions where I'd meet people with innovative ideas, the kind of creative people I enjoyed best.

On and on he extolled the virtues of his new enterprise, making me accept something he seemed to want very much. Still, I slept in his arms that night, fretting, wishing we'd never come to this house that held so many terrible memories and had caused so many tragedies.

Around midnight, unable to sleep, I got up to sit in our private sitting room that adjoined our bedroom, knitting what was supposed to end up a fluffy white baby bonnet. I almost felt like my mother as I furiously knitted on and on with such intensity I couldn't put it down. Like her I could never let anything alone until it was finished.

A soft rapping sounded on the door, soon followed by Melodie's request to come in. Delighted to have her visit, I answered, 'Of course, come in. I'm glad you saw the light under my door. I was thinking about you and Jory while I knitted, and darn if I know how to stop once I start a project.'

Falteringly she came to perch on the love seat next to me; her very uncertainty immediately put me on guard. She glanced at my knitting, looked away. 'I need someone to talk to, Cathy, someone wise, like you.'

How pitiful and young she sounded, even younger than Cindy. I put down my knitting to turn and embrace her. 'Cry, Melodie, go on. You have enough to cry about. I've been harsh with you, and I know that.'

Her head bowed down on my shoulder as she let go and sobbed with abandon.

'Help me, Cathy, please help me. I don't know what to do. I keep thinking of Jory and how terrible he must feel. I think about me and how inadequate I feel. I'm glad you made me go to see him, though I hated you for doing that at the time. Today when I went alone, he smiled as if that proved something to him. I know I've been childish and weak. Yet each time I have to force myself to enter his room. I hate seeing him lying so still on that bed, moving nothing but his arms and head. I kiss him, hold his hand, but once I start to talk about little, important things, he turns his head towards the wall and refuses to respond. Cathy . . . you may think he's learning to accept his disability, but I think he's willing himself to die – and it's my fault, my fault!'

Astonishment widened my eyes. 'Your fault? It was an accident, you can't blame yourself.'

In a breathless gush her words spilled forth. 'You don't understand why I feel as I do! It's been troubling me so much I feel haunted with guilt. It's because we're here, in this cursed house! Jory didn't want to have a baby until years from now. He made me promise before we married that until we'd been on the top for at least ten years, we wouldn't start a family – but I deliberately broke my word and stopped taking the pill. I wanted to have my first baby before I was thirty. I reasoned that after the baby was conceived he wouldn't want me to have an abortion. When I told him he blew! He stormed at me – and demanded I have an abortion.'

'Oh, no . . .' I was shocked, thinking I didn't know Jory nearly as well as I'd thought.

'Don't blame him; it was my own doing. Dancing was his world,' Melodie continued in a gasping way, as if she'd been running uphill for weeks. 'I shouldn't have done what I did. I told him I'd just forgotten. I knew on our wedding day that dancing came first with him, and I was second. He never lied or told me differently, though he loved me. Then, because I was pregnant, we abandoned our tour, came here . . . and look what happened! It's not fair, Cathy, not fair! On this very day we'd be in London but for the baby. He'd be on stage, bowing, accepting the applause, the bouquets, doing what he was born for. I tricked him, and in so doing, I brought about his accident, and what's he going to do now? How can I make up for what I've stolen from him?'

She trembled all over as I held her. What could I say? I bit down on my lip, hurting for her, for Jory. We were so much alike in some ways, for I'd caused Julian's death by deserting him, leaving him in Spain – and that had led to his end. Never deliberately harming, just coincidently doing what I felt was right, as Melodie did what she considered right.

Who ever counted the flowers that died when we pulled up the weeds? I shook my head, pulling myself out of the abyss of yesterdays and turned my full concentration on the moment.

'Melodie, Jory's just as scared as you are, much more so, and with good reason. You aren't to blame for anything. He's happy about the baby now that it's on its way. Many men protest when wives want babies, but when they see the child they helped create, they're won over. He lies there on his bed, as you lie on yours, wondering how his marriage is going to work out now that he can't dance. He's the one who is crippled. He's the one who has to face up to everyday life, knowing he can't rise from the bed when he wants to; knowing he can't sit in a regular chair and get up and down when he feels like it; nor can he walk in the rain, or run on the grass, or even go to the bathroom in a normal way.

'All the simple normal everyday things he took for granted will now be very difficult for him. And think of what he was. This is a terrible blow to his pride. He wasn't even going to try and cope for fear he'd burden you too much. But listen to this. This afternoon when I was with him, he said he was going to make a big effort to cheer up and lift himself out of his depression. And he will. He'll make it, and a lot of it will be because you've helped by just visiting and sitting there with him. Each time you go you convince him you still love him.'

Why did she draw from my arms and turn her face away? I watched her brush the tears from her face impatiently; then she blew her nose and tried to stop crying.

With effort she spoke again. 'I don't know what it is, but I keep having scary dreams. I wake up frightened, thinking something even more dreadful is going to happen. There's something weird about this house. Something strange and frightening. When everyone is gone, and Bart is in his office, and Joel is praying in that ugly, bare room, I lie on my bed and seem to hear the house whispering. It seems to call to me. I hear the wind blow as if it's trying to tell me something. I hear the floor squeak outside my door so I jump up and race to throw open the door – and no one is there, no one is ever there. I suspect it's only my imagination, but I hear, as you've said you do sometimes, so much of what isn't real. Am I losing my mind, Cathy? Am I?'

'Oh, Melodie,' I murmured, trying to draw her close again, but she put me off by moving to the far end of the sofa.

'Cathy, why is this house different?'

'Different from what?' I asked uneasily.

'From all other houses.' She glanced fearfully towards the door to the hall. 'Don't you feel it? Can't you hear it? Do you sense this house is breathing, like it has a life of its own?'

My eyes widened as a chill stole the comfort from my pretty sitting room. In the bedroom I could faintly hear Chris's regular, heavy breathing.

Melodie, usually too reticent to talk, gushed onward breathlessly. 'This house wants to use the people inside as a way to keep it living on forever. It's like a vampire, sucking our lifeblood from all of us. I wish it hadn't been restored. It's not a new house. It's been here for centuries. Only the wallpaper and the paint and the furniture are new, but those stairs in the foyer I never climb up or descent without seeing the ghosts of others . . .'

A kind of paralysing numbness gripped me.

Every word she said was only too frighteningly true. I *could* hear it breathe! I tried to pull myself back to reality. 'Listen, Melodie. Bart was only a little boy when my mother ordered it reconstructed on the foundations of the old manor home. Before she died it was up, but not completely finished inside. When her will was read, and she left this house to Bart, with Chris as trustee to manage until he came of age, we decided it was a waste not to have it completed. Chris and our attorney contacted the architects and contractors, and the job went forward until it was finished, only the inside needed furbishing. That had to wait until Bart came here in his college days and ordered the interior decorators to style it as it had been in the old days. And you're right. I, too, wish this house had been left in ashes . . .'

'Maybe your mother knew this house was what Bart would want most to give him confidence. It's so imposing. Haven't you noticed how much he's changed? He's not like the little boy who used to hide away in the shadows and lurk behind trees. He's the master here, like a baron overseeing his domain. Or maybe I should say king of the mountain, for he's so rich, so terribly rich . . .'

Not yet . . . not yet, I kept thinking. Nevertheless, her frail, whispering voice disturbed me. I didn't want to think Bart was as overbearing as a medieval lord. But she went on. 'Bart's happy, Cathy, extraordinarily happy. He tells me he's sorry about Jory. Then he telephones those attorneys and wants to know why they keep postponing the rereading of his grandmother's will. They've told him they can't read it unless everyone mentioned in the will is here to hear the reading, and so they put it off until the day when Jory comes home from the hospital. They will read the will in Bart's office.'

'How do you know so much about Bart's business?' I asked sharply, suddenly very suspicious of all that time when she was alone in this house with my second son . . . and an old man who spent most of his time in that tiny, naked room he used as a chapel. Joel would quite happily see Jory destroyed if that would satisfy Bart. In Joel's eyes a dancing man was no better than the worst sinner, displaying his body. Leaping and bounding in front of women, wearing nothing but a loincloth . . . I stared again at Melodie.

'Do you and Bart spend much time together?'

Quickly she stood. 'I'm tired now, Cathy. I've said enough to make you think I'm crazy. Do all expectant mothers have such fearful dreams – did you? I'm afraid, too, that my baby won't be normal since I've grieved so much for Jory.'

I gave her what comfort I could when I felt sick inside, and later that night while I lay beside Chris I began to toss and turn, to flit in and out of nightmares, until he wakened and pleaded with me to let him get some sleep. Turning, I wrapped my arms about him, clinging to him as if to some unsinkable raft – as I'd always clung to the only straw that kept me from drowning in the cruel sea of Foxworth Hall.

HOMECOMING

Finally the decorators I'd hired to do over Jory's suite of rooms were finished. Now everything there was planned for his entertainment and comfort and convenience. With Melodie beside me, we stood and surveyed all that had been done to make the room bright and cheerful.

'Jory likes colour and lots of light, unlike some who want only darkness because it's richer appearing,' explained Melodie with a strange look haunting her eyes. Of course I knew she meant Bart. I gave her a quizzical look, wondering again how much time she spent with Bart, and what they talked about, and if he'd tried anything. Certainly all that wistful yearning I'd seen in his eyes would force him to make advances. And what better time than while Jory was away and Melodie was desperately needing? Then my safety valve turned on . . . Melodie despised Bart. She might need him to talk to, but that was all.

'Tell me what else I can do to help,' I said, wanting her to do most of it so she'd feel needed, useful. In response she smiled for the first time with some show of happiness. 'You can help me make the bed with the pretty new sheets I ordered.' She ripped open the plastic wrappings, the movement making her fuller breasts jiggle. Her jeans were just beginning to show a slight bulge.

I was almost as worried about her as I was about Jory. An expectant mother needed to eat more, drink milk, take vitamins, and then there was this unexpected reversal of her former heavy depression. She was now completely accepting of Jory's unhappy situation. It was what I had wanted, yet it had come about too quickly, and that gave me the feeling it was false.

Then came an explanation of her newfound security. 'Cathy, Jory's going to get well and dance again. I dreamed last night he was, and my dreams always come true.'

Now I knew she was going to do what I'd done in the beginning, convince herself that Jory would recover someday, and on that kind of fantasy she was going to construct her life – and his.

I started to speak, to say what Chris had to me, but Bart stepped into the hallway outside, his large feet clumping heavily down the long, dim hall. He glowered at the once dark panelling that was now painted off-white so that paintings of the sea and shore would show up beautifully. Easy enough to see he was displeased with our changes.

'We did it to please Jory,' I said before he could object, while Melodie stood silent and stared at him with the wide-eyed, helpless look of a child caught in a sticky situation. 'I know you want your brother to be happy, and no one loves the sea, the surf, the sand and seabirds more than Jory. So, into this room we're putting a bit of the sea and shore – giving him the knowledge that all the important things in life will still exist for him. The sky above, the earth below, and the sea in between. He's not going to lack for anything, Bart. He's going to have what it takes to keep him alive and happy, and I know you want to do your part.'

He was staring at Melodie, not half listening to me. His eyes riveted to those larger breasts, moving to study the curve of the baby swelling her belly. 'Melodie, you could have come to me and asked before you did anything, since I'm the one who'll pay the bills.' I was completely ignored, as if I weren't there at all.

'Oh, no,' denied Melodie. 'Jory and I have money. We can pay for the changes we've made in here . . . and I didn't think you would mind since you seem so concerned about him.'

'You don't have to pay for anything,' said Bart with surprising warmth. 'The day Jory comes home, attorneys will be coming in the afternoon to read the will again, and this time I'll know exactly my full worth. I'm damned sick and tired of having that day postponed.'

'Bart,' I said, stepping so I was between him and Melodie, 'you know why they haven't reread the will. They want Jory to be here and fully cognizant of what's going on.'

He walked around me to deliberately lock his eyes with the huge, sad ones of Melodie. He spoke to her and her alone. 'You just tell me what you need, and I'll deliver it yesterday. You and Jory can stay as long as you like.'

They stood staring at each other across twenty feet of sea-blue velvet carpeting. Bart's dark eyes probed into her blue ones before he said softly, winningly, 'Don't worry so much, Melodie. You and Jory have a home here forever if you want. I don't really give a damn what you do with these rooms. I do want Jory to be as comfortable and happy as possible.'

Were they formula words to satisfy me – or calculated words to seduce her? Why did Melodie blush and gaze down at her feet?

Cindy's tale resounded like distant church bells in my memory. Insurance for all the guests . . . in case of accidents. Wet sand that should have been dry sand. Sand that clumped into cement and didn't instantly pour out to make the papier-mâché columns safe.

Into my thoughts flitted memories of Bart when he was seven, eight, nine and ten . . .

Wish I had legs as pretty as Jory's. Wish I could run and dance like Jory. Gonna grow taller, gonna grow much bigger, gonna be more more powerful than Jory. Someday. Someday.

Bart's mumbling boyhood wishes, said so many times I'd grown indifferent to them. Then, when he was older . . .

Who is gonna love me, like Melodie loves Jory?
Nobody. Nobody.

I shook my head to rid myself of unwelcome memories of a little boy wanting to equal the stature of his older and more talented brother.

But why was he looking now at Melodie with such significance? Her blue eyes lifted to meet his briefly; then she looked away, blushing again, positioning her hands in the ballet position all dancers used to keep from drawing attention away from the main performer – her feet toed out. On stage, Melodie was on stage, playing a role.

Bart strode off, his long legs confident and sure, as they'd never been when he was a young boy. I felt sad and sorry he had to wait until he was out of Jory's shadow before he could find even the ability to use his body co-ordination with skill. Sighing, I decided to think of the present and all that had been done to give Jory's convalescence the perfect environment.

A large colour TV was at the foot of his bed, and he had a remote control unit to change channels and turn it off and on from his bed. An electrician had arranged a way for Jory to open and close his draperies when he chose. A stereo was within his reach. Books lined the back of his adjustable bed, which would sit him up and turn him into almost any position he wanted. Melodie and I, with Chris's help, had wracked our brains to come up with every modern convenience that would enable him to do what he could for himself. Now all we had to do was to see he stayed busy with some occupation of real interest, enough to absorb his energies and challenge his innate talents.

A long time ago I'd started reading books on psychology, my poor attempt to try and help Bart. Now I could help Jory with his 'racehorse' personality that had to compete and win. He couldn't endure boredom, lying about doing nothing. There was already a barre along the wall without windows, put there recently, to give him the promise that one day he'd stand up, even if he would have to wear a back brace connected to leg braces. I sighed to think of my beautiful, graceful son stumbling along like a horse in a harness; then tears were streaking my face. Tears I quickly blinked away so Melodie wouldn't see them.

Soon Melodie was tired and left to lie down and rest. I finished up in the room, then hurried to oversee the ramps being constructed to take Jory down to the terraces and the gardens. No effort was being spared to see he would not be confined to his room. There was also a newly installed elevator put where once there had been a butler's pantry.

At last came the wonderful day when Jory was allowed to leave the hospital and come home. The cast was still on his back, but he was eating and drinking normally and had gained back his colour and a little of the weight he'd lost. My heart ached with pity to see him flat on a stretcher, being rolled to the elevator, when once he'd taken the stairs three at a time. I saw him turn his head to stare at the stairs as if he'd sell his soul to use them again.

But, smiling, he looked around the grand suite of rooms all refurbished and his eyes sparkled. 'It's great, what you've done, really great. My favourite colour combination, white and blue. You've given me the seashore – why, I can almost smell the surf, hear the seagulls. It's wonderful, truly wonderful what paint and pictures, green plants and planning can do.'

His wife stood at the foot of the narrow bed he'd have to use until the cast came off, but she took pains not to meet his eyes. 'Thanks for liking what we've done. Your mother and I, and Chris, too, really tried to please you.'

His blue eyes turned navy as he stared at her, sensing something I, too, felt. He looked towards the windows, his full lips thinning, before he drew back into his shell.

Immediately I stepped forward to hand him a huge box, saved for this kind of uncomfortable moment. 'Jory, something meaningful for you to do while you're still confined to the bed. Don't want you staring at that boob tube all the time.'

Seeming relieved not to have to trouble his wife with words she didn't want to hear, he feigned childish eagerness by shaking the huge box. 'A compressed elephant? An unsinkable surfboard?' he guessed, looking only at me. I ruffled his curly hair, leaned to hug and kiss him and ordered him to hurry and open that box. I was dying to hear what he thought of my gift that had travelled all the way from New England.

Soon he had the ribbons and pretty wrapping off and was staring down at the long box containing what appeared to be neat bundles of super-long matchsticks. Tiny bottles of paint, larger bottles of glue, with spools of thin cording, carefully packaged cloth. 'A kit to make a clipper ship,' he said with both wonder and dismay. 'Mom, there are ten pages of instructions! This thing is so complicated it will take me the better part of my life to complete. And when it's done – if ever – what will I have?'

'What will you have? My son, you will have when you are finished an heirloom that will be priceless, to leave to your son or daughter.' All said so proudly, so sure he could follow the difficult directions. 'You have steady hands, a good eye for details, a ready understanding of the written word and such determination. Besides, take a look at that empty mantel that demands a ship smack in the middle.'

Laughing, his raised head fell back on the pillow, already exhausted. He closed his eyes. 'Okay, you've convinced me. I'll give it a go – but I've not had much experience with any craft since I was a kid gluing areoplane parts together.'

Oh, yes, I remember clearly. They'd dangled down from his ceiling, infuriating Bart, who couldn't glue anything together properly at that time.

'Mom . . . I'm tired. Give me a chance to nap before the lawyers come to read that will. I don't know if I'm up to all the excitement of Bart's "coming into his own" – at last.'

It was at this moment that Bart stepped into the room. Jory sensed him there and opened his eyes. The dark brown and dark blue brotherly eyes met, locked, challenging the other for a dreadfully long time. The silence grew and grew until I became aware of my own heart throbs; the clock behind me ticked too loud, and Melodie was breathing heavily. I heard the birds outside twittering before Melodie began to rearrange another vase of flowers just for something to do.

On and on they clashed eyes, wills, when Bart should speak and welcome home the brother he'd visited only once. Still he just stood there, as if he'd keep his eyes locked on Jory until Jory broke the spell and lost the silent battle of wills.

I had my lips parted to stop this contest when Jory smiled and said warmly, without lowering his eyes or breaking the bind, 'Hi, brother. I know how much you hate hospitals, so it was doubly nice for you to visit me. Since I'm here, in your home . . . isn't it easier to say hello? I'm glad my accident didn't spoil your birthday party. I heard from Cindy that my fall only momentarily lulled the hilarity, and the party went on as if nothing had happened.'

Still Bart stood there saying nothing. Melodie put the last rose in the vase and lifted her head. A few tendrils of her fair hair had escaped the tight confinement of her ballerina bun to make her look charmingly casual and antiquely fragile. There was an air of weariness about her as if she'd surrendered to life and all its vicissitudes. Was I imagining that she sent some silent warning to Bart – and he understood? Suddenly he was smiling, even if it was stiff.

'I'm glad you're back. Welcome home, Jory.' He strode forward to clasp his brother's hand. 'If there's anything I can do, just let me know.' Then he left the room, and I was staring after him, wondering . . .

At four exactly, that very afternoon, shortly after Jory woke up and Chris and Bart lifted him on to a stretcher, three attorneys came to take over Bart's grand home office. We sat in fine milk-chocolate coloured leather chairs, all but Jory, who lay on a rolling stretcher very still and quiet. His tired eyes were half opened, showing his interest was small. Cindy had flown home to be here, as was required, for she, too, was mentioned in the will. She perched on the arm of my chair, swinging her shapely leg back and forth, treating all of this as a joke while Joel glared to see that blue high-heeled shoe moving constantly and calling attention to those remarkably lovely legs. We all sat as if at a funeral, as papers were shuffled, spectacles were put on and whisperings between the lawyers made us all uneasy.

Bart was particularly nervous, exalted looking, but suspicious of the way the attorneys kept glancing at him. The eldest of the three acted as spokesman as word by careful word the main portion of my mother's will was read once again. We'd heard it all before.

'. . . when my grandson, Bartholomew Winslow Scott Sheffield, who will eventually claim his rightful surname of Foxworth, reaches the age of twenty-five,' read the man in his late sixties with the glasses perched low on his nose, 'he will be given the annual sum of five hundred thousand dollars, until he reaches the age of thirty-five. At this stated age, the remainder of my estate, hereafter called The Corrine Foxworth Winslow Trust, will be turned over in entirety to my grandson, Bartholomew Winslow Scott Sheffield Foxworth. My firstborn son, Christopher Garland Sheffield Foxworth, will remain in his position as trustee until the aforesaid time. If he, the trustee, should not survive until the time when my grandson Bartholomew Winslow Scott Sheffield Foxworth reaches the age of thirty-five, then my daughter, Catherine Sheffield Foxworth, shall be named as replacement trustee until my aforesaid grandson reaches his thirty-fifth birthday.'

There was more, much more, but I didn't hear anything else. I filled with shock and glanced at Chris, who seemed dumbfounded. Then my eyes rested on Bart.

His face was pale, registering a kaleidoscope of changing expressions. His colour waxed and waned. He raked his long, strong fingers through his perfect hairstyle and left it rumpled. Helplessly he looked at Joel as if for guidance, but Joel only shrugged and crooked his lips as if to say, 'I told you so.'

Next Bart was glaring at Cindy as if her presence had magically changed his grandmother's will. His eyes flitted to Jory, who was lying sleepily on the stretcher, appearing disinterested in everything going on but Melodie, who stared at Bart with her pale, woebegone face flickering like a weak candle flame in the strong wind of Bart's disappointment.

Quickly Bart jerked his sizzling gaze away when her head lowered to Jory's chest. Almost silently she was crying.

An eternity seemed to pass before that elderly lawyer folded the long will, replaced it in a blue folder, then put that on Bart's desk. He stood with folded arms to wait for Bart's questions.

'What the hell is going on?' shouted Bart.

He jumped to his feet, stalked to his desk and seized up the will, which he thumbed through quickly with the eye of an expert. Finished, he hurled down the will. 'Damn her to hell! She promised me everything, everything! Now I have to wait ten more years . . . why wasn't that part read before? I was there. I was ten years old, but I remember her will stating I'd come into my own when I was twenty-five. I'm twenty-five and one month old – where is my reward?'

Chris stood. 'Bart,' he said calmly, 'you have five hundred thousand dollars a year – that kind of money isn't to be shrugged off. And didn't you hear that all your living expenses, and the cost of running this house and maintaining it, will be taken care of by the bulk of monies still in trust? All your taxes will be prepaid. And five hundred thousand a year for ten years is more money than ninety-nine point nine percent of the world will ever know in an entire lifetime. How much can you spend on supporting your own life-style after all other expenses are taken care of? Besides, those ten years will fly by, and then everything will be yours to do with as you want.'

'How much more is there in toto?' Bart fired, his dark eyes rapacious and so intense they seemed to burn. His face was magenta coloured from his rage. 'Five million paid to me over a period of ten years, but what will be left? Ten million more? Twenty, fifty, a billion – how much?'

'I really don't know,' replied Chris coolly as the lawyers stared at Bart. 'But I'd say, with honesty, that day when you finally do come into your own, all of it, you will be, beyond a doubt, one of the richest men in the world.'

'But until then – you are!' screamed Bart. 'YOU! Of all people, you! The very one who's sinned the most! It isn't fair, not fair at all! I've been misled, tricked!' Blazing his eyes at all of us first, he slammed out of his office, only to stick his head in a second later.

'You'll be sorry, Chris,' he blazed fiercely. 'You must have talked her into having that codicil added – and instructed the attorneys not to read it aloud the day I heard it first, when I was ten. *It's your fault I haven't come into everything due me!*'

As always it had been Chris's fault – or mine.

BROTHERLY LOVE

Most of the miserably hot month of August had come and gone while Jory stayed in the hospital, and September arrived with its cooler nights, only too soon starting the colourful process of autumn. Chris and I raked leaves after the gardeners had come and gone, thinking they carelessly overlooked so many. The leaves never stopped falling, and it was something we both liked to do.

We heaped them in deep ravines, dropped down a match and crouched close together on the grass to watch the fire blaze high and warm enough to heat our cold hands and faces. The fire down below was so safe we could enjoy just watching and turning often to gaze at one another and the way the glow lit up our eyes and turned our skins a lovely shade of scarlet. Chris had a lover's way of looking at me, of reaching to caress my cheek with the back of his hand, brushing my hair with his fingertips, kissing my neck, and in all ways touching me deeply with his abiding love. In the firelight of those leaves burning at night, we found each other in new ways, in mature ways that were even better than what we'd had before, and that had always been overwhelmingly sweet.

And behind us, staying forever locked within her room in that horrible house, Melodie's baby swelled her out more and more.

The month of October came to us in a stunning blaze of colours that stole my breath away, filling me with awe as only the works of nature could. These were the same trees whose tops we'd only glimpsed in our hideaway attic schoolroom. I could almost see the four of us staring out when I glanced up at the attic dormer windows, the twins only five, pining away to large-eyed gnomes, all our small, pale faces pasted wistfully to the smudgy glass, staring out, yearning to be free to do what now I took as only natural and our due.

Ghosts up there; our ghosts up there.

Colour all our days grey, was the way I'd used to think. Colour all Jory's days grey now, for he wouldn't let himself see the beauty of autumn in the mountains when he couldn't stroll the woodsy paths, or dance over the browning grass, or lean to sniff the fall flowers, or jog alongside Melodie.

The tennis courts stayed empty as Bart abondoned them for lack of a partner. Chris would have loved a Saturday or Sunday tennis game with Bart, but Bart still ignored Chris.

The large swimming pool that had been Cindy's special delight was drained, cleaned, covered over. The screens came down, the glass was cleaned before the storm windows went up. The cords of wood stacked out of sight behind the garage grew by the dozens, and trucks delivered coal to use when or if our oil furnaces failed, or our electricity went off. We had an auxiliary unit to light our rooms and keep our electric appliances working, and yet somehow I feared this winter as I'd never feared any winter but those in the attic.

Freezing cold it had been in the attic, like the Arctic zone. Now we were going to have the change to experience what it had been like downstairs, while Momma enjoyed life with her parents and friends, and the lover she found, while four unwanted children froze and starved and suffered upstairs.

Sunday mornings were the best. Chris and I gloried in our time together. We ate breakfast in Jory's room so he wouldn't feel so separate from his family, and only a few times could I persuade Bart and Melodie to join us.

'Go on,' urged Jory, when he saw me glance often at the window, 'go walking. Don't think I'm going to begrudge you and Dad your legs because mine don't work anymore. I'm not a baby, or that selfish.'

We had to go or he'd think he was inhibiting our style of living. And so we went, hoping Melodie would join him.

One day we woke up so early the frost was still thick upon the ground and pumpkins were ripening under the stacked corn stalks where farmers eked out a poor living. The frost looked sweet, like powdered sugar that would soon melt when the sun came out fully.

On our walk we stopped to stare up at the sky as Canadian geese flew south, telling us that winter would come earlier than usual this year. We heard the distant melancholy honking of those untiring birds fade as they disappeared in the morning clouds. Flying towards South Carolina – where once we had fled just before winter's sharp bite.

In mid-October the orthopaedist came to use huge electric shears to split Jory's cast halfway through; then he used handheld shears to gently cut through what remained. Jory said he felt now like a turtle without its shell. His strong body had wasted inside that cast. 'A few weeks of exercising your arms and shoulder muscles will see your chest as developed as ever,' encouraged Chris. 'You're going to need strong arms, so keep on using that trapeze, and we'll have parallel bars put in your sitting room so you can eventually pull yourself up into a standing position. Don't think life is over for you, that all challenges are behind you and nothing matters now, for you have miles and miles to go before you're done with life, don't you ever forget that.'

'Yeah,' murmured Jory bleakly, staring empty-eyed towards the door, which Melodie seldom passed through. 'Miles and miles to travel before I can find another body that works like it should. I guess I'll start believing in reincarnation.'

The quickly chilling days turned bitterly cold, with autumn nights that took us quickly towards freezing. The migrating birds stopped flying overhead now that the wind was whistling through the treetops, howling around the house, stealing inside our rooms. The moon was again a raiding Viking longboat sailing high, flooding our bed with moonlight, giving us kindling for a new kind of romance. Clean, cool, bright love that lit up our spirits, and told us we weren't really sinners of the worst kind. Not when our love could last as it had, while other marriages broke up after a few months or years. We couldn't be sinning and feel as we did towards one another. Who were we hurting? No one, not really. Bart was hurting himself, we reasoned.

Still, why was I haunted by nightmares that said differently? I'd become an expert at turning off disturbing thoughts by thinking of all the trivial details in my life. There was nothing as diverting as the startling beauty of nature. I wanted nature to heal my wounds, and Jory's – and perhaps even Bart's.

With a keen eye I studied all the signs as a farmer might and reported them back to Jory. The rabbits grew suddenly fatter. The squirrels seemed to be storing more nuts. Woolly caterpillars looked like tiny train cars of fur inching towards safety – wherever that was.

Soon I was pulling out winter coats that I'd intended to give to charities; heavy sweaters and wool skirts I'd never expected to wear in Hawaii. In September Cindy had flown back to her high school in South Carolina. This was her last year in a very expensive private school that she 'absolutely adored.' Her letters poured in like unseasonable warm rain, wanting more money for this or that.

On and on flowed Cindy's sprawling girlish script, needing everything, despite all the gifts I was constantly bombarding her with. She had dozens of boyfriends, a new one each time she wrote. She needed casual clothes for the boy who liked to hunt and fish. She needed dressy clothes for the boy who liked operas and concerts. She needed jeans and warm tops for herself, and luxury underwear and nightclothes, for she just couldn't sleep in anything inexpensive.

Her letters emphasized all that I'd missed when I was sixteen. I remembered Clairmont and my days in Dr Paul's house, with Henny in the kitchen teaching me how to cook by example, not with words. I'd bought a cookbook on how to win your man and hold him by cooking all the right dishes. What a child I'd been. I sighed. Perhaps I'd had it just as good as Cindy, after all – in a different way – after we escaped Foxworth Hall. I sniffed Cindy's pink, perfumed stationery before I put down her letter, then turned my attention to the present and all the problems in this Foxworth Hall, without the paper flowers in the attic.

Day after day of closely observing Bart when he was with Melodie was convincing me that they saw a great deal of one another, while Jory saw very little of his wife. I tried to believe that Melodie was trying to console Bart for not inheriting as much as he'd believed . . . but despite myself, I presumed there was more to it than pity.

Like a faithful puppy with only one friend, Joel followed Bart everywhere, except into his office or bedroom. He prayed in that tiny room before breakfast, lunch and dinner. He prayed before he went to bed, and prayed as he walked about, muttering to himself the appropriate quotes from the Bible to suit whatever occasion provoked him into pious mumbles.

In his own way, Chris was in Heaven, enjoying the best years of his life, or so he said. 'I love my new job. The men I work with are bright, humorous and have unending tales to tell and take away the monotony of doing a lot of drudgery. We go into the lab each day, don our white coats, check our petri dishes, expecting miracles, and grin and bear it when miracles just don't happen.'

Bart was neither friend nor foe to Jory, just someone who stuck his head in the door and said a few words before he hurried on to something he considered more important than wasting time with a crippled brother. I often wondered what he did with his time besides study the financial markets and buy and sell stocks and bonds. I suspected he was risking much of his five hundred thousand in order to prove to all of us he was smarter than Chris and craftier than the foxiest of all Foxworths, Malcolm.

Soon after Chris drove off on a Tuesday morning in late October, I hurried back up the stairs to check on Jory and see that he was properly taken care of. Chris had hired a male nurse to tend to Jory, but he was only here every other day.

Jory seldom complained about being housebound, although his head was often turned towards the windows to stare out at the brilliance of autumn.

'The summer's gone,' he said flatly, lifelessly, as the wind tossed colourful leaves playfully about, 'and it's taken my legs with it.'

'Autumn will bring you reasons for being happy, Jory. Winter will make you a father. Life still has many happy surprises in store for you, whether or not you want to believe that. I believe like Chris, that the best is still to come. Now . . . let's see what we can do to give you substitute legs. Now that you're strong enough to sit up, there's no reason why you can't move into that wheelchair your father brought home. Jory, please. I hate seeing you in bed all the time. Try the chair, maybe it won't be as obnoxious as you think.'

Stubbornly he shook his head.

I ignored that and went on with my persuasions. 'Easily we can take you outside. We can stroll through the woods as soon as Bart has workmen clear the paths that might hinder your progress, and right now you could sit on a terrace in the sunshine and gain back some of your colour. Soon it will be too cold to go outside. And when the time comes, I can push you through the gardens and the woods.'

He threw the chair, kept where he could see it every day, a hard, scornful look. 'That thing would turn over.'

'We'll buy you one of those electric chairs that's so heavy and well balanced it can't turn over.'

'I don't think so, Mom. I've always loved autumn, but this one makes me feel so sad. I feel I've lost everything that was truly important. I'm like a broken compass, spinning without direction. Nothing seems worthwhile. I've been cheated, and I resent it. I hate the days. But the nights are worse. I want to hold fast to summer and what I used to have, and the falling leaves are the tears I shed inside, and the wind whistling at night are my howls of anguish, and the birds flying south are all telling me that the summer of my life has come and gone and never, never again will I feel as happy, or as special. I'm nobody now, Mom, nobody.'

He was breaking my heart.

Only when he turned to look at me did he see this. Shame flushed his face. Guilt turned his head. 'I'm sorry, Mom. You're the only one I can talk to like this. With Dad, who is wonderful, I have to act manly. Once I spill out to you all I feel, it doesn't eat at me inside so much. Forgive me for laying all my heavy feelings on you.'

'It's all right. Never stop telling me just how you feel. If you do, then I won't know how to help. That's what I'm here for, Jory. That's why you have parents. Don't feel that your father won't understand, for he will. Talk to him like you talk to me. Say anything you need to say, don't hold back. Ask for anything within reason, and Chris and I give all we can – but don't ask for the impossible.'

Silently he nodded, then forced a weak smile. 'Okay. Maybe, after all, I can stand to sit in an electric wheelchair someday.'

Before him, spread on the table with casters that fitted over his bed, were the many parts of the clipper ship he was tediously gluing together. He seldom turned on the stereo, as if beautiful music was an abomination to his ears now that he couldn't dance. He ignored the television as a waste of time, reading when he wasn't working on the model ship. A tiny part of the wood was held by tweezers as he applied a bit of glue; then, squinting his eye, he looked at the directions and completed the hull.

Casually he asked without meeting my eyes, 'Where's my wife? She seldom comes to visit before five. What the hell does she do all day?'

It seemed a casual enough question for Jory to ask as Jory's nurse came in again to say he was off for classes. He waved a cheerful goodbye and left. During his absence either Melodie or I were supposed to do what we could to make Jory comfortable, as well as keep him entertained. Keeping him occupied was the most difficult part. His life had been a physical one, and now he had to be content with mental activities. The nearest thing he had that even approached a physical life was putting the ship together.

At least I'd presumed Melodie came in to do what she could for him.

I very seldom saw Melodie. The house was so large it was easy to avoid those whom you didn't want to see. Lately she'd taken to eating not only breakfast but lunch as well in her bedroom across the hall from Jory's suite.

Chris brought home the custom-made electric wheelchair with its joy stick for driving. Immediately the nurse began to teach Jory the methods he'd use to swing his body out of the bed and into a chair he'd have locked beside his bed, with the arm nearest the bed pulled out.

Jory had been crippled for more than three and a half long, long miserable months. For him they were more like years. He'd been forced to change into another kind of person, the kind of person I could tell he really didn't like.

Another day came without a visit from Melodie, and Jory was asking again where she was, and what she did with her time. 'Mom, did you hear my question? Please tell me what my wife does all day.' His usually pleasant voice held a sharp edge. 'She doesn't spend it with me, I know that.'

Bitterness was in his eyes as he nailed me with his penetrating dark blue eyes. 'Right this minute I want you to go to Melodie and tell her I want to see her – NOW! Not later, when she feels like it – for it seems she never feels like it!'

'I'll get her,' I said with determination. 'She's no doubt in her room listening to ballet music.'

With trepidation I left Jory still working on the model ship. Even as I looked back at him, I saw the wind was picking up and beginning to hurl the falling leaves towards the house. Golden and scarlet and russet leaves that he refused to see – and once he'd heard the music of colours.

Look, now, Jory, Look now. This is beauty you won't see again, perhaps. Don't ignore it – take it and seize the day, as you used to do.

But had I, back then . . .? Had I?

As I stood and looked at him, trying to bring him back to himself, the sky suddenly darkened and all the bright falling leaves went limp in the cold, drenching rain that plastered them against the glass. 'Daddy used to do all the chores when we lived in Gladstone. Momma used to complain the storm windows gave her twice as many to clean . . .'

'I want my wife, Mom, NOW!'

I was reluctant to go in search of Melodie for no reason I could name. In the dreary gloom Jory was forced to turn on a lamp at ten in the morning.

'Would you like a cheerful wood fire burning?'

'I only want my wife. Do I have to repeat this ten times? Once she's here, she can start the fire.'

I left him alone, realizing my presence irritated him when he wanted her – the only one who could bring him back to himself.

Melodie was not in her room as I'd expected her to be.

The halls I trod seemed the same halls I'd walked before when I was younger. The closed doors I passed seemed the same heavy, solid doors I'd stealthily opened when I'd been fourteen, fifteen. Behind me I sensed the omniscient presence of Malcolm, the malice of the hostile grandmother.

I turned to the western wing. Bart's wing.

Almost automatically my feet took me there as my mind stayed blank. Intuition had ruled most of my life, and, it seemed, would rule my future as well. Why was I going this way? Why didn't I look elsewhere for Melodie? What instinct was guiding me to my second son's rooms, where he never wanted me to go?

Before Bart's wide double doors that were heavily padded with luxurious black leather, gold-tooled with his monogram and the family crest, I called softly, 'Bart, are you in there?'

I heard nothing. However, all the doors were made of solid oak, heavily panelled beneath the ostentatious padding. Very soundproof doors and thick walls that knew how to hold secrets, so no wonder we four had been so easily hidden away. I turned the doorlatch, expecting to find it locked. It wasn't.

Almost stealthily I stepped inside Bart's sitting room, which was kept immaculate, not one book or magazine out of place. On his walls hung his sporting equipment: tennis rackets and fishing rods, a golf bag in a corner, a rowing machine inside a closet with the door partially open. I stared at the photographs of his favourite sports stars. I often thought Bart made a pretence of admiring football and baseball athletes just so he'd have something in common with the rest of his sex. To my way of thinking he'd have been more honest to plaster his walls with pictures of those who'd earned fortunes in the stock market, or wheeling and dealing in industry, or politics.

His rooms were all black and white with red accents; dramatic, but somehow cold. I sat down on his white leather sofa fully twelve feet long, my feet on his red carpet, with black velvet and satin pillows behind my back. In one corner was a marvellous bar sparkling with crystal decanters and various stemmed glasses, and every kind of liquor he kept there for his private use, along with snack foods. There was also a small fridge and a micro oven for melting cheese, or doing whatever light cooking he wanted.

Every photograph was matted in black or red and framed in gold. Three walls were of white moiré fabric. One wall was covered with padded and quilted black leather. A deceiving wall. One of those leather buttons concealed the large safe in which he kept his stock and bond certificates, for he'd proudly shown me his suite just once, soon after it was completely decorated. He'd operated the secret buttons, happy to display the complexity of all he controlled. The safe in his office downstairs was used for less permanent and important papers.

I turned my head to stare at the door to his bedroom, covered with black leather, too. Beautiful doors to a magnificent bedroom with the same decor as this room. I thought I heard something. The soft rumble of male laughter – the softer giggle of a woman. Could I be wrong? Did Bart have the ability to make Melodie laugh when none of the rest of us could?

My imagination worked overtime, picturing what they had to be doing, and I felt sick at heart, thinking of Jory in his room, hopefully waiting for a wife who never came to him. Sick because Bart would do this to him, his own brother, whom he'd loved and admired very much for a short while, such a pitifully short while . . .

Just then the door opened and Bart came striding out, wearing not one stitch of clothing. He moved swiftly, his long legs a fast blur. Embarrassed to see him naked, I shrank back into the soft cushions, hoping he wouldn't see me. He'd never forgive me. I shouldn't be here.

Due to the sudden storm, the gloom in his sitting room was so dense there was some hope he wouldn't notice me sitting on his white sofa. Straight to the fully equipped bar he stalked, and with quick, skilled hands mixed some drink using crystal decanters. He sliced lemon, filled two cocktail glasses, put those half-filled glasses on a silver tray and headed back for his bedroom. The door behind him was kicked closed.

Cocktails in the morning, before twelve . . .?

What would Joel think of that?

I sat on, hardly breathing.

Thunder rolled and lightning cracked, the rain beat on the windowpanes. Lightning zagged and lit up the gloom every few seconds.

Moving to a more secluded spot in his room, I made myself part of the shadows behind a huge plant, then waited.

It seemed an eternity passed before that door opened again, and I knew Jory was waiting anxiously, perhaps even angrily, for Melodie to show up. Two glasses, two. She was here. She had to be here.

In the dimness I finally saw Melodie step out of Bart's bedroom wearing a filmy peignoir that clearly showed she wore nothing beneath. A flash of lightning briefly illuminated her, showing the bulge of the baby that was due early in January.

Oh, Melodie, how can you do this to Jory?

'Come back,' called Bart in a slurred, satisfied voice. 'It's raining. The fire in here makes it cozier – and we have nothing better to do . . .'

'I've got to bathe and dress and visit Jory,' she said, hesitating in the doorway, looking at him with apparent longing. 'I want to stay, really I do, but Jory needs me once in a while.'

'Can he give you what I've just given you?'

'Please, Bart. He needs me. You don't know what it's like to be needed.'

'No, I don't know. Only the weak depend on others for sustenance.'

'You've never been in love, Bart,' she answered hoarsely, 'so you can't understand. You take me, use me, tell me I'm wonderful, but you don't love me, or truly need me. Someone else would serve your purpose just as well. It feels good to be needed, to know someone wants you more than he wants anyone else.'

'Leave, then,' he said, his happy tone turning quickly icy as he stayed hidden from my sight. 'Of course I don't need you. I don't need anyone. I don't know if what I feel for you is love or just desire. Even pregnant, you're very beautiful, and if your body does give me pleasure now, it might not tomorrow.'

I could tell from her profile that she was hurt. She cried out pitifully, 'Then why do you want me to come every day, every night? Why do your eyes follow wherever I go? You do need me, Bart! You do love me! You're just ashamed to admit it. Please don't talk so cruelly to me. It hurts. You seduced me when I was weak and afraid, and Jory was still in the hospital. You took me when I needed him, and told me my need was you! You knew I was terrified Jory might die . . . and I needed someone.'

'And that's all I am?' he roared. 'A need? I thought you loved me, really loved me!'

'I do, I do!'

'No, you don't! How can you love me and still talk of him? So go to him. See what he can give you now!'

She left, her frail garment fluttering behind her, reminding me of a ghost frantically fleeing to try and find life.

The door slammed behind her.

Stiffly I rose from my chair, feeling my knee throbbing with pain, like it always ached when it rained. I limped a little as I neared the closed door of Bart's bedroom. I didn't even hesitate as I threw it open. Before he could protest I'd reached inside to throw the switch and bring his cozy, firelit room into electric brightness.

Immediately he bolted up in the middle of his king-sized bed. 'Mother! What the hell are you doing in my bedroom? Get out, out!'

I strode forward, covering the large space between the door and the bed in a second.

'What the hell are you doing sleeping with your brother's wife? Your injured brother's wife?'

'Get out of here!' he bellowed, taking care to keep his privates well covered, while the mat of dark hair on his chest seemed to bristle with indignity. 'How dare you spy on me?'

'Don't you yell at me, Bart Foxworth! I'm your mother, and you are not thirty-five years old yet, so you can't order me out of this house. I'll go when I'm ready, and that time hasn't arrived. You owe me so much, Bart, so much.'

'I owe you, Mother?' he asked sarcastically, bitterly. 'Pray tell me why I owe you anything. Should I thank you for my father, whom you helped to kill? Should I say thank you for all those miserable days when I was young and neglected, and unsure of myself? Should I thank you now for putting me on such unstable ground that I don't feel I'm a normal man, capable of inspiring love?'

His voice broke as his head bowed. 'Don't stand there and accuse me with those cursed Foxworth blue eyes. You don't have to do one damned thing to make me feel guilty. I was born feeling that way. I took Melodie when she was crying and needing someone to hold her and give her confidence and love. And I found for the first time the kind of love I've been hearing and reading about all my life, from the noble type of woman who's only had one man. Do you realize how rare they are? Melodie is the first woman who has made me feel truly human. With her I can relax, put down my guard, and she doesn't try to wound me. She loves me, Mother. I don't think I've ever been happier.'

'How can you say that when I just overheard the words the two of you exchanged?'

He sobbed and fell back to roll on his side away from me, the sheet just barely covering enough. 'I'm on the defensive, and so is she. She feels she's betraying Jory by loving me. I feel much the same way. Sometimes we can let go of guilt and shame, and it's wonderful then. When Jory was in the hospital, and you and Chris were gone all the time, she didn't need a great deal of seducing. She fell with only a little reluctance into my arms, glad to have someone who cared enough to understand her feelings. Our fights all grow from the mire of guilt. Without Jory in the way, eagerly she'd run to me, be my wife.'

'BART! You can't take Jory's wife from him. He needs her as he has never needed her before! You were wrong to take her when she was weak from desperation and loneliness. Give her up. Stop making love to her. Be loyal to Jory, as he's been loyal to you. Through everything, Jory has stood behind you – remember that.'

He flipped over, clutching the black sheet modestly. Something fragile broke behind his eyes and made him seem vulnerable, a pathetic child again. A wounded, small child who didn't like himself. His voice was hoarse when he said, 'Yes, I love Melodie. I love her enough to marry her. I love her with every bone, muscle, ounce of my flesh. She's awakened me from a deep sleep. You see, she's the first woman I've loved. I have never been touched or moved by a woman as I've been touched and moved by Melodie. She slipped into my heart and now I can't push her out. She steals into my room wearing her deliate clothes, with her beautiful long and shining hair down, fresh from her bath and smelling sweet, and she just stands there, pleading with her eyes, and I feel my heart begin to beat faster, and when I dream, I dream of her. She's become the most wonderful thing in my life.

'Don't you see why I can't give her up? She's the one who has really awakened this burning desire for love and sex that I didn't even know I had. I thought that sex was a sin, and never did I pull away from a woman without feeling dirty, even dirtier than I thought I left her. When I made love to other women, I was always left feeling guilty, as if two naked bodies meeting in passion was evil – now I know differently. She's made me realize how beautiful loving can be, and now I don't know how to carry on without her. Jory can't be a real lover anymore. Let me be the husband she needs and wants. Help me to build a normal life for her and for myself . . . or else . . . I don't know . . . I just don't know what will happen . . .' His dark eyes turned my way, pleading for my understanding.

Oh, to hear him say all of that, when all his life I'd longed to have his confidence, and now that I had it, what could I do? I loved Bart, as I loved Jory. I stood there wringing my hands, twisting my conscience and tormenting myself with guilt, for somehow I must have brought this about. I had neglected Bart, favoured Jory, Cindy . . .

Now I, and Jory, had to pay the price . . . again.

He spoke, his voice lower and cracked, making him seem even younger and more vulnerable as he lay there, trying to lock his happiness away in a safe place I couldn't reach, and in this way forever shield it from killing exposure.

'Mother, for once in your life, see something from my side. I'm not bad, not wicked, or the beast you sometimes make me feel I am. I'm only a man who has never felt good about himself. Help me, Mother. Help Melodie have the kind of husband she needs now that Jory can't be a real man anymore.'

The rain beat a frantic tattoo on the window-glass. It matched the rhythm of my heart. The wind whistled and shrieked around the house, while frenzied bat wings threw themselves against the inside of my skull. I couldn't split Melodie into two equal halves and give to Jory and Bart each their share. I had to stick with what I knew was right. Bart's love for Melodie was wrong. Jory needed her most.

Still I stood there, riveted to the carpet . . . and felt overwhelmed with my second son's desperate need to be loved. So many times in the past I'd believed him capable of evil, and he'd been proven innocent. Did my own guilt for bringing him into being curse me with eyes that refused to see the good in Bart?

'Are you sure, Bart? Do you truly love Melodie – or do you just want her because she belongs to Jory?'

Turning on his back, his dark eyes met mine with more honesty than he'd ever shown. How those dark eyes pleaded for understanding. 'In the beginning I wanted Melodie only because she belonged to Jory. I honestly admit that. I wanted to take from him what he treasured most. Because he'd taken from me what I wanted most – YOU!'

I cringed as he went on. 'She rejected my advances so many times that I began to respect her, to see her as different from other women who were easy to get. The more she shoved me away, the higher burned my desire, until I had to have her or die. I love her! Yes, she's made me vulnerable . . . and now I don't know how to live without her!'

I threw my hands wide before I sank to the side of his king-sized bed. 'Oh, Bart . . . what a pity it couldn't have been another woman. Any woman but Melodie. I'm glad you've experienced love – and know it isn't dirty or sinful. Would God have made men and women the way he did if he hadn't meant for them to join together? He planned it that way. We recreate ourselves through love. But Bart, you have to promise not to see her alone again. Wait until Melodie has her baby before you and she decide anything.'

His eyes filled with hope, with gratitude. 'You'll help me?' Disbelief flooded his eyes. 'I never thought you would . . .'

'Wait, please wait. Let Melodie have her child, then go to her, and then to Jory, and face up to him, Bart. Tell him how you feel about her. Don't steal his wife without giving him a chance to have his say.'

'What can he say, Mother, that will make any difference? He's already lost. He can't dance. He can't even walk. He can't perform physically.'

Seconds ticked away before I found more useless words to speak. 'But does she honestly love *you*? I was in your sitting room. I heard her. She hasn't had her say in this matter. From what I can tell, she's torn between loving Jory and needing you. Don't take advantage of her weakness, or Jory's disabilities. Give him time to recover – then do what you must. It isn't fair to steal from Jory when he can't fight back. Give her time to adjust to Jory's condition. Then, if she still wants you, take her, for she'd only harm him more. But what would you do with Jory's child? Will you take that child from Jory, as well as take his wife? Are you planning to leave him nothing?'

Staring up at me, his eyes glittered suspiciously. Bart jerked his eyes away to stare up at the ceiling. 'I don't know yet about the baby. I haven't thought it out to that extent. I try not to think of the baby – and you don't have to go running to Chris or Jory with this. For once in your life, give me a chance to have something of my very own.'

'Bart – '

'Go now, please. Leave me alone to think. I'm tired. You can weaken a man, Mother, with your demands, with your judgments. Just give me a fair chance this time to prove to you that I'm not as bad as you think, or as crazy as I once believed myself to be.'

He didn't ask me again not to tell Jory, or Chris. As if he knew I wouldn't. Standing and turning about, I left his room.

On the way back to my room I thought about confronting Melodie, but I was too upset to face her without giving it more thought. She was already distraught enough, and I had to consider the health of her child.

Alone in my rooms, I sat before a guttering log fire and contemplated what to do. Jory's needs came first. In three months Jory's strong legs had begun to wither into thin sticks, reminding me of Bart's legs when he was very young. Short, thin legs covered with scratches, cuts and bruises, always falling, always breaking his bones. Punishing himself for being born and not living up to the standards Jory had set. That alone stood me up and headed me towards Jory's bedroom.

I stood in his doorway, my face washed clean of tear streaks, my eyes cooled by ice packs so they weren't red, and I smiled brightly at my firstborn. 'Melodie is napping, Jory. But she'll see you before dinner. I think it would be nice for the two of you to dine alone before the fireplace. The rain outside will make it very cosy in here. I've asked Trevor and Henry to carry up logs and a special small table for dining. I've planned a menu with everything you like. Now, what can I do to help you dress and look your best?'

He shrugged indifferently. Before the accident he'd always loved clothes, had always groomed himself to perfection. 'What difference now, Mom, what difference? I see you didn't bring her back with you, and why did it take you so long to come back and say she's napping?'

'The telephone rang . . . and Jory, I have to do a few things for myself once in a while. So now, what suit do you favour most?'

'None. Pyjamas and a robe will do,' he said distantly.

'Listen to me, Jory. Tonight you are going to sit in that electric wheelchair, wearing one of your father's suits, since you didn't bring a winter suit with you.' Immediately he objected, while I insisted.

Already we'd sent to New York for all of Jory's clothes, but Melodie had requested we leave hers where they were – and that had made me heat with anger inside, although I'd said nothing.

'When you look good, you feel good, and that's half the battle. You've stopped caring about your appearance. I'm going to shave your face even if you do want to grow a beard. You're much too handsome to hide behind bristly hair. You've got the most beautiful mouth, and a strong chin. Only weak-chinned men should hide behind beards.'

Eventually he gave up and smiled sardonically, agreeing to all I wanted to do to make him look more like himself. 'Mom, you're something else. You care so damned much – but I won't ask why. I'm just grateful somebody cares enough.'

About that time Chris drove home from Charlottesville, and he was eager to help. He shaved Jory's handsome face with a straight-edge razor, claiming that kind of shave did more for a man than anything else.

I sat on the bed to watch Chris finish the shaving before he splashed on lotion and cologne. All the time Jory looked so tolerant. I couldn't help but wonder what Bart was doing, and how I was going to approach Melodie and tell her that I knew what was going on between her and my second son.

Already Jory's arms were strong enough to swing his upper body into the chair. Chris and I stood back and watched, not offering to help, knowing he had to do this for himself. He seemed somewhat humiliated, and also somewhat proud that he did it easily the first time. Once he was in the chair, Jory looked pleased, despite himself. 'Not so bad,' he said as he studied his face in the mirror I held up. He activated the chair and buzzed around the room for a trial spin. He grinned at us both. 'It is better than the bed. What a fool you must think me – now it will be easier to finish the ship before Christmas, and maybe, with pampering like this, I'll struggle through.'

'As if we ever believed anything else,' said Chris happily.

'Now contain yourself, Jory . . . I'm going for Melodie,' I said, delighted with the way he looked, and the glow of happiness in his eyes, and his excitement to be mobile again, even if he had wheels instead of legs. 'Melodie is probably dressed and ready for dinner downstairs. As you know, our formerly sloppy Bart is now a stickler for all the niceties of living elegantly.'

'Tell her to hurry,' called Jory behind me, sounding more like his old self. 'I'm famished. And the sight of that fire burning makes me want her very badly.'

With many trepidations I headed for Melodie's room, knowing I was going to face her down with what I'd found out – and when I was finished, I might very well have driven her straight into Bart's ready arms. That was the chance I took.

One brother would win.

The other would lose.

And I wanted them both to win.

Softly I rapped on Melodie's door. I could hear faintly through the heavy wood the music from *Swan Lake*. She must have had it playing very loud, or else I wouldn't be hearing it at all. I knocked again. She didn't respond. This time when she didn't answer I opened her door and stepped inside, quietly closing the door behind me. Her room was messy with clothes dropped on the floor; cosmetics littered the dressing room table. 'Melodie, where are you?'

Her bathroom was empty. Oh, damn! She'd gone to Bart. In a flash I was off and running back to Bart's wing. On his door I banged furiously. 'Bart, Melodie . . . you can't do this to Jory.'

They weren't there.

I flew down the back stairs, heading for the dining room, half expecting they'd start dinner without Chris and me. Trevor was setting the table for two, measuring with his eye the distance of the plate from the edge of the table with such precision it was as if he used a ruler. I slowed down to walk into the dining room. 'Trevor, have you seen my second son?'

'Oh, yes, my lady,' he said in his polite British way, beginning to lay out the silver flatware. 'Mr Foxworth and Mrs Marquet just left to eat in a restaurant. Mr Foxworth requested that I tell you he'd be back . . . soon.'

'What did he really say, Trevor?' I asked, feeling sick at heart.

'My lady, Mr Foxworth was just a wee bit drunk. Not too drunk, so don't worry about the rain and accidents. I'm sure he can control the car, and Mrs Marquet will be just fine. It's a lovely night for driving if you like rain.'

I hurried on towards the garage, hoping to be in time to stop them. Too late! And it was just as I'd feared. Bart had taken Melodie in his small, fast, sports car, the red Jaguar.

My steps were snail-like as I headed back up the stairs. Jory was glowing from the champagne he'd sipped as he waited. Chris had gone on to our room to change for dinner.

'Where is my wife?' asked Jory, seated at the small table Henry and Trevor had carried up. Fresh flowers from our greenhouse centred the table, and with the champagne cooling in a silver ice bucket the atmosphere was festive and seductive, especially with the log fire burning to chase away the damp chill. Jory looked very much like himself with his legs hidden, and the chair he'd hated was hardly noticeable.

Should I make up a lie this time, as I had before?

All the brightness in his eyes faded. 'So she's not coming,' he said in a flat way. 'She never comes here anymore – at least not inside the room. She lingers in the doorway and speaks to me from a distance.' His husky voice cracked, then broke entirely and he was crying.

'I'm trying, Mom, really trying to accept this and not be bitter. But when I see what's happening between me and my wife, I come apart inside. I know what she's thinking even when she says nothing. I'm not a real man anymore, and she doesn't know how to cope with that.'

I fell upon my knees at his side and took him into my arms. 'She'll learn, Jory, she'll learn. We all have to learn how to cope with what can't be helped. Give her time. Wait until after the baby comes. She'll change. I promise she'll change. You will have given her your child. There's nothing like a baby of your own to hold in your arms to put joy in your heart. The sweetness of a baby, the thrill of having one small, tiny bit of humanity entirely dependent on you to shape and mould. Jory, just you wait and see how Melodie changes.'

His tears had stopped, but the anguish in his eyes stayed.

'I don't know if I can wait,' he whispered hoarsely. 'When there are others around to see, I smile and act content. But I'm thinking all the time about putting an end to this and setting Melodie free of all obligations. It's not fair to expect her to stay on. I'm going to tell her tonight that she can go if she wants, or she can stay until after the baby is born and then leave, and file for divorce. I won't contest.'

'No, Jory!' I flared. 'Say nothing to upset her more – just give her time. Let her adjust. The baby will help her adjust.'

'But, Mom, I don't know if I can live through to the end now. I think all the time about suicide. I think of my father and wish I had the courage to do what he did.'

'No, darling, hang on. You'll be never be alone.'

Chris and I sat down at the small table to keep him company. He didn't speak a dozen words during the meal.

At bedtime, I stealthily put away all the razors and everything with which he could harm himself. I slept on the couch in his room that night, fearful he was so despondent he might try to end his life just to give Melodie freedom to leave without guilt. His moans reached me even as I dreamed.

'Mel . . . my legs ache!' he cried out in his sleep. I got up to comfort him. He wakened and stared at me in a disoriented way. 'Every night my back and my legs ache,' he answered sleepily in reply to my questions. 'I don't need sympathy for my phantom pains. I just want a full night's rest.'

All through the night he writhed in agony. The legs that he couldn't feel during the day by night tormented him with constant pain. The lower part of his back stabbed him with repeated jabs.

'Why do I feel pain at night, when I feel nothing during the day?' he cried out, sweat pouring down his face, sticking his pyjama jacket to his chest. 'I still wish I had the nerve my father did – that would solve all our problems!'

No, no, no. I clung to him, covering his face with kisses, promising him everything and anything to make him cling to life. 'It will work out, Jory, it will! Hang in there. Don't give up and lose the greatest challenge of your life. You have me and you have Chris and sooner or later Melodie will come around and be your wife again.'

Bleakly he stared at me, as if I spoke of pipe dreams made of nothing but smoke.

'Go sleep in your own room, Mom. You make me feel more like a child by staying here. I promise not to do anything to make you cry again.'

'Darling, be sure and ring for your father or me if you need anything. Neither one of us minds getting up. Don't call for Melodie, for she might trip and fall in the dark now that she's kind of unsteady on her feet. I've always been a light sleeper, and it's easy for me to fall asleep again. Are you listening, Jory?'

'Sure, I'm listening,' he said with his eyes blank and remote. 'If there's one thing I'm good at now, it's listening.'

'And soon the physical therapist will come to start you on the road to recovery.'

'Recovery, Mom?' His eyes looked tired, very shadowed and dark. 'You mean that back brace I'll be fitted for? Indeed, I am looking forward to using that thing. The leg braces are going to be a real joy to wear. Isn't it fortunate I won't feel them? And I'm not even going to mention that harness contraption that will make me think of myself as a horse. I'll just think it will keep me from falling . . .' He paused, covered his face with his hands briefly, threw back his head and sighed. 'Lord, give me strength to endure – are you punishing me for having too much pride in my legs and body? You've done a damned good job of bringing me low.'

His hands came down. Tears shone in his eyes, streaked his cheeks. In a moment he was apologizing. 'Sorry about that, Mom. Tears of self-pity aren't very manly, are they? Can't be brave and strong all the time. Got my moments of weakness just like everyone else. Go back to your room. I'm not going to do anything to cause you and Dad more grief. I'll see this thing through to the end. Good night. Say good night to Melodie for me when she comes in.'

I cried in Chris's arms, causing him to ask a thousand questions that I refused to answer. Frustrated and more than a bit angry, he flipped away. 'You can't fool me,

Catherine. You're holding something back, thinking it will add another burden, when not to know what's going on is the heaviest of all burdens!'

He waited for me to reply. When I didn't, he quickly fell asleep on his side. He had the most irritating habit of being able to sleep when I couldn't. I wanted him awake, forcing me to answer the questions I'd just avoided. But he slept on and on, turning to embrace me in his sleep, burying his face in my hair.

Every hour I was up and checking to see if Bart had brought Melodie home, checking to see if Jory was all right. Jory lay on his bed with his eyes wide open, apparently waiting, as I did, for Melodie to come home.

'Has the phantom pain eased up?'

'Yes, go back to bed. I'm fine.'

I met Joel in the hallway outside Bart's room. He flushed to see me in my lacy white negligee. 'Joel,' I said, 'I thought you changed your mind about living under this roof and went back to that small cell over the garage . . .'

'Used to, Catherine, used to,' he muttered. 'Bart ordered me into the house, saying a Foxworth shouldn't be treated like a servant.' His watery eyes reproached me for not objecting when he'd informed us he liked the garage cell better than the nice room in Bart's wing of the house.

'You don't know what it's like to be old and lonely, niece. I've suffered from insomnia for years and years, troubled by bad dreams, with vague aches and pains that kept me from ever reaching that deep sleep I yearn for. So I get up to tire myself, I roam about . . .'

Roam about? Spying, that's what he did! Then, looking at him more closely, I felt ashamed. Standing there in the gloom of the hall, he appeared so frail, so sickly and thin – was I being unfair to Joel? Did I dislike him only because he was Malcolm's son? – and had that detestable habit of muttering to himself incessant quotes from the Bible to take me back in time to our grandmother, and her insistence that we learn a quote each day from the holy book.

'Good night, Joel,' I said with more kindness than usual. Still, as he continued to stand there, as if to win me to his side, I thought of Bart, who had said many a painful thing to me when he was a boy, but not since he'd been an adult. Now he, too, was reading the Bible, using the words written in there to prove some moot point. Had Joel helped bring life back to what I thought was dormant? I stared at the old man, who edged away from me almost fearfully.

'Why do you look like that?' I asked sharply.

'Like what, Catherine?'

'Like you're afraid of me.'

His smile was thin, pitiful. 'You are a fearsome woman, Catherine. Despite all your blond prettiness, you can sometimes act as hard as my mother.'

I started, stunned that he could think that. I could not possibly be like that mean old woman.

'You also remind me of your mother,' he whispered in his thin, brittle voice, drawing his old bathrobe more tightly about his skinny frame. 'And you seem far too young to be in your fifties. My father used to say the wicked always managed to stay young and healthy longer than those who had a place waiting for them in Heaven.'

'If your father went on to Heaven, Joel, then I will gladly go in the opposite direction.'

He eyed me as if I were a pitiful object who just didn't understand before he ambled away.

Once I was back beside Chris, he woke up long enough for me to spill out the scene between Joel and me. Chris glared at me in the dimness. 'Catherine, how rude of you to talk to an old man like that. Of course you can't drive him out. In a way he has more right here than all of us, and it is Bart's home legally, even if we do have lifetime residency privileges.'

Anger filled me. 'Can't you recognize that Joel has become the father figure Bart has been looking for all his life?' And there I'd gone and hurt him. He stiffened and turned away from me.

'Good night, Catherine. Perhaps you should stay in bed and mind your own business for a rare change. Joel is a lonely old man who is grateful to have a champion like Bart and a place where he can live out the rest of his life. Stop imagining you see Malcolm in every old man you meet, for eventually, if I live long enough, I'll be another old man.'

'If you look and act like Joel, I'll be glad to see the end of you as well.'

Oh, how could I say that to the man I loved? He shifted farther away, then refused to respond to my touch on his arm. 'Chris, I'm sorry. I didn't mean that.' My hand caressed his arm, then moved to slip inside his pyjama jacket.

'I think it best if you keep your hands to yourself. I'm not in the mood now. Good night, Catherine, and remember, when you look for trouble, you usually find it.'

I heard a distant door close. My illuminated wristwatch read three-thirty. Drawing on a robe, I slipped into Melodie's room and sat down to wait. It was four before she managed the long trip from the garage to her bedroom. Did she and Bart stop to embrace and kiss? Did they whisper love words they couldn't save for tomorrow? What else could be taking her so long? Faint hints of dawn approaching showed over the rimming mountains. I paced the floor of her room, growing terribly impatient. Finally I heard her coming. Stumbling in the door of her room, Melodie held her high-heeled silver slippers in one hand, and in her other hand she held a small silver clutch.

She was six months pregnant, but in her loose-fitting black dress it was hardly noticeable. She jerked when she saw me rise from a chair, then choked as she backed away. 'Well, Melodie,' I said cynically, 'don't you look pretty.'

'Cathy, is Jory all right?'

'Do you really care?'

'You sound so angry with me. You look at me so hard – what have I done, Cathy?'

'As if you don't know,' I said to her with angry emphasis, forgetting the tact I'd intended to use. 'You slip out on a rainy night with my second son, and you come home hours later with red strawberry marks on your neck, with your lipstick smeared and your hair unbound, and still you ask, what . . . have . . . you . . . done. Why don't you tell me . . . what you have done.'

She stared at me with huge eyes of disbelief, half-blended with guilt, with shame, but there was some element of hope there as well. 'You've been like my mother, Cathy,' she cried, her eyes tearing as they pleaded for my understanding. 'Please don't fail me now – now when I need a mother more than I ever have before.'

'But you forget, I am Jory's mother first and foremost. I am also Bart's mother. When you betray Jory, you betray me.'

Melodie cried out again, pleading with me to listen to her.

'Don't turn away from me now, Cathy. I have no one but you who will understand. Certainly you of all people have to understand! I love Jory, I'll always love him – '

'And so you go to bed with Bart? What a fine way to show your love,' I interrupted. My voice sounded cold and hard.

Her face lowered into my lap as her arms wrapped around my waist. She clung to me. 'Cathy, please. Wait until you hear my side.' Her face lifted, already stained with tears, black tears because of her mascara. Somehow this served only to make her look more pitifully vulnerable. 'I'm part of the ballet world, Cathy, and you know what that means. We are the dancers who take music into our bodies and souls and make it visible for all to see, and for that we pay a price, a heavy price. You know the price. We dance with our souls bared for all to view and criticize if they will, and when the dance ends, and we hear the applause, and we accept the roses, and take the bows and the curtain calls, and hear the calls of *bravo*! *bravo*! finally we end up backstage to take off the makeup, to put on everyday mundane clothes, and then we know the best of what we are isn't real, only fantasy. We float on wings of sensuality so powerful nobody can realize as we do the pain of all that's so insensitive and cruel and brutal in reality.'

She hesitated to gain the strength to go on, while I sat stunned with her acuteness, for I knew the truth when I heard it – who would know better than I?

'Out there in the audience they think most of us are gay. They don't realize we're borne on the music, sustained by the music, made bigger than life by the sets, the applause, the adulation, and least of all do they realize that lovemaking is all that keeps us really nourished. Jory and I used to fall passionately into each other's arms the minute we were alone and only then could we find the release we needed to wind down enough to fall asleep. Now I have no release, nor does he. He won't listen to the music, and I can't turn it off.'

'But you have a lover,' I said weakly, fully understanding every word she'd said. Once, I, too, had flown on the joyous wings of music, and drifted downward, sick because there was no one to love me and lend reality to the fantasy world I loved best of all.

'Listen, Cathy, please. Give me a chance to explain. You know how boring it is in this house, with no one ever visiting, and the only time the phone rings it's Bart they want. You and Chris and Cindy were always in the hospital with Jory, while I was a coward and hung back, scared, so scared he'd see my fright. I tried to read, tried to entertain myself with knitting like you do, but I couldn't do it. I gave up and waited for the telephone to ring. Nobody from New York ever calls me. I took walks, pulled weeds from the garden. Cried in the woods, stared at the sky, watched the butterflies, and cried some more.

'Several nights after we found out that Jory would never walk or dance again, Bart came to my room. He closed the door behind him and just stood there looking at me. I was on the bed, crying as usual. I had ballet music playing, trying to recreate the feeling of how it had been with Jory, and Bart was there, staring at me with those dark, mesmerizing eyes. He stood waiting, just looking at me, until I stopped crying and he came closer to wipe the tears from my face. His eyes turned soft with love when I sat up and just stared at him. I'd never seen his eyes so kind, so full of tenderness and compassion. He touched me. My cheek, my hair, my lips. Shivers began to race up and down my spine. He put his hands in my hair, stared into my eyes, and slowly, ever so slowly he inclined his head until his lips brushed over mine. I'd never guessed he could be so gentle. I'd always presumed he'd take a woman by brutal force. Maybe if he had touched me with rough, uncaring hands I would have turned away. But his gentleness was my undoing. He reminded me of Jory.'

Oh, I didn't want to hear any more. I had to stop her before I felt pity and sympathy for her, for Bart.

'I don't want to hear anymore, Melodie,' I said coldly, jerking my head so I didn't have to look at the love marks that Jory might notice if she went to him now. 'So now when Jory needs you most, you intend to fail him and turn to Bart,' I said bitterly. 'What a wonderful wife you are, Melodie.'

She sobbed louder, covering her face with her hands.

'I remember your wedding day when you stood before the altar and made your vows of fidelity, for better or for worse – and the first worse that turns up, you find a new lover.'

While she sniffled and tried to find better words to win me to her side, I thought of how lonely this mountainside home was, how isolated. And we'd left Melodie here thinking she was too upset to want to drive anywhere. Thoughtless about what she and Bart could be doing, never suspecting she'd turn to him – the very one she'd seemed to dislike so much.

Still sniffling and crying, Melodie fiddled with her strap, while her washed-out eyes took on a certain wariness. 'How can you condemn me, Cathy, when you have done even worse?'

Stung, I rose to leave, feeling that my legs had turned to lead along with my heart. She was right. I wasn't any better. I, too, had failed, and more than once, to do the right thing. 'Will you forget Bart and stay away from him, and convince Jory you still love him?'

'I do still love Jory, Cathy. It may sound strange, but I love Bart in a different way, a strange way that has nothing at all to do with the way I feel about Jory. Jory was my childhood sweetheart and my best friend. His younger brother was someone I never really liked, but he's changed, Cathy, he has, really. No man who really hates women can make love as he does . . .'

My lips tightened. I stood in the open doorway condemning her, as once my grandmother had condemned me with her pitiless steel-grey eyes alone telling me I was the worst kind of sinner.

'Don't go before I make you understand!' she cried, putting forth her arms and beseeching me. I closed the door, thinking of Joel, and backed against it. 'All right. I'll stay, but I won't understand.'

'Bart loves me, Cathy, really loves me. When he says it, I can't help but believe him. He wants me to divorce Jory. Bart has said he will marry me.' Her tearful voice diminished to a husky whisper. 'I don't truthfully know if I can live out my life with a husband confined to a wheelchair.'

Sobbing more than before, she broke and from her kneeling position fell in a crumpled heap on the floor. 'I'm not strong like you are, Cathy. I can't give Jory the support he needs now. I don't know what to say, or what to do for him. I want to turn back the clock and bring back the Jory I used to have, for I don't know this one. I don't even think I want to know him . . . and I'm ashamed, so ashamed! Now all I want to do is vanish.'

My voice took on the steely edge of a razor. 'You're not going to escape your responsibilities that easily, Melodie. I'm here to see that you live up to your marriage vows. First, you will cut Bart out of your life. You will never allow him to touch you again. You will say no every time he tries anything. I am going to confront him again. Yes, I've already faced him down, but I'm going to be tougher. If I have to, I will go to Chris and tell him what's going on. As you know, Chris is a very patient, understanding man with a great deal of control, but he won't condone what you're doing with Bart.'

'Please,' she cried. 'I love Chris like a father! I want him to keep on respecting me.'

'*Then leave Bart alone*! Think of your child, which should come first. You shouldn't be having sex now anyway, it's sometimes not safe.'

Her huge eyes closed, squeezed back the tears; then she was nodding and promising never to make love with Bart again. Even as she vowed, I didn't believe her. I didn't believe Bart either when I spoke to him before I went to bed.

Morning came and I hadn't slept at all. I rose, tired and listless, putting on a false smile for Jory before I tapped on his door, announcing myself. He invited me to come in. He appeared happier than he had last night for some reason, as if overnight thought had calmed him down. 'I'm glad Melodie has you to lean on,' said Jory as I helped him to turn over.

Each day Chris, the nurse and took turns moving his legs and massaging them when the therapist wasn't there to do it for him. This way his muscles wouldn't atrophy. His legs, due to the massaging, had regained a little of their former shape.

I took that as a huge step forward. Hope . . . in this house of dark misery we were always clinging to hope we coloured yellow – like the sun we'd seldom seen.

'I was expecting Melodie to come in this morning,' Jory said with a bit of wistfulness, 'since she failed to even stop by and say good night last night.'

Days passed. Melodie disappeared often, as did Bart. My faith in Melodie had eroded. No longer could I meet her eyes and smile. I stopped trying to talk to Bart and turned to Jory for companionship. We watched TV together. We played games together. We competed in silly jigsaw competitions to see who could find the right pieces faster. We sipped wine in the afternoon, grew sleepy by nine and pretended, pretended that everything would work out fine.

There was something about being in bed most of the time that made him exceptionally fatigued. 'It's the lack of proper exercise,' he said, pulling on the trapeze fastened to his headboard. 'At least I'm keeping my arms strong – where did you say Melodie was?'

I put down the bootee I'd just finished and picked up the

yarn to make another. In between games I knitted and watched TV. When I wasn't with Jory, I was in my room typing the journal I was keeping of our lives. My last book, I told myself. What more did I have to say? What else could happen to us?

'Mom! Don't you ever listen to me? I asked if you knew where Melodie was, and what she's doing.'

'She's in the kitchen, Jory,' I said quickly. 'Busy preparing just the kind of dinner you like most.'

A look of relief brightened his face. 'I'm worried about my wife, Mom. She comes in and does small things for me, but her heart doesn't seem in it.' A shadow fleeted through his eyes, quick to disappear when he saw my piercing look. 'I say to you all the things I need to say to her. It hurts to watch her pulling away from me bit by bit. I want to speak out and say I'm still the same man inside, but I don't think she wants to know that. I believe she wants to think that I'm different because I can no longer dance or walk, and that makes it easier for her to break away and release all the ties that bind us. She never talks to me about the future. She hasn't even discussed names for our child. I've been looking in books for just the right names for our son or daughter. I tell myself, like you said, that she's pregnant, and I've been reading up on that subject, too. Just to make up for my former lack of interest . . .'

On and on he talked, convincing himself with his own words that it was her pregnancy that was responsible for all the changes in his wife.

I cleared my throat and used my chance. 'Jory, I've been giving this serious thought. Your doctor said once you'd be better off in the hospital than staying here and having someone come to help with your rehabilitation. You and Melodie can rent a small apartment near the hospital, and she can drive you each day to Rehab. It's almost winter, Jory. You don't know about winters in this western mountainous part of Virginia. They're freezing. The wind never stops blowing. It snows often. The roads leading here from the village are often blocked. The state keeps the highways and expressways open, but the small private roads to this estate are often closed. I'm thinking of the days when your nurse won't be able to come, or your physical therapist, and you need daily exercise. If you live near the hospital, all your physical needs can easily be met.'

He stared at me in hurt surprise. 'You mean you want to get rid of me?'

'Of course not. You've got to confess you don't like this house.'

His eyes darted to the windows where the rain was coming down hard, driving dead leaves and late-blooming roses into the earth. All the summer birds had flown away.

The wind whipped around the house, finding its way through small crevices, shrieking and howling in this replica just as much as it had in the old, old original.

Jory said from behind me, as I just continued staring out, 'I like what you and Mel did to these rooms. You've given me a haven safe from the scorn of the world, and right now, I don't want to leave and face those who used to admire my grace and skill. I don't want to be separated from you and Dad. I feel we've grown closer than we've ever been, and the holidays are coming up.

'And if the roads from here to there might be closed for my nurse and my therapist, they'll also be closed for you and Dad. Don't put me out, Mom, when I most want to stay. I need you. I need Dad. I even need this chance to grow closer to my brother. I've been thinking a lot about Bart recently. Sometimes he comes and sits nearby, and we talk. I think, at last, we're beginning to be the kind of friends we were before your mother moved into that house next door, way back when he was nine . . .'

Uneasily I fidgeted, thinking of Bart's dual face, coming in to be his brother's friend and seducing his wife behind his back.

'If it's what you want, Jory, stay. But give it more thought. Chris and I could move to the city just to be with you and Melodie, and we can make things as comfortable for you there as they are here.'

'But you can't give me another brother at this late date, can you, Mom? Bart's the only brother I'm going to have.

Before I die, or he does, I want him to know I care what happens to him. I want to see him happy. I want him to have the kind of married life I share with Mel. Someday he's got to wake up to the fact that money can't buy everything, and most certainly, it can't buy love. Not the kind of love Mel and I have.'

He looked thoughtful, as I inwardly cried for him and his 'love'; then a blush rose up from the neck of his sports shirt covered with a red sweater that put colour in his wan cheeks. 'At least, I should add, the kind of marriage we used to have. It's not much of a marriage now, I'm sorry to admit. But that's not her fault.'

A week later I was alone in my room, furiously writing in the journal, when I heard the pounding of Chris's footfalls as he ran and burst in on me. 'Cathy,' he said excitedly, throwing off his topcoat, hurling it to a chair, 'I've got wonderful news! You know that experiment I was assisting with? There's been a breakthrough.' He pulled me up from the desk, shoved me into a chair before the roaring fire. He explained in minute detail all that he and other scientists were trying to accomplish. 'It means I'll be away from home five nights a week, now that winter's come. The snow isn't cleared until around noon, and that gives me so little in the lab. But don't look sad, I'll be here on weekends. But if you object, tell me honestly. My first duty is to you and our family.'

His excitement over this new project was so evident I couldn't dash his enthusiasm with my fears. He'd given so much to me, to Jory and Bart, and received so little appreciation. My arms went automatically around his neck. I scanned over his dear, familiar face. I saw faint etchings around his blue eyes that I hadn't noticed before. My fingers in his hair found silver that was coarser in texture than the gold. There were a few grey hairs in his eyebrows.

'If this is going to make you unhappy, I can always quit and forget about research, and devote all my time to my family. But I'll be very grateful if you give me this opportunity. I thought when I gave up my practice in California that I would never find anything to interest me more, but I was wrong. Perhaps this was meant to be – but, if necessary, I *can* give it up and stay here with my family.'

Give up medicine entirely? He'd centred the major portion of his life on the study of medicine. To feel useful gave added zest to his life. To keep him here just to please myself, doing nothing that would contribute to mankind at this crucial point when he felt vulnerable by being middle-aged, would destroy him.

'Cathy,' Chris said, interrupting my thoughts as he pulled on his heavy woollen coat again, 'are you all right? Why do you look so strange? So sad? I'll be back every Friday evening and won't leave until Monday morning. Explain to Jory everything I've told you. No, on second thoughts, I'll stop by his room and explain myself.'

'If it's what you want, then it's what you have to do. But we're going to miss you. I don't know how I can sleep without you beside me. You see, I talked to Jory, and he doesn't want to move to Charlottesville. I think he's grown to like his rooms very much. He's almost finished that clipper ship. And it would be a pity to deprive him of all the comforts he has here. And Christmas isn't too far away. Cindy will be coming home for Thanksgiving to stay until the New Year. Chris, promise to make real efforts to come home every Friday. Jory needs your strength as well as mine since Melodie fails him entirely.'

Oh, I'd said too much.

His eyes narrowed. 'What's going on that you're not telling me?' He pulled off the heavy coat and carefully hung it up. Swallowing first, I started to speak, faltered, tried to pull my eyes from the strong hold of his . . . but those blue eyes forced me to say, 'Chris, would you think it terrible if you knew that Bart has fallen in love with Melodie?'

His lips twitched. 'Oh, that. I know Bart's been infatuated with her since the day she came here. I've seen him watching her. One day I found the two of them in the back salon, seated on the sofa. He had her dress open and was kissing her breasts. I walked away. Cathy, if Melodie didn't want him, she'd slap his face and make him stop. You may think their affair is stealing Jory's wife when he needs her most, but he doesn't need a woman who doesn't love him anymore. Let him have her – what good can she do Jory now?'

I glared at him with total disbelief. 'You're defending Bart! Do you think it's fair what he's done?'

'No, I don't think it is fair. When is life fair, Cathy? Was it fair when Jory's back was broken, and now he can't walk? No, it's not fair. I've been in medicine too long not to know justice isn't doled out equally. The good often die before the bad. Children die before grandparents, and who is to say that's right? But what can we do about it? Life is a gift, and perhaps death is another kind of gift. Who am I, or you, to say? Accept what has happened between Bart and Melodie, and stay close to Jory. Keep him happy until the day comes when he can find another wife.'

Reeling from his words, I felt hazy and unreal. 'And the baby, what of the baby?'

Now his voice turned hard. 'The baby is another matter. He or she will belong to Jory, no matter which brother Melodie chooses. That child will help see Jory through – for he may never be able to sire another.'

'Chris, please. Go to Bart and tell him to let Melodie go. I cannot stand the thought of Jory losing his wife at this point in his life.'

He shook his head, telling me that Bart had never listened to him, and it wasn't likely he would now. And already he'd spoken without my knowledge to Melodie.

'Darling, face up to the facts. In her heart Melodie doesn't want Jory now. She won't come out and say that, but behind every word she doesn't say, behind all her excuses, is the plain fact that she just does not want to stay married to a man who can't walk. In my way of thinking it would be cruel to force her to stay, and even harder on Jory in the long run. If we do try to force her to stay, sooner or later she'd strike back at him for not being the man he was and I want to spare him that. Better to let her go before she hurts him even worse than by just having an affair with Bart.'

'Chris!' I cried, shocked that he would think as he did. 'We can't let her do this to Jory!'

'Cathy, who are we to judge this matter? Right or wrong, should we, who are considered sinners by Bart, sit in judgment on him?'

In the morning Chris drove away after telling me he'd be back Friday evening around six. I watched from my bedroom window until his car was out of sight.

How empty the days when Chris was away, how bleak the nights without his arms to hold me and his whispers to assure me everything would work out fine. I smiled and laughed for Jory, not wanting him to know that I was suffering from the lack of having Chris in my bed every night. Jory slept alone, I told myself, and I could manage if he could. I knew that Melodie and Bart were still lovers; however, they were discreet enough to try and hide that from me. But I knew from the way Joel glared at Jory's wife that he considered her a bitch. Strange that he didn't glare at Bart, when he was just as guilty. But then men had a way of thinking what was right for the gander was wrong for the goose, even pious religious ones like Joel.

We were two weeks into November, and our plans for Thanksgiving were complete. Our weather turned more severe and hurled blustery winds and snow our way, stacking snow around our doors, freezing it overnight to ice so we couldn't leave the garage in one of our many cars. One by one our servants deserted until there was only Trevor to prepare the meals with my off-and-on help.

Cindy flew home and helped cheer our hours with her easy laughter, her winning ways that charmed everyone but Bart and Joel. Even Melodie seemed a bit happier. Then she took to her bed, to stay there all day long, trying to keep warm now that our electricity went off so often, and that meant our furnaces controlled by electric thermostats refused to give out heat. We then had to resort to our coal furnace auxiliary.

Freely Bart carried in the wood he wanted to burn in his office fireplace and forgot the rest of us would enjoy a fire.

Bart was secreted away with Joel, whispering of the Christmas ball he planned, so I had to carry in enough logs to build a fire in Jory's room, where Cindy was playing a game with him. He sat in his chair, wrapped with an afghan, his shoulders covered with a jacket, and smiled at my futile attempts to set the kindling ablaze. 'Open the damper, Mom, that always helps a little.'

How had I forgotten that?

Soon I had a fire going. The bright glow cheered up the room, which seemed so right in summer but not so right in winter, just as Bart had predicted. Now the dark panelling would have made Jory feel cosier.

'Mom,' Jory said, suddenly looking very cheerful, 'I've been thinking about something for days. I'm a fool to act as I am. You're right – been right all along. I'm not going to feel sorry for myself the minute I'm alone and no one can see, as I've been doing since the accident. I am going to accept what can't be helped and make the most of a difficult situation. Just like you and Dad did when you were locked away, I'm going to turn my idle moments into creative moments. I'll have plenty of time to read all the books I've never had time to read before, and I'm going to say yes to Dad the next time he offers to teach me how to paint with watercolours. I'll go outdoors and try landscapes. Perhaps I'll even venture into oils, other mediums. I want to thank you both for giving me the incentive to go on. I'm a lucky guy to have parents like you and Dad.'

Feeling proud enough to cry myself, I embraced him, congratulating him for coming back to being his natural, enthusiastic self.

Cindy had set a bridge table for two, but Jory soon turned back to the clipper ship he was determined to finish before Christmas. He was stringing the threadlike cords to the rigging, which was the last step before the little touch-up painting here and there.

'I'm going to give this to someone very special, Mom,' he informed me. 'On Christmas day, one person in this house is going to have my first difficult piece of handicraft.'

'I bought it for you, Jory, to become an heirloom to pass

down to your children . . .' I blanched when I heard myself say 'children.'

'It's all right, Mom, for with this gift I am going to win back the younger brother who loved me before that old man came and changed him. He wants it badly; I see it in his eyes every time he comes in and checks to see my progress. Besides, I can always put together another one for my child. Right now I want to do something for Bart. He thinks none of us need him or like him. I've never seen a man as uncertain about himself . . . and that's such a pity.'

HOLIDAY JOYS

Thanksgiving Day came, and with it arrived Chris early in the morning. Jory's nurse ate Thanksgiving dinner with us, keeping his lovesick eyes glued on Cindy as if she had him under a spell. She couldn't have behaved more like a lady, making me tremendously proud of her. The next day she eagerly accepted our invitation to go shopping in Richmond. Melodie shook her head. 'Sorry, I just don't feel up to it.'

Chris, Cindy and I drove off with a clear conscience, knowing Bart had flown to New York and wouldn't be with Melodie. Jory's nurse had promised to stay with Jory until we returned.

Our three-day holiday in Richmond refreshed our minds and souls, gave me the sense of being still beautiful and very much in love, and Cindy had the time of her life spending, and spending, and spending some more. 'You see,' she said proudly, 'I don't waste all the allowance you send me on myself. I save to buy wonderful gifts for my family . . . and Momma, Daddy, you just wait until you see what I bought for you both. And I certainly hope Jory likes his gift. As for Bart, he can take what I give and like it or not.'

'What about your Uncle Joel?' I asked with curiosity.

Laughing, she hugged me. 'Wait until you see.'

Hours later Chris turned on to the private road that would wend its crooked way up to Foxworth Hall. In one of the boxes that filled our trunk and rear seat of the car, I had an expensive dress to wear to the Christmas ball I'd overheard Bart arranging with the same caterers who'd taken care of his birthday party. In her own huge box, Cindy had chosen a spectacular dress, daring but at the same time wonderfully appropriate. 'Thank you, Mom, for not objecting,' she'd whispered before she kissed me.

Nothing unusual had occurred during our absence, except Jory had finally completed the clipper ship. It stood proud and exquisitely finished down to the last detail, its tiny brass helm gleaming, its sails full and bulging with invisible and unfelt high winds. 'Sugar stiffening,' revealed Jory with a small laugh, 'and it worked. I took the sails and shaped them around a bottle like the instructions read, and now our maiden voyage is well under way.' He was proud of his work, smiling as Chris stepped over to admire his meticulous craftmanship more closely. Then we had to help him lift the ship into a styrofoam form-fitting mould that would hold it securely until it reached the hands of the new owner.

His beautiful eyes turned to me. 'Thanks for giving me something to do during all these long, boring hours, Mom. When I first saw it I was overwhelmed, thinking I'd never be able to do something that appeared so difficult. But I took one step at a time, and now I feel I won over those hideously complicated directions.'

'That's the way all life's battles are won, Jory,' said Chris as I hugged Jory close. 'You don't look at the overall picture. You take one step, then another, and another . . . until you arrive at your destination. And I must say, you did a magnificent job on this ship. It's as professionally made as any I've seen. If Bart doesn't appreciate all the effort you put into this, he'll really disappoint me.'

Standing, Chris beamed at Jory. 'You're looking healthier, stronger. And don't give up on the watercolour. It is a difficult medium, but I thought you would enjoy it more than oils. I think one day you are going to be a fine artist.'

Downstairs, Bart was on the phone directing a bank official to take over a failing business. Then he was talking to someone else about the Christmas party he was planning, a ball to make up for the tragedy of his birthday party. I stood in his open doorway thinking it was a good thing that all he ordered did not come from his personal fund but from the Corrine Foxworth Winslow Trust, which left Bart his annual five hundred thousand as 'pin' money to spend only on himself. It more than irked Bart to be forced to confer with Chris each time he spent over the named figure of ten thousand.

Bart slammed down the receiver, glared at me. 'Mother, do you have to stand in the doorway and eavesdrop? Haven't I told you before to stay away from me when I'm busy?'

'When do I see you if I don't do this?'

'Why do you need to see me?'

'Why does any mother need to see her son?'

His dark eyes softened. 'You've got Jory – and he always seemed more than sufficient.'

'No, you're wrong there. If I had never had you, Jory would have been sufficient. But I did have you, and that makes you a vital part of my life.'

Uncertain looking, he stood up and strode to a window, keeping his back towards me. His voice came to me deep and gruff, with a melancholy sadness. 'Remember when I used to keep Malcolm's journal stuffed inside my shirt? Malcolm wrote so much about his mother, and how much he loved her until she ran off with her lover and left him alone with a father he didn't like. Some of Malcolm's hate for her rubbed off on me, I'm afraid. Each time I see you and Chris head up those stairs together, I feel the need to cleanse myself from the shame I feel and you two don't. So don't you start lecturing to me about Melodie, for what I do with her is far less sinful than what you do with Chris.'

He was no doubt right, and that's what hurt worse than anything.

More or less I grew unhappily accustomed to seeing Chris only on the weekends, although my heart ached and my bed felt huge and lonely without him, and all my mornings alone were wistful, wishing I could hear him whistling as he shaved and showered, missing his cheerfulness, his optimism. When the weather kept him away on the weekends, even then, I grew used to that. How adaptable we humans were, how willing to suffer through any horror, any adjustment, any deprivations, just to gain those few minutes of priceless joy.

To stand at the window and watch Chris drive up filled me with surprising youthful excitement so overwhelming it was as if I were waiting for Bart's father to steal away from Foxworth Hall and meet me in the cottage. Certainly I didn't act as placidly accepting as when I'd seen him every night, every morning. The weekends were something to be anticipated and dreamed about. However, Chris was both more and less to me – more a lover and less a husband. I missed the brother who'd been my other half, and loved the lover-husband who didn't remind me as much of the brother I'd known.

There was no way and there were no words that could separate the two of us now that I'd accepted him and taken him as my husband, defying all scorn and society's moral rules.

Still, my unconscious was trying peculiar tricks to give my conscious relief. With determination I was separating Chris the man from Chris the boy who'd been my brother. An unconscious, unplanned game we both began to play with some finesse. We didn't discuss it, we didn't have to. No longer did Chris call me 'my lady Cath-er-ine'. No more did he say teasingly, 'Don't let the bedbugs bite.' All the charms and enchantments of those yesterdays when we were locked up, meant to keep away evil spirits, we let go, at last, in the middle years of our contentment.

He came home late one Friday night in December, stomping his feet in the foyer as I lingered in the shadows of the rotunda watching him take off his topcoat and hang it neatly in the guest closet before he raced up the stairs two at a time, calling my name. I stepped out of the shadows and threw myself into his eager arms. 'You're late again!' I cried. 'Who do you see in your lab that sends shivers up and down your spine?'

No one! No one! his passionate kisses assured.

The weekends were so short, so dreadfully short.

I was spilling out all that troubled me, about Joel and his weird ways of roaming about the house, scowling his disapproval at everything I did. I told him about Melodie and Bart, and Jory, who was depressed and yearning for

Melodie, hating her indifference, loving her even so, while I was trying constantly to remind Melodie of her responsibilities, which hurt him even more grievously than the loss of the use of his legs.

Chris lay beside me and listened to my long tirade with quiet impatience before he said sleepily and bit out of patience, 'Catherine, sometimes you make me dread coming home.' He rolled on his side away from me. 'You spoil everything wonderful and sweet we have between us with your incessant, unpleasant, suspicious tales. And most of all that troubles you is in your imagination. Haven't you always had too much of it? Grow up, Catherine. You are contaminating Jory with your suspicions as well. Once you learn to expect only good from people, then perhaps that's all you'll get.'

'I've heard your philosophy before, Christopher,' I said with a flash of bitterness that shot through my brain like a laser beam, bringing to mind his faith in our mother, and the good he'd expected from her by his devotion. *Chris, Chris, don't YOU ever learn?* But I didn't say it, didn't dare to say it.

There he was, middle-aged, even if he didn't look it, presenting me with his same old rosy-glow boyish optimism. Though I could ridicule him verbally for this, inside I longed for his kind of redeeming faith . . . for it gave him peace, while I lived day in and day out, juggling from one foot to another on a hot frying pan.

Bart sat before the roaring fire, trying to concentrate on *The Wall Street Journal* as Jory and I wrapped Christmas gifts on a long table we'd cleared of all accessories. All of a sudden it occurred to me as I tied fancy bows and cut foil paper to size that since Cindy had arrived, she'd drifted dreamlike throughout the house, lost in her own world, so that she seemed almost not there. Because of the peace this brought, I had more or less forgotten her needs as I attended to Jory's. I hadn't been surprised when she wanted to go with Chris into Charlottesville to finish up her shopping and see a movie before she came back with him on Friday. Chris had a one-bedroom apartment and planned to sleep Cindy on his sofa bed.

'Really, Momma, my special Christmas surprise will please you.' Only when she was gone did I wonder what put that secret smile of pleasure on her pretty face.

As Jory and I topped off all his presents with huge satin bows and name tags, I heard the banging of car doors, the stomping feet on the portico, and then the sound of Chris calling out. It was only about two in the afternoon as he strolled into our favourite salon with Cindy at his side – and, to my amazement, a strikingly handsome boy about eighteen was with them. I already knew Cindy considered any boy less than two years older too young for her. The older and more experienced the better was the way she liked to tease me.

'Mom,' said Cindy happily, her face radiant, 'here is the surprise you said I could bring home.'

Startled, I still managed a smile. Cindy had not once said her 'secret' surprise was a guest she'd invited without asking anyone's permission. I stood so Chris could introduce the boyfriend Cindy had met in South Carolina as Lance Spalding. The young man had considerable poise as he shook hands with me, with Jory, with Bart, who glowered.

Chris kissed my cheek and briefly embraced Jory before he hurried towards the door. 'Cathy, forgive me for leaving so soon, but I'll be back tomorrow early. Cindy couldn't wait until tomorrow to bring her houseguest home. I've got a few things to wrap up at the university. And I haven't finished my shopping.' He flashed me a brilliant smile full of charm. 'Darling, I've got two weeks off for the holidays. So take it easy and keep your imagination under lock and key.' He turned to Lance. 'Enjoy your holiday, Lance.'

Cindy, very full of herself, pulled her boyfriend closer to the very one who was least likely to be hospitable to her guest. 'Bart, I knew you wouldn't mind if I invited Lance. His father is president of the chain of Chemical Banks of Virginia.'

Magic words. I smiled at Cindy's cleverness. Instantly Bart's hostile attitude changed into interest. It was embarrassing to see the way he tried to milk every bit of information he could from the young man, who was obviously very much infatuated with Cindy.

Cindy was lovelier than ever, glowing like a winter rose in her tight white sweater banded with strips of rose to match her tight knit pants. She had a wonderful figure she was determined to display.

Laughing and full of joy, she caught hold of Lance's hand and tugged him away from Bart. 'Lance, you just wait until you see all of this house. We have authentic suits of armour – two of them – and they would be too small for me to wear. Momma, maybe, but not me. And just think, knights were supposed to be big, powerful men, and they weren't big. The music room is larger than this room, and my room is the prettiest room of all. The suite my parents share is incredible. I've not been invited to view Bart's rooms, but I'm sure they must be fabulous.' Here she half turned to toss Bart a wicked, teasing smile. His scowl deepened.

'Stay out of my rooms!' he ordered harshly. 'Don't go near my office. And Lance, while you are here, you will remember you are under my roof and I expect you to treat Cindy with honour.'

The boy's face turned red before he meekly said, 'Of course. I understand.'

The second the two of them were out of sight, though we could still hear Cindy singing the praises of Foxworth Hall, Bart hurled at me his opinion of Cindy's boyfriend. 'I don't like him. He's too old for her and too slick. She or you should have told me. You know I don't want unexpected guests just dropping in.'

'Bart, I agree with you entirely. Cindy should have warned us, but perhaps she was fearful that if she did, you would say no. And he seems a very nice young man to me. Remember how sweet Cindy has been since Thanksgiving. She hasn't given you one second of trouble. She's growing up.'

'Let's hope she continues to behave herself,' he grumbled before he smiled faintly. 'Did you see him looking at her? She's got that poor kid snowed under.'

Relieved, I settled back to smile at Bart, then at Jory, who was fiddling with the Christmas lights before he began to quietly arrange his gifts beneath the tree.

'The Foxworths had a tradition for always throwing a Christmas ball on Christmas night,' said Bart in a pleasant tone, 'and Uncle Joel himself drove to mail my invitations two weeks ago. I'm expecting at least two hundred if the weather remains fairly decent. Even if a blizzard blows in, I still think half will manage to get here. After all, they can't afford to slight me when I give them so much business. Bankers, attorneys, brokers, doctors, businessmen and their wives and girlfriends, as well as the best of the local society. And a few of my fraternity brothers will be showing up. So for once, Mother, you shouldn't complain that our lives are lonely in this isolated area.'

Jory went back to reading his book, seemingly determined not to let anything Bart said or did upset him. In the firelight his profile was classically perfect. His dark hair curled softly around his face, turning up at the collar of his knit sports shirt. Bart lounged in a business suit, as if at any moment he'd be up and away to attend a corporation meeting. That's when Melodie drifted in wearing a shapeless grey garment that hung from her shoulders and bulged out as if she had a watermelon beneath it. Her eyes went immediately to Bart, who jumped up, turned his eyes away and hastily he left the room, leaving behind him an uncomfortable silence.

'I met Cindy upstairs,' said Melodie huskily, her forlorn eyes avoiding contact with Jory's. She sat down near the fire and stretched forth her hands to warm them. 'Her boyfriend seems very pleasant and well bred, and also very handsome.' She kept her eyes on the fire while Jory diligently tried to force her to look at him. His heart was in his eyes as he wistfully gave up and turned back to his book. 'It seems Cindy likes dark-haired men who look like her brothers,' she went on in a vague, distant way, as if nothing mattered and she was only making an effort, for a change.

Angrily Jory jerked his eyes up. 'Mel, can't you even say hello to me?' he asked hoarsely. 'I'm here, I'm alive. I'm doing my best to survive. Can't you say or do something to tell me you remember that I'm your husband?'

Reluctantly turning her head his way, Melodie gave him a vague smile of recognition. Something in her eyes said she didn't see him anymore as the husband she'd so passionately loved and admired. She saw only a crippled man in a wheelchair and as he was now, he made her uneasy and embarrassed.

'Hello, Jory,' she said dutifully.

Why didn't she get up and kiss him? Why didn't she see the pleading in his eyes? Why couldn't she make an effort, even if she didn't love him anymore? Slowly Jory's wan face reddened before he bowed his head and stared down at all the gifts he'd so beautifully wrapped.

I was about to say something cruel to Melodie when Cindy and Lance came strolling back, both with starry eyes and flushed faces. Bart wasn't long in following them in. He raked the room with his eyes, saw that Melodie was still there and turned to leave again. Instantly Melodie rose and quickly disappeared. Bart must have seen her leave, for shortly he returned and sat down and crossed his legs, looking relieved now that Melodie was gone.

The boy-friend spoke up, looking at Bart and smiling widely. 'I hear all this belongs to you, Mr Foxworth.'

'Call him Bart,' ordered Cindy.

Bart frowned.

'Bart . . .' began Lance hesitatingly, 'truly this is a remarkable house. Thank you for inviting me.' I glanced at Cindy, who stood her ground as Bart threw her an angry look, even as Lance went on innocently, 'Cindy didn't show me your suite of rooms, or your office, but I hope you will do that. Someday I hope to own something like this . . . and I have a passion for electronic gadgets, as Cindy tells me you have.'

Instantly Bart was on his feet, seemingly proud to show off his electronic equipment. 'Sure, if you want to see my rooms, and my office, I'll be delighted to show you. But I'd rather Cindy didn't accompany us.'

After a sumptuous dinner, which Trevor served, we conversed in the music room with Jory and Bart. Melodie was upstairs, already in bed. Soon Bart said he had to rise early and he was going to bed. Instantly the conversation dwindled to nothing as we all stood and headed for the stairs. I showed Lance into a lovely room with its own connecting bath. It was in the eastern wing, not so far from Bart's own rooms, while Cindy's was near my own. Cindy smiled sweetly and kissed the cheek of Lance Spalding. 'Good night, sweet prince,' she whispered. 'Parting is such sweet-sweet sorrow.'

His arms folded over his chest, as Joel folded his, Bart stood back and watched this tender scene with scorn. 'Let it be a true parting,' he said meaningfully, looking directly at Lance, then at Cindy, before he stalked off towards his rooms.

First I saw Cindy to her room and we exchanged a few words and our regular good night kisses. Then I paused outside Melodie's door, wondering if I should rap and go in and try to reason with her. I sighed, knowing it wouldn't do any good, not when I'd tried so many times before. Next I was crossing over to Jory's room.

He lay on his bed, staring up at the ceiling. His dark blue eyes rolled my way, shiny with unshed tears. 'It's been so long since Melodie came in to kiss me good night. You and Cindy always find the time to do that, but my wife ignores me as if I don't exist for her. There's no real reason now why I couldn't sleep in a larger bed, and she could sleep beside me, but she wouldn't even if I asked. Now I've finished the clipper ship, and I don't know what to begin next to occupy my time. I really don't want to start another ship for our child. I feel so unfulfilled, so at odds with life, with myself, and most of all, with my wife. I want to turn to my wife, but she turns from me. Mom . . . without you, Dad and Cindy, I wouldn't know how to live through the days.'

I held him in my arms, ran my fingers through his hair as I had when he was a little boy. I said all the things that should have come from Melodie. I pitied her, disliked her for being weak, hated her for not loving enough, for not knowing how to give even when it hurt.

'Good night, my sweet prince,' I said from Jory's doorway. 'Hold tight to your dreams, don't abandon them now, for life offers many chances at happiness, Jory. It's not all over for you.'

He smiled, said good night, and I headed for the southern-wing suite I shared with Chris.

All of a sudden Joel was in front of me, blocking my passage. He wore a shabby old bathrobe of some faded colour that seemed more grey than anything else. His thin, pale hair stood up in small peaks like horns, while the long end of his corded sash trailed behind him like a limp tail.

'Catherine,' he said sharply, 'do you realize what that girl is doing this very minute?'

'That girl? What girl?' I answered just as sharply.

'You know who I mean, that daughter of yours. Right now, at this moment, she is entertaining that young man she brought home with her.'

'Entertaining? What do you mean?'

His smile came crooked and mean. 'Why, if anyone should know, it should be you. She's got that boy in her bed.'

'I don't believe you!'

'Then go and see for yourself!' he answered quickly, with some delight. 'You never believe anything I say. I was in the back hall and just happened to see this boy stealing down the halls, and I followed. Before he reached Cindy's door, she had it open and was welcoming him inside.'

'I don't believe you,' I said again, more weakly this time.

'Are you afraid to check and find out I might be telling the truth? Would that convince you then that I am not the enemy you presume me to be?'

I didn't know what to say or think. Cindy had promised to behave herself. She was innocent, I knew she was. She'd been so perfect, helping with Jory, resisting her natural tendency to argue with Bart. Joel had to be lying. Spinning about, I headed towards Cindy's room with Joel close at my heels.

'You are lying about her, Joel, and I intend to prove that to you,' I said as I almost ran.

Just outside her door I paused and listened, hearing nothing at all. I lifted my hand to knock. 'No!' hissed Joel. 'Don't give them any warning if you want to know the full truth. Just throw open the door and step inside the room and see for yourself.'

I paused, not wanting to even think he could possibly be right. And I didn't want Joel to tell me what to do. I glared at him before I knocked sharply just once, waited a few seconds, then threw open Cindy's bedroom door and stepped inside her room, which was lit my moonlight flooding in through her windows.

Two totally naked bodies were entwined on Cindy's virgin bed!

I stared, shocked, feeling a scream in my throat that just stayed there. Before my amazed eyes Lance Spalding sprawled over my sixteen-year-old daughter, jerking spasmodically. Cindy's hands clutched at his buttocks, her long red fingernails digging in, her head rolling from side to side as she moaned with pleasure, telling me this was not their first time.

What should I do now? Close the door and say nothing? Fly into a towering rage and drive Lance out of our home? Helplessly caught in a web of indecision I stood there as only seconds must have passed, until I heard a faint noise behind me.

Another gasped. I whirled around to see Bart, who was staring at Cindy, who'd rolled on top of Lance and was lustily riding him, crying out four-letter word vulgarities in between her moans of ecstasy, entirely unaware of anything but what she was doing and what was being done to her.

Bart had no indecision.

He strode directly to the bed and caught hold of Cindy around the waist. With a mighty heave he tore her off the boy, who seemed helpless in his nakedness and the bliss of what had been going on. Bart ruthlessly hurled Cindy to the floor. She screamed as she fell face downward on the carpet.

Bart didn't hear.

He was too busy handling the youth. Again and again his fists slammed into Lance's handsome face. I heard the crack of his nose as blood spurted everywhere. 'Not under my roof!' he roared, repeatedly battering Lance's face. 'No sinning under my roof!'

A moment ago I felt like doing the same thing. Now I ran to save the boy. 'Bart, stop! You'll kill him!'

Cindy kept screaming hysterically even as she tried to cover her nudity with the clothes she'd dropped on the floor. They were all mixed up with Lance's discarded garments. Joel was now in the room, raking his eyes scornfully over Cindy; then he was turning to smile at me with gloating satisfaction that said over and over again: *See, I told you so. Like mother, like daughter.*

'See what you've raised with your pampering?' Joel intoned, as if behind a pulpit. 'It was evident from the first time I saw her that that girl was nothing but a harlot under the roof of my father's house.'

'You fool!' I stormed. 'Who are you to condemn anyone?'

'You are the fool, Catherine. Just like your mother, in more than one way. She, too, wanted every man she saw, even her own half-uncle. She was like this naked girl crawling lewdly around on the floor – ready to bed down with anything in pants.'

Unexpectedly Bart dropped Lance on the bed and hurled himself at Joel. 'Stop it! Don't you dare tell my mother she's like her mother! She isn't, she isn't!'

'You'll see it my way eventually, Bart,' said Joel in his softest, most sanctimonious tone. 'Corrine got what she deserved. Just as your mother will get hers one day. And if justice and right still rule in this world, and God is in his Heaven, that indecent, naked girl on the floor trying to cover herself will meet her end in fiery flames, as she deserves.'

'Don't you say anything like that again!' bellowed Bart, so furious with Joel he forgot all about Cindy and Lance, who were both hastily pulling on the nightclothes they'd abandoned. He hesitated, as if shocked to find himself defending the girl he incessantly denied was his sister. 'This is my life, Uncle,' he said sternly, 'and my family more than it is yours. I will deal out what justice is demanded, and not you.'

Seemingly very distressed and shaken, shuffling lamely like an old man, Joel ambled off down the hall, bent over almost double.

The moment Joel was out of sight, Bart turned his furious temper on me. 'YOU SEE!' he roared. 'Cindy has just proven what I suspected she was all along! She's no good, Mother! NO GOOD! All the time she played the game of being sweet, she was planning how she'd enjoy herself when Lance came. I want her out of this house and out of my life forever!'

'Bart, you can't send Cindy away – she's my daughter! If you have to punish someone more than you have, send Lance away. You're right, of course, Cindy shouldn't have done what she did, nor should Lance have taken advantage of our hospitality.'

Somewhat mollified, he managed to simmer down a little. 'All right, Cindy can stay since you insist on loving her no matter what. But that boy is going tonight!' He yelled at Lance, 'Hurry and pack your things – for in five minutes I'm driving you to the airport. If you ever dare touch Cindy again, I'll break the rest of your bones! And don't think I won't know. I have friends in South Carolina, too!'

Lance Spalding was very pale as he hurried to throw his clothes back into suitcases he'd just emptied. He couldn't even look at me as he hurried by and whispered huskily, 'I'm sorry and so ashamed, Mrs Sheffield . . .' and then he was gone, with Bart right behind him, shoving him on faster from time to time.

Now I turned to Cindy, who had donned a very modest granny gown and was huddled under the covers of her bed, staring at me wide-eyed and scared looking. 'I hope you are satisfied, Cindy,' I said coldly. 'You have truly disappointed me. I expected more from you . . . you promised me. Don't your promises mean anything at all?'

'Momma, please,' she sobbed. 'I love him, and I wanted him, and I think I waited long enough. It was my Christmas gift to him – and to myself.'

'Don't lie to me, Cynthia! Tonight wasn't your first time with him. I'm not as stupid as you presume I am. You and Lance have been lovers before.'

She wailed loudly, 'Momma, aren't you going to love me anymore? You can't just turn it off, 'cause if you do, then I'll want to die! I don't have any parents but you and Daddy . . . and I swear it won't happen again. Please forgive me, please!'

'I'll think about it,' I said coldly as I closed her door.

The next morning as I dressed, Cindy came running into my room, crying out hysterically, 'Momma, please don't let Bart force me to leave, too. I've never had a happy Christmas when Bart was around. I hate him! Really hate him! He's ruined Lance's face, ruined it.'

More than likely she was right. I had to teach Bart how to hold back his rage. How terrible for such a good-looking boy to have his beautiful nose broken, to say nothing of his black eyes and many cuts and bruises.

However, after Lance was gone, something peculiar laid a ghostly hand on Bart and turned him very quiet. Lines I hadn't seen before etched from his nose to his beautifully shaped lips, and he was too young for face lines. He refused to look or talk to Cindy. He treated me as if I weren't there, either. He sat sullen and quiet, staring at me, then rested his dark eyes fleetingly on Cindy, who was weeping, and I couldn't remember another time when Cindy had allowed any of us to see her cry.

Through my mind flitted all kinds of dreary thoughts. The place where owls and foxes resided, remembering the Bible we used to have to study every day. Where could understanding be found? There was a time for planting, a time for reaping, a time to gather in . . . where was our time for joy?

Hadn't we waited long enough?

Later that morning I had a talk with Cindy. 'Cindy, I am shocked at your behaviour. Bart had every right to be enraged, even though I disapprove of the way he was so rough on that boy. I can understand *his* actions, but not yours. Any young man would have entered your room when you willingly opened your door and invited him in. Cindy, you have to promise not to do anything like that again. Once you are eighteen, you become your own boss – but until that day, and while you are under this roof, you will not play sex games with anyone here or anywhere else. Do you understand?'

Her blue eyes widened, took on the shine of forthcoming tears. 'Momma, I don't live in the eighteenth century! All the girls are doing it! I held out much longer than most do, and from all I've heard about you . . . you went after men, too.'

'Cindy!' I snapped sharply. 'Don't you ever throw my past or present in my face! You don't know what I had to endure – while you have had nothing but happy days full of everything that was denied me.'

'Happy days?' she asked bitterly. 'Have you forgotten all the nasty, mean things Bart did to me? Maybe I wasn't locked up, starved or beaten, but I've had my problems, and don't think I haven't. Bart makes me feel so unsure about my femininity that I have to test all the boys I meet . . . I just can't help it.'

We were at that time in her bedroom, while Bart was downstairs.

I stepped foward to take Cindy into my arms. 'Don't cry, darling. I do understand how you must feel. But you must try to understand how parents feel about their daughters. Your father and I want only the best for you. We don't want you to be hurt. Let this experience with Lance teach you a lesson, and hold back until you are eighteen and able to reason with more maturity. Hold out longer than that if you can. When you grab at sex too soon, it has a way of biting back and giving you exactly what you don't want. It did that to me, and I've heard you say a thousand times you want a stage and film career, and husbands and babies have to wait. Many a girl has been thwarted by a baby that started because of uncontrollable passion. Be careful before committing yourself to anyone. Don't fall in love too soon, for when you do you make yourself vulnerable to so many unforeseen events. Give romance a try without sex, Cindy, and save yourself all the pain of giving too much too soon.'

Her arms were tight about me, her eyes turned soft and told me we were again mother and daughter.

Later Cindy and I stood side by side downstairs, watching everything whiten with snow, grow misty with distance, cruelly isolating us even more from the rest of the world. 'Now all roads from Charlottesville will be blocked,' I said tonelessly to Cindy. 'What's more, Melodie is acting so strangely she makes me fear for the good health of her child. Jory's staying in his room as if he doesn't want to encounter her, or any of us. Bart saunters around like he owns all of us as well as the house. Oh, I wish Chris were here. I hate it when he's gone.'

I turned to find Cindy staring at me with a kind of wonderment. She flushed when she met my eyes. When I asked why, she murmured, 'I just wonder sometimes how the two of you hang on to what you have, when I fall in and out of love so often. Momma, someday you've got to tell me how to make a man really love me, and not just my body. I wish boys would look first into my eyes like Daddy looks into yours; I wish they'd look at my face at least once in a while, for it's not an ugly face, but they all stare at my boobs. I wish their eyes would follow me around like Jory's follow Melodie . . .'

Cindy put her arm around me and buried her face against my shoulder. 'I'm so sorry, Momma, really so sorry I caused all that trouble last night. Thank you for not scolding me more than you did. I've been thinking about what you said, and you're right. Lance has paid a heavy price, and I should have known better.' Pleadingly she gazed into my eyes. 'Momma, I was serious, all the girls at school started way back when they were eleven, twelve and thirteen, and I love Lance. And I held back, although all the boys chased after me more than they did the others. The girls thought I was doing it when I wasn't. I pretended to be really with it, but then one day I heard some boys comparing notes and they were all saying they hadn't scored all the way with me. They talked as if I were some kind of freak –

or maybe a lesbian. That's when I decided I'd let Lance have his way this Christmas. The special gift I had for him.'

I stared at her hard, wondering if she told all the truth, as she went on to tell me she was the only girl in her group to hold out until sixteen, and that was really old for a girl in today's world. 'Please don't be ashamed, for if you are, then I'll be. I've wanted to do it since I was twelve but held back because of what you said. But you've got to understand that what I did with Lance wasn't casual. I love him. And for a while, before you and Bart came in . . . it felt . . . felt . . . so good.'

What could I say now?

I had my own wilful youth clearly tucked in a memory closet, ready to jump forward and put the vision of Paul before me . . . and the way I'd wanted him to teach me all the ways of love, especially when my first experience with sex had been so devastating, filling me with the kind of guilt that even now I could cry to look up at the moon that had seen Chris's sin, and mine.

About six Chris called to say he'd been trying to reach me all day but the limes had been down. 'You'll be seeing me Christmas Eve,' he said cheerfully. 'I've hired a snowplough to precede me to the Hall, and I'll be right behind. How are things going?'

'Fine, just fine,' I lied, telling him Lance's father had fallen down the stairs and he had to fly home immediately. Then I rattled on and on, saying we were all set for Christmas, gifts wrapped, tree up, but Melodie was, as usual, clinging to her rooms as if they offered her the only sanctuary in the world.

'Cathy,' said Chris in a tight voice, 'how nice it would be if you'd only level with me on occasion. Lance didn't fly home. All the planes are grounded. Lance is, at this moment, not ten feet away from this very phone booth. He came to me and confessed everything. I took care of his broken nose, his other wounds, and cursed Bart all the time. That boy is a mess.'

Early the next morning, we heard on the radio that all roads to the village and the nearest city were snowed under.

Travellers were warned to stay home. We kept the radio on all day, listening to the weathermen who seemed to control our lives. 'Never before has there been a winter more dramatic than this one,' went the sing song male voice, extolling the virtues of weather. 'Records are being broken . . .'

Hour by miserable hour Cindy and I stood at the windows, with Jory often joining us to stare as we did at the snow coming down with relentless determination to isolate us.

Behind my eyes I saw the four of us, locked in that room, whispering about Santa Claus and telling the twins that surely he would find us. Chris had written him a letter. Oh, the pity of those little twins waking up on Christmas morning, not even remembering the good times that had gone on before.

Hearing Jory cough brought me back to the present. Every few minutes Jory suffered through paroxysms of racking coughs. I glanced at him fearfully.

Soon he was heading his chair for his room, saying he could put himself back into bed. I wanted to go with him but knew he wanted to do all he could for himself.

'I'm beginning to hate this place,' grumbled Cindy. 'Now Jory's got a cold. That's why I brought Lance home with me, knowing it would be this. I was hoping every night we'd have a party, and being slightly drunk would take away the pall of living under the shadows of Bart and that creepy old Joel. I was expecting Lance to keep me happy while I was here. Now I've got no one but you, Momma. Jory seems so aloof and alone, and he thinks I'm too young to understand his problems. Melodie never says anything to me, or anybody. Bart stalks around like the grim reaper – and that old man sends shivers up my spine. We don't have any friends. No one ever calls unexpectedly. We're all alone, getting on each other's nerves. And it's Christmas. I'm looking forward to that ball Bart says he's throwing. At least that would give me the chance to meet some people and brush off the moss I feel creeping up my legs.'

Suddenly Bart was there, yelling at Cindy. 'You don't have to stay. You're just the bastard my mother had to have.'

Cindy blushed deeply red. 'Are you trying to hurt me again, jerk? You can't hurt me *now*! I'm through with that!'

'Don't you ever call me jerk again, bastard!'

'Creep, jerk, creep, jerk!' she taunted, backing up and dodging behind chairs and tables, deliberately baiting him to give chase, and in this way, give her dull day a bit of excitement.

'Cindy!' I stormed, furious now. 'How dare you talk to Bart that way? Now, say you're sorry . . . say it!'

'No, I won't say it, for I'm not sorry!' she yelled not at me but at Bart. 'He's a brute, a maniac, a crazy, and he's trying to drive us all as batty as he is!'

'Stop!' I yelled, seeing Bart's face go very pale. Then he lunged forward and caught her by her hair. She tried to run, but he had her held too securely. I rushed forward to prevent him from striking her by clinging on to his free arm. Above her he towered. 'If you ever so much as speak to me again, little girl, you'll rue the day. You're very proud of your body, of your hair, of your face. One more insult and you'll hide in closets and break all the mirrors.'

His deadly tone of voice said he was serious. I moved to help Cindy stand. 'Bart, you don't mean that. All your life you've tormented Cindy. Can you blame her for wanting her revenge?'

'You take her side, after what she said to me?'

'Say you're sorry, Cindy,' I pleaded, turning to her. Then I turned appealing eyes on Bart. 'You say it, too, please.'

Indecision flashed in Bart's fiery dark eyes as he saw how upset I was, but it vanished the moment Cindy screamed out, 'NO! I'm *not* sorry! And I'm not afraid of him! You're just as creepy and senile as that old jerk who wanders around muttering to himself. Boy, do you have a thing for old men! Maybe that's your hang-up, brother!'

'Cindy!' I whispered, very much shocked, 'apologize to Bart.'

'Never, never, never! – not after what he did to Lance!'

The anger on Bart's face frightened me.

Just then Joel ambled into the room. He stood with his long arms crossed over his chest and met Bart's fiery eyes. 'Son . . . let it go. The Lord sees and hears all and, in time, wreaks his own justice. She's a child like a bird chirping in the trees, led by instincts that know nothing of morality. She acts, speaks, moves, all without thinking. She's nothing compared to you, Bart. Nothing but a hank of hair, a bone and a rag – you are born to lead.'

As if transfixed, Bart's anger simmered down. He followed Joel from the room without looking our way. To see Bart follow that old man so obediently and without question filled my head with fresh fears. How had Joel gained such control?

Cindy fell into my arms and began to cry. 'Momma, what's wrong with me, with Bart? Why do I say such hateful things to hurt him? Why does he say them to me? I want to hurt Bart. I want to pay him back for every ugly thing he's done to hurt me.'

In my arms she sobbed out her anxieties until she was limp.

In many ways Cindy reminded me of myself, so eager to love and be loved, to live a full, exciting life even before she was mature enough to accept the emotional responsibilities.

I sighed and held her closer. Someday, somehow, all family problems would be resolved. I held to that belief, praying that Chris would come home soon.

CHRISTMAS

As it had in the past, Christmas Eve arrived with its charm and festive peace to reign over troubled spirits and gave even Foxworth Hall its own beauty. The snow still fell, but it was not so wild and wind driven. In our favourite room for getting together, Bart and Cindy, with Jory directing, were decorating the gigantic Christmas tree. Cindy was up on a ladder on one side, Bart was on the second ladder, as Jory sat in his wheelchair, fiddling with strings of lights meant for our door wreaths. Decorators were working in other rooms to make them festive enough for the hundreds of guests Bart expected to entertain at the ball. He was terribly excited. To see him happy and laughing added joy to my heart, especially when Chris came in the door loaded down with all he'd purchased at the last moment, as was his customary procrastinating way.

I ran to greet him with hungry arms and eager kisses that Bart couldn't see from his position behind the tree. 'Whatever took you so long?' I asked, and he laughed, indicating the beautifully wrapped gifts.

'Out in the car I've got more,' he said with a happy smile. 'I know what you're thinking, that I should do my shopping earlier, but I never seem to find the time. Then all of a sudden it's Christmas Eve, and I end up paying twice as much, but you're going to be very pleased – and if you're not, don't tell me.'

Melodie was crouched down on a low stool near the fireplace in the salon just off the foyer, looking miserable. In fact, when I studied her more closely she appeared to be in pain. 'Are you all right, Melodie?' I asked. She nodded to say she was fine, and I foolishly took her word for that. When Chris questioned her, she stood and denied anything was wrong. She threw Bart an imploring glance he didn't see, and then she was heading for the back stairs. In her shapeless, dull-coloured garment, she seemed a drab thing that had aged ten years since July. Jory, who always kept a close eye on Melodie, turned to watch her drift away, a terrible haunted sadness in his eyes that stole his pleasure from the happy occupation at hand. The string of lights slid from his lap to entangle the wheels of his chair. He didn't notice, only sat with clenched fists, as if he'd like to smash Fate in the face for taking away the use of his marvellous body, and in so doing stealing from him the woman he loved.

On the way to the stairs, Chris stopped to clap Jory heartily on the back. 'You're looking fit and healthy. And don't worry about Melodie. It's normal for a woman in the last weeks to become irritable and moody. So would you if you were carrying around all that extra weight.'

'She could at least speak to me occasionally,' complained Jory, 'or look at me. She doesn't even cosy up to Bart anymore.'

I looked at him with alarm. Could he know that only a short while ago Bart and Melodie had been lovers? I didn't believe they were anymore, and that was the true explanation of Melodie's miserable state. I tried to read his eyes, but he lowered his lids and pretended to be interested in decorating the tree again.

Long ago Chris and I had established a tradition of opening at least one gift on Christmas Eve. When night came, Chris and I sat alone in the best of our downstairs salons, toasting one another with champagne. We lifted our glasses high. 'To all our tomorrows together,' he said with his warm eyes full of love and happiness. I repeated the same words before Chris handed me my 'special' gift. I opened the small jewellery box to find a two-carat pear-shaped diamond suspended on a fine gold chain.

'No, don't object and say you don't like jewellery,' Chris said hastily when I just stared at the object that glittered and refracted rainbow colours. 'Our mother never wore anything like this. I really wanted to buy you opera-length pearls like the ones she used to wear, because I think they are both elegant and understated. But knowing you, I forgot the pearls and settled for this beautiful diamond. It's tear-shaped, Cathy – for all the tears I would have cried inside if you had never let me love you.'

The way he said that put tears in my eyes and swelled my heart with the guilty sadness of being us, the special joy of being us; the complications of being us sometimes were just too overwhelming. Silently I handed him my 'special' gift – a fine star-sapphire ring to fit his forefinger. He laughed, saying it was ostentatious but beautiful.

No sooner were those words out of his mouth than Jory, Melodie and Bart joined us. Jory smiled to see the glow in our eyes. Bart frowned. Melodie sank into a deep-cushioned chair and seemed to disappear in the depths. Cindy came running in with bells that she shook merrily, her pants and sweater bright red. Finally Joel slunk into the room to stand in a corner with his arms folded over his chest, casting his own pall, like a somber judge overseeing wicked and dangerous children.

It was Jory who first responded to Cindy's charm by raising his glass of champagne high and toasting. 'Hail to the joys of Christmas Eve! May my mother and father always look at one another as they do this night, with love and tenderness, with compassion and understanding. May I find that kind of love in the eyes of my wife again . . . soon'.

He was directly challenging Melodie and in front of all of us. Sadly, his timing was bad for this kind of confrontation. She drew herself into a tighter knot and refused to meet his eyes; instead, she leaned forward to stare more intensely into the fire. The hope in Jory's eyes faded. His shoulders sagged before he swivelled his chair so that he couldn't see her. He put down his champagne and fixed his eyes on the fire just as intensely as his wife, as if to read what symbolism she was seeing. In a distant dim corner, Joel smiled.

Cindy tried to force gaiety. Bart, by attrition, gave in to the corroding gloominess that Melodie emitted like a grey fog. Truly our little family get-together in a gloriously festive room was a flop. Bart refused even to look at Melodie now that she was so grossly out of shape.

Soon he was pacing the room restlessly, glancing at all the

gifts under the 'family' tree. His eyes accidently found Melodie staring at him hopefully, and only too quickly he looked away, as if embarrassed by her too overt pleading. In a few minutes Melodie excused herself, saying in a low voice that she didn't feel well.

'Anything I can do?' Chris asked immediately, jumping up to assist her up the stairs. She plodded along heavily, flat footed. 'I'm all right,' she snapped near one newel post. 'I don't need you help – or anyone's!'

'And a merry Christmas was had by all,' intoned Bart, much in the manner of Joel, who still stood in the shadows, watching, always watching.

The moment Melodie was gone from the room, Jory slumped forward in his chair before he stated, too, that he was tired and not feeling too well. His next prolonged bout of coughing revealed that. 'I've got just the medicine you need,' said Chris, jumping up and heading for the stairs. 'You can't go to bed yet, Jory. Stay a while longer. We have to celebrate. Before I dose you with something that might not be appropriate, I need to listen to your lungs.'

Bart leaned casually against the mantel, watching this caring scene between Jory and Chris as if jealous of their relationship. Chris came to me. 'Perhaps it is better if we retire now, so we can be up at dawn to eat breakfast, open our presents, and then have naps before we start getting ready for the ball tomorrow night.'

'Oh, glory hallelujah!' cried Cindy, whirling around the room in a small dance. 'People, hordes of people, all dressed in their best – I can hardly wait for tomorrow night! Laughter, how I long to hear it. Jokes and small talk, how my ears crave that. I'm so tired of being serious, looking at grim faces that don't know how to smile, hearing sad talk. I hope all those old fuddy-duds bring along their college-aged sons – or any son as long as he's over twelve. I'm that desperate.'

Bart wasn't the only one of us to throw her disapproving looks, which Cindy ignored. 'I'm gonna dance all night, I'm gonna dance all night,' she sang, whirling around by herself, pretending to have a partner, refusing to let her anticipations be diminished by anything anyone of us could say. 'And then I'll dance some more . . .'

Despite himself, Chris and Jory were charmed with her actions, her bright, happy song. Chris smiled before he said, 'There should be at least twenty young men here tomorrow night. Just try to contain yourself. Now, since Jory looks so beat, let's head for bed. Tomorrow will be a long day.'

It seemed a good idea.

All of a sudden, falling into a chair, Cindy sagged as limp as Melodie had, looking sad and near tears. 'I wish Lance could have stayed. I'd rather have him than any other.'

Bart threw her a furious look. 'That particular young man will never enter this house again.' He turned to me next. 'We don't need Melodie at the party,' he went on with determination and continued anger, 'not when she's acting so miserable and sick. Let her sulk in her room tomorrow morning so we can enjoy opening our gifts. I think afternoon naps are a good idea, so tomorrow night we'll look fresh from plenty of rest and bright and happy for my party.'

Jory had gone on ahead, entering the elevator by himself, as if to prove his independence. The rest of us seemed reluctant to part. As I sat there hearing the Christmas carols that Bart had put on the stereo to play, I thought of all his newly acquired fastidious habits.

As a boy he'd loved being not just dirty, but filthy. Now he took several showers a day, kept himself immaculately groomed. He couldn't retire until he'd checked over 'his house' from top to bottom, seeing that the doors were locked, the windows, too, and that the new kitten Trevor had as his pet hadn't stained a carpet. (Trevor had been fired a dozen times by Bart, but still he stayed on, and Bart didn't insist that he go.)

Even as I watched, Bart got up to fluff the throw pillows, smoothed wrinkles out of downy sofa cushions, picked up magazines and arranged them in neat piles. All the things the servants forgot to do, he did. Then he'd jump on Trevor in the morning and order the maids to do better – or out they'd go without severance pay. No wonder we couldn't keep servants. Only Trevor remained loyal, ignoring the rudeness of Bart, whom he looked at with pity, although Bart didn't know that.

All this was on my mind as I took note of Bart's growing enthusiasm for tomorrow night's party. I glanced towards the windows and saw the snow was still falling, and already two feet of snow were on the ground. 'Bart . . . the roads are going to be icy tomorrow night, perhaps closed, and many of your guests might not be able to make it here for the traditional Foxworth ball.'

'Nonsense! I'll fly them in if they call to cancel. A helicopter could land on the lawn.'

I sighed, for some reason made uneasy by the strangely malicious look of Joel, who chose that time to leave the room.

'Your mother is right, Bart,' said Chris kindly, 'so don't feel disappointed if only a few are able to show up. I had a devil of a time reaching here a few hours ago, and it's snowing harder now.'

It was as if Chris hadn't said a word. Bart bade me good night, then strode towards the stairs. Shortly afterwards, Chris, Cindy and I ascended the stairs.

While Chris went in to say a few words to Jory, I waited for Cindy to come from her bath. Another shower (at least two a day with shampoos) brought her fresh and bright from the bath, wearing the briefest little red nightie. 'Momma, don't you lecture me again. I just can't take any more. When I first came to this house, I thought it like a fairy tale palace. Now I think of it as a gloomy fortress to keep us all prisoners. As soon as this ball is over, I'm leaving – and to hell with Bart! I love you and Daddy and Jory, but Melodie has turned into a boring pain in the neck and Bart will never change. He'll always hate me, so I'm going to stop even trying to be nice to him.'

She slipped between the sheets, pulled the covers high, turned on her side away from me. 'Good night, Momma. Please turn out the light when you leave. Don't ask me to behave myself tomorrow night, for I intend to be the model of ladylike decorum. Wake me three hours before the ball begins.'

'In other words, you don't even want to share Christmas morning with us?'

'Oh,' she said indifferently, 'I guess I can wake up long enough to open my gifts . . . and watch the rest of you open yours. Then back to bed so I can be the belle of the ball tomorrow night.'

'I love you, Cindy,' I said as I switched off her lamp, and then bent to lift her hair and kiss the warm nape of her neck.

Flipping over, her slim young arms tightened around my neck as she sobbed, 'Oh, Momma, you're the best! I promise to be good from now on. I won't let any boy so much as hold my hand. But let me escape this house and fly to New York and attend that New Year's party my best friend is throwing in a grand hotel ballroom.'

Silently I nodded. 'All right. If you want to enjoy yourself at the home of your friend, that's fine, but please do your best not to rile Bart tomorrow. You know his problem, and he has worked hard to overcome all those disturbing ideas planted in his head when he was very young. Help him, Cindy. Let him realize he has a family backing him up.'

'I will, Momma, I promise I will.'

I closed the door and was soon saying good night to Jory. He was unusually quiet. 'It's going to be all right, darling. Just as soon as the baby is here, Melodie will see you again.'

'Will she?' he asked bitterly. 'I doubt it. She'll have the baby then to occupy her time and thoughts. She'll need me even less than she does now.'

Half an hour, Chris opened his arms to me, and eagerly I surrendered to the only love in my life that had lasted long enough to let me know I had a firm grip on happiness . . . despite everything that could have ruined what we had cultivated and grown in the shade.

The morning light crept eerily into my room, bringing me out of sleep even before the alarm sounded. Quickly I was up and staring out the windows. The snow had stopped.

Thank God for that; Bart would be pleased. I hurried back to the bed to kiss Chris awake. 'Merry Christmas, darling Doctor Christopher Sheffield,' I whispered in his ear.

'I'd rather you call me just darling,' he mumbled as he came awake and looked around in a disoriented way.

Determined that this day was going to be successful, I tugged him out of bed, and soon we were both dressed and heading for the breakfast room.

For two days men and women had been coming to the house, repeating what had been done in the summer, only this time the entire downstairs had been transformed into a Christmas fantasy.

I watched with a certain indifference as the workers from the caterer Bart had hired finally finished making our home look like a wonderland. Cindy stood at my side watching all they did to turn the rooms into extraordinarily festive rooms, full of colour, candles, wreaths, garlands, a towering Christmas tree that outdid our family tree by ten feet.

All she saw soon had Cindy convinced she didn't want to spend the better part of her day in bed. She forgot Lance and loneliness, for Christmas Day worked better magic than Christmas Eve.

'Look at that pie, Momma! It's huge. Four and twenty blackbirds baked in a pie,' she sang, all of a sudden glowing with life. 'Sorry I've acted ugly. I've been thinking, there'll be boys here tonight, and lots of handsome rich men. Oh, maybe this house can give more than misery after all.'

'Of course it can,' Bart said as he came in to stand between us, his eyes shining as he surveyed all that had been done. He seemed thrilled by his expectations. 'You just be sure and wear a decent dress, and don't do anything outrageous.' Then he was following the workmen and giving directions, laughing often, even including Jory, Cindy, Melodie and me, as if all were forgiven now that it was Christmas.

Day after day, like some dark, gloomy shadow, Joel had trailed behind Bart, his old voice cracking as he intoned words from the Bible. He said again this morning, fully dressed at six-thirty, 'It is easier for a camel to go through the eye of a needle than for a rich man to enter the kingdom of God . . .'

'What the hell are you trying to say, old man?' shouted Bart.

Momentarily Joel's watery eyes flared with anger, like a spark ready to ignite from a brisk, unexpected wind.

'You're throwing away thousands of dollars hoping to impress someone – and no one will be impressed, for the others have money, too. Some live in finer homes. Foxworth Hall was the best of its kind in its day, but its day has come and gone.'

Bart turned on him with fury. 'Shut up! You're trying to spoil whatever happiness I reach for. Everything I do is a sin! You're an old man and have done your share; now you try to spoil mine. This is my time to be young and fully enjoy my life. Keep your religious quotes to yourself!'

'Pride goeth before a fall.'

'Pride goeth before destruction,' corrected Bart, glaring at his great-uncle and giving me delicious satisfaction.

At last, at last, Bart was seeing Joel as a threat and not as the respectable father he'd sought all his life.

'Pride is the never-failing vice of fools,' extolled Joel, looking with disgust at all that had been done. 'You have wasted money that would be better off given to charities.'

'Get out! Go to your room and polish your pride, Uncle! For obviously you have nothing in your heart but jealousy!'

Joel stumbled from the room, muttering to himself, 'He'll find out. Nothing is forgotten or forgiven here in the hills. I know. Who would know better than I? Bitter, bitter are the days of the Foxworths despite all their wealth.'

I stepped forward to hug Bart. 'Don't listen to him, Bart. You'll have a wonderful party. Everyone will come now that the sun is shining and melting the snow. God is on your side this day, so rejoice and have the time of your life.'

The look in his eyes when I said that, oh, that grateful look. He stared at me, trying to say something – but the words couldn't form. Finally he could do nothing but briefly embrace me; then he was striding away as if embarrassed. Such a wonderful-looking man, so wasted, I was thinking. There had to be someplace where Bart fitted.

Rooms that had been closed off since winter began were opened, the dustcovers removed and freshened so that no one would know we ever made an effort to conserve heat or money. Bathrooms and powder rooms were given special attention to make them both immaculate and attractive. Expensive soaps and lavish guest towels were put out. Every toiletry item that a guest might need was displayed. Special Christmas china and crystal were taken from the party cabinets, along with seasonal decorations too expensive for the caterer to supply.

We gathered around the Christmas tree about eleven o'clock. Bart was freshly shaven, splendidly well groomed, as was Jory. Only Melodie looked stale in her worn maternity dress that she wore day in and week out. Trying as always to ease tensions, I picked up the Christ child from the realistic manger and held the baby in my arms. 'Bart, I haven't seen this before. Did you buy this? If so, I've never seen a more beautifully carved set of Biblical figures.'

'It just arrived yesterday, and only today I unpacked it,' Bart answered. 'I bought it in Italy last winter and had them ship it over.'

I gushed on, happy to see him so animated. 'This Christ child looks like a real baby, when most don't, and the virgin Mary is absolutely beautiful. Joseph looks so kind and understanding.'

'He'd have to be, wouldn't he?' asked Jory, who was leaning forward to put more of his gifts under our family tree. 'After all, it must have seemed a bit incredible for him to believe a virgin could be impregnated by an invisible, abstract God.'

'You're not supposed to question,' answered Bart, his eyes lovingly caressing the almost life-sized figures he'd purchased. 'You just blindly accept what is written.'

'Then why did you argue with Joel?'

'Jory . . . don't push me too far. Joel is helping me find myself. He's an old man who lived in sin when he was young and is redeeming himself in his old age through good deeds. I am a young man who wants to sin, feeling my traumatic childhood has already redeemed me.'

'I suggest a few orgies in some big city will have you running back here, as old and hypocritical acting as your greatuncle Joel,' answered Jory fearlessly. 'I don't like him. And you'd be wise to drive him out, Bart. Give him a few hundred thousand and say goodbye.'

Something yearning struggled in Bart's eyes, as if he'd like to do exactly this. He leaned forward to stare into Jory's eyes. 'Why don't you like him?'

'I can't really say, Bart,' said Jory, who'd always forgiven easily. 'He looks around your home like it should be his. I've caught him glaring at you when you aren't paying attention. I don't believe he's your friend, only your enemy.'

Deeply distressed and disturbed looking, Bart left the room, tossing back his cynical remark. 'When have I ever had anything but enemies?'

In a few moments Bart was back, bearing his own heavy stack of gifts. It took him three trips from his office to put all he'd bought under the family tree.

Then it was Chris. Carefully arranging all his presents, and that took some doing. The gifts were stacked up three feet high and spreading to fill most of one corner.

Melodie crept dismally into the cheerful room like a dark shadow and settled down near the fireplace, close enough to feel the warmth, crumpled like a rag in her chair, still everlastingly finding more fascination in the dancing flames than in anything else. She appeared sullen, moody, withdrawn and determined to be there in physical appearance only as her spirit roamed free. Her abdomen was tremendously swollen, and she still had a few weeks to go. Her eyes were darkly shadowed.

Soon all of us were making an effort to be a loving family as Cindy played Santa Claus. Christmas, as I'd learned a long time ago, had its own gifts to give. Grudges could be forgotten, enemies forgiven as we all united around the tree, even Joel, and one by one shook our packages, made our guesses, then tore into our packages, laughing and drowning out the carols I'd put on the stereo. Soon glittering paper and shining ribbons littered the floor.

Cindy at last handed Joel the gift she had for him. He accepted it tentatively as he'd taken all our gifts, as if we were heathen fools who didn't know the real meaning of a Christmas that didn't need gifts. Then his eyes were bulging at the white nightshirt and the peaked sleeping cap Cindy must have really hunted to find. Definitely he would look like Scrooge wearing those things. Included was an ebony walking stick, which he hurled to the floor along with the nightshirt and cap. 'Are you mocking me, girl?'

'I only wanted you to have warm sleeping garments, Uncle,' she said demurely, her sparkling eyes downcast, 'and the walking stick would hurry your steps.'

'Away from you? Is that what you mean?' He stopped painfully to pick up the stick and brandished it wildly in the air. 'Maybe I will keep this thing after all; great weapon in case I'm attacked one night when I stroll the gardens . . . and long corridors.'

Silent for a moment, not one of us could speak. Then Cindy laughed. 'Uncle, I thought of that in advance. I knew one day you'd feel threatened.'

He left the room then.

Only too soon all the gifts were unwrapped, and Jory was staring worriedly at the litter on the floor, then scanning all around the room. 'I didn't forget you, Bart,' he said with concern. 'Cindy and Dad helped me wrap it once, but then I undid the wrapping, touched up again, wrapped it myself the last time after Cindy helped me lift it in.' He kept looking through the rubble of discarded foil and ribbons. 'Early this morning, before the rest of you were up, I came down here and I put it under the tree. Where the hell did it go, I wonder? It's a huge box wrapped in red foil, tied with silver ribbons – and by far the largest box under the tree.'

Bart didn't say a word, as if he'd grown accustomed to disappointments and the lack of Jory's gift was of no importance.

Of course I knew Jory had worked for months and months to finish the clipper ship that had ended up three feet in length and just as tall, with all its fragile riggings exactly right. He'd even sent for special copper fittings and a solid brass wheel for the helm. Desperately Jory looked around. 'Has anyone seen the big box wrapped in red foil, with Bart's name on the tag?' he asked.

Immediately I was on my feet and scrambling through the piles of boxes, papers, ribbons, tissue, with Chris soon joining me in the search. Cindy began her own search on the other side of the room. 'Oh,' she cried out. 'Here it is, behind this red sofa.' She carried it to Bart and put it on the floor near his feet, bowing in mocking obeisance. 'For our lord, our master,' she said sweetly, backing away. 'I think Jory's a fool to give it to you after all the hard work he put into this thing, but maybe you'll be appreciative, for once.'

Suddenly I noticed Joel had slipped back into the room to observe Bart. How strange his expression, how strange.

Bart dropped his sophistication like an unwanted garment and became childishly eager to open this particular gift. Already he was tearing into the package Jory had so beautifully and carefully wrapped. He glanced up at Jory, his smile warm, wide and happy, his dark eyes lit with boyish anticipation. 'Ten to one it's that clipper ship you made, Jory. You really should keep that yourself . . . but thanks, thanks a heap – ' He paused, then sucked in his breath.

He stared down in to the box, paling before he looked upward, his happiness vanished. Now his eyes were full of bitterness. 'It's broken,' he said in a dull tone. 'Smashed to small pieces. There's nothing in this box but broken matchsticks and tangled rigging.'

His voice cracked as he stood up and dropped the box to the floor. Violently he kicked it aside before he threw a hard look at Melodie, who hadn't said a word even when she opened her gifts, only thanked us with nods and weak smiles. 'I should have known you would find the perfect way to repay me for sleeping with your wife.'

Stunned silence rumbled louder than thunder. Melodie sat on, bleakly staring, seeming an empty shell, even as she mumbled on and on about how much she hated this house. Jory's eyes went starkly blank.

Had he guessed all along? All of Jory's colour vanished before finally he could force his eyes to look at Melodie. 'I don't believe you, Bart. You've always had a nasty, hateful way of kicking where it hurts most.'

'I'm not lying,' lashed out Bart, disregarding the pain he was inflicting on Jory, on me and Chris. 'While you lay on your hospital bed, inside your cast, your wife and I shared one bed, and eagerly enough she spread her legs for me.'

Chris jumped to his feet, his face angrier than I'd ever seen it. 'Bart, how dare you say such things to your brother? Apologize to Jory and Melodie, immediately! How can you hurt him like this, when already he's hurt enough? Do you hear me? You tell him every word you just said is a lie! A damned lie!'

'It's not a lie,' raged Bart. 'If you never believe anything I say again, believe me when I say that Melodie was a very co-operative bed companion.'

Cindy squealed, then jumped up to slap Melodie's stricken white face. 'How dare you do that to Jory?' she screamed. 'You know how much he loves you!'

Then Bart was laughing, hysterically laughing. Chris thundered, 'Stop that! Face up to this situation, Bart – the loss of the clipper ship is not a good excuse for trying to destroy your brother's marriage. Where is your honour, your integrity?'

Almost instantly Bart's laughter faded. His eyes turned crystal hard and cold as they surveyed Chris from head to toe. 'Don't *you* talk to me about honour and integrity. Where was yours when it came to your sister? Where is it now when you continue to sleep with her? Don't you realize yet that your relationship with her has warped me so that I don't care about anything but seeing the two of you separated? I want my mother to finish out her life as a decent, respectable woman . . . and it's you who keeps her from that! You, Christopher, you!'

His face full of disgust and no remorse, Bart spun on his heel and left the room.

Left us all in the shambles of our Christmas joy.

Eager to do the same, Melodie rose awkwardly, stood trembling with her head bowed, before Cindy yelled, 'Did you sleep with Bart? Did you? It isn't fair for you to just say nothing when Jory's heart is breaking.'

Melodie's darkly shadowed eyes seemed to sink deeper into her skull even as they grew larger and larger, her pupils dilating as if with fear. 'Why can't you leave me alone?' she cried pitifully. 'I'm not made of the same iron as the rest of you! I can't take one tragedy after another. Jory lay stricken in the hospital, unable to ever walk or dance again, and Bart was here. I needed someone. He held me, comforted me. I closed my eyes and pretended he was Jory.'

Jory fell forward in his chair. I ran to hold him, only to find him gasping so rackingly he couldn't even control his shaking hands. I held him in my arms as Chris tried to stop Melodie from running up the stairs. 'Be careful!' he called. 'You could fall and lose your baby!'

'I don't care,' came back her pitiful wail before she disappeared from sight.

By this time Jory had gained enough control to wipe away his tears and find a weak smile. 'Well, now I know,' he said in a cracked voice. 'I guessed a long time ago that she and Bart had something going on, but I hoped it was only my suspicions working overtime. But I should have known better. Mel can't live without a man beside her, especially in bed . . . and I can hardly blame her, can I?'

Stricken to the bone, I began to pick up the wrappings that had been so carefully applied and so ruthlessly ripped off. Like life, and how carefully we tried to maintain our illusions when things were seldom what they had appeared to be.

Soon Jory excused himself, saying he needed to be alone.

'Who could have smashed that wonderful ship?' I whispered. 'Cindy helped Jory wrap that gift the last time he touched up the paint, and I was there watching. The ship was carefully put in a special plastic foam shell to hold it upright. It shouldn't have had one crack, one thing broken.'

'How can I ever explain what goes on in this house?' answered Chris in a throaty voice full of pain. He looked up to see Bart standing in the doorway, his long legs spread wide, his fists on his hips as he glared at me. In a louder tone Chris addressed Bart. 'What's done is done, and I'm sure it's not Jory's fault the clipper ship was broken. He meant well. All along he told us he was putting that ship together for your office mantel.'

'I'm sure Jory did mean well,' said Bart evenly, his control regained. 'But there is my dear little adopted sister who hates me and no doubt wants to punish me for giving her boyfriend what he deserved. Next time it will be her I punish.'

'Maybe Jory dropped the box,' said Joel in a saintly way. I stared at that old man with his glittering weak eyes and waited my opportunity to say what I had to when no one else was around.

'No,' denied Bart. 'It had to be Cindy. I have to admit my brother has always given me fair treatment, even when I didn't deserve it.'

And all the while he said this, I was staring at Joel with his smirky face, his glittery, satisfied eyes.

Just before retiring, I had my chance. We were in a back second-floor hallway. 'Joel, Cindy wouldn't have destroyed all Jory's work and ruined Bart's gift. But you like to drive wedges between members of our family. I believe it was you who smashed the ship, then rewrapped it.'

He said nothing, only put more hatred in his unrelenting stare.

'Why did you come back, Joel?' I shouted. 'You claim you hated your father and were happy in your Italian monastery. Why didn't you stay there? Certainly in all those years you made a few friends. You must have known you wouldn't find any here. My mother told me you always hated this house. Now you walk through it as if you owned it.'

Still he said nothing.

I followed him into his room and looked around for the first time. Biblical illustrations on his walls. Quotes from the Bible put in cheap frames.

He moved so that he was behind me. I felt his wheezy warm breath on my neck, smelling old and faintly sick. I sensed when he moved his arms he meant to choke me. Startled, I whirled about to find him inches away.

How silently and quickly he could move. 'My father's mother was named Corrine,' he said in the sweetest possible voice, enough to make me doubt my reasoning. 'My sister had the same name, given to her as a form of punishment, a constant reminder to my father of his unfaithful mother, proving to him again and again that no beautiful woman could be trusted – how right he was.'

He was an old man, in his late seventies, yet I slapped him, slapped him hard. He staggered backwards, then lost his balance and fell to the floor.

'You'll regret that slap, Catherine,' he cried with more anger than he'd as yet shown. 'Just as much as Corrine regretted all her sins. You, too, will live long enough to regret yours!'

I fled his room, fearing what he said was only too true.

THE TRADITIONAL FOXWORTH BALL

On Christmas night our dinner was served around five in order to give the family plenty of time to prepare for the big event that would begin at nine-thirty. Bart wore a glow of happiness. His warm hand reached to cover mine, sending a shock of pleasure through me, for so seldom did he show affection by touching. 'If I can't have all my wealth right away, then I should have at least all the prestige due the owner of this house.'

I smiled and covered the hand that held mine with my free hand. 'Yes, I understand, and we'll do everything possible to see that your party is a huge success.'

Joel sat nearby, sending out invisible vibes. He was smiling cynically. 'Lord help those fools who deceive themselves,' he muttered half under his breath. Bart closed his ears and pretended not to hear, but I was worried. Someone had broken Jory's clipper ship, which had been meant as a reconciliation gift to Bart. It had to be Joel who had heartlessly ruined that ship that Jory had slaved over for months and months. What else would he do?

My eyes met Joel's. I couldn't quite put my finger on how Joel looked at this moment, except sanctimonious. He daintily picked at his food, cutting his fruitcake into tiny morsels that he picked up with his long fingers. These he chewed with intense concentration, using only his front teeth, much as a rabbit ate a carrot.

'I'm going to bed now,' announced Joel. 'I don't approve of tonight's party, Bart, you might as well know that. Remember what happened at your birthday party, and you should have known better. Again I say it's a waste of good money entertaining people you don't know well enough. I also disapprove of people who drink, who cavort and act wild on a day meant for worship. This day belongs to the Lord and his son. We should all go down on our knees and stay there from dawn until midnight, like we did in my monastery, as we gave silent thanks for just being alive.'

Since not one of us said a word, Joel went on. 'I know drunken men and women will eventually try to fornicate with someone other than whom they came with. I remember your birthday party and what went on. Sinful modern life makes me realize how pure the world was when I was young. Nothing is the same as it used to be. People knew how to act decently in public then, no matter what they did behind closed doors. Now nobody cares who sees them do what. Women didn't bare their bosoms when I was a boy, nor pull up their skirts for every man who wanted them.'

He riveted his cold blue eyes on me, and then on Cindy. 'Those who sin, and sin again, always pay dearly, as some here should already know.' Next he was staring at Jory meaningfully.

'The old son of a bitch,' murmured Cindy, watching him slip out of the room with the same stealth as he had entered.

'Cindy, don't you ever let me hear you say anything like that again!' fired Bart. 'Nobody uses obscenities under *my* roof.'

'Well, I'll be damned!' flared Cindy. 'Just the other day I overheard you calling Joel the same thing. And what's more, Bart Foxworth, I'll call a spade a spade – even under your roof!'

'Go to your room and stay there!' bellowed Bart.

'Everybody continue having fun,' said Jory, guiding his chair towards the elevator. 'As for me, damned if I don't want to turn in my Christian membership.'

'You've never been a Christian to begin with,' called Bart. 'Nobody here goes to church. But there will come a day in the near future when everyone here will attend church.'

Chris stood up and precisely put down his napkin, fixing Bart and Cindy with commanding eyes. 'I've had enough of this childish quibbling. I'm surprised that all of you who think you are adults can revert to children in a wink of the eye.'

But Jory was not to be stopped this time. He wheeled his

chair about abruptly, rage flaming his usually controlled face, flaring wide his nostrils. 'Dad, I'm sorry, but I've got to have my say.' He turned towards Bart, who had risen to his feet. 'Now, you listen to me, little brother.' His strong hands released the joy stick to clench into fists. 'I believe in God . . . but I don't believe in religion. Religion is used to manipulate and punish. Used in a thousand ways for profit, for even in the church, money is still the real God.'

'Bart,' I implored, so afraid he'd harm Jory again, 'it's time we all headed upstairs.'

Bart had paled. 'No wonder you sit there in that chair if you believe what you just said. You are being punished by God, just as Joel says.'

'Joel,' sneered Jory. 'Who the hell cares what an old fool like Joel says? I'm punished because some stupid idiot wet the sand! God didn't pour down rain to do that. A garden hose took God's place, and that's why I'm in this chair and not where I belong. As soon as possible, I'm leaving here, Bart! I'm forgetting you're my brother, whom I've always tried to love and help. I'm not going to try again.'

'Hooray for you, Jory!' cried Cindy, jumping to her feet and applauding.

'Stop!' I yelled, seizing Cindy by the arm while Chris grabbed her other arm and we dragged her away from Bart. Still she twisted and fought to free herself. 'You damned freaky hypocrite!' she yelled back at Bart. 'I heard at your birthday party that you do your share of using the local brothel . . .'

Thank God the elevator door closed behind us and we were on our way up before Bart could reach Cindy.

'Learn to keep your mouth shut,' said Jory. 'You only make him worse, Cindy – and I regret what I just said. Did you see his face. I don't think he's pretending about religion. He's deadly serious. He seems to truly believe. If Joel is a hypocrite, Bart is not.'

Chris fixed his strong regard on both before he stepped out of the elevator. 'Jory, Cindy, you listen to me carefully. I want you both to do your best tonight to see that Bart's party is successful. Forget your enmity, at least for one night. He was a troubled little boy, and he has grown into a more troubled man. He needs help, and badly. Not from more sessions with psychiatrists, but help from those who love him most – and despite everything, I know you both love him. Just as his mother and I love him and care what happens to him. As for Melodie, I visited her before dinner, and she's not feeling well enough to attend the party. She wouldn't let me examine her, though I tried to insist, and she says she feels too big, too clumsy and won't be coming out where guests can stare at her enormous size. I think that might be the best solution for her. But if you would, look in on her and say a few kind words of encouragement, for that poor girl is coming apart from worry . . .'

Jory steered his chair down the hall, turning directly into his room, ignoring Melodie's closed door. I sighed, as did Chris.

Dutifully Cindy tried to say a few consoling words to Melodie outside of her locked door before she came prancing back to join Chris and I. 'I'm not going to let Melodie spoil my fun. I think she's acting like a damned selfish fool. As for me, I intend to have the time of my life tonight,' said Cindy in parting. 'I don't give a damn about Bart and his party except what pleasure it gives me.'

'I'm concerned about Cindy,' said Chris when we were sprawled on our wide bed, trying to catch a short nap. 'I have the feeling Cindy is not stingy with her favours.'

'Chris, don't you dare say that! Just because we caught her with that boy Lance doesn't mean she is loose. She's looking, looking all the time at each young man she meets, hoping he's the one. If one says he loves her, she believes because she needs to believe. Don't you realize Bart has stolen her confidence? She's afraid she is exactly what Bart thinks she is. She's torn between being as wicked as he thinks and being as nice as we want her to be. Cindy's a beautiful young woman . . . and Bart treats her like filth.'

It had been a long day for Chris. He closed his eyes and turned on his side to embrace me. 'Eventually Bart will straighten out,' he murmured. 'For the first time I'm seeing in his eyes the need to find a compromise. He has the desperate desire to find someone or something to believe in. Someday he will find what he needs, and when he does, he'll be set free to be the fine man he is under that hateful exterior.'

Sleep and dream of impossible things, like harmony in the family, like brothers and a sister who found love for each other. Dream on, dreamer . . .

I heard the grandfather clock down the hall chiming the hour of seven when we were supposed to rise from our naps to bathe and dress. I shook Chris awake and told him to hurry and dress. He stretched, yawned, lazily got up to shower while I took a quick tub bath; then he was shaving before donning his custom-tailored tux. Chris stared at himself in a pier glass. 'Cathy, am I gaining weight?' he asked with concern.

'No, darling. You look terrif – as Cindy would say.'

'What do you say?'

'You grow more handsome with each passing year.' I stepped closer to encircle his waist with my arms as my cheek rested against his back. 'I love you more each year . . . and even when you are as old as Joel, I will see you as you are now . . . standing twelve feet tall, in your shining suit of armour, soon to ride your white unicorn. In your hand you'll carry a twelve-foot spear with a green dragon's head perched upon its point.'

In the mirror I saw his reflection; tears had come to glisten in his eyes. 'After all this time, you remember,' he whispered hoarsely. 'After all these many years . . .'

'As if I could forget . . .'

'But it's been so long ago.'

'And today the moon shone at noon,' I murmured, moving to face him and slide my arms up around his neck, 'and a blizzard blew in your unicorn . . . and I saw to my own delight that you've always had my respect. You didn't need to earn it.'

Those two tears trickled slowly down his cheeks. I kissed them away. 'So you forgive me, Catherine? Say now, while we have the chance, that you forgive me for putting you through so much hell. For Bart would have turned out differently if I had stayed only his uncle and found another wife.'

I was careful not to smudge his jacket with my makeup as I rested my cheek over his heart, which I heard thumpity-thump-thumping. Just as I'd heard it the first time our love changed and became more than it should have been. 'If I blink my eyes just once, I'm twelve years old again, and you're fourteen. I can see you as you were then . . . but I can't see me. Chris, why can't I see me?'

His crooked smile was bittersweet. 'Because I've stolen all the memories of what you were and stored them in my heart. But you haven't said you forgive me.'

'Would I be here, where I am, if I didn't want to be?'

'I hope and pray not,' and I was held, held so tightly in his arms my ribs ached.

Outside the snow began to fall again. Inside my Christopher Doll had turned back the clock, and if there was no magic for Melodie in this house, and Lance's departure had stolen romance from Cindy, there was more than enough magic for me when Chris was there to cast his spell.

At nine-thirty we sat, all ready to stand when Trevor hurried to open the door. He stood anxiously looking at his watch, glancing at us with great pride. Bart, Chris, Jory and myself in our elegant expensive formal clothes faced the front windows with their splendid draperies. The towering Christmas tree in the foyer sparkled with a thousand tiny white lights. It had taken five people hours to decorate that tree.

As I sat there like some middle-aged Cinderella who had already found her prince and married him and was caught in the spell of the happy-ever-after, which wasn't all that perfect, something pulled my eyes upward. In the shadows of the rotunda where two knights in full armour stood on pedestals opposite each other, I saw a dark shadow move. Even in the shade of that smaller closer knight, I thought I knew who it was. Joel, who was supposed to be in bed asleep, or on his knees praying for all our sinning un-Christian souls.

'Bart,' I whispered to my second son, who moved to stand beside my chair, 'wasn't this supposed to be the special party to reintroduce Joel to all his old friends?'

'Yes,' he whispered back, putting his arm over my shoulders. 'But that was just my excuse. I knew he wouldn't want to come. The truth of the matter is, few of his old friends are still alive, although many of my grandmother's schoolchums are still around.' His strong fingers bit down into my shoulder's tender flesh. 'You look lovely – like an angel.'

Was that a compliment, or a suggestion?

He smiled at me cynically, then snatched his arm away as if it had betrayed him.

I laughed nervously. 'Oh, someday when I'm as old as Joel I suppose I'll take on a dowager's hump and shuffle my feet along, and when my sinning is over, I'll put on the halo I lost way back when I was in puberty . . .'

Both Bart and Chris scowled to hear me talk that way, but I felt good when I saw the shadow of Joel slink away.

Liveried servants readied the buffet tables as Bart got up to pace the floor, looking exceptionally handsome in his black tux with the pleated formal shirt.

I reached for Jory's hand, squeezed it. 'You're looking just as handsome as Bart,' I whispered.

'Mom, have you given him a compliment? He looks great, really great, the very man his father must have been.'

Blushing, I felt ashamed. 'No, I haven't said a word because he seems so devilishly pleased with himself that I think he'd burst with any praise he might hear from me.'

'Mom, you're wrong. Go on, say to him what you say to me. You may think I need it more, but I think he does.'

Standing, I strode over to where Bart was peering out on to the drive, which curved gradually downward. 'Can't see a single headlight,' he gruffily complained. 'It's not snowing now. The roads have been cleared. Ours is sprinkled over with gravel; where the hell are they?'

'I've never seen you look more handsome than you do tonight, Bart.'

He turned to stare into my eyes, then he glanced at Jory. 'More handsome than Jory?'

'Equally as handsome.'

Scowling, he turned back to the window. Out there he saw something to take his mind off of himself. 'Hey – look, here they come!'

I watched the string of headlights in the distance, heading up the hill. 'Get ready, everybody,' called Bart, giving Trevor an excited gesture to be ready to swing wide the doors.

Chris strolled beside Jory's chair, which he guided expertly, as I caught hold of Bart's arm and went to form a receiving line. Trevor hurried up to give us all a bright smile.

'I just love parties, I always have, I always will. Makes the heart beat faster. Makes old bones feel young again. I can tell it's going to be a jolly smashing one tonight.'

Two or three times Trevor said that – with less conviction each time, as still not one pair of those headlights climbed high enough to reach our drive. No one rang our bell, banged our door knocker.

The musicians were in position under the rotunda, on a dais that had been constructed especially for them, centred directly between the curving dual stairways. They tuned their instruments over and over again as my feet in their high-heeled fancy slippers began to ache. I sat again on an elegant chair and wiggled my shoes off under the folds of my gown, which was growing heavier and more uncomfortable by the minute. Eventually Chris sat beside me, and Bart took the righthand chair, all us us very silent, almost holding our breaths. Jory had his own special chair that could buzz him around tirelessly. From window to window he drove, looking out and reporting.

I knew that Cindy was upstairs, all dressed and ready, waiting to be 'fashionably' late and impress everyone when finally she drifted down the stairs. She had to be growing very impatient.

'They must be coming soon – ' Jory said when the hour reached ten-thirty. 'There's lots of banked snow on the side roads to confuse them . . .'

Bart's lips were tight and grim, his eyes stony cold.

No one said anything. I was afraid to even speculate on why no one had arrived. Trevor looked very anxious when he thought we weren't noticing.

To give myself something pleasant to think about, I fixed my eyes on the buffet tables, which reminded me so much of that first ball I'd seen in the original Foxworth Hall.

Very much like what I was staring at.

Red linen tablecloths, silver dishes and bowls. A fountain spraying champagne. Huge, gleaming, chafing dishes emitting delicious odours. Heaps and heaps of food on fancy tiered plates of crystal, porcelain, gold and silver. At last I could resist no longer and got up to taste of this and that while Bart frowned and complained I was ruining the beautiful designs. I wrinkled my nose his way and handed Chris a plate full of everything I knew he'd like best. Soon Jory was helping himself.

Red beeswax bayberry candles burned lower and lower. Towering gelatin masterpieces began to sag. Melted cheeses began to toughen, and the heating sauces thickened. Crêpe batter waited to be poured on turned over thin pans, while chefs eyed each other curiously. I had to look away from all that was going bad.

Fires cheered all our main rooms, making them cosy, exceptionally lovely. Extra servants grew restless and anxious-looking as they fidgeted and began to mill about, whispering amongst themselves, not knowing what to do.

Down the stairs drifted Cindy in a crimson hooped-skirted gown, so elaborate it put my delicately beaded gown to shame. Hers had a tight bodice, with a flounce of fluted ruffles to cover a little of her upper arms, displaying her shoulders to advantage and creating a magnificent frame for her creamy, swelling breasts. The red gown was cut very low. The skirt was a masterpiece of ruffles, caught with white silk flowers rain-dropped with iridescent crystals. A few of these white silk blossoms were tucked in her upswept hair, duplicating something Scarlett O'Hara might have liked.

'Where's everybody?' she asked, looking around, her radiant expression fading. 'I waited and waited to hear the music playing, then sort of dozed off, thinking when I woke that I was missing out on all the fun.'

She paused and glanced around before a look of dismay flooded her expression. 'Don't tell me nobody's going to come! I just can't stand another disappointment!' Dramatically she threw her hands about.

'No one has as yet arrived, Miss,' said Trevor tactfully. 'They must have lost their way, and I must say you look a dream of loveliness, as does your mother.'

'Thank you,' she said, floating his way and brushing his cheek with a daughterly kiss. 'You look very distinguished yourself.' She dashed past Bart's look of astonishment and ran to the piano. 'Please, may I?' she asked a young, good-looking musician who seemed delighted to have something happening, at last.

Cindy sat down beside him, put her hands on the keys, threw back her head and began to sing: 'Oh, holy night, Oh, night when stars are shining.'

I stared, as did all of us, at the girl we thought we knew so well. It wasn't an easy song to sing, but she did it so well, with so much emotion even Bart stopped pacing the floor to turn and stare at her in amazement.

Tears were in my eyes. Oh, Cindy, how could you keep that voice a secret for so long? Her piano playing was only adequate, but that voice, the feeling she put into her phrasing. All the musicians then joined in to drown out her piano playing, if not her voice.

I sat, stunned, hardly believing that my Cindy could sing so beautifully. When she'd finished, we all applauded enthusiastically. As Jory called out, 'Sensational! Fantastic! Absolutely wonderful, Cindy! You sneak – you never told us you continued with your voice lessons.'

'I haven't. It's just me expressing the way I feel.'

She cast her eyes down, then took a sly, hooded look at Bart's astonished expression, which showed not only his surprise but some pleasure as well. For the first time he had found something to admire about Cindy. Her small smile of satisfaction fleeted quickly by, kind of a sad smile, as if she wished Bart could like her for other reasons as well.

'I love Christmas carols and religious songs, they do something for me. Once in school I sang "Swing Low, Sweet Chariot", and the teacher said I had the kind of emotional feeling to make a great singer. But I still want most to be an actress.'

Laughing and happy again, she asked us to join in and we'd make this a real party, even if no one showed up. She began to bang out a tune resembling 'Joy to the World'. Then 'Jingle Bells'.

This time Bart was not moved.

He strode again to the windows to stare out, his back straight. 'They can't ignore my invitations, not when they responded,' he mumbled to himself.

I couldn't understand how his business friends could dare to offend him when he had to be their most important client, and everyone loved a party, especially the kind of party they had to know would be sensational.

Somehow or other, Bart was accomplishing miracles with that five hundred thousand a year, making it grow in ways that Chris would have found too risky. Bart risked everything . . . calculated gambles that paid off handsomely. Only then did I realize that perhaps my mother had meant it to be this way. If she had given Bart all the fortune in one grand huge sum, he wouldn't have worked as hard to build his own fortune, which would, if he kept it up, far exceed what Malcolm had left him. And in this way Bart would find his own worth.

Yet what did money matter when he was so disappointed he couldn't eat a thing that was lavishly displayed? However, disillusionment drove him to the liquor, and in a short while he'd managed to swallow half a dozen strong drinks as he paced the floors, growing angrier by the second.

I could hardly bear to watch his disappointment, and soon, despite myself, tears were silently wetting my face.

Chris whispered, 'We can't go to bed and leave him here alone. Cathy, he's suffering. Look at him pacing back and forth. With every step he takes his anger grows. Somebody is going to pay for this slight.'

Eleven-thirty came and went.

By this time Cindy was the only one having a good time. The musicians and servants seemed to adore her. Eagerly they played and she sang. When she wasn't singing, she was dancing with every man there, even Trevor and other male servants. She gestured to the maids, inviting them to dance, and happily they joined in the festivity she created around her as they took turns to see that she, at least, was entertained.

'Let's all eat, drink and be merry!' Cindy cried, smiling at Bart. 'It's not the end of the world, brother Bart. What do you care? We're too rich to be well liked. We're also too rich to feel sorry for ourselves. And look, we have at least twenty guests . . . let's dance, drink, eat, have a ball!'

Bart stopped pacing to stare at her. Cindy held high her glass of champagne. 'My toast to you, brother Bart. For every ugly thing you've said to me, I give you back blessings of good will, good health, long life and much love.' She touched his highball glass with her champagne glass and then sipped, smiling into his eyes charmingly before she offered another toast. 'I think you look absolutely terrif, and the girls who don't show up tonight are missing the chance of their lifetimes. So here it is, another toast to the most eligible bachelor in the world. I wish you joy, I wish you happiness, I wish you love. I would wish you success, but you don't need that.'

He couldn't move his eyes away. 'Why don't I need success?' he asked in a low tone.

'Because what more could you want? You have success when you have millions, and soon enough you'll have more money than you know what to do with.'

Bart's dark head bowed. 'I don't feel successful. Not when no one will even come to my party.' His voice cracked as he turned his back.

I got up to go to him. 'Will you dance with me, Bart?'

'No!' he snapped, hurrying to a distant window where he could stand and stare again.

Cindy had a wonderful time with the musicians and the men and women who'd come to serve Bart's guests. However, I was deeply downcast, feeling sorry for Bart, who had counted so much on this. Out of sympathy for him, all of us but Cindy and the hired help moved into the front parlour, and there we sat in our fabulous expensive clothes and waited for guests who obviously had accepted, only to trick Bart later on – and in this way tell us what they thought of the Foxworths on the hill.

The grandfather clock began to toll the hour of twelve. Bart left the windows and fell upon the sofa before the guttering log fire. 'I should have known it would turn out this way.' He glanced bitterly at Jory. 'Perhaps they came to my birthday party only to see you dance, and now, when you can't – to hell with me! They've snubbed me – and they're going to pay for it,' he said in a hard, cold voice, louder and stronger than Joel's but with the same kind of zealot's fury. 'Before I'm through, there won't be a house in a twenty-mile radius that doesn't belong to me. I'll ruin them. All of them. With the power of the Foxworth trust behind me I can borrow millions, and then I'll buy out the banks and demand they pay off their mortgages. I'll buy out the village stores, close them down. I'll hire other attorneys, fire the ones I have now and see that they're disbarred. I'll find new stock brokers, hire new real estate agents, see that real estate property values are undermined, and when they sell cheap, I'll buy. By the time I'm through, there won't be one old aristocratic Virginia family left this side of Charlottesville! And not one of my business colleagues will be left with anything but debts to pay off!'

'Then will you feel satisfied?' asked Chris.

'No!' flared Bart, his eyes hard, glaring. 'I won't be satisfied until justice has ruled! I have done nothing to deserve this night! Nothing but try to give them what our ancestors did – and they have rejected me! They'll pay, and pay, and then pay some more.'

He sounded like me! To hear my very own words coming from the mouth of the child I'd carried when I'd said them made all my blood drain into my feet. Shivering, I tried to appear normal. 'I'm sorry, Bart. But it wasn't a total loss, was it? We're all together under one roof, a united family for once. And Cindy's music and singing made this a festive occasion after all.'

He wasn't listening.

He was staring at all the food that had yet to be eaten. All the champagne with the bubbles gone flat. All the wine and liquor that could have loosened many a tongue and given him information he wanted to use. He glared at the maids in their pretty black and white uniforms, drunken and staggering around, some still dancing as the music played on and on. He glowered at the few waiters who still held trays of drinks gone warm. Some stood and looked at him and waited for his signal to say the night was over. The impressive centrepiece of an ice crystal manger, with the three shepherds, the wise men and all the animals, had melted into a puddle and spilled over to darken the red cloth.

'How lucky you were when you danced in *The Nutcracker*, Jory,' said Bart as he headed fast for the stairs. 'You were the ugly nutcracker that turned into the handsome prince. You dominated every male role – won the prettiest ballerina every time. In *Cinderella*, in *Romeo and Juliet*. In *The Sleeping Beauty*, *Giselle*, *Swan Lake* – every time but the last time. And it's the last time that counts, isn't it?'

How cruel! How very cruel! I watched Jory wince, and for once he allowed his pain to show, making my heart ache for him.

'Merry Christmas,' Bart called as he disappeared up the stairs. 'We'll never again celebrate this holiday, or any other in this house as long as I run it. Joel was right. He warned me not to try and conform and be like others. He said I shouldn't try to make people like or respect me. From now on, I'll be like Malcolm. I'll gain respect by inflicting my will on others, with fists of iron, and with ruthless determination. All who have alienated me tonight will feel my might.'

I turned to Chris when he was out of sight. 'He sounds crazy!'

'No, darling, he's not crazy – he's just Bart, young and vulnerable again and very, very hurt. He used to break his bones when he was a child to punish himself because he failed socially and in school. Now he's going to break the lives of others. Isn't it a pity, Cathy, that nothing works out for him?'

I stood at the newel post looking upward to where an old man hid in the shadows, seeming to shake from his silent laughter.

'Chris, you go on up, and I'll follow in a few seconds.' Chris wanted to know what I was planning, so I lied and said I was going to have a few words with our housekeeper about cleaning up the mess. But I had something far different in mind.

As soon as everyone was out of sight, I ducked into Bart's huge office, closed the door and was soon rifling through his desk to find the RSVP cards that had dutifully arrived weeks ago.

They must have been fingered many a time from the ink smudges on the envelopes. Two hundred and fifty cards had accepted. My teeth bit down on my lower lip. Not one rejection, not even one. People didn't do things like this, even to someone they disliked. If they hadn't wanted to come, they would have tossed the invitations into the trash along with the return card, or sent back the card declining.

Carefully I replaced the cards and then headed up the back stairs to Joel's room.

Without even a preliminary knock I opened his door to find him sitting on the edge of his narrow bed, doubled over in what appeared to be a terrible stomach cramp, or that hateful silent laughter. He was in quiet convulsion, quivering, jerking, hugging himself with skinny arms.

Quietly I waited until his hysteria was over, and only then did he see the long shadow I cast. Gasping, his mouth sunken because his teeth were in a cup by the bed, he stared up at me. 'Why are you here, niece?' he asked in that whiny but raspy voice, his thin hair rumpled into devil horns that stood straight up.

'Downstairs, a while ago, I looked up and saw you in the rotunda shadows, laughing. Why were you laughing, Joel? You must have seen that Bart was suffering.'

'I don't know,' he mumbled, half turning to replace the teeth in his mouth. When he had them in, he ran a hand over his spikey hair, smoothing it down. Only his cowlick refused to behave. Now he could meet my eyes. 'Your daughter made so much racket down there I couldn't sleep. I guess the sight of all of you in your fancy clothes waiting for guests that didn't come tickled my sense of humour.'

'You have a very cruel sense of humour, Joel. I thought you cared for Bart.'

'I do love that boy.'

'Do you?' I asked sharply. 'I don't think so, or else you would have sympathized.' I glanced around his sparsely furnished room, thinking back. 'Weren't you the one who mailed off the party invitations?'

'I don't remember,' he said calmly. 'Time doesn't mean much to an old man like me when it's growing so short. What happened years ago seems clearer than what happened a month ago.'

'My memory is much better than yours, Joel.'

I sat down in the one chair he had in his room. 'Bart had an important appointment, and, as I recall, he turned over that stack of invitations to you. Did you mail them, Joel?'

'Of course I mailed them!' he snapped angrily.

'But you just said you couldn't remember.'

'I remember that day. It took so long, dropping them in the slot one by one.'

All the time I'd closely watched his eyes. 'You're lying, Joel,' I said, taking a wild shot in the dark. 'You didn't mail those invitations. You brought them up here, and in the privacy of this room, you opened each one, filled in the blank places for "Yes, we will be happy to attend," and then mailed those in the provided envelopes back to Bart. You see, I found them in Bart's office. I never saw such a strange assortment of crooked handwriting, all in various shades of blue, violet, green, black and brown ink. Joel, you changed pens to make it seem those cards were signed by different guests, when it was you who signed them all!'

Slowly Joel stood. He gathered about him the handwoven invisible brown habit of a saintly monk, thrusting his gnarled hands up those imaginary sleeves. 'I think you have lost your mind, woman,' he said coldly. 'If you wish, go to your son and tell him your barbaric suspicions, and see if he belives you.'

Jumping up, I headed for the door. 'I intend to do just that!' I slammed the door hard behind me and hurried off.

In his study Bart was seated behind his desk, now wearing pyjamas covered by a black woollen robe piped in red. Drunkenly he was tossing the RSVP cards one by one into the roaring fire. I saw to my dismay the last of the pile go up in flames as I watched Bart pour another drink.

'What do you want?' he asked in a slurred way, narrowing his eyes and seeming surprised to see me.

'Bart, I've got to say this, and you have to listen. I don't think Joel mailed your invitations, and that is why your guests didn't show up.'

He tried to focus his eyes and his intellect, which must have reeled under the influence of all he'd drunk. 'Of course he did. Joel always does as I order.' He leaned back in his swivel chair with its back that lowered automatically from the pressure he applied and closed his eyes. 'Tired now. Go away. Don't stand and stare at me with eyes of pity. And they did accept . . . didn't I just burn their replies?'

'Bart, listen to me. Don't fall asleep before I finish. Didn't you notice how strangely they were signed? All the different coloured ink? The crooked, awkward handwriting? Joel did not mail your invitations, but instead took them to his room, opened them, extracted the RSVP cards and envelopes, and since you had put stamps on all of them, all he had to do was drive to the post office and mail them back to you a few each day.'

His closed eyes slotted. 'Mother, I think you should go to bed. My greatuncle is the best friend I've ever had. He'd never do anything to hurt me.'

'Bart, please. Don't put too much faith in Joel.'

'Get out!' he roared. 'It's your fault they didn't come! Yours and that man you sleep with!'

I stumbled as I turned away, feeling defeated and so afraid this could very well be true – and Joel was just what Bart and Chris believed him to be, a harmless old man who wanted to live out his days in this house, near the one person who respected and loved him.

UNTO US IS BORN . . .

Christmas Day was over. I was in bed curled up beside Chris, who could always fall easily into deep sleep, leaving me to fret and stew and flip and turn. Behind me the great one-eyed swan kept its ruby eye alert, causing me to look around often at what it could be seeing. I heard the deep, mellow tones of the grandfather clock at the end of our hall strike three o'clock. A few minutes ago I'd got up to watch Bart's red car speed down the drive, heading towards the local tavern where no doubt he'd drown his sorrows in additional liquor and end up in some whore's bed. More than once he'd come home reeking of liquor and cheap perfume.

Hour after hour passed as I waited for Bart to come home. I pictured all sorts of calamities. On a night like this the drunks were out, deadlier than arsenic.

Why lie here doing nothing? I slipped out of the bed, arranged the covers neatly over Chris's sleeping bulk, kissed his cheek, then arranged his heavy arms around a pillow that I presumed he'd think was me, and he did from the way he snuggled it close. It was my intention to wait for Bart in his room.

It was almost five on a cold, blustery, winter morning before I heard his car approaching. I was huddled in a deep pile robe of red-rose, curled up on one of his white sofas with his black and red pillows behind my back.

I dozed, then heard him climbing the stairs, heard him moving drunkenly from room to room, bumping into furniture as he had when he was a child. He was dedicated to checking each room to see if it had been neatly tidied before the servants retired. And to my dismay, from the length of time it was taking him to appear in his own rooms, he was doing that now. No newspapers could be left in sight. No magazines not neatly stacked in their respective piles. No articles of clothing left on the floor, or coats on doorknobs or draped on chair backs.

Minutes later Bart was in his room, flicking the switch to light the lamps. He swayed to and fro before he stared at me sitting in the dimness of his room, where I'd started a fire that crackled cheerfully in the darkness. Shadows danced on the white walls, turning them orange and rosy, the black leather of another wall catching red highlights, creating a kind of fake inferno.

'Mother, what the hell is going on? Didn't I tell you to stay out of my wing?' Yet, in his drunken state, he looked glad to see me.

He wove his way uncertainly to a chair, took careful aim and fell down, closing his darkly shadowed eyes. I got up to massage the back of his neck while he drooped his head forward and held it as if it pained him dreadfully. His hands cupped his face as my hands took away the pain. Then he sighed, leaned back and stared fuzzily up into my eyes. 'I should know better than to drink,' he murmured in a slurred way, sighing as I stepped back and sat before him. 'It always makes me do crazy things, and then I feel sick. Stupid to keep it up when liquor has never done anything for me but add to my problems. Mother, what's wrong with me? I can't even drink myself into a forgetful stupor. I'm always too sensitive. I overheard Jory tell you one day he was building that wonderful clipper ship to give to me, and I was secretly thrilled. No one has ever spent months and months making me a gift – and then it's broken. He did such a great job, taking so many pains to see that everything was exactly right. Now all that work is in the trash pile.'

He sounded childlike, vulnerable, easy to reach and I was going to try, try to give him every ounce of love I had. Not mean when he was drunk, not silly but loveable, touching in his humanity. 'Darling, Jory will gladly make you another,' I volunteered, not sure he would be glad to do all that tedious work a second time.

'No, Mother, I don't want it now. Something would happen to that one, too. That's the way my life goes. Life has a cruel way of taking from me what I want most.

There's no happiness or love waiting for me around the bend of tomorrow. No gaining what I want – my heart's desire, as I used to call the impossible dreams of my youth. Wasn't that childish and silly? No wonder you pitied me – I wanted so much. Too much. I was never satisfied. You and that man you love gave me everything I ever said I wanted, and many things I didn't even mention, and still you never gave me happiness. So I've decided not to care about anything anymore. The Christmas ball wouldn't have given me pleasure even if the guests had showed up. I still would have failed to impress them. Inside, all along, I knew my party would prove just another failure, like all the other parties you used to give me. Still I went ahead and hypnotized myself into believing that if tonight was successful it would set a precedent, so to speak, and all my life would then change for the better.'

My second son was talking to me as he'd never done before. Liquor was loosening his tongue.

'Stupid, aren't I?' he went on. 'Cindy's right when she calls me a jerk and a creep. I look in my mirrors and see a handsome man, very much like my father, whom you say you loved more than any other man. But I don't feel I am handsome inside. I'm uglier than sin inside. Then I wake up, feel the fresh morning mountain air, see the dew sparkling on the roses, see the winter sun shining on the snow, and that tells me maybe life is going to offer me my chance after all. I have hopes of one day finding the real me – the one I can like, and that's why, months ago, I decided to make this the happiest Christmas of all our lives, not only for Jory, who deserves it, but for you and for myself. You think I don't love Jory, but I do.'

He bowed his head into his waiting hands and sighed heavily. 'Confession time, Mother. I hate Jory, too, I don't deny that. But I hold no love at all for Cindy. She's done nothing but steal from me – and she isn't even one of us. Jory's always had the largest portion of your love, the part you've got left over after giving your brother the best. I've never had the major portion of anyone's love. I thought that Melodie had given me that. Now I know she'd have taken any man just to replace Jory. Any man at all who was available and willing, and that's why I hate her now, just as much as I hate Cindy.'

His hands came down to show how bitterly his dark eyes glowed; the reflection from the fire made them like red-hot coals. Those drinks had made his breath reek. My heart almost stopped beating. What would he want? I stood up, moved behind his chair and slid my arms around his neck before my head lowered to rest on top of his dishevelled hair. 'Bart, you drove away tonight and left me sleepless and waiting for you to come home. Tell me what can I do to help. Nobody here hates you like you think. Not even Cindy. Often you make us angry because you disappoint us, not because we want to reject you.'

'Send Chris away,' he said tonelessly as if he said this without hope of ever seeing Chris gone from my life. 'That will tell me you love me. Only when you break with him can I feel good about myself, and you.'

Pain stabbed me. 'He'd die without me, Bart,' I whispered. 'I know you can't understand the way it is between us, and I myself can't explain why he needs me, and why I need him, except we were young and alone and in a terrifying situation, and we had only each other. We created a fantasy dreamlike world when we were locked away and trapped ourselves in so doing, and now that we're both middle-aged we still live in that fantasy. We can't survive without it. To lose him now would destroy not only him, but me as well.'

'But Mother!' he cried out passionately, turning to hold me, to press his face between my breasts, 'you'd still have me!' He gazed up into my face, his arms around my waist. 'I want you to purify your soul before it's too late. What you do with Chris is against the rules of God and society. Let him go, Mother. Please let him go – before someone does something terrible, let go of your brother's love.'

I drew away, brushed back a fallen wisp of my hair. Feeling defeated and hopeless, for it was so impossible, what he asked. 'Would you hurt me, Bart?'

He bit down on his lip, a childish habit that came back when he was disturbed. 'I don't know. Sometimes I want to. More than I want to hurt him. You smile at me with such sweetness, and my heart reaches out, wanting you never to change. Then I go to bed and hear whispers in my head that tell me you are evil and deserve to die. When I think of you dead and in the ground, tears fill my eyes and my heart feels empty and broken, heavier than lead – and I'm undone. I feel so cold, so alone and scared. Mother, am I crazy? Why is it I can't fall in love with confidence that it will last? Why can't I forget about what you do?

'I thought for awhile that Melodie and I had it made. She seemed to me so perfect, and then she began to turn fat and ugly. She whined and nagged, and complained about my home. Even Cindy was more appreciative. I took her to the best restaurants, to plays and movies, and tried to take her mind off Jory, but she wouldn't let it go. She kept talking of the ballet and how much it means to her, and that's when I found out I was only a substitute for Jory and she never loved me, never loved me at all. She used me as a way to forget her loss for a while. Now she doesn't even look like the girl I fell in love with. She wants pity and sympathy, not love. She took my love and turned it around, so now I can't stand to look at her.'

Sighing, he lowered his eyes and said in such a low voice I could hardly hear him, 'I see that kid, Cindy, and realize she must look the way you used to, and a little bit of me knows why Chris fell in love with you. That makes me hate her worse. She teases me, you know. Cindy would like to creep under my skin and make me do something as wicked as what Chris does with you. She strolls around in her bedroom wearing nothing but bikini bra and bottoms. And she knows I check her rooms before I retire. Tonight she had on a nightgown so transparent I could see right through it. She just stood there and let me stare. Joel tells me she's nothing but a whore.'

'Then don't go to her bedroom,' I said with control. 'Lord knows we don't have to see anyone who lives here if we don't want to – and Joel is a bigoted, narrow-minded fool. All Cindy's generation wears next-to-nothing undergarments. But you're right, she shouldn't parade around in them. I'll speak to her about that in the morning. You're sure she displayed herself deliberately?'

'You must have done the same thing,' he said, dully accusing. 'All those years locked up with Chris – did you show him your body deliberately?'

How could I tell him how it had been and make him understand? He'd never understand. 'We all tried to be decent, Bart. It's so long ago and I don't like to remember. I try to forget. I want to think that Chris is my husband and not my brother. We can't have children, never could. Doesn't that make it better – a little better?'

Shaking his head, his eyes darkened. 'Go away. You just give me excuses, and you bring it all back, the sickness I used to feel when I found out about you and him. I was just a kid wanting to feel clean and wholesome. I still want to feel that way. That's why I keep showering, shaving, picking up, ordering the servants to scrub, vacuum, dust and dust, and do it every day. I'm trying to eliminate the dirt you and Chris put in my life – and I can't do it!'

There was no comfort in Chris's arms as I tried to sleep. I drifted into an uneasy dream. Then I bolted awake to hear distant screams. Leaving my bed for the second time in the same night, I raced towards the screams.

Disoriented, I stared down at Melodie on the floor of the long corridor. She seemed to be wearing a white nightgown with ragged red stripes. She crawled along, moaning, causing me to think I was still dreaming. Her long hair was in damp disarray, her brow dripped sweat – and behind her was a trail of blood!

Blindly she stared up at me, imploring. 'Cathy, my baby is coming . . .' She screamed, then slowly, slowly, her pleading eyes went blank before she keeled over in a dead faint.

I ran for Chris, shaking him awake. 'It's Melodie!' I cried as he sat up and rubbed at his tired eyes. 'She's in labour. Right now she's fainted, lying face down in the hall with a trail of blood behind her . . .'

'Take it easy,' he soothed, leaping out of bed and pulling on his bathrobe. 'First babies are notoriously slow in arriving.' Nevertheless there was a look of anxiety in his eyes, as if he were mentally calculating just how long Melodie had been in labour. 'I've got everything I'll need in my bag,' he said as he rushed about gathering up blankets, clean sheets, towels. He still had the same black doctor's bag they'd given him when he graduated from medical school, as if that bag were sacred to him. 'No time to get her to the hospital if she's haemorrhaging like you say. Now all *you* have to do is rush down to the kitchen and put on all that hot water all doctors in the movies seem to need.'

I yelled impatiently, thinking he just wanted me out of his way. 'We're not in the movies, Chris!'

We were in the hall now, and he was bending over Melodie. 'I know that – it would help if you did something except run beside me and act hysterical. Now move aside, Catherine,' he barked as he leaned to pick Melodie up. In his arms she seemed to weigh no more than a feather, while her middle seemed a mountain high.

In her room he stuffed pillows under her hips, asked for more white towels, sheets, newspapers, even as he glared at me. 'Move, Catherine, move! From the position of the baby, its head is down and is already well on its way. RUN! I do have to sterilize a few instruments. Damn her for not speaking up and telling me she'd started her contractions early. While we were opening our gifts, she just sat there and said nothing. What the hell is wrong with everybody in this house? All she had to do was speak up and say something!'

Even before he finished muttering all this, as if to himself more than to me, I fled down the long dim halls, dashed recklessly down the back stairs closest to the kitchen. I drew hot water from the tap, put the kettle on to boil. Anxiously I waited, thinking Melodie enjoyed pity and wanted to punish us, and perhaps even wanted her baby to die so she could go back to New York unencumbered by a crippled husband and a fatherless child.

A watched pot takes so long to boil. A thousand thoughts went through my mind, ugly thoughts as I peered into the water to see the slightest roll. What was Chris doing? Should I waken Jory and tell him what was going on? Why had Melodie done this? Was she in some ways like Bart – inflicting punishment on herself for her sins? Finally, after what seemed an hour, the water began to bubble, then roll furiously. With steam pouring from the spout, I sprinted up the stairs and down more endless halls until I came to Melodie's bedroom.

Chris had arranged Melodie so she was sitting up, backed with many pillows. Her knees were shoved upward and held spread wide apart by pillows he used to support them. She was naked from the waist down, and I could see blood still trickling from her body. Feeling peculiar to see something like this, I fixed my eyes on the pads of towels and sheets he'd spread over newspapers to catch the blood. 'I can't stop the bleeding,' he said in a worried way. 'Scares me to think the baby might swallow some.' He threw me a glance. 'Cathy, put on that extra pair of rubber gloves and use the calipers you see in my bag to dip each instrument I've laid out into that boiling water. I expect you to hand me what I need when I ask for it.'

I nodded, terribly afraid I wouldn't remember the instrument names, when it had been so long ago, before he'd even graduated from medical school.

'Wake up, Melodie,' he said over and over. 'I need your help.' Lightly he slapped her face. 'Cathy, wet a facecloth in cold water. Wipe her face with that to bring her around so she can bear down and help push the baby out.'

The cold cloth on her head brought Melodie back to reality filled with pain. Right away she began to scream, to try and shove Chris away, to pull the covers over herself. 'Don't fight me,' said Chris in a fatherly way. 'Your baby is almost here, Melodie, but you have to bear down and take deep breaths, and I can't see what I'm doing if you cover yourself.'

Still screaming in a jerky, spasmodic way, she tried to obey Chris's orders as the sweat streamed off her face and wet her hair and chest. Her gown, which was shoved up to her waist, was soon sopping. 'Help her, Cathy,' ordered Chris, fiddling with what I thought were forceps. I put my hands where he told me and bore down.

'Please, darling,' I whispered when she stopped yelling long enough to hear me, 'you have to help. Right now your baby is struggling to survive and get out.'

Her wild eyes fraught with pain and fear struggled to focus on reality. 'I'm dying!' she yelled before she squinched her eyes shut, pulled in a deep breath and then, with my hands assisting the shove, bore down with more determination.

'You're doing fine, Melodie,' encouraged Chris. 'Now another hard shove and I should be able to see the top of your baby's head.' Sweating, holding on to my hands and squinting her eyes even tighter, Melodie gave one last might effort.

'Fine . . . you're doing fine! I can see the top of the baby's head,' said Chris in a happier tone, throwing me a look of pride. At that moment Melodie's head fell to the side and her eyes closed.

She'd fainted again. 'It's all right,' said Chris, glancing at her face. 'She's done a good job, and I can do my part now. She's through the worst part and can rest. I was thinking I'd have to use forceps, but it won't be necessary.'

With confident, kind hands, he carefully slid his hand inside the birth canal and somehow drew out a very small baby and handed it to me. I held the tiny, slimy, red baby and stared down in awe at Jory's son. Oh, how perfect this miniature little boy who flailed the air with his tiny fists and kicked with incredibly small feet, and screwed his apple-sized face into a knot as he prepared to let go with a howl as Chris tied off and severed the umbilical cord. Thrills that felt cold made my spine shiver. Out of the joining of my son with his wife came this perfect little grandson who had already seized my heart even before he cried. With tears in my eyes, my heart beating joyously for Jory, who would be so happy, I glanced up to see Chris working over Melodie and drawing from her what must be the afterbirth.

Again, I stared down at the crying, doll-sized, slimy infant that seemed to weigh less than four pounds. A child born from the passion and beauty of the ballet world . . . born on the music that must have played when he was conceived. I hugged the child to my heart, thinking this was a God's finest miracle, more beautiful than a tree, more lasting than a rose, a human born in His likeness. Tears flowed down my cheeks, for, like God's son, this child was born almost on Christmas day. My grandson! 'Chris, he's so little. Will he live?'

'Absolutely,' he said in an absorbed, abstracted tone as he continued to work over Melodie, frowning with some perplexity. 'How about using the mail scales and weighing him in. Then, if you would, give him a nice bath in tepid water. He'll begin to feel much better. Use the solution I mixed and put in a blue bowl to wash out his eyes, and use the solution in the pink bowl to clean his mouth and ears. There should be diapers and receiving blankets around here somewhere. He needs to be kept very warm.'

'In her suitcase,' I called out as I hurried into the adjacent bath and held the little boy in the cradle of my arm and began filling a pink plastic basin. 'For weeks she's had baby things packed and ready.'

I was excited, feeling exalted, wishing now I'd gone to Jory and given him the chance to see his child born. I sighed then, thinking this would be his one and only child. The chances were very slim that he could father another. How lucky he was to be blessed with this little boy.

The baby I held was so frail, with just a fuzz of blond making the top of his small head softly hazy. Miniature hands and incredibly small feet flailed the chilly air. His rosebud mouth worked in sucking motions even as he tried to open eyes that seemed glued together. Despite all the slime of childbirth smeared on his red skin, my heart went out to him.

Beautiful little baby. Dear, sweet little boy to make my Jory happy. I wanted to see the colour of his eyes, but he kept them tightly closed.

I was nervous, as if I'd never had a newborn of my own, and in a way, I hadn't. This baby was so small, so delicate looking. My two had been full term and had been cared for by experienced nurses immediately after their birth.

'Wrap him up tight,' reminded Chris from the other room. 'Be sure to run your finger around in his mouth to take out any blood clots or mucous you'll find. Newborns can choke on what's in their mouths.'

The baby's cries were distraught over the loss of the warm, familiar fluid of the womb, but as soon as I gently eased him into the warm water, he stopped crying and seemed to fall asleep. This little babe was so new, so raw looking that he seemed pitiful as I did what I had to. Even asleep his tiny, doll-like hands reached to find his mother and her breasts. His tiny penis stood straight up as I poured warm water over his genitals. Then, to my astonishment, I heard another baby cry!

Quickly wrapping my clean little grandson in a thick white towel, I hurried into the bedroom to see Chris staring down at a second child.

Chris looked up with the strangest expression. 'A girl,' he said softly. 'Blond hair, blue eyes. I talked to her obstetrician myself, and he didn't mention anything about hearing two heartbeats. Sometimes that happens because one child is behind the other . . . but how odd that not once – ' He broke off before he changed the subject and continued. 'Twins are usually smaller than other babies, and their small size, plus the weight of the second bearing down, helps the first come quicker than a single birth – usually. Melodie was lucky this time . . .'

'Ohhh,' I breathed, taking the small girl into my free arm and gazing down at her. I knew immediately who they were. Carrie and Cory born all over again!

'Chris, how fantastically marvellous!' I laughed, then saddened as I thought of my beloved twin brother and sister, now dead for so long. Still I could see them behind my eyes, racing through the backyard garden in Gladstone; running through the pitiful attic garden of paper flora and fauna. 'The same twins. Doppelgangers.'

Chris looked up, his rubber gloved hands quite bloody. 'No, Cathy,' he stated firmly, 'not doppelgangers. These are not the same twins born again. Remember that. Carrie came first then; this time the boy was first. This is not an unlucky, doomed set of children. These two will have only the best. Now, would you please stop staring and get busy? She needs a bath, too. And diaper that boy before he sprays everything.'

Handling such slippery tiny babies wasn't at all easy. Still, I managed, feeling overwhelmingly happy. Despite what Chris had said, I knew who these twins were – Cory and Carrie, reborn to live the kind of wonderful lives that were their due, the happy lives stolen from them by greed and selfishness.

'Don't you worry,' I whispered as I kissed each small red cheek and then their sweet tiny hands and feet. 'Your grandmother will see that you're happy. No matter what I have to do, you two are going to have everything that Carrie and Cory didn't.'

I glanced towards the bedroom where Melodie lay spent, just pulling out of her faint.

Chris called in to say he thought Melodie could use a nice sponge bath now, before he strode into the bathroom to take both babies from me. He sent me out to tend to the new mother while he gave the newborn twins a more complete inspection.

As I bathed Melodie and then slipped a fresh pink gown over her head, she awakened to stare at me with blank, disinterested eyes. 'Is it over?' she asked in a weak, weary way. I picked up her hairbrush and went to work to unsnarl her damp, stringy hair.

'Yes, darling, it's over. You have delivered.'

'What is it? A boy?' There was hope in her eyes, the first I'd seen in many a day.

'Yes, darling, a boy . . . and a girl. You have just given birth to beautiful, perfect twins.'

Her eyes grew huge, dark, full of anxieties so numerous she seemed about to faint again.

'They are perfect, with everything where it's supposed to be.'

She stared at me until I hurried to show her the twins.

She stared with the look of utmost amazement before she smiled faintly. 'Oh, they're cute . . . but I thought they'd be dark like Jory.'

I placed the two babies in her arms. She gazed down at them as if all this was totally unreal. 'Two,' she whispered weakly again and again, 'two!' Her eyes fixed somewhere in space. '*Two*. I used to tell Jory we'd stop having children when we had two. I wanted a boy and a girl . . . but not twins. Now I have to be both mother and father to two! Twins! It's not fair, not fair!'

Gently I smoothed back her hair. 'Darling, this is God's way of blessing both you and Jory. He has delivered to you the complete family you wanted, and you won't have to go through this again. And you're not alone in this; we'll do all we can to help you. We'll hire nurses, maids, the best. Neither you nor they will lack for anything.'

Hope came to her eyes before she closed them. 'I'm tired, Cathy, so tired. I guess it is nice to have both a boy and a girl, now that Jory can't make more. I just hope this will make up for a little that he's lost . . . and he'll be pleased.'

With those words she fell into deep sleep, even as I finished brushing her hair. Once her hair had been so lovely; now it was dull, lifeless. I'd have to shampoo it before Jory saw her. When next Jory saw his wife, he'd see again the lovely girl he'd married.

For I was going to reunite this pair if it was the last thing I did.

Chris stepped up beside me and took the twins from her arms. 'Leave now, Cathy. She's exhausted and needs a long rest. Time to shampoo tomorrow.'

'Did I say that aloud? I was only thinking about it.'

He laughed. 'You did only think it, but you were also fingering her hair, and in your eyes your thoughts shone clearly. I know how you feel about clean hair – the remedy for all depressions.'

Kissing him first and hugging him tight, I left him with Melodie, then went to shake Jory awake. He came back from dreams, rubbing at his eyes, squinting at me. 'What's up now? More trouble?'

'No trouble this time, darling.' I stood and grinned at him until he must have thought I'd lost my mind. He looked so perplexed as he shoved himself up on his elbows. 'I have belated Christmas gifts for you, Jory, my love.' He shook his head in a bewildered way.

'Mom, couldn't that gift have waited until morning?'

'No, not this one. You're a father, Jory!' I laughed and hugged him again. 'Oh, Jory, God is kind. Remember when you and Melodie planned your family, you said you wanted two children, first a boy, then a girl? Well, as a special gift, sent straight from Heaven, you have twins! A boy, a girl!'

Tears flooded his eyes. He choked out his first concern. 'How is Mel?'

'Chris is in there now, taking care of her. You see, ever since the wee hours of yesterday, Melodie was in labour and she didn't say a word.'

'Why?' he bemoaned, his hands covering his face. 'Why, when Dad was here all the time and he could have helped?'

'I don't know, son, but let's not think about that. She'll be fine, just fine. He says she won't even need to go to the hospital, although he does want to drive the twins in for a checkup just to be safe. Such tiny babies need more care than full-term ones. And he also said it wouldn't hurt if Melodie had the attention of an obstetrician. He had to cut her, an episiotomy he called it. Without the surgery she would have torn. He sewed her up nicely, but it hurts, Jory, until the stitches come out. No doubt he'll bring them and her back the same day.'

'God *is* good, Mom,' he whispered hoarsely, swiping at the tears as he tried to smile. 'I can't wait to see them. It will take me too much time to get up and go to them – will you bring them here to me?'

First he had to sit up to be ready to receive the twins into his arms. I turned to look at him from the doorway, thinking I'd never seen a happier-looking man.

During my absence, Chris had fashioned cribs out of two drawers pulled open and lined with soft blankets. He immediately wanted to know how Jory took my news and smiled when he heard of Jory's delight. Tenderly he put both babies in my arms. 'Walk carefully, my love,' he whispered before he kissed me. Then I was hurrying back to my eldest son with his firstborn. He received them as tender gifts to cherish forever, staring down with pride and love at the children he'd created.

'They look so much like Cory and Carrie did,' I said softly in the warm glow of his dimly lit room. 'So beautiful, even if they are very small. Have you thought about names?'

He flushed and continued to admire the babies in his arms. 'Sure, I've got names all ready, although Mel failed to tell me there was a chance of twins. This makes up for so much.' He looked up, his eyes shining with hope. 'Mom, all the time you've been saying Mel would change after the baby came. I can't wait to see her, to hold her in my arms again.'

That's when he paused and blushed. 'Well, at least we can sleep together, if nothing more.'

'Jory, you'll find ways . . .'

He went on as if he hadn't heard. 'We constructed out lives around a plan, thinking we'd dance until I was forty, and then we'd both go into teaching or choreography. We didn't include the chance of accidents, or sudden tragedies, no more than your parents did, and on the whole, I think my wife has held up rather well.'

He was being kind, overly generous! Melodie had been his brother's lover, but perhaps he didn't want to believe that.

Or, more likely, he understood her need and had already forgiven not only Melodie but Bart as well. Reluctantly Jory allowed me to take the twins away.

In Melodie's room, Chris said, 'I'm taking Melodie and the twins to the hospital. I'll be back as soon as possible. I'd like another doctor to check Melodie over, and, of course, the twins need to be put in incubators until they weigh five pounds. The boy weighs three pounds thirteen ounces and the girl three pounds seven ounces . . . but nice healthy babies, even so.

'In your heart you'll fit the new twins and love them just

as much as you did Cory and Carrie.' How did he know each time I looked at those small babies, visions of 'our' twins came to haunt me?

Glowing, Jory was at the breakfast table seated beside Bart when I entered our sunny room saved for special mornings. The plates were bright red on a white tablecloth, and a bowl of fresh holly was the centrepiece. Poinsettias were everywhere, both red and white.

'Good morning, Mom,' said Jory as he met my eyes. 'I'm a very happy man today . . . and I saved my news to tell Bart until you and Cindy and Dad arrived.'

Small happy smiles played about Jory's mouth. His bright eyes pleaded with me not to hold anger, as once Cindy stumbled in, all sleepy and tousled looking, Jory proudly announced that he was now the father of twins, both a girl and a boy whom he and Melodie had decided to name Darren and Deirdre. 'Once there were C-named twins. We're following precedent a little, but travelling further through the alphabet.'

The frown on Bart's face was envious, scornful, too. 'Twins, twice the trouble as one. Poor Melodie, no wonder she grew so huge. What a pain – as if she didn't have enough problems.'

Cindy let out a squeal of delight. 'Twins? Really? How wonderful! Can I see them now? Can I hold them?'

But Jory was still bristling from Bart's cruel remark. 'Don't count me out, Bart, just because I'm down. Mel and I have no problems we can't overcome – once we're gone from this place.'

Bart got up and left his breakfast uneaten.

Jory and Melodie were going to leave and take the twins with them? My heart sank. My hands on my lap worked nervously.

I didn't see the hand that took mine and pressured my fingers. 'Mom, don't look so sad. We'd never cut you or Dad out of our lives. Where you go, we'll go – only we can't stay on here if Bart doesn't start acting differently. When you need to see your grandchildren, all you have to do is yell – or whisper.'

Around ten Chris drove home with Melodie, who was put immediately to bed. 'She's fine now, Jory. We would have liked to keep her in the hospital for a few days, but she made such a fuss that I brought her back. We left the twins in the nursery, put in separate incubators until they gain weight.'

Chris leaned to kiss my cheek, then beamed brightly. 'See, Cathy. I told you everything would work out fine. And I do like those names you and Melodie chose, Jory. Really fine names.'

Soon I carried a tray up to Melodie, who was out of bed and staring out of a window at the snow. She began to speak immediately.

'I'm thinking of when I was a child and how much I wanted to see snow,' she said dreamily, as if babies out of sight were also out of mind. 'I always wanted a white Christmas away from New York. Now I have a white Christmas, and nothing has changed. No magic to give Jory back the use of his legs.'

She went on in that strange, dreamlike way that frightened me. 'How am I going to manage with two babies? How? One at a time was the way I planned it. And Jory won't be any help . . .'

'Didn't I say we'd help?' I said with some irritation, for it seemed Melodie was determined to feel sorry for herself no matter what. Then I understood, for Bart stood in the open doorway.

His unsmiling face showed no expression. 'Congratulations, Melodie,' he said calmly. 'Cindy made me drive her to the hospital to see your twins. They're very . . . very . . .' He hesitated and finished – 'small.'

He left.

Melodie stared vacantly at the place where he'd stood.

Later Chris drove Jory, Cindy and me to the hospital to again look at the twins. Melodie was left in her bed, deeply asleep and looking very worn. Cindy took another look at the tiny babies in their little glassed-in cages. 'Oh, aren't they adorable? Jory, how proud you must feel. I'm going to make the best aunt, you just wait and see. I can't wait to hold them in my arms.' She was behind his chair, leaning over to hug him. 'You've been such a special brother . . . thank you for that.'

Soon we were home again, and Melodie was asking weakly about her children, then falling asleep as soon as she knew they were fine. The day wore on without guests who dropped in, without the telephone ringing with friends to congratulate Jory on becoming a father. How lonely it was on this mountainside.

Miserable winter days slipped by, filled with myriad trivial details. We'd gone to a party on New Year's Eve, taking Cindy and Jory with us. Cindy finally had her chance to meet all the young men in the area. She'd been an overwhelming hit. Bart had failed to join us, thinking he'd have a better time in an exclusive men's club he'd joined.

'It's not a club for only men,' whispered Cindy, who thought she had all the answers. 'He's going to some cathouse.'

'Don't you ever say anything like that again!' I reprimanded. 'What Bart does is his own business. Where do you hear such gossip?'

At that New Year's Eve party a few of the guests that Bart had invited to his party had showed up, and soon enough I was tactfully finding out if they'd received Bart's invitation. No, everyone said, though they stared at Chris and me, then at Jory in his chair, as if they had many secret thoughts they'd never speak.

'Mother, I don't believe you,' said Bart coldly when I told him the guests I'd met hadn't received his invitations. 'You hate Joel, you see only Malcolm in him, and therefore you want to undermine my faith in a good and pious old man. He's sworn to me he did mail off the invitations, and I believe him.'

'And you don't believe me?'

He shrugged. 'People are tricky. Maybe those you talked to only wanted to appear polite.'

Cindy left for school the second of January, eager to escape the boredom of what she considered Hell on earth. She'd finish high school this spring and had no intentions of going on to college as Chris had tried to persuade her.

'Even an actress needs culture.' But it hadn't worked. Our Cindy was just as stubborn in her own way as Carrie had been in hers.

Melodie was quiet, moody and melancholy, and so tediously boring to be around that everyone avoided her. She resented caring for the small babies I had thought would give her pleasure and something meaningful to do. Soon we had to hire a nurse. Melodie also did very little to help with Jory, so I did for him what he couldn't do for himself.

Chris had his work that kept him happy and away until Fridays around four when he'd come in the door, much as Daddy had once returned to us on Fridays. Time repeating itself. Chris was in his own busy world, we on the mountainside stayed put in ours. Chris came and went, looking fresh, breezy, confident and overjoyed to be with us on the weekends. He brushed aside problems as if they were lint not worth noticing.

We in Foxworth Hall stayed, never going anywhere now that Jory didn't want to leave the security of his wonderful rooms.

Soon it would be Jory's thirtieth birthday. We'd have to do something special. Then it came to me. I'd invite all the members of his New York ballet company to come to his party. First, of course, I'd have to discuss this with Bart.

He swivelled his office desk chair away from the computer. 'No! I don't want a group of dancers in my house! I'm not ever going to throw another party and waste my good money on people I don't even want to know. Do something else for him – but don't invite them.'

'But Bart, once I heard you say you'd like to have his ballet company entertain at your parties.'

'Not now. I've changed. Besides, I've never really approved of dancers. Never have, never will. This is the Lord's house . . . and in the spring a temple of worship will be raised to celebrate his rule over all of us.'

'What do you mean, a temple will be raised?'

He grinned before he turned his attention back to the computer. 'A chapel so near you can't avoid it, Mother. Won't that be nice? Every Sunday we'll rise early to attend services. *All* of us.'

'And who will be on the podium delivering those sermons? You?'

'No, Mother, not me. As yet I am not washed clean of my sins. My uncle will be the minister. He is a very saintly, righteous man.'

'Chris enjoys sleeping late on Sunday mornings, and so do I,' I said despite my will to always keep him placated. 'We like to eat breakfast in bed, and in the summers, the bedroom balcony is the perfect place to start off a happy day. As for Jory and Melodie, you should discuss the subject with them.'

'I already have. They will do as I say.'

'Bart . . . Jory's birthday is the fourteenth. Remember, he was born on Valentine's Day.'

Again he looked at me. 'Isn't it weird and meaningful that babies come often to our family on holidays – or very near them? Uncle Joel says it means something – something significant.'

'No doubt!' I flared. 'Dear Joel thinks everything is significant – and offensive in the eyes of his God. It's as if he not only owns God but controls him as well!' I whirled to confront Joel, who was never more than ten feet away from Bart. I shouted because for some reason he made me afraid. 'Stop filling my son's head with crazy notions, Joel!'

'I don't have to fill his head with those kind of notions, dear niece. You established his brain patterns long before he was born. Out of hatred came the child. And out of need comes the angel of salvation. Think of that before you condemn me.'

One morning the headlines of the local paper told of a family who'd gone bankrupt. A notable family that my mother had often mentioned. I read the details, folded the newspaper and stared thoughfully before me. Had Bart had anything to do with that man's fortune suddenly disappearing? He'd been one of the guests who hadn't shown up.

Another day the newspaper told of a father who killed his wife and two children because he'd put the main part of his savings into the commodity market, and wheat had dropped drastically in price. There went another of Bart's enemies – once an invited guest to that unhappy Christmas ball. But if so, how was Bart manipulating the markets, the bankruptcy?

'I know nothing about any of that!' flared Bart when I questioned. 'Those people dig their own graves with their greed. Who do you think I am, God? I said a lot of things Christmas night, but I'm not quite as crazy as you think. I have no intention of putting my soul in jeopardy. Fools always manage to trip themselves.'

We celebrated Jory's birthday with a family party; Cindy flew home to stay two days, happy to celebrate with Jory. Her suitcases were full of gifts meant to keep him busy. 'When I meet a man like you, Jory, I'm going to grab him so quickly! I'm just waiting to see if any other man is half as wonderful. So far Lance Spalding hasn't proved to be half the man you are.'

'And how would you know?' joked Jory, who had not heard the details of Lance's sudden departure. He flashed his wife a hard look as she held Darren and I held Deirdre. We were both supporting nursing bottles as we sat before the cozy log fire. The babies gave all of us reasons for feeling the future held great promise. I think even Bart was fascinated with how swiftly they grew, how sweet and cuddly they felt when on a few occasions he held them for several uncomfortable seconds. He'd looked at me with a certain pride.

Melodie put Darren in the large cradle Chris had found in an antique shop and had refinished so it looked almost new. With one foot she rocked the baby as she glared hard at Bart before once again gazing pensively into the roaring fire. Seldom did she speak, and she showed no real interest in her children. Only negligently did she pick them up, as if for show, as she showed no interest in any one of us, or anything we did.

Jory shopped by mail for gifts that were delivered almost daily to surprise her. She'd open each box, faintly smile and say a weak thank you, and sometimes she even put the package down unopened, thanking Jory without even looking his way. It pained me to see him wince, or bow his head to hide his expression. He was trying – why couldn't she try?

Each passing day saw Melodie withdrawing not only from her husband but, much to my amazement, also from her children. Hers was an indecisive love, without strong commitment, like the frail flutterings of moth wings beating at the candle flame of motherly love. I was the one who got up in the middle of the night to feed them. I was the one who paced the floor and tried to change two diapers at once, and it was I who raced down to the kitchen to mix their formula and held them on my shoulder for burping, I who took the time and trouble to rock them to sleep as I sang soft lullabies while their huge blue eyes stared up at me with fascination until they grew sleepy and with great reluctance closed their eyes. Often I could tell they were still listening from their small, pleased smiles. It filled me with joy to see them growing more and more like Cory and Carrie.

If we lived isolated from society, we did not live isolated from the malicious rumours that the servants brought home with them from the local stores. Often I overheard their whispers as they chopped onions, green peppers, and made the pies and cakes and other desserts we all loved to eat. I knew our maids lingered too long in back halls and deliberately made our beds when we were still upstairs. Thinking we were alone, we'd let out many secrets for them to feed their gossip.

Much of what they speculated on I speculated on as well. Bart was so seldom home, and sometimes I was grateful for that. With him out of the house, there was no one to create arguments; Joel stayed in his room and prayed, or so I presumed.

It came to me one morning that maybe I should try the servants' tricks and hang out near the kitchen . . . and when I did, our cook and maids filled my ears with knowledge gained from those in the village. Bart, according to them, was having many affairs with the prettiest and richest society ladies, both married and unmarried. Already he'd ruined one marriage that just happened to be one of the couples that had been on his Christmas guest list. Also, according to what I overheard, Bart often visited a brothel ten miles away, not within any city's limits.

I had evidence that some of those tales might be true. Often I saw him come home drunk and in mild, happy moods that made me wish, regretfully, that he'd stay drunk. Only then could he smile and laugh easily.

One day I had to ask. 'What are you doing all those nights you stay out so late?'

He giggled easily when he drank too much; he giggled now. 'Uncle Joel says the best evangelists have been the worst sinners; he says you have to roll in the gutter filth to know what it's like to be clean, and saved.'

'And that's what you're doing all those nights, rolling in the gutter filth?'

'Yes, Mother darling – for damned if I know what it's like to feel clean, or saved.'

Spring approached cautiously like a timid bluebird. Blustery cold winds softened to warm southern breezes. The sky turned that certain shade of blue that made me feel young and hopeful. I was often out in the gardens raking leaves and pulling up weeds that the gardeners overlooked.

I couldn't wait to see the crocuses peek from the ground in the woods, couldn't wait to see the tulips and daffodils and watch pink and white dogwood blossoms spring forth. Couldn't wait for the azaleas everywhere to make my life a fairyland of many delights, for the twins, for all of us. I'd look up and admire the wonder of the trees that never seemed depressed or lonely. Nature – how much we could learn if only we would.

I took Jory with me as far as he could easily guide his sturdy electric chair with the huge balloon wheels that climbed most gradual grades. 'We've got to find a better way to get you deeper into the woods,' I said thoughtfully. 'Now, if we laid flagstones everywhere, they'd be very lovely, but if they freeze in the winter they'd poke up and could possibly snag your chair and tip you over. As much as

I hate cement, we'll have to use that or blacktop. Somehow I like blacktop better, what about you?'

He laughed at my silliness. 'Red bricks, Mom. Brick walks are so colourful, and besides, this chair of mine is a real marvel.' He looked around, smiling with pleasure, then tilted his face so the sun could warm it. 'I only wish Mel would accept what's happened to me and show more interest in the twins.'

What could I say to that, when already I'd had it out with Melodie more than a dozen times, and the more I said the more resentful she grew. 'This is MY life, Cathy!' she'd shouted. 'MY LIFE – not yours!' Screaming at me, her face a red mask of fury.

Jory's physical therapist showed Jory how to lower himself to the ground without so much effort, and then he taught Jory how to get back into his chair without assistance. And all so Jory could help me plant more rose bushes. His strong hands used the trowel much better than mine.

The gardeners eagerly taught Jory how to prune our shrubbery, when to fertilize, how to mulch and with what. He and I made gardening not just a hobby but a life-style to save us both from going crazy. The greenhouse was enlarged so we could grow exotic flowers, and in there we had a world of our own to control, full of its own kind of quiet excitement. But it wasn't enough for Jory, who decided he had to stay in the arts in one form or another.

'Dad is not the only one in this family who can paint a hazy sky and make you feel the humidity, or put a dewdrop on a painted rose so real you can smell it,' he said to me with a broad smile. 'I'm growing as an artist, Mom.'

Even with Melodie in the same house, Jory was making a life without her. He fashioned slings to his chair that fitted over his shoulder so he could carry his twins with him. His delight to see them smile when they saw him coming touched my heart, just as it drove Melodie from the nursery. 'They love me now, Mom! It's in their eyes!'

They knew Jory better than they knew their mother. They gave her void and somehow pitiful hopeful smiles, perhaps because her expression was so blank and thoughtful when she stared at them.

Yes, the twins not only loved and knew who was their father, they also trusted him fully. When he reached to pick them up, they didn't flinch or fear he'd drop them. They laughed as if they knew he'd never, never drop them.

I found Melodie sulking in her room, really thin now, her once beautiful hair dull and stringy. 'It takes time, Melodie, to develop motherly instincts,' I said as I sat down unasked and, apparently, unwanted. 'You allow me and the maids to wait upon them too much. They don't recognize you as their mother when you stay away. The day you see their small faces light up when you come in, and they smile from the happiness they feel to see you, their mother, you'll find the love you're searching for. Your heart will melt. Their needs will give you something nothing else can, and never again will you feel anything but an all-encompassing love for your children, when they love you, and you love them.'

Her faint smile flashed bittersweet and was quickly gone. 'When do you give me the chance to mother my children, Cathy? When I get up in the night, you are already there. When I rise early, you've already bathed and dressed them. They don't need a mother when they have a grandmother like you.'

I was stunned by her unfair attack. Often I lay on my bed and heard the twins cry and cry before I got up to tend to their needs. In torment while I waited and waited for Melodie to go to them. What was I supposed to do, ignore their cries? I gave her time enough. Her room was across the hall from theirs, and mine was in another wing.

She apparently saw my thoughts, for her voice came almost like the hiss of a venemous snake. 'You always come out on top, don't you, mother-in-law? You always manage to get what you want, but there's one thing you will never get, and that's Bart's love and respect. When he loved me – and once he did love me – he told me he hated you, really despised you. I felt sorry for him then, and sorrier for you.

Now I understand why he feels as he does. For with a mother like you, Jory doesn't need a wife like me.'

The next day was Thursday. I felt heavy-hearted to think of all the ugly words Melodie had screamed and hissed at me yesterday. I sighed, sat up and swung my legs off the bed, slipping my feet into satin mules. A busy day ahead since this was the day all our servants but Trevor had off. On Thursdays I was like Momma had been, preparing myself for Friday, coming fully alive only when the man I loved strolled through the door.

Jory was quietly sobbing when I entered his room with the freshly bathed and diapered twins held one in each of my arms. In his hands he loosely held a creamy long sheet of stationery.

'Read this,' he choked, putting the paper on the table beside his chair before he reached for his children. When he had them both in his arms, he bowed his face into the soft hair of his son, then his daughter's hair.

I picked up the creamy sheet; always bad news on cream-coloured paper came from Foxworth Hall.

My dearest darling Jory,

I'm a coward. I've always known that, and hoped you'd never find out. You were always the one with all the strength. I love you, and no doubt will always love you, but I can't live with a man who can never make love to me again.

I look at you in that horrible chair that you've grown to accept, when I cannot accept it, or your handicap. Your parents came to my room and confronted me and urged me to face up to you and say everything I feel. I'm unable to do that, for if I do, you might say or do something that would change my mind, and I've got to leave, or lose my mind.

You see, my love, I already feel half insane from being in this house, this horrible, hateful house with all its deceiving beauty. I lie on my lonely bed and dream of the ballet. I hear the music playing even when it isn't. I've got to go back to where I can hear it play, and if that is ugly and selfish, as I know it is, forgive me, if you can.

Say kind things about me to our children when they are old enough to ask questions about their mother. Say those nice words even if they aren't true, for I know I've failed you just as much as I've failed them. I've given you every reason to hate me, but please don't remember me with hate. Remember me as I used to be when we were younger, and very much in control of our lives.

Don't blame yourself for anything, or blame anyone else for what I have to do. Everything is my own fault. You see, I'm not real, I névер was, and I never will be. I can't face up to the kind of cruel reality that destroys lives and leaves behind broken dreams. Then, too, remember this: I'm the fantasy you helped created out of your desire and my own.

So farewell, my love, my first and sweetest love, and sadly perhaps my only true love. Find someone rare like your mother who can take my place. She's the one who gave you the ability to copy with reality, no matter how harsh.

God would have been kind if he had given me your kind of mother.

Yours regretfully,
Mel

The note fell from my hand, fluttering its pathetic certain way to the carpet. Both Jory and I stared at it lying there, so sad – and so final.

'It's over, Mom,' he said tonelessly, his voice deep and gruff. 'What began when I was twelve and she was eleven, all over. I built my life around her, thinking she'd last until we were old. I gave her the best I had to offer, and still it wasn't enough once the glamour was gone.'

How could I tell him that Melodie wouldn't have lasted even if he was still on stage dancing. Something in her resented his strength, his innate ability to cope with situations beyond her ability to comprehend.

I shook my head. No. I was being unfair. 'I'm sorry, Jory, so terribly sorry.' I didn't say, perhaps you'll be better off without her.

'I'm sorry, too,' he whispered, refusing to meet my eyes. 'What woman will want me now?'

Perhaps he would never perform sexually again in the normal way, and I knew he needed someone in the bed with him during all those long, lonely nights. I could tell from his morning face that the nights were the worst part of his life, leaving him feeling isolated, vulnerable emotionally, as well as physically helpless. He was like me, needing arms to hold me safe during the darkness, wanting kisses on my face to put me to sleep, to wake me up, to put over me a safe parasol of love.

'Last night I heard the wind blowing,' he confided to me as the twins sat in their highchairs and smeared their faces with warm, mushy cereal. 'I woke up. I thought I heard Mel breathing beside me, but there was nothing. I saw the birds happily building their nests, heard them chirping to greet the new day, and then I saw her note. I knew without reading what was inside, and I went on thinking about the birds, and all their love songs suddenly turned into only territorial rights.' His voice broke again as he lowered his head to hide his face. 'I've heard that geese, once mated, never mate again, and I keep seeing Melodie as the swan, loyal forever, no matter what the circumstances.'

'Darling, I know, I know,' I soothed, stroking his dark curls. 'But love can come again, you hold on to that – and you're not alone.'

He nodded, saying, 'Thanks for always being here when I need you. Thank Dad for me, too . . .'

Brusquely, fearing I'd cry as well, I put my arms about him. 'Jory, Melodie is gone, but she's left you with a son and a daughter, be grateful for that. Because she did leave you, that makes them all yours now. She walked out not only on you, but also on her own children. You can divorce her and use your strength to help your children develop your own kind of courage and determination. You'll manage without her, Jory, and as long as you need us, you have your parents' willing help.'

And all the time I was thinking that Melodie had deliberately withdrawn from her own children in order to make the break easier; she hadn't allowed herself to love them, or them to love her. Her parting gift of love to her childhood sweetheart was his own children.

Jory brushed the tears from his eyes and tried to grin. When he did it was full of irony.

BOOK THREE

THE SUMMER OF CINDY

All of a sudden Bart was taking business trips, flying off to return in a few days, never staying away more than two or three days, as if afraid that during his absence as he wheeled and dealed we would run away with his fortune. As he put it, 'I have to keep to top of things. Can't trust anyone more than I trust myself.'

He had just happened to be gone the day that Melodie slipped out of Foxworth Hall and left that pitiful note for Jory to find on his night table. Bart's expression didn't change when he came home and found Melodie's chair at the dining table empty. 'Upstairs moping again?' he asked indifferently, indicating her chair, which was a constant reminder of her absence.

'No, Bart,' I answered when Jory refused to look his way or even answer. 'Melodie decided she wanted to resume her career, and she left, leaving Jory a note.'

His left eyebrow quirked upward cynically; then he flashed Jory a glance, but not one word to say he was sorry to find her gone, or one word of condolence to his brother.

Later, when Jory was upstairs and I was changing diapers, Bart came in and stood at my side. 'Too bad I was in New York at the time. I would have enjoyed seeing Jory's expression when he read her note. By the way, where is it? I'd like to read what she had to say.'

I turned to stare at him. For the first time it occurred to me that Melodie might have arranged to meet him in New York. 'No, Bart, you will never read that note . . . and I hope to God you had nothing to do with her decision to go.'

Angry, his face reddened. 'I went on a business trip! I haven't said two words to Melodie since Christmas. And as far as I'm concerned, it's good riddance.'

In some ways it was better without Melodie always sitting around moodily, shadowing the rooms with her dreary depression. I made it a practice to visit Jory just before bedtime, tucking him in, opening his window, dimming the lights and seeing he had water where he could reach it. My kiss on his cheek tried to substitute for a wife's kiss.

Now that Melodie was gone, I soon found out that she had helped a little just by getting up early once in a while to change and feed the babies. She'd even bothered to diaper them several times a day.

Often Bart drifted into the nursery, as if irresistibly drawn, and stared down at the tiny twins, who had learned how to smile and had found out to their delight that those waving shadowy things were their own feet and their own small hands. They reached for the mobiles of pretty colourful birds, struggled to pull them down and put them in their mouths.

'They are kind of cute,' Bart commented in a musing way that pleased me, even doing a little to help by handing me the baby oil and talcum. Unfortunately, just when the twins almost had him won over, Joel strode into the nursery and scowled down at the beautiful babies, and all the kindness and sympathy growing in Bart vanished completely, leaving him standing beside me looking guilty.

Joel gave the twins one hard, quick glance before he turned away his offended eyes. 'Just like the first twins, the evil ones,' muttered Joel. 'Same blond hair and blue eyes . . . no good will come of this pair either.'

'What do you mean by that?' I raged. 'Cory and Carrie never harmed anyone! They were the ones who were harmed. They suffered what was inflicted on them by your own sister, mother and father, Joel. Don't you ever dare to forget that.'

With silence Joel answered before he left the room, taking Bart with him.

* * *

In mid-June, Cindy flew home to stay the summer. She made determined efforts to keep her rooms neater, hanging up her own clothes, which she used to drop on the floor. She helped me by changing the twins and holding their bottles as she rocked them to sleep. It was sweet to see her sitting in the rocker, a baby in the crook of each arm, struggling to hold two bottles at the same time while she wore baby doll pyjamas, her lovely long legs bare and tucked under her. She seemed very much a child herself. She bathed and showered so often I thought she'd shrivel into a dried prune.

One evening she came from her luxurious bath and dressing room looking radiantly fresh and alive, smelling like an exotic flower garden. 'I love twilight,' she gushed, twirling around and around. 'Just adore strolling the woods when the moon is on the rise.'

By this time we were all seated on our favourite terrace, sipping drinks. Bart pricked up his ears and glared at her. 'Who's waiting for you in the woods?'

'Not who, dear brother, but what.' She turned her head to smile at him in an innocent, charming way. I'm going to be nice to you, Bart, no matter how nasty you are to me. I've decided I cannot win friends by tossing out rude and nasty remarks.'

He glared suspiciously. 'I still think you're meeting some boy in the woods.'

'Thank you, brother Bart, for only thinking of punishing me with nasty suspicions. I expected more – and worse. There's a boy in South Carolina that I've fallen madly for, and he's a nature lover. He's taught me how to appreciate all that money can't buy. I adore sunrises and sunsets. When rabbits run, I follow. Together we catch rare butterflies and he mounts them. We picnic in the woods, swim in the lakes. Since I'm not allowed to have a boyfriend here, I'm going to stand alone at the top of a hill and try just strolling down. It's fun to challenge gravity and try not to run all breathless and out of control.'

'By what name do you call gravity? Bill, John, Mark or Lance?'

'I'm not going to let you annoy me this time,' she said arrogantly. 'I like to stare up at the sky, count the stars, find the constellations, watch the moon play hide-and-seek. Sometimes the man in the moon winks at me, and I wink back. Dennis has taught me how to stand perfectly still and absorb the feel of the night. Why, I'm seeing wonders I didn't even know existed because I'm in love – madly, passionately, ridiculously, insanely in love!'

Envy flashed through his dark eyes before he growled, 'What about Lance Spalding? I thought you felt that way about him. Or did I ruin his pretty face permanently so you can't bear to look at him?'

Cindy paled. 'Unlike you, Bart Foxworth, Lance is beautiful inside and out, like Daddy, and I do still love him, and Dennis, too.'

Bart's frown deepened. 'I know all about your nature loving! You want to sprawl on your back and spread your legs for some village idiot – and I won't have it!'

'What's going on here?' asked Chris, appearing dumbfounded to come back from the telephone and find all the peace gone.

Cindy jumped to her feet, took her stance and put her hands on her hips. She glared down into Bart's face, struggling to hold fast to that adult control she was determined to have with him. 'Why do you always presume the worst about me? I just want to walk in the moonlight, and the village is ten miles away. What a pity you don't understand what it's like to be human.'

Her answer and her glare seemed to infuriate him more. 'You're not my sister, just a smart-ass little bitch in heat – the same as your mother!'

This time it was Chris who jumped up from the table and slapped Bart hard. Bart drew back and raised his fists, as if ready to punch Chris in the jaw – when *I* jumped to my feet and placed myself in front of Chris. 'No, don't you dare ever hit the man who's tried to be the best father possible! If you do, Bart, you and I are through forever!' That was enough for him to turn his dark, fiery eyes on me, so furious his look could have started a blaze.

'Why can't you see that little whore for what she is? You both see everything wrong about me, but you close your eyes to the sins of your favourites! She's nothing but a tramp, a goddamned tramp.' He froze, his eyes wide and startled.

He'd taken the Lord's name in vain. He looked around to see Joel, who for once was out of sight and hearing. 'You see, Mother, what she does to me? She corrupts – and in my own home, too.'

Looking at Bart disapprovingly, Chris sat down again. Cindy disappeared into the house. I stared forlornly after her, as Chris spoke harshly, confronting Bart. 'Can't you see that Cindy is doing her best to please you? She's been trying since she came home to do her utmost to appease you, but you won't let her. How can you take a stroll in these lonely woods as anything but innocent? From now on, I want you to treat her with respect – for if you don't you may well drive her into doing something rash. Losing Melodie is quite enough for one summer.'

It was just as if Chris had no voice and Bart had no ears, from all the effect those words had. Chris ended by giving Bart an even harder look and more reprimanding words before Chris stood and disappeared inside the house. I suspected he would follow Cindy upstairs and do what he could to comfort her.

Alone with my second son, I tried to rationalize, as I always did. 'Bart, why do you talk so ugly to Cindy?' I began. 'She's at a very vulnerable age and is a decent human being who needs to be appreciated. She's not a tramp, a whore or a bitch. She's a lovely young girl who is very thrilled to be pretty and attracting so much attention from the boys. That doesn't mean she's giving in to every one. She has scruples, honour. That one episode with Lance Spalding has not corrupted her.'

'Mother, she was corrupted long ago, only you don't want to believe that. Lance Spalding wasn't the first.'

'How dare you say that?' I asked, really enraged. 'What kind of man are you, anyway? You sleep with whom you please, do what you please, but she's supposed to be an angel with a halo and wings on her back. Now you go upstairs and apologize to Cindy!'

'An apology is something she'll never get from me.' He sat down to finish his meal. 'The servants talk about Cindy. You don't hear them, for you're too busy with those two babies you can't leave alone. But I hear them as they clean and dust. Your Cindy is a red-hot number. The trouble is you think she's an angel. You think that just because she looks like one.'

I sank down to lean my elbows heavily on the glass-topped wrought-iron white table, feeling overwhelmingly tired, just as Jory did, and he hadn't said one word for or against Cindy. To be for any length of time around Bart was so exhausting; the tension of saying one wrong thing kept you wired tight.

My eyes fixed on the crimson roses that were this evening's centrepiece. 'Bart, has it ever occurred to you that Cindy may feel she's been contaminated, so that now she doesn't care? And certainly you don't give her any reason to value her self-esteem.'

'She's a wanton, loose slut.' Said with absolute conviction.

My voice turned as uncompromising as his. 'Apparently from what I overhear when the servants whisper, you are drawn to the very type of woman you condemn.'

Standing, he threw down his napkin and stalked purposefully into the house. 'I'll fire every damn one who gossips about me!'

I sighed. Soon we wouldn't be able to hire any servants if he kept hiring and firing.

'Mom, I'm going to hit the sack,' said Jory. 'This pleasant evening meal on the terrace has turned out just as I could have predicted.'

That very evening Bart fired every servant but Trevor, who seldom said anything except to me or Chris. If Trevor had left every time Bart fired him, he'd have been gone long ago. Trevor had an understanding way of knowing just when to believe Bart was serious. Never, never did he rebuke Bart, nor did he meet Bart's eyes squarely. Perhaps because of this, Bart thought he had Trevor cowed. I thought Trevor forgave Bart, because he understood and pitied him.

I headed for Cindy's room, meeting Chris as he came down. 'She's very upset. Try to calm her down, Cathy. She's talking about leaving here and never coming back.'

Cindy was face down on her bed. Small grunts and groans came from her throat. 'He ruins everything,' she wailed. 'I never knew my own father and mother – and Bart wants to chase me away from you and Daddy,' she sobbed as I perched on the side of her bed. 'Now he's determined to spoil my summer, drive me away like he did Melodie.'

I held her slight body in my arms and comforted as best I could, thinking I'd have to send her away to keep her safe from being hurt again by Bart. Where could I send Cindy and not injure her feelings, which didn't need another cruel blow? I went to bed thinking about that, as Cindy escaped the house to meet a boy from the village.

I was to hear about this later.

As Bart had predicted, Cindy's nature-loving experience did have a name. Victor Wade. And while I lay on my bed, and Chris slept beside me, pondering what to do with Cindy, and still keep her love, how to keep Bart from being his worst self, our Cindy sneaked out of the house and went with Victor Wade to Charlottesville.

In Charlottesville Cindy had a glorious time, dancing with Victor Wade until she wore holes in the thin soles of her fragile, sparkling sandals with the four-inch glass heels (really only lucite and not as heavy as glass). Then Victor, true to his word, drove back towards Foxworth Hall. Near one of the roads leading to our hill, he parked and drew Cindy into his arms.

'I've fallen in love,' he whispered huskily, raining kisses expertly on her face, behind her ears, travelling down her neck to end up on her breast that he bared. 'I've never met a girl who was half the fun you are. And you were right. They don't grow 'em better in Texas . . .'

Half drunk on too much wine, intoxicated, too, with the expertise of his foreplay, Cindy's efforts to resist his lovemaking were weak, ineffectual. Soon her own passionate nature was responding, and eagerly she helped him to undress as he unzipped her dress and soon had it off, along with everything else. He fell upon her – and that's when Bart showed up.

Bellowing like an enraged bull, Bart rushed the parked car, catching Cindy and Victor in the very act of copulating.

Seeing their naked bodies with arms and legs entwined on the back seat confirmed all his suspicions and enraged him more. Bart threw open the door and yanked Victor out by the ankles, forcefully dragging him off the top of Cindy so he fell face downward upon the rough gravel of the roadside.

Not giving the boy chance to recover, Bart attacked, using his fist brutally.

Screaming her anger, disregarding her nudity, Cindy hurled her dress directly into Bart's face, blinding him momentarily. This gave Victor the chance to jump to his feet and deliver his own blow that momentarily gave Bart pause, but already Victor's nose was bleeding and he had a black eye.

In the moonlight his nakedness seemed blue in Cindy's eyes. 'And Bart was so ruthless, Momma! So awful! He seemed like a madman – especially when Victor managed to smash a good right hook into his jaw. Then he tried to kick Bart in the groin. It did hit him there, but not hard enough. Bart doubled up, cried out, then rushed Victor with so much fierce anger that I was scared he'd kill him! He came out of that pain so fast, Momma, so fast – and I'd always heard that stopped a man cold.' Cindy sobbed with her head on my lap.

'He was like the Devil straight from hell, screaming abuse at Victor, using all the obscene words he never wants me to use. He knocked Victor down, then beat him into unconsciousness. Then he came at me! I was terrified he'd batter my face and break my nose and make me ugly, like he's always threatened to do. Somehow I'd managed to pull on that dress, but the zipper was wide open down the back. He grabbed me by the shoulders, shook me so hard the dress fell to my ankles and I was naked – but he didn't look to see anything. He kept his eyes on my face as he slapped one cheek and then the other and my head was rocked from side to side, until I felt dizzy and faint. My head was reeling before he picked me up like a sack of grain, threw me over his shoulder and took off through the woods, leaving Victor lying on the ground.

'It was awful, Momma, so humiliating! To be carried like that, as if I were cattle! I cried all the way, pleading with Bart to call an ambulance in case Victor was seriously hurt . . . but he wouldn't listen. I begged him to put me down and let me cover myself, but he ordered me to shut up or else he'd so something terrible. Then he took me to – '

She cut off her words abruptly, staring before her as if mesmerized by fear.

'Where did he take you, Cindy?' I asked, feeling sick, as if her humiliation was mine, and so furious with Bart, feeling sorry for her shocking plight. At the same time I was so angry that she'd brought this upon herself by disobeying and disregarding everything I'd tried to teach her.

In a small, weak voice, with her head lowered so her long hair fell to hide her face, she finished, 'Just home, Mom . . . just home.'

There was more to it, but she refused to tell me anything else. I wanted to scold her, to chastise her, remind her again that she knew all about Bart and his fierce temper, but she was too traumatized to hear more.

I got up to leave her room. 'I'm taking away all your privileges, Cindy. I'll send up a servant to take out your telephone so you can't call one of your boyfriends to help you escape. I've heard your side of the story now, and Bart just this morning told me his side. I don't agree with his method of punishing you or that boy. He was much too brutal, and for that, I apologize. However, it seems you are very free with your sexual favours. You can't deny that any longer, for I've seen you with my own eyes when that boy Lance was here. It hurts to know that you've heeded so little of what I've tried to teach you. I realize it's hard to be young and different from your peers, but still I was hoping you'd wait until you knew how to handle intimate relationships. I couldn't bear for an unknown man to lay a finger on me – much less take me totally – and you just met that boy, Cindy! A complete stranger who might have hurt you!'

Her pitiful pretty face lifted. 'Momma, help me!'

'Haven't I done my best to help you all your life? Listen to me, Cindy, for once really listen. The best part of loving comes with learning to know a man, by allowing him to know you as a person before you begin to think about sex – you don't pick up the first man you meet!'

Bitterly she railed back. 'Momma, all the books write about sex. They don't mention love. Most psychiatrists say there is no such thing as love. You've never explained to me exactly what love is. I don't even know if it really exists. I think that sex is as necessary at my age as water and food, and love is nothing but excitement; it's your blood heating up; your pulse racing, your heart pounding, your breath coming faster, heavier, and in the end it's only a natural need no worse than wanting to sleep. So despite you and your old-fashioned ideas, I give in when a boy I like wants to make out. Victor Wade wanted me . . . and I wanted him. Now, don't blaze your eyes at me that way! He didn't force me. Didn't rape me – I just let him! I wanted him to do what he did!'

Her blue eyes defied me as she jumped up and stared me in the eyes. 'Now go on and call me a sinner like Bart did! Yell and scream and say I'll go to hell, but I don't believe you any more than I believe him! If so, ninety-nine percent of the world's population are sinners – including you and your brother!'

Stunned, deeply hurt, I turned and left.

The beautiful summer days dragged by while Cindy sulked in her room, angry at Bart, at me, even at Chris. She refused to eat at the table if Bart or Joel were there. She stopped showering two and three times a day and allowed her hair to become just as stringy and dull as Melodie's, as if proving to us she was now on her way to abandoning us as Melodie had, and it was Melodie's manner she tried to duplicate as much as possible. However, even in sullenness her eyes still sparked with fire, and she managed to look pretty even when she looked messy.

'You're not accomplishing anything but making yourself miserable,' I said when I saw her quickly turn off the TV set she had in her bedroom, as if she wanted me to believe she didn't have a single pleasure left to enjoy when her room contained every luxury but the telephone, which I'd removed so she couldn't arrange secret dates with Victor Wade or anyone else.

She sat on the bed, staring at me resentfully. 'You just let me go, Momma. You go and tell Bart to let me go and I'll never bother him again. I'll never come back to this house again! NEVER!'

'Where will you go and what will you do, Cindy?' I asked with concern, afraid she'd slip out one night and we'd never hear from her again. And I knew she didn't have enough money saved to see her through longer than two weeks.

'I'll do what I have to!' she screamed, tears of self-pity streaking her pale face, which was already losing its rosy tan. 'You and Daddy gave to me generously, so I won't have to sell my body if that's what you're thinking. Unless I just want to. Right this moment I feel like being everything Bart doesn't want me to be, and that would show him, really show him.'

'Then you stay in this room until you feel like being everything I want you to be. When you can speak to me with respect, without yelling, and express to me some mature decisions on what you intend to do with your life, I'll help you escape this house.'

'Momma!' she wailed. 'Don't hate me! I can't help it if I like the boys and they like me! I'd like to save myself for that special Mister Right, but I've never met anyone that special. When I refuse to let them, they go straight from me to some other girl who doesn't refuse. How did you manage it, Momma? What did you do to keep all those men loving you, and only you?'

All those men? I didn't know how to answer.

Instead, like other parents put on the spot, I avoided giving the straight answer I didn't have anyway. 'Cindy, your father and I love you very much, you should know that. Jory loves you. And the twins smile just to see you come near them. Before you decide to do something rash, let's sit down with your father, with Jory, and then you have your say, and let us know what you want for yourself. And if it is at all reasonable, we will do what we can to see that you obtain your goals.'

'You won't let Bart in on any of this?' she asked suspiciously.

'No, darling. Bart has proven he doesn't reason when it comes to you. Ever since the day you joined our family he's resented you, and at this late date there doesn't seem to be much any of us can do about that. As for Joel, I don't like him, either, and he has no place in our family discussion about your future.'

Suddenly she flung her arms about my neck. 'Oh, Momma, I'm so ashamed I said so many ugly things. I wanted to hurt you the other day because Bart had shamed me so much. Save me from Bart, Momma. Find a way, please, please.'

After Chris, Jory, Cindy and I talked, we found a way to save Cindy not only from Bart but from herself. I tried to calm Bart, who wanted to punish her more drastically.

She's only adding fuel to the fire already burning in the village,' he shouted when I entered his office. 'I try to lead a decent, God-fearing life – now don't you yell at me and say you've heard differently. I'll admit I was rolling in filth for a while, but things have changed. I didn't enjoy those women. Melodie was the only one who gave me anything that approached love.'

I tried to keep the frown from my face. How easily he had turned away from her once he knew he had her loving him . . .

Looking around at all the valuables in his office, I wondered again if Bart didn't love things more than he loved people; I stared at the luxurious antique Orientals that he'd purchased at auctions, costing hundreds of thousands. His furniture put that in the White House to shame. He would be the wealthiest man in the world if he kept doubling his five hundred thousand a year every few months, the way he was somehow managing to do now. Even before he came fully 'into his own' he'd have made his billion or so. He was clever, quick, brilliant. What a pity he couldn't be more to mankind than just another greedy, selfish millionaire.

'Leave now, Mother. You waste my time.' He swivelled his chair around and stared out at the beautiful gardens now in full bloom. 'Send Cindy away – anywhere. Just get her out of my hair.'

'Cindy told us last night she'd like to spend the remainder of the summer in a New England drama school. She had the name and address of the one she preferred. Chris called to check them out, and they seem reliable and have a good reputation. So she's leaving in three days.'

'Good riddance to rubbish,' he said indifferently.

Standing, I threw him a look of pity. 'Before you condemn Cindy so harshly, Bart, think about yourself. Has she done any worse than you have?'

He began to use his computer without replying.

I slammed the door behind me.

Three days later I was helping Cindy finish her packing. We'd been shopping, so she had more than enough casual clothes, six pairs of new shoes and two new swimsuits. She kissed Jory goodbye, then lingered with the twins cuddled in her arms. 'Dear little babies,' she crooned, 'I'll be back. I'll sneak in and out and won't let Bart even see me. Jory, you should get away from here, too. Momma, you and Daddy go with him.' Reluctantly she put the twins back in their play pen and came to hug and kiss me. I was already crying. I was losing my daughter. I knew from the way she looked at me that nothing between us would ever be quite the same again.

Still she came to me and hugged me. 'Daddy's going to drive me to the airport,' she said as she bowed her head on my shoulder. 'You can come, too, if you don't cry and feel sorry for me, because I'm happier than any lark to be free of this damned house. And take me seriously for once – get Jory and yourselves free of this house. It's an evil house, and now I hate its spirit just as much as once I loved its beauty.'

We drove to the airport without Cindy bidding Bart or Joel farewell.

Without another word to me, her remote expression told me everything. She was warmer with Chris, kissing him goodbye. She only waved to me as she raced towards her departure gate. 'Don't hang around and wait for my plane to take off. I'm boarding it gladly.'

'You will write?' Chris asked.

'Naturally, when I can find time.'

'Cindy,' I called despite myself, wanting to protect her again, 'write at least once a week. We care about what happens to you. We'll be here to do what we can when you need us. And sooner or later, Bart will find what he's looking for. He'll change. I'll see to it that he changes. I'll do anything I have to so we can be a family again.'

'He won't find his soul, Momma,' she called back coolly, backing away even farther. 'He was born without one.'

Before her plane left the ground, my tears stopped flowing and my determination hardened into concrete. Indeed, before I died, I was going to see my family united, made whole and healthy – if it took the rest of my life.

Chris made attempts to pull me out of my depression as he drove me back to what had to be called 'home'. 'How's the nurse making out?'

My concern for Cindy had kept me so involved that I'd paid little attention to the beautiful, dark-haired nurse Chris had recently hired to live in and help with the twins and Jory. She'd been in the house a few days and I'd hardly said more than six words to her.

'What does Jory think of Toni?' he asked. 'I took considerable pains looking for just the right one. In my opinion, she's a real find.'

'I don't think he's even looked at her, Chris. He stays so busy with his painting and the babies. They're just beginning to crawl without so much effort. Why, yesterday, I saw Cory – I mean Darren – pick up a bug from the grass and try to put it in his mouth. It was Toni who ran to prevent that. I don't recall Jory even looking at her.'

'He will, sooner or later. And Cathy, you've got to stop thinking of his twins as Cory and Carrie. If Jory hears you call them Cory or Carrie he'll be angry. They are not our twins – they are Jory's.'

Chris said nothing more during the long drive back to Foxworth Hall, not even when he turned into our long drive and then drove slowly into the garage.

'What's going on in this crazy house?' Jory asked as soon as I stepped on to the terrace, where he was seated on an athletic mat put on the flagstones. The twins were with him, playing happily in the sunshine. 'Shortly after you left to drive Cindy to the airport, a crew of construction workers arrived and knocked and banged away in that downstairs room Joel likes to pray in. I didn't see Bart, and I didn't want to talk to Joel. And then there's something else – '

'I don't understand . . .'

'It's that damned nurse you and Dad hired, Mom. She's gorgeous and she's good at her job – when I can get hold of her. I've been calling for ten minutes and she hasn't responded. The twins are dripping wet, and she didn't bring out enough diapers so I can change them again. I can't go in the house and get more without leaving them alone. They scream now when I try to put them in the slings. They want to be on their own. Especially Deirdre.'

I diapered the twins myself and put them down for naps, then went in search of the newest member in our household.

To my astonishment I found her in the new swimming pool with Bart, both of them laughing, splashing water at one another.

'Hi, Mother!' called Bart, looking tan and healthy, and happier than I'd seen him since the days when he had believed himself in love with Melodie. 'Toni plays a super game of tennis. It's great having her here. We were both so hot after all that exercise that we decided to cool off in the pool.'

The look in my eyes was read clearly by Antonia Winters. Immediately she clambered out of the pool and began to dry off. She towelled her dark curly hair dry, then wrapped her red bikini with the same white towel. 'Bart has asked me to call him by his first name. You won't mind if I do that, will you, Mrs Sheffield?'

I looked her over appraisingly, wondering if she was truly responsible enough to take care of Jory and the twins. I liked her dark hair that sprang immediately into soft waves and curls to frame her face becomingly without makeup. She was about five eight and had as many voluptuous curves as Cindy, curves that Bart had despised on his sister. But from the way he was looking at the nurse, he approved of her figure very much.

'Toni,' I began with control, 'Jory, who I hired you to help, tried to call you to bring more diapers for the twins. He was out on the terrace with his children, and you should have been with *him*, not Bart. We hired you expecting you'd see that neither Jory or his children would be neglected.'

Embarrassment heated her face. 'I'm sorry, but Bart . . .' and here she hesitated, seeming flustered as she glanced at him.

'It's all right, Toni. I accept the blame,' said Bart. 'I told her Jory was fine and able to take care of himself and the twins. It seems to me he has made a big point of being independent.'

'See that this doesn't happen again, Toni,' I said, disregarding Bart.

That damned man was going to drive all of us batty! Then I had a brilliant idea. 'Bart, you and Toni would have done Jory a great favour if you had included him in your swimming party. He has full use of his arms. In fact, he has very powerful arms. And you should remember, Bart, that it's rather dangerous to have a pool like this without a fence, when two small children are around. So, Toni, with Jory's help, I'd like you both to begin teaching the twins how to swim . . . just in case.'

Thoughtfully Bart stared at me, seeming to read my mind. He glanced again at Antonia, who was striding towards the house. 'So you're going to stay on – why?'

'Don't you want us to stay?'

His smile radiated his dead father's charm. 'Why, yes, of course I do. Now that Toni has come to brighten up my lonely hours.'

'You leave her alone, Bart!'

He grinned at me wickedly and began to backpaddle in the pool, performing a backward flip that brought him up near my feet to grasp my ankles so hard it hurt. For a moment I feared he'd pull me in the pool and ruin the silk dress I wore.

I stared down and met his dark, suddenly menacing, eyes, not flinching. 'Let go of my ankles. I've already had my morning swim.'

'Why not swim with me sometimes?'

What did he see that made the threat leave and sadness come, a look so wistful he leaned to kiss my toes with the pink nails that peaked through the sandals? Then he was breaking my heart. Speaking with the exact tones of his dead father: 'I think that I shall never see, anyone quite as lovely as thee . . .' He looked up. 'See, Mother, I've got a bit of artistic talent, too.'

This was my moment. He was vulnerable, touched by something he saw on my face. 'Yes, of course you do, but Bart, don't you feel just a little sorry that Cindy is gone?'

His dark eyes grew hard, remote. 'No, not sorry. I'm glad she's gone. Did I prove to you what she really was?'

'You proved just how hateful you can be.'

His eyes darkened more. A fiercely determined look came to frighten me. He glanced towards the house on hearing some slight shuffling noise. I looked that way. Joel had come out on to the grassy area that enclosed our long oval pool.

Silently Joel condemned us with his pale blue eyes, his long-fingered bony hands steepled beneath his chin. He tilted back his head and stared heavenwise. His weak, sweet voice came to us falteringly. 'You keep the Lord waiting, Bart, while you waste your time.'

Helplessly I watched Bart's eyes flood with guilt before he scampered from the pool. For a moment he stood in all his youthful male glory, his long, strong legs deeply bronze, his belly hard and flat, his shoulders wide, his muscles firm, rippling beneath his skin, the hair on his chest curling, and for a flashing second I thought he was flexing his strong muscles, preparing them for a lion's charge that would lunge him straight at Joel's throat. I tensed, wondering if he would even consider striking his uncle.

A cloud drifted over the sun. Somehow it caused shadows from the unlit poolside lamps to form a cross on the ground. Bart stared downward.

'You see, Bart,' said Joel in a compelling voice I'd never heard before, 'you neglect your duties and the sun disappears. God gives you his sign of the cross. He's always watching. He hears. He knows you. For you have been chosen.'

Chosen for what?

Almost as if Joel had him hypnotized, Bart followed his great uncle into the house, leaving me standing alone beside the pool. I hurried to tell Chris about Joel. 'What can he mean, Chris – by saying that Bart has been chosen?'

Chris had just come in from visiting Jory and the twins. He forced me to sit, to relax. He even handed me my favourite mixed drink before he sat beside me on our small balcony overlooking the gardens and the mountains all around. 'I had a few words with Joel minutes ago. It seems Bart hired workers to construct a small chapel in that small, empty room he favours for his prayers.'

'A chapel?' I asked with bewilderment. 'Why do we need a chapel?'

'I don't think it is meant for us, it's for Bart and Joel. A place where they can worship without going into the village and facing up to all the villagers who despise Foxworths. And if it's what Bart thinks will help him to find himself, for God's sake, don't say a word to condemn what he's doing with Joel. Cathy, I don't think Joel is an evil man. I think, more than anything he's trying to make himself a candidate for sainthood.'

'A saint? Why, that would be like putting a halo above the head of Malcolm!'

Chris grew impatient with me. 'Let Bart do what he wants. I've decided it's time we left here, anyway. I can't talk to you in this house and expect a sane answer. We'll move to Charlottesville and take Jory, the twins and Toni with us, just as soon as I can find a house that's suitable.'

Unknown to me, Jory had rolled himself into our suite of rooms, and he startled me when he spoke up. 'Mom, Dad may be right. Joel could be the kind, benign saint he often appears. Sometimes I think we are both overly suspicious, and then again, you are so often right. I study Joel when he isn't watching. I think in many ways he's trying not to be what we most fear – a duplicate of the grandfather you both hated.'

'I think all of this is ridiculous! Of course Joel isn't like his father, or else he wouldn't have hated him so much,' Chris flared with sudden and unusual anger, his expression hard and totally out of patience not only with me but with Jory. All this talk about souls being born again in later generations is absolute nonsense. We don't need to add complications to our lives when they're complicated enough already.'

The next Monday Chris drove off again, heading back to the job he now loved just as much as he'd loved being a practicing physician. I stood staring after his car, feeling my rival was his blossoming love affair with biochemistry.

The dinner table seemed lonely without Chris or Cindy there, and Toni was upstairs putting the twins to bed, a fact that annoyed Bart greatly. He said several things to Jory about Toni, meant to imply she was already madly in love with him. This information didn't affect Jory one way or another; he was too deep in his own thoughts. He didn't say two words during the entire meal, even when eventually Toni did join us.

Another Friday evening came, and with it Chris returned, as once Daddy had come home every Friday. Somehow or other I was disturbed by the similarities of our lives compared to our parents' lives. Saturday we spent most of the day in the pool with Jory and the twins, with Toni and I supporting the babies as Chris helped Jory, who really didn't need much help. He took off across the water, expertly swimming, his strong arms more than making up for his legs that trailed limply behind. In the pool, with his legs under the water, he appeared so much himself that it showed on his happy face.

'Hey, this is great! Let's not move away from here yet. There aren't many houses in Charlottesville with pools like this. And I need the wide hallways and the elevator. And I've grown accustomed to Bart, and even to Joel.'

'I might not be coming next weekend.' Chris didn't meet my eyes as he gave out this startling information at our Sunday breakfast table. He went on, steadfastly refusing to look my way or meet anyone's eyes. 'There's a convention of biochemists in Chicago and I'd like to fly there. I'll be gone two weeks. If you want to join me, Cathy, I'd be grateful.'

Bart keened his ears my way, digging his spoon into his ripe melon. His dark eyes held a quiet, waiting look, as if his entire life depended upon my answer. I wanted to go with Chris. In the worst way I wanted to escape this house, its problems, and to be alone with the man I loved. I wanted to be near him, but I had to deny him and make this last-ditch effort to save Bart. 'I'd like very much to go with you, Chris. But Jory is embarrassed to ask Toni to do some intimate things for him. He needs me here.'

'For Christ's sake! That's why we hired her! She's a nurse!'

'Chris, not under my roof do you take the Lord's name in vain.'

Glaring at Bart for saying this, Chris rose to his feet. 'I've suddenly lost my appetite. I'll eat breakfast in town, if I can regain an appetite for anything again.'

He glared at me accusingly, flashed angry eyes at Bart, put his hand briefly on Jory's shoulder, and then he was off.

It was a good thing I'd asked him to find a nurse before this happened. Now he'd more than likely close his ears to what I wanted to do for my two sons who were, in one way or another, driving a wedge between us. Yet I couldn't leave

Jory when I wasn't really sure Toni would take good care of him, not yet.

Toni joined us at our luncheon table wearing a fresh white uniform. The three of us at the table talked of the weather and of other mundane things while she sat with her eyes fixed on Bart. Beautiful soft, luminous, grey eyes filled with awe – and infatuation. It was so obvious I wanted to warn her to look at Jory, to see him and not the man who was most likely to destroy her.

Sensing her admiration, Bart turned on his charm, laughing and telling her some silly stories that mocked the little boy he'd been. Each word he said entranced her more, as Jory sat unnoticed in his detested chair, pretending to read the morning newspaper.

Day by day I could see Toni's infatuation with Bart growing, even as she kindly tended to the twins and patiently did what she could for Jory. My firstborn son stayed in a sullen mood, waiting constantly for telephone calls from Melodie, waiting for letters that didn't come, waiting for someone to help with things he used to do for himself and no longer could. I sensed his impatience when it took the servants so long to make up his bed, to tidy his rooms, to get out of his way and leave him alone.

He drove himself relentlessly, hired an art instructor to come three times a week and teach him different techniques. Work, work, work . . . he was driving himself to become the best artist possible, as once he'd dedicated himself to practicing his ballet exercises morning, night and noon.

The four *D*s of the ballet world never died in some of us. Drive, Dedication, Desire, Determination.

'Do you think Toni is an adequate nursemaid for the twins?' I asked one evening as she took off down the road, pushing the twins in a double stroller. They loved being outdoors. Just to see the stroller brought squeals of pleasure and excitement. No sooner were the words out of my mouth than both Jory and I saw Bart racing to catch up with the nurse. Then the two of them were pushing Jory's children.

Uneasily I waited for Jory to speak. He said nothing. I glanced to see his bitter expression as he stared after Bart, now taking charge of his children, and the nurse I'd hired for him. It was as if I could read his thoughts. He didn't stand a chance with any woman now that he was in that chair. Now that his legs didn't dance, or even walk. Yet his doctors had told Chris and me that many handicapped men married and lived more or less normal lives. The percentages for marriage were much higher for disabled men than for handicapped women. 'Women have more compassion than men. Most normal men think more of their own needs. It takes an exceptionally compassionate and understanding man to marry a woman who isn't physically normal.'

'Jory, do you still miss Melodie?'

He stared gloomily before him, deliberately turning his eyes away from Toni and Bart, who'd paused to sit on a tree stump, apparently talking.

'I try not to do much thinking at all. It's a good way to keep from worrying about the years ahead, and how I'm going to manage. Eventually I will be alone, and I fear that day, fearing it's more than I can handle.'

'Chris and I will always be with you, as long as you need us, and as long as we live; but long before either of us die, you will have found someone else. I know that will happen.'

'How do you know that? I'm not sure I even want anyone. I'd be embarrassed now to have a wife. I'm trying to find something to do to fill the empty place that dancing left, and so far I haven't. The best thing in my life now are my twins and my parents.'

I glanced again at the pair on the tree stump, just in time to see Bart jump up to lift the twins out of their double stroller, and then he was playing with them on the roadside grass. They liked everyone and even tried to charm Joel, who never touched them, never spoke to them as we did. Faintly we could hear the laughter of the little boy and girl who grew prettier and prettier each day. Bart looked and acted happy. I told myself that Bart needed someone, too, just as desperately as Jory did. In a way, he needed someone even more than Jory. Inevitably Jory would find his way, with or without a wife.

We sat on and on, watching the pair who played with the twins. A full moon rose, appearing exceedingly large and golden in the twilight. A bird over the lake not so far away made its lonely cry. 'What's that?' I asked, sitting up straighter. 'I never heard a bird like that before down here.'

'It's a loon,' said Jory, looking in the direction of the lake. 'Sometimes a storm blows them down this way. Mel and I used to rent a cottage on Mount Desert Isle, and we'd hear the cries of the loons and think them romantic. I wonder why we thought that. Now that cry just sounds forlorn, even eerie.'

Out of the dark near the shrubbery, Joel spoke up. 'There are some who say that lost souls inhabit the bodies of loons.'

I asked sharply, turning to stare at him, 'What is a *lost* soul, Joel?'

His benign voice said softly, 'Those who can't find peace in their graves, Catherine. Those who hesitate between Heaven and Hell, looking back to their time on earth to see what they left unfinished. By looking back, they are trapped forever, or at least until their life's work is done.'

I shivered as if a cold wind blew from the cemetery.

'Don't try to digest that, Mom,' said Jory impatiently. 'I wish I could use some of the descriptive adjectives that Cindy's age group can throw out with so much ease and not feel crass. Funny,' he added more thoughtfully as Joel disappeared again in the darkness, 'when I was in New York and I was disgusted, impatient or angry, I used gutter language, too. Now, even when I think about saying those words, something keeps me from doing it.'

He didn't have to explain. I knew exactly what he meant. It was all around us, in the atmosphere, the clarity of the mountain air, the closeness of the stars . . . the presence of a strict and demanding God. Everywhere.

They met in the shadows. They kissed in the halls. They haunted the sunny, spacious gardens, roamed there in the moonlight, too. They swam together, played tennis together, strolled hand in hand by the lakeshores; they walked and jogged in the woods, had picnics by the pool, by the lake, in the woods; went dancing, to restaurants, then the theatre, the movies.

They lived in their own world while we were apparently invisible, not seen or heard by them, not when they could look at each other across the dining table with dazzled eyes, as if they had the world by its tail and would never let it go. I was caught up in their romance, despite myself, thrilled to be around such glowing, beautiful young lovers, a matched pair with their dark hair almost the same colour. I was happy and I was unhappy, delighted, yet so sad that it was not Jory who had found another woman to love. I wanted to warn Toni she was on treacherous ground, that Bart was not to be trusted, but then I'd look at Bart's radiant face, free of guilt or shame. This time he wasn't stealing anything that belonged to his brother. My critical words would fade away unspoken. Who was I to tell him whom he could love? I, of all people, had to stay quiet and let him have his chance. This was different than it had been with Melodie; Toni didn't belong to Jory.

Bart showed his happiness by becoming more confident, and with the security in his newfound love he forgot all his peculiar habits and his obsessive concern for neatness and allowed himself to relax in sports clothes. In the past, a thousand-dollar suit worn with expensive silk shirts and ties had given him his status symbols; now he didn't care, for Toni had given him his sense of worth. I could tell that for the first time in his life he seemed to have found stable ground to stand on.

He smiled and kissed me several times on the cheek. 'I know what you wanted to happen, I do! I do! But it's me she loves, Mother! Me! Toni sees something wonderful and noble in me! Do you realize how that makes me feel? Melodie used to say she saw these qualities in me, too, but I didn't feel noble or wonderful when I knew what harm I was doing to Jory. Now it's different. Toni's never been married, never had a lover before, although she's had lots of boyfriends. Mother, think of that! I am her first lover! It makes me feel so special to be the one she waited for. Mother, we have something wonderfully special. In me she sees the same things that you see in Jory.'

'I think that's wonderful, Bart. I am happy for you both.'

'Are you really?' His dark eyes turned serious as they sought to delve the truth of my statement. Before I could reply, Joel spoke from the open doorway of Bart's study.

'You stupid fool! You think that nurse really wants *you*? That woman sees the nobility of your money! It's your bank accounts she's after, Bart Foxworth! Have you observed the way she strolls through this house, her eyes half closed, obviously pretending that she's the mistress here! She doesn't love you. She is using you to get what every woman wants – money, control, power, and then more money – and once you marry her, she'll be set for life, even if you divorce her later on.'

'Shut up!' barked Bart, turning to glare furiously at the old man. 'You're jealous because I have no time left to spend with you. This is the cleanest, purest love of my life – and I'm not going to allow you to spoil it!'

Joel bowed his head meekly, appearing crestfallen as he templed his palms together under his chin before he slipped down the hall, obviously headed for that special small room that Bart had converted into a family chapel, although only Joel and Bart ever prayed there. I'd never even bothered to look inside.

I stood on my toes to kiss Bart's cheek, to hug him and wish him good luck. 'I'm happy for you, Bart. Sincerely happy. I truthfully admit I had hopes that Toni might fall in love with Jory and make up for his loss of Melodie. I wanted the twins to have a mother while they are still babies. She would have the chance to learn to love them like her own, and they wouldn't remember any mother but her. But since it hasn't happened that way, seeing your happiness and hers makes me feel warm and good inside.'

Delving, delving, those dark eyes that tried to read my soul. I had to ask: 'Will you marry her?'

His hands rested lightly on my shoulders. 'Yes, I'll ask her soon, after I make sure she isn't deceiving me. I have a method all planned to test her.'

'Bart, that's not fair. When you love you have to trust.'

'To have blind faith in anyone but God is idiotic.'

Only too well I remembered what Chris was always telling me. Seek and you shall find. I knew that well enough. I'd always been suspicious of the best that life gave me, and soon enough the best had disappeared.

'Mother . . .' he began with surprising candour, 'if Jory had kept his dancing legs, I know now that Melodie would never have let me touch her. She loved him, not me. She may have even pretended I was him, for sometimes I see a certain resemblance between us. I also think Melodie saw what she wanted to see, and she turned to me because he couldn't satisfy her physical needs any longer. I was a substitute lover for my brother, just as I've always come in second to Jory. Only with Toni have I come first.'

'You're right this time, Bart. Jory is here and Toni isn't seeing him. She sees you, only you.'

His lips took on an ironic twist. 'Yeah . . . but you're not mentioning that I'm up on my legs and he's down. I've got the most money, and he's got a pittance in comparison. And he's already burdened with two children that won't be hers. Three strikes against Jory . . . so I win.'

Now I was wanting him to win; he needed Toni ten times more than Jory did. My Jory was strong even when he was down, and Bart was so vulnerable and uncertain while he was perfectly healthy. 'Bart, if you can't love yourself for what you are, how do you expect anyone else to? You've got to start believing that even without money Toni would still love you.'

'We will soon find out,' he said tonelessly, a certain something in his eyes that reminded me of Joel. He turned to dismiss me. 'I've got work to do, Mother. See you later . . .' and he was smiling at me with more love than he'd shown since he was nine.

Contrary, complex, perplexing, challenging, the man my little troubled Bart had grown into . . .

Cindy had written to tell us how fabulous her summer days in the New England drama class were going. 'We act in real productions, Momma, in real barns that are temporarily converted into theatres. I love it, really love every aspect of show biz.'

Often I missed Cindy as the summer days passed. We all swam in the lake or pool, introducing the rapidly growing twins to all the wonders of nature. They had small teeth now and were both fast crawlers to wherever they wanted to go, and that was everywhere. Nothing was safe from their small, grasping hands that considered every object a food item. Flaxen blond hair turned into ringlets on their heads, pink lips turned rosy from the sun, and their cheeks stayed flushed with colour, while their wide, innocent, blue eyes devoured all faces, swallowed down all first impressions.

We swept the glorious hot summer days away like iridescent dust settling into photograph albums that would never let the days and happy moments truly disappear. Snap snap snap went three different kinds of cameras, as Chris, Jory and I took picture after picture of our wonderful twins. They adored being outdoors, sniffing the flowers, feeling the tree bark, watching the birds, squirrels, rabbits, racoons, the ducks and geese that often invaded our swimming pool, only to be chased off quickly by the adults.

Before I knew it, summer was gone and autumn was upon us again. This year Jory could enjoy this glorious season of splendour in the mountains. The trees foresting the mountainside flamed into spectacular colours.

'A year ago I was in Hell,' said Jory, staring at the trees and mountains and glancing down at his left hand, which no longer wore a wedding band of gold. 'My final divorce papers came, and you know, I didn't feel anything but numb. I lost my wife the day I lost the use of my legs, and still I'm surviving and finding that life does go on and it can be good, even when experienced from a chair.'

My arms went around him. 'Because you have strength, Jory, and determination. You have your children, so your marriage was not without its rewards. You still have celebrity status, don't forget that, and you can, if you want, start teaching ballet classes.'

'Nope, I can't neglect my son and daughter, not when they don't have a mother.' Then he tilted his head back to smile at me. 'Not that you don't make a super mother figure, but I want you and Dad to live your own lives, not be burdened down with small children who might hamper your life-style.'

Laughing, I tousled his dark curls. 'What life-style, Jory? Chris and I are happy where we are, with our sons and grandchildren.'

The bright fall days slowly chilled, bringing the acrid scent of woodfires burning. I was drawn outside early each day, taking Jory and the twins with me. The twins were pulling themselves up to stand by holding on to hands or furniture. Deirdre had even taken a few faltering, wide-legged steps, her bottom fat with diapers and plastic panties, covered by other pretty panties that she seemed to adore. Darren seemed more than content with his fast crawl that took him speedily wherever he wanted to go – which was everywhere. I'd even caught him crawling backwards down those high front stairs, with Deirdre close behind him.

On this fine early October day, Deirdre rode on Jory's lap, happily jabbering to herself, as I carried a more subdued Darren, using the new dirt trails that Bart had considerately ordered levelled so Jory could drive his chair through the woods. Tree roots that might have tripped up his chair had been removed at considerable cost. Now that Bart had a love of his own, he treated his brother with much more consideration and respect.

'Mother, Bart and Toni are lovers, aren't they?' Jory shot out unexpectedly.

'Yes,' I admitted with reluctance.

He said something then that startled me. 'Isn't it odd how we're born into families and have to accept what we're given? We don't ask for each other, yet we're glued all our lives to those whom we'd never speak to twice if they weren't blood related.'

'Jory, you don't really dislike Bart that much, do you?'

'I'm not speaking of Bart, Mom. He's been rather decent lately. It's that old man who says he's your uncle that I dislike. The more I see of him the more I detest him. At first when he showed up, I pitied him. Now I look at Joel and see something evil beneath those faded blue eyes. Somehow or other he reminds me of John Amos Jackson. I believe he's using us, Mom. Not just for practical reasons of having a home and food to eat . . . he has something else in mind. Just today, I happened to hear Joel whispering to Bart in the back hall. I think from what I overheard, Bart is going to tell Toni the complete truth about his past – his psychological problems – and the fact that if he's ever committed to an institution he'll lose his entire inheritance. He's being urged to do this by Joel. Mom, he shouldn't tell her! If Toni truly love him, she'll accept the fact he's had his problems. From all I can see, he's normal now, and very brilliant at making money grow.'

My head bowed. 'Yes, Jory. Bart told me himself, but he keeps putting off that revelation, as if he himself believes it's his money she's after.'

Jory nodded, holding fast to Deirdre, who was trying to climb down from his lap and explore by herself. Just seeing his sister do that made Darren anxious to be free as well.

'Has Joel ever said anything to indicate he might try to break his sister's will and take the money that Bart expects to inherit the day he's thirty-five?'

Jory's laugh was short, dry. 'Mom, that old man never says anything that isn't a double entendre. He doesn't like me and avoids me as much as possible. He disapproves of the fact that once I was a dancer and wore skimpy costumes. He disapproves of you. I see him watching you with narrowed eyes, and he mutters to himself, "Just like her mother . . . only worse, far worse." I'm sorry to tell you that, but he's scary, Mom, really a sinister old man. He looks at Dad with hatred. And he prowls the house at night. Since I've been disabled, my ears have become very sharp. I hear the floorboards in the hall outside my door squeak, and sometimes my door is opened ever so slightly. It's Joel, I know it's him.'

'But why would he be peeking in on you?'

'I don't know.'

I bit down on my lower lip, imitating Bart's nervous habit. 'Now you are frightening me, Jory. I have reasons to think he means harm for all of us, too. I believe it was Joel who smashed the ship you made for Bart, and I truly believe Joel never mailed off those Christmas invitations. He wanted Bart to be hurt, so he took them up to his room, removed the RSVP cards, signed them as if the invitations were accepted and then mailed them back to Bart. It's the only explanation of why no one showed up.'

'Mom . . . why didn't you tell me this before?'

How could I tell him of all my suspicions about Joel without his reacting much like Chris had? Chris had completely rejected my story of how Joel might have planned to hurt Bart. And sometimes even I thought I was much too imaginative and gave Joel credit for being more evil than he actually was.

'And what's more, Jory, I think it was Joel who overheard the servants in the kitchen talking about Cindy meeting that boy, Victor Wade, and he quickly passed that information along to Bart. How else would Bart have known? Servants are to Bart like designs on the wallpaper, not worthy of his notice – it's Joel who does the eavesdropping so he can report what they say to Bart.'

'Mom . . . I think you could very well be right about the ship, the invitations and Cindy, too. Joel has something in mind for all of us, and I'm afraid it's not for our good.'

Deep in thought, Jory had to tell me twice that I should put his son on his lap, to ride on his other leg, and we'd make better progress through the woods. Even one twin was a load to carry for a long distance, and more than willingly I lowered Darren to his father's lap. Deirdre squealed her delight and hugged her small brother. 'Mom, I believe if Toni really loves Bart enough, she'll stay, no matter what his background – or how much he inherits.'

'Jory . . . that's exactly what he's trying to prove.'

Around midnight, when I was almost asleep, a soft tapping sounded on my door. It was Toni.

She came in wearing a pretty rosy peignoir, her long dark hair loose and flowing, her long legs appearing as she neared my bed. 'I hope you don't mind, Mrs Sheffield . . . I waited for a night when your husband wasn't with you.'

'Call me Cathy,' I said as I sat up and reached for my own robe. 'I'm not sleeping. Just lying here thinking, and I appreciate another woman to talk to.'

She began to pace the floor of my large bedroom. 'I've got to speak to a woman, someone who can understand more readily than a man, so that's why I'm here.'

'Sit down. I'm ready to listen.' Tentatively she perched on a love seat, twisting a tress of her dark hair over and over, sometimes pulling it in between her lips.

'I'm terribly upset . . . Cathy. Bart's told me some very disturbing facts today. He mentioned that you already know about us, that he loves me and I love him. I think you have caught us a few times in one room or another in rather intimate moments. And I thank you for pretending not to notice, so I wouldn't feel embarrassed. I've got all kinds of notions that most people think are obsolete.'

She gave me a nervous smile, seeking my understanding. 'The moment I looked at Bart I fell in love. There's something so magnetic about his dark eyes, so mystical and compelling. And then tonight he took me into his office, sat down behind his desk and like a cold and distant stranger told me a long story about himself, as if he were talking about someone else, someone he didn't like. I felt like a business client whose every reaction was being judged. I didn't know just what he thought I'd reveal. It occurred to me he expected me to appear shocked or disgusted, and at the same time his eyes were so beseeching.

'He loves you, Cathy . . . loves you almost to the point of obsession,' she said, making me sit up straighter, stunned with her crazy notion. 'I don't even think he realizes how much he adores you. He thinks he hates you because of your relationship with your brother.' She flushed and lowered her eyes. 'I'm sorry I have to even mention this, but I'm trying to be open.'

'Go on,' I urged.

'Because Bart feels he should hate you for that, he tries to. Still, something in you, in him, keeps him from ever really deciding which emotion will reign, love or hatred. He wants a woman like you, only he doesn't know that.' She paused, looked up to meet my wide and interested eyes. 'Cathy, I told him what I honestly thought, that he was looking for a woman like his mother. He went pale, almost dead white. He appeared totally shocked at the idea.'

She paused to watch my reaction. 'Toni, you have to be wrong. Bart doesn't want a woman like me, but the exact opposite.'

'Cathy, I've studied psychology, and Bart does protest too much about you, so while I listened, I tried to keep an open mind. Bart impounded also the fact that he's never been mentally stable, and that any day he could lose his mind and, with it, his inheritance. Why, it's as if he wants me to hate him, to cut all ties and run away . . . so I am going to run,' she sobbed, her hands covering her face so that her tears trickled between her long, elegant fingers. 'As much as I love him and I thought he loved me, I can't continue to love and sleep with a man who has so little faith in my integrity – and worse than that, in his own.'

Quickly I was on my feet and striding to comfort her. 'Don't go, please, Toni, stay. Give Bart another chance. Give him time to think this through. Bart has always been inclined to act on impulse. He also has that old greatuncle who whispers in his ears, telling him you love him for his money alone. It's not Bart who is crazy, but Joel, who tells Bart what he should look for in a future wife.'

Hopefully she stared at me, trying to check her flow of tears. I went on, determined to help Bart escape the childhood sense of being unworthy and the adult influence of Joel. 'Toni, the twins adore you, and there's only so much I can do. Stay to help with Jory and help me keep him entertained. He needs professional help to maintain physical progress, too. And keep in mind that Bart is unpredictable, sometimes unreasonable, but he loves you. He's told me several times how much he loves and admires you. He's testing your love for him by telling you what is the truth. He was unstable mentally when he was a child, but there were good reasons that caused his mental disturbance. Hold fast to your belief in him and you can save him from himself and his greatuncle.'

Toni stayed.

Life went on as usual.

Deirdre, before her first birthday, was walking anywhere she chose to go, or we'd allow. Small and dainty, her golden curls bobbing, she charmed us all with her incessant babbling, which soon turned into simple words, leading the way for Darren to follow. Once she heard herself speak, she couldn't stop. Although Darren was slower to walk, he was not slower to investigate dark, dim places that scared his twin sister. He was the incessant explorer, the one who had to pick everything up and examine it, so I was forced to put expensive and delicate objets d'art on shelves he couldn't reach.

A letter came from Cindy stating that she was homesick for her family and wanted to come home and spend Thanksgiving through Christmas, but she was invited to a fabulous New Year's Eve party and would fly back to attend that.

I gave the letter to Jory to read. Smiling, he looked up. 'Have you told her about Bart and his love affair with Toni?'

'No,' I said, for I was going to let her see and find out for herself. Of course, before she'd left last summer, Toni had been with us only two days, but at that time Cindy had been so discontented she hadn't paid attention to what she thought was just more hired help.

The day came when we were expecting Cindy home for the holidays, a bitterly cold day. Chris and I were at the airport when she came through the gate, dressed in bright crimson, looking so beautiful all the people in the airport turned to stare her way. 'Mom! Dad!' she cried happily, flinging herself first into my arms and then into Chris's. 'I'm so happy to see you. And before you warn me, I promise to do and say nothing that will upset the applecart named Bart. This Christmas I'm going to be the perfect sweet little angel he wants me to be . . . and no doubt even then he'll find something to criticize, but I won't care.' Then she was asking about Jory, about the twins, and had we heard from Melodie? And how was the new nurse working out? And was our chef the same? Was Trevor still as sweet as ever?

Somehow or other, Cindy gave me the feeling we were, after all, a real family . . . and that was enough to make me very happy. Once she was in the grand foyer, Toni and Bart, with Jory holding the twins on his lap, were all waiting to sing out greetings. Only Joel hung back and refused to welcome our daughter home. Bart shook her hand in a warm fashion, and that gave me such relief and pleasure. Cindy laughed. 'Someday, brother Bart, you are going to be really overjoyed to see me, and maybe then you can allow your chaste lips to kiss my unholy cheek.'

He flushed and glanced uneasily at Toni. 'I've got a confession, Toni. In the past, Cindy and I haven't always gotten along.'

'To say the least,' said Cindy. 'But rest easy, Bart, I'm not here to make trouble. I didn't bring a boyfriend. I'm going to behave myself. I've come because I love my family and can't stand being away during the holidays.'

The holidays that year couldn't have been better, unless we could have turned back the clock and made Jory whole again, and restored Melodie to him.

In a matter of a few days, Cindy and Toni became close friends. Toni went shopping with us as Jory took care of the twins with the help of a maid. Time flew as it never did when Cindy wasn't around. The four years' difference between her age and Toni's didn't matter. Generously Cindy loaned Toni one of her prettiest dresses for that Christmas Eve trip into Charlottesville where she could dance with one of the doctor's sons she'd met the year before. Jory went as well but sat looking unhappy while Bart danced with Toni.

'Mom,' whispered Cindy when she came back to our table, 'I think Bart has changed. He's a much warmer person now. Why, I'm even beginning to think he's human.'

Smiling, I nodded, but still I couldn't help thinking of Joel and the way he and Bart spent so much time in that small room they'd converted into a chapel. Why? There were churches all around.

New Year's Eve came and Bart and Toni decided to fly to New York with Cindy and celebrate there. Leaving Chris, Jory and I to do the best we could without them. We used this opportunity to invite a few of Chris's colleagues to our home, along with their spouses, knowing that Joel would report this to Bart when he came back. Still I didn't care.

I bumped into Joel that night as I left the nursery. Smiling, I met his eyes. 'Well, Joel, it seems my son won't be as dependent on you once he marries Toni.'

'He'll never marry her,' said Joel in his harsh, forecasting way. 'He's like all young men in love, a fool who can't see the truth. She wants his money, not him, and he'll soon find that out.'

'Joel,' I said softly, pityingly, 'Bart is a very handsome young man, and a passionate one, and even if he were a ditch digger, the girls would fall for him. When he lets go of his determination to show the world how brilliant he is, he's a very likeable young man. Leave him alone. Stop trying to mould him into something that will please you but might not suit him. Let him find his own way . . . for that will be what's the right thing for him, even if it's not what you have in mind.'

Scornfully he looked me over. 'What do you know about what's right and what's wrong, niece? Haven't you already proved you have no perception of morality? Bart will never find himself without my guidance. Hasn't he been searching all his life and failed? Did you help him then – do you help him now? God will provide for Bart, Catherine, while you continue to plague Bart with your sins.'

He turned from me and shuffled off down the hall.

While Bart was in New York with Toni and Cindy, Jory completed his most impressive watercolour depicting Foxworth Hall. He'd darkened the rosy bricks to a dusty and dreary old ash rose, made the immaculate gardens overgrown with weeds; the cemetery was moved in closer so that tombstones showed off to the left, casting long shadows that snared the Hall in their web. Foxworth Hall looked two thousand years old and full of spectres.

'Put that thing away, Jory, and try a happier subject,' I said, feeling strange. I think that was the only watercolour Jory painted that didn't please me.

Bart and Toni flew home from New York, and immediately I noticed the difference. They didn't look or speak to each other but went quietly to their rooms without spilling out happy tales of the fun they'd had. When I tried to broach the subject, both refused to give me details. 'Leave me alone!' stormed Bart. 'She's just another woman after all.'

'I can't tell you, Cathy,' cried Toni. 'He doesn't love me, that's all!'

January fled by, and then came the February when we celebrated Jory's thirty-first birthday. We had a huge cake baked for him in the shape of a heart covered with red frosting to represent the Valentine gift he'd been, with his name in white icing, trimmed with white roses. The twins were delighted, squealing when they saw him blow out the candles. Both were seated in highchairs, one on each side of him, and before Jory could slice down into the cake, Deirdre and Darren reached simultaneously and grabbed great handfuls of the soft fresh cake. We all stared at the mess they'd made of a work of art, while they jammed the cake into their mouths and smeared their faces with red.

'What's left is still edible,' said Jory with a laugh.

Silently Toni got up to wash the hands and faces of two very messy little one-year-olds. Bart followed her every movement with sad, wistful eyes.

We were trapped, all of us, in the winter blizzards, caught in frozen time, making do with each other when others would have been welcomed, even as some of us kept on loving the wrong person.

The day came when the snow stopped and Chris could drive back to his cancer research team, which worked on and on without ever reaching any conclusions that were absolute.

Another blizzard kept Chris in Charlottesville, and two weeks dragged slowly by, although we talked every day when the lines weren't down – but they weren't comfortable conversations. Always I had the sensation that someone was listening in on another telephone.

Chris called on the next Thursday to say he'd be home, have the home fires burning, the steak charcoaled, the salad fresh, '. . . and wear that new white nightgown I gave you for Christmas.'

Eagerly I waited at an upstairs window to spot Chris's blue car coming around the drive, and when I did, I raced down the stairs to the garage to be there when he left his car. We came together like long separated lovers who might never have the chance to kiss and hug again. But it wasn't until we were in the sanctuary of our rooms with the doors closed that my arms slipped around his neck again. 'You still feel cold. So, just to warm you up, you are going to hear all the dull things that go on here – and in exquisite detail. Last night I overheard Joel telling Bart again that Toni is only after his money.'

'Is she?' he asked, nibbling on my ear.

'I don't think so, Chris. I think she sincerely loves him, but I'm not sure how long her love will last, or his. It seems when they went with Cindy to New York for New Year's Eve, Bart scolded Cindy ruthlessly again, humiliating her in a night-club, and Cindy's letter said he later on jumped on Toni for dancing with another man. He so shocked Toni with his brutal accusations that she hasn't been the same since. I think she's afraid of his jealousy.'

His eyebrows shot up quizzically, though he said nothing to remind me he was 'my Bart'. 'And Jory, how is he?'

'He's adjusting marvellously, but he's lonely and melancholy, wanting Melodie to write. He wakes up in the night and calls her name. Sometimes he inadvertently calls me Mel. I found a small article about Melodie in *Variety*. Melodie has rejoined their old ballet company and has a new partner. I showed that to Jory just today, feeling he should know. His eyes went blank. He put away his watercolours just when he'd washed in the most beautiful winter sky and refused to finish the painting. Anyway, I put the painting in a safe place, thinking he can finish it later.'

'Yes . . . everything will work out.' And with that we surrendered to each other, forgetting our problems in the ecstasy we knew so well how to create.

Time flew by, wasted by small, trivial things. Daily arguments between Bart and Toni concerning his attitude towards Cindy, whom Toni really liked, as well as his suspicions of her loyalty to him and only him. 'You shouldn't have danced with that man you just met!' and on and on. There were also daily fights between them about the twins and how they should be handled, and soon enough the narrow gulf between them widened into an ocean.

We wore on each other's nerves. The sight, the sound, the closeness of living so tightly knit had its toll.

I contributed nothing to help and nothing to harm as Bart and Toni fought it out. I felt they had to solve their differences between themselves, and I would only have added complications. Once again Bart started visiting the local bars, often staying out all night. I suspected he spent many a night in brothels, or else he'd found someone else in the city. Toni spent more time with the twins, and since Jory was trying to teach them to dance and speak more clearly, naturally she spent more time with him as well.

March finally arrived with its fierce rains and winds, but also with welcome faint heralding signs of spring. I watched Toni carefully for signs of taking notice of Jory as a man and not as a patient. His eyes followed wherever she went. There were a few weeks that year when I was under the weather with a severe cold, and she took over all duties, including washing Jory's back, massaging his long legs that were bit by bit losing their fine shape. I hated seeing his beautiful legs turn into thin sticks. I suggested to Toni that she massage them several times a day. 'He was always very proud of his legs, Toni. They served him so well and looked so great in tights. So, even if they don't walk or dance, or even move, do what you can to see they don't lose all their shape. Then he can retain a bit of his pride.'

'Cathy, his legs are still beautiful; thin, but well shaped. He's a wonderful man, so kind and understanding and naturally cheerful. And you know, for the longest time I didn't see anyone but Bart.'

'Do you think of Bart as beautiful?'

Her expression changed and grew hard. 'I used to. Now I'm seeing that he's very handsome, but not beautiful in the way that Jory is. Once I thought he was perfect, but during our stay in New York, he showed so much ugliness towards me and Cindy that I began to see him differently. He was nasty and cruel to both of us. Before I knew what was happening, he embarrassed me in a nightclub by jumping on me about my dress, when it was a perfectly nice dress. Maybe it was cut a little low, but all the girls wear dresses like that. I came home from that trip a little afraid of him. Every day my fear of him grows; he seems too harsh about harmless events and believes that everyone is wicked. I think he corrupts himself with his thoughts and forgets that beauty comes from the soul. Just last night he accused me of trying to arouse his brother sexually. He couldn't talk like that to me if he really loved me. Cathy, he'll never love me as I want and need to be loved. I woke up this morning feeling a huge emptiness in my heart, realizing that what I felt for Bart is over. He's ruined what we had by letting me know what I'm in for if I marry him,' she went on brokenly. 'He's got an invisible model of the perfect woman, and I'm not perfect. He thinks your one flaw is your love for Chris . . . and if he ever found a woman he believed is perfect in the beginning, I'm sure he'll keep looking until he finds something he can hate about her. So I've given up on Bart.'

I felt embarrassed to ask what I did, but still I had to know. 'But . . . are you and Bart still lovers, despite your disagreements?'

Furiously she shook her head. 'NO! Of course not! He's changing every day into someone I really can't even like. He's found religion, Cathy, and according to the way he tells it, religion is going to be his salvation. Every day he tells me I should pray more, go to church . . . and stay away from Jory. If he keeps it up I think I may well end up hating him, and I don't want that to happen. We had something so beautiful between us in the beginning. I want to keep that special time like a flower I can press between the pages of my memory.'

She stood up to go, smearing her tears with her balled handkerchief, tugging down her tight white skirt and trying to smile. 'If you want me to quit so you can hire a new nurse for Jory and his children, I'll do that.'

'No, Toni, stay on,' I answered quickly, afraid she'd go anyway. I didn't want her to leave now that I knew without a doubt that she didn't love Bart anymore, and Jory had finally given up hope of Melodie returning to him. And with the final hope dead, Jory had at last turned his eyes on the woman he believed was his brother's mistress.

As soon as possible I was going to inform him differently. But . . . even as Toni left the room, I sat on and on, thinking of Bart and how sad it was that he couldn't hold on to love once he had it. Did he deliberately destroy love, afraid it would enslave him as he often accused me of having enslaved Chris, my own brother?

The endless days crept by. No longer did Toni's eyes follow Bart with wistful yearning, pleading mutely with him to love her again as he had in the beginning. I began to admire the way she could keep her poise regardless of some of the insulting innuendoes Bart made during meal times. He took her former love for him and turned it against her, making it seem she was loose, depraved, immoral and he'd been wrongfully seduced.

Dinner after dinner, sitting there and watching the two drift further and further apart, driven there by all the ugly words Bart found so easy to say.

Toni took my place and played the games I used to entertain Jory with . . . only she could do so much more to light up his eyes and make him feel a man again.

Bit by bit the days began to mellow, the brown grass showed spikes of fresh green, the crocus came up in the woods, the daffodils blossomed, the tulips fired into flame and the Grecian windflowers that Jory and I had planted everywhere the grass didn't grow turned the hills into paint-smeared pallets. Chris and I stood again on the balcony watching the geese return north as we stared up at our old friend and sometimes enemy, the moon. I couldn't take my eyes from the winged skein as they disappeared beyond the hills.

Life grew better with the coming of summer, when the snow couldn't keep Chris away during the weekends. Tensions eased now that we had the great outdoors to escape to..

In June the twins were one year and six months old and able to run freely anywhere we would permit. We had swings hung from tree limbs from which they couldn't fall, and how happy they were to be swung high . . . or what they considered high enough to be dangerous. They pulled the blossoms off the best of my flowers, but I didn't care – we had thousands blooming, enough to fill all the rooms with daily fresh bouquets.

Now Bart was insisting that not only the twins should attend church services but Chris and I and Jory and Toni as well. It seemed a small enough thing to do. Each Sunday we sat in our front row pews and stared up at the beautiful stained-glass window behind the pulpit. The twins always sat between Jory and me. Joel would don a black robe as he preached fire-and-brimstone sermons. Bart sat beside me, holding my hand in such a tight grip I had to listen or have my bones broken. Next to Toni, deliberately separated from me by my second son, was Chris. I knew those sermons were meant for us, to save us from eternal hellfires. The twins were restless, like all children their age, and didn't like the pew, the confinement, the dullness of the overlong services. Only when we stood up to sing hymns did they stare up at us and seem enchanted.

'Sing, sing,' encouraged Bart, leaning to pinch tiny arms or tug on golden locks.

'Take your hands off my children!' snapped Jory. 'They will sing or not sing, as is their choice.'

It was on again, the war between brothers.

Autumn again, then Halloween when Chris and I took the twins by their small hands and led them to the one neighbour we considered 'safe' enough not to recriminate us or our children. Our little goblins timidly accepted their first Halloween trick-or-treat candy, then screamed all the way home with the thrill of having two Hersey bars and two packs of chewing gum of their very own.

Winter came, and Christmas and the New Year started without anything special happening, for this year Cindy didn't fly home. She was too busy with her budding career to do more than call long distance or write short but informative letters.

Bart and Toni now moved in different universes.

Perhaps I was not the only one who guessed that Jory had fallen deeply in love with Toni, now that all attempts at restoring a brotherly relationship with Bart had failed. I couldn't blame Jory, not when Bart had taken Melodie and driven her away and was even now trying to hold fast to Toni just because he could detect Jory's growing interest. To keep Jory from having her, he was turning again towards Toni . . .

Loving Toni gave Jory new reasons for living. It was written in his eyes, written on his new zeal for getting up early and beginning all those difficult exercises, standing for the first time, using parallel bars we'd had put in his room. As soon as the water was warm enough, he swam the length of our large swimming pool three times in early mornings and late evenings.

Maybe Toni was still waiting for Bart to make her his wife, though she often denied this. 'No, Cathy, I don't love him now. I only pity him for not knowing who or what he is and, more importantly, what he wants for himself but money and more money.' It occurred to me that, inexplicably, Toni was as rooted here as any one of us.

The Sunday church services made me nervous and tired. The strong words shouted from the weak lungs of an old man brought back terrifying memories of another old man I'd never seen. *Devil's issue. Devil's spawn.* Evil seed planted in the wrong soil. Even wicked thoughts were judged the same as wicked deeds – and what wasn't sinful to Joel? Nothing. Nothing at all.

'We're not going to attend anymore,' I stated firmly to Chris, 'and we were fools to even try to please Bart. I don't like the kind of ideas Joel is planting in the twin's impressionable young heads.' True to Chris's agreement, he and I refused to attend 'church' services or allow the twins to hear all that shouting about Hell and its punishments.

Joel came to the play area in the gardens, under the trees where there was a sandbox, swings, a slide and a spin-a-round that the twins loved to play on. It was a fine sunny day in July, and he looked rather touching and sweet as he sat between the twins and began to teach them how to do cats cradle, twining the string and intriguing the curious twins. They abandoned the sandpile with the pretty awning overhead and sat beside him, looking up at him in bright anticipation of making a new friend out of an old enemy.

'An old man knows many little skills to entertain small children. Do you know I can make aeroplanes and boats out of paper? And the boats will sail on the water.'

Their round eyes of amazement didn't please me. I frowned. Anyone could do that.

'Save your energies for writing new sermons, Joel,' I said, meeting his meek, watery eyes. 'I grew tired of the old ones. Where is the New Testament in your sermons? Teach Bart about that. Christ was born. He did deliver his Sermon on the Mount. Deliver to him that particular sermon, Uncle. Speak to us of forgiveness, of doing unto others as you would have done unto you. Tell us off the bread cast upon the waters of forgiveness returning to us tenfold.'

'Forgive me if I have been neglectful of our Lord's one truly begotten son,' he said humbly.

'Come, Cory, Carrie,' I called, getting up to leave. 'Let's go see what Daddy is doing.'

Joel's lowered head jerked upright. His faded blue eyes took on heaven's deeper blue. I bit down on my tongue to observe the twisted smile that Joel displayed. He nodded sagely. 'Yes, I know. To you they are the "other twins" – those born of evil seed planted in the wrong soil.'

'How dare you say that to me!' I flared.

I didn't realize then that by occasionally calling Jory's twins by the names of my beloved dead twins I was only adding fuel to the fire – a fire that was already, unknown to me, sending up small red sparks of brimstone.

COMES A MORNING DARK

A storm threatened a perfectly lovely summer day with dark ominous clouds, forcing me to hurry outdoors to cut my morning flowers while they were still fresh with dew. I drew up short when I saw Toni snipping yellow and white daisies that she brought to Jory in a small milkglass vase. She put them near the table where Jory was working on another watercolour showing a lovely dark-haired woman very much like Toni picking flowers. I was hidden by the dense shrubbery and could take a peek now and then without either one seeing me. For some strange reason, my intuitiveness warned me to stay quiet and say nothing.

Jory thanked Toni politely, gave her a brief smile, swished his brush in clean water, dipped it in his blue mixture and added a few touches here and there. 'Never can seem to mix the exact colour of the sky,' he murmured as if to himself. 'The sky is always changing . . . oh, what I could give to have Turner for my teacher . . .'

She stood watching the sun play on Jory's waving blue-black hair. He hadn't shaved, and that made him look twice as virile, although not as fresh. Suddenly he looked up and noticed her overlong stare. 'I apologize for the way I look, Toni,' he said as if embarrassed. 'I was very anxious to be up and busy this morning before the rain sets in and spoils another day for me. I hate the days when I can't stay outside.'

Still she said nothing, only stood there, the peekaboo sun glorifying her beautifully tanned skin. His eyes drifted over her clean, fresh face even before he briefly dropped his eyes and took in the rest of her. 'Thank you for the daisies. They're not supposed to tell. What is the secret?'

Swooping down, she picked up a few sketches he'd tossed at the waste basket and missed. Before she could drop them in the can, she gave the subjects her attention, and then her lovely face flushed. 'You've been sketching me,' she said in a low tone.

'Throw them away!' he said sharply. 'They're no good. I can paint flowers and hills and make fairly good landscapes, but portraits are so damned difficult. I can never capture the essence of you.'

'I think these are very good,' she objected, studying them again. 'You shouldn't throw away your sketches. May I keep them?'

Carefully she tried to flatten out the wrinkles, and then she was placing them on a table and stacking heavy books upon them. 'I was hired to take care of you and the twins. But you never ask me to do anything for you. And your mother likes to play with the twins in the mornings, so that gives me extra time, time enough to do many things for you. What can I do for you?'

The brush dripping with grey coloured the bottoms of clouds before he paused and turned his chair so he could look at her. A wry smile moved his lips. 'Once I could have thought of something. Now I suggest you leave me alone. Crippled men don't play very exciting games, I'm sorry to say.'

Appearing weary with defeat, she crumpled down on a long, comfortable chaise. 'Now you're saying to me what Bart does all the time – "Go away," he shouts, "Leave me alone," he yells. I didn't think you'd be the same.'

'Why not?' he asked with his own bitterness. 'We're brothers, half-brothers. We both have our hateful moments – and it's better to leave us alone then.'

'I thought he was the most wonderful man alive,' she said sadly. 'But I guess I can't trust my own judgment anymore. I believed Bart wanted to marry me – now he yells and orders me out of sight. Then he calls me back and begs forgiveness. I want to leave this house and never come back – but something holds me here, keeps whispering that it's not time for me to go . . .'

'Yes,' said Jory, beginning to paint again with careful strokes, tipping the board to make his washes run and create 'accidental' blendings that sometimes worked out beautifully. 'That's Foxworth Hall. Once you enter its portals, you seldom are seen again.'

'Your wife escaped.'

'So she did; more credit to her than I believed when it happened.'

'You sound so bitter.'

'I'm not bitter, I'm sour, like a pickle. I enjoy my life. I am caught between Heaven and Hell in a kind of purgatory where ghosts of the past roam the hallways at night. I can hear the clank and clonk of their restraining chains, and I can only be grateful they never appear, or perhaps the silent tread of my rubber-rimmed wheels scares them off.'

'Why do you stay if you feel that way?'

Jory shoved away from his painting table, then riveted his dark eyes on her. 'What the hell are you doing here with me? Go to your lover. Apparently you like the way he treats you, or easily enough you could escape. You aren't chained here with memories, with hopes or dreams that don't come true. You aren't a Foxworth, nor a Sheffield. This Hall holds no chains to bind you.'

'Why do you hate him?'

'Why don't you hate him?'

'I do sometimes.'

'Trust your sometime judgment and get out. Get out before you are made, by osmosis, into one of us.'

'And what are you?'

Jory drove his chair to the rim of the flagstones, where the flowerbeds began, and stared off towards the mountains. 'Once I was a dancer, and I never thought beyond that. Now that I can't dance, I have to presume that I am nothing of importance to anyone. So I stay, thinking I belong here more than I belong anywhere else.'

'How can you say what you just did? Don't you believe you're important to your parents, your sister, and most of all to your children?'

'They don't really need me, do they? And my parents have each other. My children have them. Bart has you. Cindy has her career. That leaves me the odd man out.'

Toni stood, stepped behind his chair and began to massage his neck with skilful fingers. 'Does your back still bother you at night?'

'No,' he said in a hoarse voice. But it did, I knew it did. Hidden behind the shrubs, I went right on snipping roses, sensing they didn't know I was there.

'If ever your back aches again, buzz for me and I'll give you a massage to take away the pain.'

Whirling his chair around in a full about-face, Jory confronted her fiercely. She had to jump back out of the way or be knocked down. 'So, it seems if you can't get one brother, you'll settle for the other – the crippled one who can't possibly resist your many charms? Thanks, but no thanks. My mother will massage my aching back.'

Slowly she drifted away, turning twice to look back at him. She didn't know that she left him staring after her with his heart in his eyes. She closed a French door behind her quietly. I stopped cutting roses for the breakfast table and sat on the grass. Behind me the twins were playing 'church'.

Following Chris's instructions, we were doing what we could to increase their vocabulary daily, and our instructions seemed to be working wonders.

'And the Lord said to Eve, go forth from this place.' Darren's childish voice was full of giggles.

I turned to look.

Both children had removed their brief sunsuits and taken off small white sandals. Deirdre stuck a leaf on her brother's small male organ, then stared down at her own private place. She frowned. 'Dare . . . what's sinning?'

'Like running,' answered her brother. 'Bad when you're barefoot.'

They both giggled and jumped up to run towards me. I caught them in my arms and held their soft, warm, nude bodies close, raining kisses on their faces. 'Have you eaten your breakfast?'

'Yes, Granny. Toni fed us grapefruit, which we hate. We ate everything but the eggs. Don't like eggs.'

That was Deirdre who did most of the talking for Darren, just as Carrie had been Cory's voice most of the time.

'Mom – how long have you been there?' called Jory. He sounded annoyed, a bit embarrassed.

Rising, I held the naked twins in my arms, and headed for Jory. 'I found Toni in the pool teaching the twins how to swim, so I took over and asked her to look in on you. They're doing very nicely in the water now, paddling all around with confidence. Why didn't you join us this morning?'

'Why did you keep yourself hidden?'

'Just snipping my morning roses, Jory. You know I do that every day. It's the one thing that makes this house cozy, the cut flowers I put in every room the first thing in the mornings.' Playfully I stuck a red rose behind his ear. Quickly he snatched it away and stuffed it in with the daisies Toni had brought him.

'You heard Toni and me, didn't you?'

'Jory, when I am outdoors in August knowing September isn't far away, I just grab each moment and value it for what it is. The rose scent is in my nostrils, making me think I am in Heaven, or in Paul's garden. He had the most beautiful gardens. All kinds. He divided sections into those that held English gardens, Japanese, Italian – '

'I've heard all that before!' he said impatiently. 'I asked if you heard us?'

'Yes, as a matter of fact, I did hear every fascinating thing, and when I had the chance, I peeked above the roses to watch the two of you.'

He scowled very much like Bart as I moved to put the twins on their feet, then gave their bare bottoms small spanks, telling them to find Toni, who would help them dress. They scuttled away, little naked dolls.

I sat down to smile at Jory, who glowered at me accusingly. He seemed even more like Bart when he looked angry. 'Really, Jory, I didn't mean to eavesdrop. I was there before either of you came out.' I paused and looked at his frowning face. 'You love Toni, don't you?'

'I don't love her! She's Bart's! Damned if I want to take Bart's leavings again.'

'Again?'

'Come off it, Mom. You know as well as I do the real reason why Mel left this house. He made it plain enough, and so did she that Christmas morning when the clipper ship was mysteriously broke. She'd have stayed on here forever if Bart had kept his position as replacement for me. I think she fell in love with him inadvertantly, while trying to satisfy her need for me and the sex we shared. I used to hear her crying in the night. I'd lie on my bed, wanting to go to her but unable to move, feeling sorry for her, sorrier for myself. It was hell then. It's hell now. A different kind of hell.'

'Jory – what can I do to help?'

He leaned forward, meeting my eyes with such intensity I was reminded of Julian and the many ways in which I had thwarted him.

'Mom, despite all this house represents to you, it's grown to feel like home to me. The halls and doorways are wide. There's the elevator to take me up and down. There're the swimming pool, the terraces, the gardens and the woods. Actually, a kind of paradise on earth – but for a few flaws. I used to think I couldn't wait to get away. Now I don't want to go, and I don't really want to worry you any more than you already are, yet I must speak.'

I waited with dread to hear about those few 'flaws'.

'When I was a child, I believed the world was full of many wonders, and miracles could still happen, and blind men would one day see, and the lame would one day walk, and so forth. Thinking like that made all the unfairness I saw all around, all the ugliness, much better. I think the ballet kept me from fully growing up, so I maintained the idea that miracles could truly happen if you believed in them enough – like that song "When you wish upon a star, your dreams come true." And in the ballet miracles do happen all the time, so I stayed childlike even after I became an adult. I still believed that in the outside world, the real world, everything would work out fine in the long run if I believed enough. Mel and I had that in common. There's something about ballet that keeps you virginal, so to speak. You see no evil, hear no evil, though I won't mention speak no evil.

You know what I mean, I'm sure, for it was your world, too.' He paused and glanced up at the threatening sky.

'In that world I had a wife who loved me. In the outside world, the real world, she quickly found a replacement lover. I hated Bart for taking her when I needed her most. Then I'd hate Mel for allowing him to use her as just another way to get back at me. He's still doing it, Mom. And I wouldn't trouble you with what's going on if I wasn't sometimes afraid for my life. Afraid for my children.'

I listened to him, trying not to show shock as he spoke of all he'd never hinted at before.

'Remember the parallel bars I exercise on, in order to use the back and leg braces? Well, somebody scraped the metal to that when I slip my hands along the rails I get metal splinters in both hands. Dad dug them out for me and made me promise not to tell you.'

I shivered, shrank inside. 'What else, Jory? That's not all, I can tell from the way you look.'

'Nothing much, Mom. Just little things to make my life miserable, like insects in my coffee, tea and milk. My sugar bowl filled with salt, and my salt cellar full of sugar . . . dumb tricks, childish pranks that could be dangerous. Tacks appear in my bed, in the seat of my chair . . . oh, it's Halloween time all the time in this house for me. At times I want to laugh, it's so silly. But when I slip on a shoe and there's a nail in the toe that I can't feel, and it gives me an infection because my leg circulation isn't top-notch, it's not a laughing matter. It could cost me a leg. I waste so much time looking everything over before I use it, like my razor with new blades that are suddenly rusty.'

He looked around as if to see if Joel or Bart were in earshot, and even though he saw nothing, for I looked, too, still his voice lowered to a whisper. 'Yesterday was very warm, remember? You yourself opened three of my windows so I'd have fresh, cool breezes – then the wind shifted and blew from the north, and it turned dramatically cold. You came on the run to close my windows, to cover me with another blanket. I fell back to sleep. Half an hour later I woke up from a dream of being at the North Pole.

The windows – all six of them – were wide open. Rain blew in and wet my bed. But that wasn't the worst of it. My blankets had been removed. I turned to ring for someone to come to my assistance. My buzzer was gone. I sat up and reached for my chair. It wasn't where I usually put it, right beside my bed. For a moment I panicked. Then, because I'm much stronger now in my arms, I lowered myself to the floor, used my arms to pull myself over to a regular chair that I could shove near the windows. Once I was on the chair seat, I could have easily pulled the windows down. But the first one refused to budge. I moved the chair to another window, and that wouldn't close any more than the first one would. Stuck with the fresh coat of paint applied a few weeks ago. I knew then it was useless to try the other four and brave that fiercely cold wet rain and wind, for my leverage wasn't right, even if my arms are strong. Yet, foolhardy as you often say I am, I persisted. No luck. That's when I put myself on the floor again and made my way to the door. It was locked. I dragged myself along by pulling on furniture legs until I was in the closet, and there I pulled down a winter coat, covered myself and fell asleep.'

What had happened to my face? It felt so numb that I couldn't move my lips and speak, nor could I manage to show shock. Jory stared at me hard.

'Mom, are you listening? Are you thinking? Now . . . don't try to comment until I complete this story. As I just said, I fell asleep in the closet, on the floor, soaking wet. When I woke up, I was back on my bed. A dry bed, the sheet and blankets covered me, and I was wearing a fresh pair of pyjamas.' He paused dramatically and met my horrified eyes.

'Mom . . . if someone in this house wanted me to catch pneumonia and die, would that someone have put me back in bed and covered me up? Dad wasn't home to pick me up and carry me, and certainly you don't have the strength to do that.'

'But,' I whispered, 'Bart doesn't hate you that much. He doesn't hate you at all . . .'

'Perhaps it was Trevor who found me, and not Bart. But somehow I don't think Trevor is young and strong enough to lift me. Still, somebody here hates me,' Jory stated firmly. 'Somebody who would like to see me gone. I've thought about this considerably and come to the conclusion that it had to have been Bart who found me in the closet and put me back to bed. Has this occurred to you: if you, Dad, I and the twins were out of the way, Bart would have our money as well as his own?'

'But he's already filthy rich! He doesn't need more!'

Jory spun his chair so that it faced east, staring at the faded sun. 'I've never really been afraid of Bart before. I have always pitied him and wanted to help him. I think about taking the twins and leaving with you and Dad . . . but that's a coward's way. If Bart did open those windows to let in the rain and wind, he later changed his mind and came back to rescue me. I think about the clipper ship and how it was broken, and certainly Bart couldn't have been responsible for that, not when he wanted it so much. And I think about Joel, whom you think was responsible – and again I think about who influences Bart more than anyone here. Someone is taking Bart and twisting him and turning back the clock, so he's again like that tormented ten-year-old kid who wanted you and his grandmother to die in fire and be redeemed . . .'

'Please, Jory, you said you'd never mention that period in our lives again.'

Silence came, stretched out interminably before he went on. 'The fish in my aquarium died last night. Their air filter was turned off. The temperature control smashed.' Once again he paused, watching my face closely. 'Do you believe any of what I've just told you?'

I fixed my eyes on the blue-misted mountains with their soft, rounded tops to remind me of ancient, gigantic, dead virgins laid out in jagged rows, their upthrust, moss-covered bosoms all that remained. My eyes lifted to the sky, deeply blue, and the feather-brushed storm clouds with wisps of shimmering gold clouds behind them, heralding a better day.

Under such skies as this, surrounded by the same mountains, Chris, Cory, Carrie and I had faced terrors while God watched. My fingers nervously wiped away those invisible cobwebs, trying to find the right words to say.

'Mom, as much as I hate to say this, I think we have to give up on Bart. We can't trust his now-and-then love for us. He needs professional help again. Truthfully, I've always believed he had a great deal of love within him that he didn't know how to release or express. And here I am, now thinking he's beyond saving. We can't drive him out of his own home – unless we want him declared insane and put in an institution. I don't want that to happen, and I know you don't. So, all we can do is leave. And isn't it funny – now I don't want to go, even when my life is threatened. I've grown accustomed to this house; I love it here, so I risk my life, the lives of all of us. The intrigue of what might happen today keeps me from ever being bored. Mom, the worst thing in my life is boredom.'

I wasn't half listening to Jory.

My eyes widened as I saw Deirdre and Darren following Joel and Bart to the small chapel, which had its own outside door that could be reached from the gardens. They disappeared inside, and the door closed.

I forgot my basket of cut roses and jumped to my feet. Where was Toni? Why wasn't she protecting the twins from Bart, from Joel? Then I felt foolish, for why should she feel that Bart or Joel was a threat to two such small, innocent children? Still I said a hasty goodbye to Jory, told him not to worry, I'd be back in a few minutes with Darren and Deirdre so we could all eat lunch together. 'Jory, you will be all right if I leave you alone for a few moments?'

'Sure, Mom. Go after my kids. I spoke to Trevor this morning, and he gave me a battery-operated two-way intercom. Trevor can be fully trusted.'

Believing wholeheartedly in our butler's loyalty, I sped after the foursome already in the chapel.

* * *

Minutes later I sneaked through the small downstairs inside door to enter the chapel that Joel had told Bart was truly necessary if he were to redeem his soul from sin. It was a small room that tried to duplicate what many old castles and palaces contained for family worship. There was Bart kneeling behind the first pew, with Darren on one side and Deirdre on the other. Joel stood behind the pulpit, his grey head bowed as he began to pray. Stealthily I inched myself closer to hide in the shadow of an arch strut.

'We don't like it here,' complained Deirdre in a loud whisper to Bart.

'Be quiet. This is God's place,' Bart warned.

'I hear my kitty crying,' said Darren weakly, cringing away from Bart.

'You cannot possibly hear your cat, or any cat crying from such a distance. Besides, it's not your kitty. It's Trevor's kitten, which he only allows you to play with.'

Both the twins began to sniffle, trying to hold back cries of distress. They both adored kittens, puppies, birds, anything that was little and cute. 'Silence!' roared Bart. 'I don't hear anything from the outside, but if you listen carefully, God will speak and tell you how to survive.'

'What's survive?'

'Darren, why do you let your sister ask all the questions?'

'She likes questions better.'

'Why is it so dark in here, Uncle Bart?'

'Deirdre, like all females, you talk too much.'

She began to wail louder. 'I do not! Gramma likes my talk . . .'

'Your gramma likes anyone's talk as long as it isn't mine,' answered Bart bitterly, pinching Deirdre's small arm to make her stay quiet.

Dozens of candles burned on the podium where Joel lifted his head. The architects had arranged for ceiling spots to converge on whomever was behind the pulpit, placing Joel squarely in the centre of a mystical, artificial, light cross.

In a clear and loud voice he said, 'We will stand and we will sing the praises of the Lord before today's sermon begins.' His voice was resonant, assured and authoritative.

I had eased myself by this time to a position behind a supporting pillar from which I could spy and not be seen. Like two small robots, the twins, who'd obviously been here many times before without their father, Chris, me or Toni, were well trained and intimidated. They stood obediently, one on each side of Bart, who kept his hands restrainingly on their small shoulders, and they began, with him, to sing hymns. Their voices were frail, faltering, unable to carry the tune well. Yet they made mighty efforts to keep up with Bart, who stunned me with his surprisingly good baritone singing voice.

Why hadn't Bart sung out like that when we attended the chapel services? Did Chris and I, with Jory, so intimidate Bart that he held back what had to be a God-given natural gift? When we'd praised Cindy for her singing voice, he had just frowned and said nothing to indicate that he had a wonderful voice as well. Oh, the complexity of Bart was likely to drive me crazy.

Under other, less sinister circumstances I would have been thrilled to hear Bart's voice lifted so joyously, his whole heart in it. Some filtering sunlight fell through the stained glass windows to glorify his face with colours of purple, rose and green. How beautiful he appeared as he sang, with his eyes lit up, as if he truly had the power of the Holy Ghost.

I was touched by his faith in God. Tears came to my eyes as a sense of relief washed over me and made me feel clean.

Oh, Bart, you can't be all evil if you can sing like that, and look like that. It isn't too late to save you, it can't be.

No wonder Melodie had loved him. No wonder Toni was unable to turn her back and leave such a man.

'Oh, sing this song . . . this song of love to thee,
In God we trust, in God we trust . . .'

His voice soared, overwhelming the thin voices of the twins. I was lifted up and out of myself, willing to believe in the powers of God. I sank down on my knees, bowing my head.

'Thank you, God,' I whispered. 'Thank you for saving my son.'

Then I was staring at him again, catching the Holy Spirit and willing to believe in anything he did. Words came out of the past. Bart had been with us at the time. 'We've got to be careful with Jory,' warned Chris. 'His immunity system has been impaired. We can't allow him to catch a cold that might fill his lungs with fluid . . .'

Still I knelt on, transfixed. Now I could not believe Bart was anything but a very troubled young man trying desperately to find what was right for himself.

Bart's powerful singing voice drew to the end of the hymn. Oh, if only Cindy could have heard him. If only they could both sing together, the two of them friends at last, joined by their equal talents. There was no one to applaud when his song ended. There was only silence and the thud of my beating heart.

The twins stared up at Bart with wide, innocent, blue eyes. 'Sing again, Uncle Bart,' pleaded Deirdre. 'Sing about the rock . . .'

Now I knew why they came to this chapel – to hear their uncle sing, to feel what I was feeling, an unseen presence that was warm and comforting.

Without any accompaniment, Bart sang 'Rock of Ages'. I was by this time a limp rag of emotions. With a voice like that he could have the world at his feet, and he locked away his talent in an office.

'That's enough, nephew,' said Joel when the second song was over. 'Everyone will sit, and we will begin today's sermon.'

Obediently, Bart sat and pulled the twins down beside him. He kept his arm about each in such a protective way that I was again moved to tears. Did he love Jory's twins? Had he, all this time, only pretended to dislike them because they resembled the *evil* twins of yesterday?

'Let us bow our heads and pray,' instructed Joel.

My head bowed as well.

I listened to his prayer with incredulity. He sounded so professional, so concerned for those who had never experienced the joy of being 'saved' and belonging entirely to Christ.

'When you open your heart and let Christ enter, he fills you with love. When you love the Lord, love his son who died for you, and you believe in the righteous ways of God and his son crucified so cruelly on that cross, you will find the peace of fulfilment that's always eluded you before. Lay down your sins, your swords, your shields, your thirsts for power and money. Put away your earthly lusts that crave the pleasures of flesh. Lay down all your earthly appetites that can never be satisfied and believe, believe! Follow in the footsteps of Christ. Follow where he led, believe in his teachings and you will be saved. Saved from the evils of this world of sin and lust for sex and power. Save yourselves before it is too late!'

His zealot's fire was frightening. Why couldn't I believe in his fiery sermon as I believed in Bart's beautiful singing voice? Why were visions of wind and rain pouring in on Jory washing me clean of Joel's evangelist oratory? I felt I'd betrayed Jory by my moment's belief that even Joel was what he seemed to be at this moment.

There was more to his sermon. I was startled at the casual, conversational tone he now assumed, as if he were talking directly to Bart. 'The voices in the village are momentarily lulled because we have constructed in this great mountain mansion a small temple dedicated to the worship of God. The workmen who constructed this divine house of worship and created the elaborate embellishments have told them what we have done, and others spread the word that the Foxworths are trying to salvage their souls. They no longer speak of revenge upon the Foxworths, who have ruled over them for more than two hundred years. They bear deep in their hearts many grudges for deeds done to them in the past by our self-serving, self-centred ancestors. They have not forgotten or forgiven the sins of Corrine Foxworth, who married her half-uncle, nor have they forgotten the sins of thy mother, Bart, and the brother she loves. Under your very roof she still gives him the pleasure of enjoying her body, as she takes her pleasure with him . . . and under God's own heavenly blue sky, those two lie naked in the sun before they blend one with the other. They are addicted to one another, as surely as if they were addicted to one of the many drugs that abound in today's immoral, headstrong, selfish, heedless society.

'He, the doctor, her very own brother, redeems himself somewhat in his efforts to serve mankind, dedicating his professional life to medicine and science. So he can be more easily forgiven than the sinful woman, thy mother, who gives nothing to the world but a perverted daughter who will turn out perhaps even worse, and a firstborn son who danced indecently for money! For glorifying his body! And for that sin he has paid, and dearly paid, by losing the use of his legs, and in losing his legs, he lost his body, and in losing his body, he lost his wife. Fate has infinite wisdom when it comes to deciding whom to punish and whom to assist.' Again he paused, as if for dramatic effect, before he fixed his piercing zealot's eyes on Bart, as if to burn his will into the brain of my son by pure force. 'Now, my son, I know you love your mother and you would at times forgive her anything . . . wrong, wrong – for will God? No, I don't think so. Save her, for how can God forgive *her* when she is responsible for luring her brother into her arms?'

He paused, his pale eyes lit with religious zeal, waiting for Bart to respond.

'I'm hungry!' wailed Deirdre suddenly.

'Me, too,' cried Darren.

'You'll stay, and you will do what you have to do, or suffer the consequences!' shouted Joel from the pulpit.

Immediately the twins shrank into small, tight shells, staring at Joel with immense eyes of fear. What had Joel done to put that fear there? Oh, God, had I given Joel or Bart an opportunity to hurt them in some way?

Long minutes passed, as if Joel were deliberately testing them. I wanted to jump up and cry out to stop Joel from implanting foul ideas in the heads of innocent babes. But there sat Bart, as if not hearing Joel's words at all. He had his dark eyes riveted on the magnificent stained-glass window directly behind the pulpit. Stained glass that showed Jesus with the little children at his feet, leaning against his knees, staring up into his face with adoration. That same adoration was on Bart's face. He wasn't listening to his great uncle. He was filling himself with the presence even I could feel in this place.

God did exist, had always been there even when I wanted to deny him.

The words of Christ did have meaning in today's world – and somehow his teachings had reached out and found a place in Bart's maze of troubled brain waves.

'Bart, your niece and nephew are falling asleep!' roared Joel angrily. 'You neglect your duty! Wake them up! Immediately!'

'Suffer the little children, Uncle Joel,' said Bart. 'Your sermons last too long and they become bored and restless. They are not evil or contaminated. They were born within the holy vows of marriage. They are not the first twins, the blood-related twins, Uncle – not the evil twins . . .'

Even as I saw Bart lifting Darren and Deirdre up into his arms, holding them in a protective way, I felt fear confused with hope. Bart was proving himself to be just as fine and noble as his father. No sooner did I think that when I heard words that chilled my blood. I froze in the shadows.

Bart had risen with the twins in his arms. 'Put them down,' ordered Joel, his sermon over and his strong voice diminished to his habitual thin whisper. Had he drained his supply of energy so that now he was ineffective? I prayed so.

'Now, children who have not learned how to control physical demands, repeat the lessons I have tried to teach you. Speak, and tell me, Darren, Deirdre! Speak the words you are supposed to keep forever in your minds and hearts. Speak, and let God hear.'

They had such babishly small voices that seldom said more than a few words at a time. They sometimes used the wrong syntax . . . but this time they intoned as correctly and as seriously as adults.

Bart listened carefully, as if he'd helped coach them.

'We are children born of evil seed. We are the Devil's issue, the Devil's spawn. We have inherited all the evil genes that lead to inces . . . incestuous relationships.'

Pleased with themselves, they grinned at each other for having said it right, not understanding in the least the meaning of the words. Then both twins turned serious blue eyes on that forbidding old man behind the pulpit.

'Tomorrow we will continue with our lessons.' So said, Joel closed his huge black Bible.

Bart picked up the twins, kissed their cheeks and told them that now they could put on clean, dry pants, eat lunch, take baths and have nice naps before they attended chapel services again.

That's when I stood up and stepped into full view. 'Bart, what are you trying to do to Jory's children?'

My son stared at me, his sun-bronzed skin going very pale. 'Mother, you aren't supposed to come here except on Sundays . . .'

'Why? Do you hope to keep me away so you can mould the twins into warped human beings you can punish later on? Is that your purpose?'

'Who warped you into what you are?' asked Joel coldly, his eyes small and hard.

In a wild fury of rage, I spun to confront him. 'Your parents!' I screamed. 'Your sister, Joel, locked us up and kept us there, living on promises year after year, while Chris and I were turning into adults with no one to love but each other. So place the blame on those who made Chris and I what we are. But before you say one more word, I'm having my say.

'I love Chris, and I am not ashamed. You think I have given nothing of importance to the world, yet there stands your greatnephew, holding my grandchildren, and on the terrace is another of my sons. And they are not contaminated! They are not Devil's issue, or Devil's spawn – and don't you ever, as long as you live, dare to say those words again to anyone who belongs to me or I will see that you are put away and declared senile!'

Colour came to Bart's face as what colour he had left

departed from Joel's pasty skin. His desperate, faded, blue eyes sought to meet Bart's, but Bart was staring at me as if he'd never seen me before. 'Mother,' he said weakly, and would have said more, but the twins tore from his arms and ran to me.

'Hungry, Gramma, hungry . . .'

My eyes locked with Bart's. 'You have the most beautiful singing voice I have ever heard,' I said, backing away and taking the twins with me. 'Be your own man, Bart. You don't need Joel. You have found your talent, now use it.'

He stood there frozen, as if he had volumes to say, but Joel was tugging on his arm, imploring, just as the twins were crying for lunch.

HEAVEN CAN'T WAIT

Jory fell very ill a few days later with a cold that just wouldn't go away. The cold, wet rain and winds had done their work. He lay on his bed with his temperature soaring, his brow glistening with beads of perspiration, writhing and turning his head incessantly from side to side, as he moaned, groaned and called repeatedly for Melodie. I saw Toni wince each time he did that, even as she did her best to nurse him.

As I watched her with him, I saw that she truly did care for Jory; it was clear in every caring thing she did, in her soft, compassionate eyes and her lips that brushed his face whenever she thought I wasn't looking.

She turned to give me a brave smile. 'Try not to worry so much, Cathy,' she pleaded, bathing Jory's bare chest with cool water. 'Most people don't realize that a fever is usually very helpful in burning up viruses. As a doctor's wife I'm sure you already know this and are just worried that he will go into pneumonia. He won't. I'm sure he won't.'

'Let's pray he won't . . .'

I still worried; she was only a nurse without the medical expertise of Chris. I called him every hour, trying to find him in that huge university lab. Why wasn't Chris responding to my urgent calls? I began to feel not only worried but angry that Chris couldn't be reached. Hadn't he promised to always be here when he was needed?

Two days had passed since Joel preached his sermon, and Chris had not called home.

The sweltering, humid weather and intermittent rain and electrical storms did nothing but create more misery and havoc in my mind. Thunder crashed overhead. Lightning flashed, momentarily lighting up dark, forbidding skies. Near my feet the twins were playing and whispering about it being time for lessons in the chapel. 'Please, Gramma. Uncle Joel says we must come.'

'Deirdre, Darren, I want you to listen to me and forget what your Uncle Joel and Uncle Bart tell you. Your father wants you to stay with me and Toni, near him. You know your daddy is sick, and the last thing he'd want is for his son and daughter to be visiting that chapel where . . . where . . .' and here I stumbled. For what could I say about Joel that wouldn't somehow rebound later? He was teaching what he believed was right. If only he had not taught them those phrases . . . Devil's issue. Devil's spawn.

Instantly the two of them wailed, as if of one mind. 'Will Daddy die?' they cried out simultaneously.

'No, of course he won't die. What do you two know about death, anyway?' I went on to explain that their grandfather was a wonderful doctor and he'd be coming home any second.

They stared at me without comprehension before I realized they often mouthed words they'd learned by rote and had no understanding of what they said. Death – what could they know about that?

Toni turned to give me a strange look. 'You know something? As I help those two on and off with their clothes and give them baths, they keep up a constant chatter. They're really very remarkable and bright children. I guess being around adults so much has taught them more swiftly than playing with other children would have. Most of what they say while playing alone is silly gibberish. Then out of this silly gibberty-junk come serious words, adult words. Their eyes widen. They speak in whispers. They look around and seem afraid. It's as if they are expecting to see someone, or something, and in low tones they suddenly warn each other of God and his wrath. It alarms me.' She looked from me and the twins back to Jory.

'Toni, listen carefully. Never allow the twins out of your sight. Keep them with you at all times during the day, unless you know positively they are with me or Jory, or my husband. When you're caring for Jory and are too preoccupied to keep an eye on them, call me and I'll take them over. Above all, don't let them go off with Joel,' and as much as I hated to, I had to add Bart's name.

She threw me another worried look. 'Cathy, I think it was not only that thing that happened in New York with Cindy, and with me, but also what Joel had to say when we came back that made Bart start looking at me as if I were the worst kind of sinner. It hurts to have the man you think you love hurl such ugly accusations.'

Again she was bathing Jory's arms and chest. 'Jory would never say such ugly things, no matter what I did. Sometimes he looks fierce, but even then he's thoughtful enough to say nothing to damage my ego. I never knew a man so thoughtful and compassionate.'

'Arc you saying now that you love Jory?' I asked, wanting to believe she did but afraid her disappointment was rebounding and making Jory only a substitute love.

She blushed and bowed her head. 'I've been in this house almost two years, and I've seen and heard a great many things. In this house I found sexual satisfaction with Bart, but it wasn't romantic or sweet, just exciting. Only now am I beginning to feel the romance of a man who tries to understand me and give me what I need. His eyes never condemn. Never do his lips shout out terrible things, when I haven't done anything I think is terrible. My love for Bart was a burning hot fire, kindled to a blaze the first day we met, while my feet stayed in quicksand, never knowing what he wanted, or what he needed, except he wanted someone like you . . .'

'I wish you'd stop saying that, Toni.' I objected with discomfort. Bart still disliked himself so much he feared a woman turning away from him first, and to keep that from happening, he discarded Melodie before she had the chance to turn against him. Later, he turned his self-loathing against Toni before she could hate him and leave him. Again I sighed.

Toni agreed never to discuss Bart with me again, and then she began with my help to slip a clean pyjama jacket on to Jory. We worked together as a team while the twins played on the floor, shoving little cars and trucks along just like Cory and Carrie had done.

'Just be sure which brother it is you love before you hurt

both of them. I'm going to talk to my husband and Jory again, and I'm doing my damndest to see that we move out of this house just as soon as Jory recovers. You can go with us if that is your choice.'

Her pretty grey eyes widened. She looked from me back to Jory, who had rolled on his side and was murmuring incoherently in his delirium. 'Mel . . . is that our cue?' I think he was saying.

'No, it's Toni, your nurse,' she said softly, caressing his hair and brushing it back from his beaded brow. 'You have a very bad cold . . . but soon you'll feel just fine.'

Jory stared up at her in a disoriented way, as if trying to distinguish this woman from the one he dreamed about every night. During the day he had eyes only for Toni, but in the night, Melodie came back to haunt him. What was there about the human condition that made us hold on to tragedy with such tenacity and easily forego the happiness we could reach readily?

He began to cough violently, choking and pulling up huge wads of phelgm. Tenderly Toni held his head, then threw away the soiled tissues.

Everything she did for him she did with tenderness, fluffing his pillows, massaging his back, moving his legs to keep them supple even if he couldn't control them. I couldn't help but be impressed with all that she did to make him comfortable.

I backed off towards the door, feeling I was an intruder during a very important private moment as Jory's eyes came into focus enough for him to pick up her hand and meet her eyes. Even as sick as he was, something in his eyes spoke to her. Quietly I caught hold of Darren's hand, and then Deirdre's. 'Got to go now,' I whispered even as I watched Toni tremble before her head bowed.

To my surprise, just before I closed the door, she put his hand to her lips and kissed each of his fingers. 'I'm taking advantage of you,' she whispered, 'at a time when you can't fight back, but I need to tell you what a fool I've been. You were here all the time, and I never saw you. Never saw you at all when Bart stood in the way.'

Weakly Jory answered, his eyes warm as they drank in the sincerity of her words and most of all, her loving, warm expression. 'I guess it's easy to overlook a man in a wheelchair, and perhaps that alone was enough to make you blind. But I've been here, waiting, hoping . . .'

'Oh, Jory, don't hold it against me because I let Bart dazzle me with his charm. I was overwhelmed and sort of flabbergasted that he found me so desirable. He swept me off my feet. I think every woman secretly wants a man who refuses to take no for an answer, and pursues her relentlessly until she has to give in. Forgive me for being a fool, and an easy conquest.'

'It's all right, all right,' he whispered, then closed his eyes. 'Just don't let what you feel for me be pity – or I'll know.'

'You're what I wanted Bart to be!' she cried out as her lips neared his.

This time I did close the door.

Back in my own rooms, I sat down near the telephone waiting for Chris to call in response to my many urgent messages. On the verge of sleep, with the twins tucked neatly in my bed for their naps, the phone rang. I snatched up the receiver, said hello. A deep, gruff voice asked for Mrs Sheffield, and I identified myself.

'We don't want you and your kind here,' said that frightening, deep voice. 'We know what's going on up there. That little chapel you built don't fool us none. It's a sham to hide behind while you flaunt God's rules of decency. Get out – before we take God's will into our own hands and drive every last one of you away from our mountains.'

Unable to find a clever reply, I sat stunned and very shaky before he hung up. For long moments I just sat there with the receiver in my hand. The sun broke through the clouds and warmed my face . . . only then did I hang up. I looked around me at the rooms I myself had decorated to please my own taste, and found, much to my surprise, that these rooms no longer reminded me of my mother and her second husband. In here were only remnants of the past that I wanted to remember.

Cory and Carrie's baby pictures in silver frames on my dresser, placed next to those of Darren and Deirdre. They were look-alike twins, but when you knew them well, you could see they weren't the same. My eyes moved to the next silver frame, and there was Paul smiling at me, and Henny was in another. Julian sulked in a way he used to think sexy from a gold frame, and I also had a few snapshots of his mother, Madame Marisha, framed to keep near her son. But nowhere did I have a photograph of Bartholomew Winslow. I stared at the picture of my own father, who'd died when I was twelve. So much like Chris, only now Chris looked older. Turn around, and the boy you knew so well was a man. The years flew by so swiftly; once a day had seemed longer than a year did now.

Again I looked at the two sets of twins. It would take only someone very familiar with both sets to recognize the slight differences. There was a hint of Melodie in Jory's children, a vague resemblance. I stared at another picture, with Chris and myself, taken when we still lived in Gladstone, Pennsylvania. I'd been ten, he'd just turned thirteen. We stood in three feet of snow beside the snowman we'd just finished, smiling at Daddy as he took yet another picture. A photograph turning brown, one that our mother had put in her blue album. Our blue album now.

Little snippets of our lives were caught in all those little squares and oblongs of slick paper. Frozen forever in time, that Catherine Doll who was on an attic windowsill, wearing a flimsy nightgown as Chris in the shadows took a time lapse photo. How had I managed to sit so still, and hold that expression – how? Through the nightgown I could see the tender form of young breasts – and in that girlish profile all the wistful sadness I'd felt back then.

How lovely she was – I'd been. I stared at her hard and long. That frail, slender girl had long ago disappeared in the middle-aged woman I was now. I sighed for the loss of her, that special girl with her head full of dreams. I tried to tear my gaze away; instead, I got up to pick up the picture that Chris had carried with him to college, to medical school. When he was an intern, still he had this photograph with him. Was it this paper in my hand that had kept his love for me so strong? This attic face of a girl of fifteen, sitting in the moonlight? Longing, always longing for love that would last forever? I no longer looked like this girl I held in my hand. I looked like my mother the night she burned down the original Foxworth Hall.

Shrill telephone rings startled me back to the here and now. 'I've had a flat tyre,' said Chris on hearing my small voice. 'I had driven to another lab and spent a few hours there, so when I came back I saw all those messages from you about Jory. Jory can't be worse, can he?'

'No, darling, he's no worse.'

'Cathy, what's wrong?'

'I'll tell you when you get here.'

Chris reached home an hour later and rushed in to embrace me before he hurried to Jory. 'How's my son?' he asked even as he sat on Jory's bed and reached to feel his pulse. 'I hear from your mother that someone opened all your windows and the rain soaked you.'

'Oh!' cried Toni. 'Who could have done such an awful thing? I'm so sorry, Doctor Sheffield. It's my habit to check on Jory, I mean Mister Marquet, two or three times during the night, even if he doesn't call for me.'

Jory grinned at her in a happy way. 'I think you can stop calling me Mister Marquet now, Toni.' His voice was very weak and hoarse. 'And this happened on your day off.'

'Oh,' she said, 'that must have been the morning I drove into the city to visit my girlfriend.'

'It's just a cold, Jory,' said Chris, checking his lungs again. 'There's no hint of fluid in your lungs, and from your symptoms you don't have the flu. So swallow your medicine, drink the fluids Toni brings you and stop fretting about Melodie.'

Later, sprawled in his favourite chair in our sitting room, Chris listened to everything I had to say. 'Did you recognize the voice?'

'Chris, I don't know any of the villagers well enough. I do my damndest to stay away from them.'

'How do you know it was a villager?'

That thought had never occurred to me. I'd just presumed. Nevertheless, as soon as Jory was well enough, we both determined to leave this house.

'If it's what you want,' said Chris, looking around with some regret. 'I like it here, I must admit. I like all the space around us, the gardens, the servants who wait on us, and I'll be sorry to leave. But let's not flee too far. I don't want to leave my work in the university.'

'Chris, don't worry. I won't take that away from you. When we leave here, we will go to Charlottesville and pray to God nobody there will know that I'm your sister.'

'Cathy, my dearest, sweetest wife, I don't think even if they knew, they'd give a damn. And besides, you look more like my daughter than my wife.'

Wonderfully sweet as he was, he could say that with honesty in his eyes. I knew then he was blind when he looked at me. He saw what he wanted to see, and that was the girl I used to be.

He laughed at my doubting expression. 'I love the woman you've become. So don't you go looking for the tarnish when I deliver to you eighteen-carat-gold honesty. I'd say twenty-four carat, but you'd then say it was too soft and therefore useless functionally. So I give to you the best there is: my eighteen-carat love that truly believes you are beautiful inside, outside and in between.'

Cindy flew in for one of her whirlwind visits, breathlessly gushing out every detail of her life in exquisite minute detail since last she'd seen us. It seemed incredible that so much could happen to one girl of nineteen.

The instant we were inside the grand foyer, she raced up the stairs, hurling herself into Jory's arms with such abandon I thought she might tip over his chair. 'Really,' he laughed, 'you weigh more than a feather, Cindy.' He kissed her, looked her over, then laughed. 'Wow! What kind of outfit is that, anyway?'

'The kind that is going to fill the eyes of a certain brother named Bart with horror. I picked this out just to annoy him and dear Uncle Joel.'

Jory turned solemn. 'Cindy, if I were you, I'd stop deliberately baiting Bart. He's not a little boy anymore.'

Unknown to Cindy, Toni had stepped into the room and stood patiently waiting to take Jory's temperature.

'Oh,' said Cindy, turning to see Toni. 'I thought after that terrible scene Bart made in New York that you'd see him for what he really is and leave this place.' The look in Toni's eyes made Cindy glance again at Jory, then back to Toni again, and she laughed. 'Well, now you've got good sense! I can read your eyes, Toni, Jory. You're in love! Hooray!' She rushed to hug and kiss Toni before she settled down near Jory's chair and stared up at him with adoration. 'I met Melodie in New York. She cried a lot when I told her how pretty the twins are . . . but the day after your divorce went through, she married another dancer. Jory, he looks a lot like you, only not nearly as handsome, and he doesn't dance as well, either.'

Jory kept his small smile, as if Melodie had been put on the shelf and there she'd stay. He turned his head to grin at Toni. 'Well, there goes my alimony payment. At least she could have let me know.'

Again Cindy was staring at Toni. 'What about Bart?'

'What about me?' asked a baritone voice from the open doorway.

Only then did we all notice that Bart was in the doorway, lounging insolently against the frame, taking in all we said and did as if we were specimens in his special zoo of family oddities.

'Well,' he drawled, 'as I live and breathe, our breathless little imitation Marilyn Monroe has come to thrill us all with her stagey presence.'

'That's not how I'd describe my feelings on seeing you again,' Cindy said with her eyes flashing. 'I'm chilled, not thrilled.'

Bart looked her over, taking in her skin-tight gold leather pants, her striped cotton knit sweater of white and gold. The horizontal stripes emphasized her breasts which jiggled freely each time she moved, and knee-high gold boots decorated her feet and legs.

'When are you leaving?' asked Bart while he stared at Toni sitting on Jory's bed and holding his hand. Chris sat next to me on a love seat, trying to catch up on some mail that had been delivered to the house and not to his office.

'Dear brother, say what you will, I don't care. I've come to see my parents and the rest of my family. I'll be leaving soon enough. Chains of steel couldn't keep me here longer than necessary.' She laughed and stepped closer and looked up into his face. 'You don't have to like me, or approve of me. And even if you open your mouth and say something insulting I'll just laugh again. I've found a man to love me that makes you look like something drug up from the Dismal Swamp!'

'Cindy!' said Chris sharply, putting down his unopened mail. 'While you are here, you will dress appropriately, and you will treat Bart with respect, as he will treat you. I'm sick of these childish arguments about nothing.'

Cindy looked at him with hurt eyes, making me say apologetically, 'Darling, it is Bart's home. And sometimes I would like to see you in clothes that aren't too small.'

Her blue eyes changed from those of a woman to those of a child. She wailed, 'You're both taking his side – when you know he's nothing but a crazy creep out to make us all unhappy!'

Toni sat uncomfortably until Jory leaned to whisper something in her ear, and then she was smiling. 'It doesn't mean anything,' I heard him say in an undertone. 'I believe Bart and Cindy enjoy tormenting one another.'

Unfortunately Bart's attention was drawn from Cindy to take notice of Jory with his arm about Toni's shoulders. He scowled, then beckoned to Toni. 'Come with me. I want to show you the inside of the chapel with all its new additions.'

'A chapel? Why do we need a chapel?' asked Cindy, who had not been informed of the newest room transformed.

'Cindy, Bart wanted a chapel added to this house.'

'Well, Mom, if anybody ever needed a chapel close at hand, it's the creep of the hill and the Hall.'

My second son didn't say a word.

Toni refused to go with him. She gave him the excuse of needing to bathe the twins. Anger lit up Bart's eyes before it died, leaving him standing there, strangely desolate looking. I got up to take his hand. 'Darling, I'd love to see what new additions you've made in the chapel.'

'Some other time,' he said.

I watched him covertly at the dinner table as Cindy taunted Bart in rather ridiculous ways that might have made the rest of us laugh if he could only see the humour she displayed. However, Bart had never been able to laugh at himself, more the pity. He took everything so seriously. Her grin was triumphant. 'You see, Bart,' she teased, 'I can put away my childish foibles, even physical ones. But you can't put away anything that sours your guts and chews away on your brain. You're like a sewer, ready to hold all that's stinking and rotten and never give it up.'

Still he said nothing.

'Cindy,' spoke up Chris, who'd remained quiet during our evening meal, 'apologize to Bart.'

'No.'

'Then get up and leave the table, and eat in your room until you can learn to speak pleasantly.'

Her eyes flashed balefully again, this time at Chris. 'ALL RIGHT! I'll go to my room – but tomorrow I'm leaving this house and I'm never coming back! NOT EVER!'

Finally Bart had something to say. 'The best news I've heard in years.'

Cindy was in tears before she reached the dining room archway. I didn't jump up to follow her this time. I sat on, pretending nothing was amiss. Always in the past I'd shielded Cindy, chastised Bart, but I was seeing him with new eyes. The son I'd never known had facets that weren't all dark and dangerous.

'Why don't you go to Cindy, as you always have in the past, Mother?' asked Bart, as if challenging me.

'I haven't finished my dinner, Bart. And Cindy has to learn to respect the opinions of others.'

He sat staring at me as if completely taken off guard.

Early the next morning, Cindy stormed into our room without knocking, catching me wrapped in a towel, fresh from my bath, and Chris was still shaving. 'Mom, Dad, I'm leaving,' she said stiffly. 'I won't enjoy myself here. I'm wondering why I even bothered to come back. It's clear you've decided to take Bart's side on every issue, and if that's the case, then I'm finished. I'll be twenty next April, and that's old enough not to need a family.'

Her eyes smeared with the tears that came unbidden. Her voice turned small and broken. 'I want to say thanks to both of you for being wonderful parents when I was little and needed someone like both of you. I'm going to miss you and Daddy, and Jory and Darren and Deirdre, but every time I come here, I leave feeling sick. If ever you decide to live somewhere far from Bart, maybe you'll see me again . . . maybe.'

'Oh, Cindy!' I cried, rushing to embrace her. 'Don't leave!'

'No, Momma,' she said staunchly. 'I'm going back to New York. My friends there will throw me a party, the best kind. They do everything better in New York.'

But her tears were coming faster, harder. Chris wiped his face free of shaving lather and came to hug her close. 'I can understand how you feel, Cindy. Bart can be irritating, but you did go too far last night. In a way you were very funny, but sadly, he can't see that. You have to judge whom you can tease, and whom you cannot. You've outgrown Bart, Cindy. And we won't object if you want to leave so soon. But, before you go, we want you to know your mother and I are taking Jory and his children, and Toni, too, and moving to Charlottesville. We'll find a large house there and settle down in the midst of people, so when you come again, you won't be lonely, and Bart will still be here, high on this hill and far from you.'

Sobbing, she clutched Chris. 'I'm sorry, Daddy. I was nasty to him, but he always says such mean things to me, and I have to hit back or feel like a doormat. I don't like for him to wipe his feet on me – and he is like a sewer, he is.'

'Someday I hope you'll see him differently,' said Chris softly, tilting up her pretty tear-stained face and kissing her lightly. 'So kiss your mother, say goodbye to Jory, Toni, Darren and Deirdre . . . but don't say you won't come back to see us again. That would make us both very unhappy. You give us a great deal of joy, and nothing should spoil that.'

I helped Cindy pack the clothes she'd just unpacked. And even as we did this together, I saw that she was undecided and wanted to stay on if only I'd plead. Unfortunately we'd left her door open, and I looked around to see Joel standing in the doorway watching us.

Joel turned pale eyes on Cindy. 'Why are you red-eyed, little girl?'

'I'm not a little girl!' she screamed. She turned wrathful eyes on him. 'You're in league with him, aren't you? You help make him what he is. You stand there and gloat because I'm packing my bags, don't you? Glad I'm leaving – but before I go, I'm telling you off, too, old man. And I don't care if my parents scold me for not showing respect for old age.' She stepped closer, her posture dominating his cringing form. 'I hate you, old man! Hate you for preventing my brother from being normal, and he could have been without you! I HATE YOU!'

Hearing this, Chris, who'd been seated near the window, became furious. 'Cindy, why? You could have gone and said nothing.' Joel had disappeared by this time, leaving Cindy staring at Chris, bleak-eyed. 'Cindy,' Chris said softly, reaching out to caress her hair. 'Joel is an old man dying of cancer. He won't be around much longer.'

'What do you mean?' she asked. 'He looks healthier than when he came.'

'Perhaps he's had a remission. He refuses to see a doctor and won't let me check him over. He says he's resigned to dying soon. So, I take him at his word.'

'I expect now you want me to apologize to him – well, I won't! I meant every word! That time in New York, when Bart was so happy with Toni, and they seemed so much in love, we were at a party, when suddenly an old man appeared that looked like Joel – and instantly Bart changed. He turned mean, hateful, like a spell had been cast, he began to criticize my clothes, Toni's pretty dress that he said was shameless . . . and only a few minutes before, he'd complimented the way she looked in that very same dress. So don't tell me that Joel doesn't have a great deal to do with Bart's nutty behaviour.'

Instantly I was with Cindy. 'You see, Chris. Cindy believes just as I do. If Joel weren't here using his influence, Bart would straighten out. Drive Joel out, Chris, before it's too late.'

'Yes, Daddy, make that old man leave. Pay him off, get rid of him.'

'And what do I say to Bart?' asked Chris, looking from one to the other of us. 'Don't you realize he has to be the one who sees Joel for what he is? We can't tell him Joel's not a healthy influence. Bart has to discover that for himself.'

Soon after this we drove to Richmond to see that Cindy caught a plane back to New York. In another week she was moving to Hollywood to try and begin a film career. 'I won't be coming to Foxworth Hall again, Momma,' she repeated. 'I love you, and I love Dad, even if he is angry with me for speaking my mind. Tell Jory again that I love him and his children. But hate and ugly thoughts come into my mind the minute I step inside that house. Leave there, Momma. Daddy. Leave before it's too late.'

Numbly I nodded.

'Momma, remember the night when Bart beat up Victor Wade? He carried me home naked – and he took me up to Joel's room. He held me so Joel could look me over, and that old man spat on me, cursed me. I couldn't tell you then. The two of them scare me when they get together. Alone, Bart might straighten out. With Joel there to influence him, he could be dangerous.'

She was soon on the plane and we were on the ground watching her fly away again.

She flew towards morning. We drove home towards night.

This couldn't go on any longer. To save Jory, Chris, the twins and myself, we had to leave, even if it meant we'd never see Bart again.

Poor Cindy, I was thinking, how would she fare in Hollywood? I sighed, then began to look around for the twins. They sat solemnly in their sandbox with the rainbowed canopy overhead, although in early September the weather was steadily cooling off. They sat without shovelling sand into pretty buckets, not building sand castles. Not doing anything. 'Just listening to the wind blow,' said Deirdre.

'Don't like the wind,' added Darren.

Before I could speak, Chris was striding towards us, and soon I was telling him, 'Cindy just called from Hollywood. She says she has lots of friends there already. I don't know if she does or not. But she does have plenty of money. Already I've called one of my friends who will check on her.'

'It's better so,' he said with a troubled sigh. 'It seems nothing can work out for Cindy here. She can't get along with Bart, and now she's started on Joel as well. In fact, she seems to think Joel is worse than Bart.'

'He is, Chris! Don't you know that by now?'

He grew impatient with me, just when I thought I had him convinced. 'You're prejudiced because he is Malcolm's son, and there's all it is. For a while when Cindy was berating him, too, the two of you almost convinced me, but Joel is not doing one thing to influence Bart. Bart, from all I hear, is a full-blooded young stud, having the time of his life, only you don't know that. And Joel can't have much longer to live. That cancer is devouring him day by day, even if he does maintain his weight. He can't possibly hold on more than a month or two more.'

I wasn't distressed. I didn't even feel guilty or ashamed at that moment, I told myself with sincerity, that Joel was getting out of life exactly what he deserved. 'How do you know he's ill with cancer?' I asked.

'He told me that's why he came back to die on home ground, so to speak. He wants to be buried in the family cemetery.'

'Chris, like Cindy said, he does look better now than when he came.'

'Because he's well fed and well housed. He lived in poverty at that monastery. You see him in one way, I see him in another. He confides in me, Catherine, and tells me how hard he's tried to win you to his side. Tears come into his eyes. "And she's so much like her dear mother, my dear sister" he'll say over and over again.'

Not for one minute, after witnessing Joel in that chapel, would I ever believe in that evil old man. Even when I told Chris about the chapel incidence in great detail, he didn't think it so terrible until I mentioned what had been taught to the twins.

'You heard that? Actually heard those babies say they were Devil's issue?' Disbelief was clear in his blue eyes.

'Does it ring a familiar bell? Do you see Cory and Carrie on their knees by their beds, praying for God to forgive them for being born Devil's spawn? Even when they didn't know what that meant? Does anyone know more than you and I what harm can be done from ideas like that planted in such young minds? Chris, we have to leave soon! Not after Joel dies, but soon as possible!'

He said exactly what I'd feared he would. We had to think of Jory, who needed special quarters, special equipment. 'He'll have to have an elevator. Doors will have to be enlarged. The halls must be wide. And there is another consideration – Jory may marry Toni. He asked me what I thought about it, wanting to know if I believed he had a chance of making Toni happy. I said yes, of course he could. I can see the love between them growing day by day. I like the way she treats him, as if she doesn't see the wheelchair, or what he can't do – only what he can.

'And Cathy, it wasn't love between Toni and Bart. It was infatuation, glands calling to glands – call it whatever you will, but it wasn't love. Not our kind of everlasting love.'

'No . . .' I breathed, 'not the kind that lasts forever . . .'

Two days later Chris called from Charlottesville, telling me he'd found a house.

'Exactly how many rooms?'

'Eleven. It's going to seem small after Foxworth Hall. But the rooms are large, airy, cheerful. It has four baths and a powder room, five bedrooms, a guest room and another bath over the garage, and also on the second floor is a huge room we can convert into a studio for Jory, and one of the extra bedrooms can be my home office. You're going to love this house.'

I doubted that, he'd found it too quickly, even though that's what I'd asked him to do. He sounded so happy, and that gave me happy expectations. He laughed, then explained more. 'It's beautiful, Cathy, really just the kind of house I've always heard you say you wanted. Not too big, not too small, with plenty of privacy. Three acres with flowerbeds everywhere.'

It was settled.

As soon as we could pack our bags and many personal possessions accumulated over the years we'd lived in Foxworth Hall, we would move out.

I felt sad in some ways as I sauntered through the grand rooms that I'd gradually made cosy with my own decorating ideas. Bart had complained more than once that I was changing what should never change. But even he, once he'd seen the improvements that made this a home rather than a museum, had finally agreed to let me have my way.

Chris came to me Friday evening, looking at me with soft eyes. 'So, my beautiful, hold on for just a few more days and let me drive back to Charlottesville and check out that house more thoroughly before we sign the contract bid. I've found a nice apartment we can rent until we can close on the house. Also, I have a few things to clear up at the lab, so I can take off several days and help get us settled. As I was telling you on the phone, I think two weeks of work, after the closing, and our new home will be ready for all of us – ramps, elevator and all.'

He graciously didn't mention all the years he'd lived with Bart, knowing it was like living with an explosive hidden somewhere, bound to go off sooner or later. Never a word to reproach me for giving him a defiant, disrespectful son who refused to care how much love was given him.

Oh, how much agony he'd suffered because of Bart, and still he didn't say a word to condemn me for going with deliberate intentions after my mother's second husband. I put my hands to my head, feeling that deep ache beginning again.

My Christopher drove away in the early morning, leaving me to fret through yet another anxiety-ridden day. Over the years I'd grown more and more dependent on him, when once I'd prided myself for being independent, able to go my own way and not need anyone nearly as badly as they needed me. How selfishly I'd looked at life when I was younger. My needs had come first. Now it was the needs of others that came first.

Restlessly I roamed about, checking on all those I loved, staring at Bart when he came home, dying to throw all kinds of accusations his way, yet somehow feeling so much pity for him. He sat behind his desk, looking absolutely the perfect young executive. No guilt. No shame as he bargained, manipulated, negotiated, making more and more money just by talking over the telephone, or communicating with his computer. He looked up at me and smiled. A genuine smile of welcome.

'When Joel told me Cindy had decided to leave, it cheered my whole day, and I still feel that way.' Yet what was that oddness behind the darkness of his eyes? Why did he look at me as if soon he'd cry? 'Bart, if ever you want to confide in me – '

'I have nothing to confide, Mother.'

His voice was soft. Too soft, as if he spoke to someone that would soon be gone – forever gone.

'You may not know this, Bart, but the man you so hate, my brother and your uncle, has done the best he could to be a good father replacement.'

Shaking his head, he denied this. 'To do his best would have been abandoning his relationship with you, his sister, and he hasn't done that. I could have loved him if he'd only stayed my uncle. You should have known better than try to deceive me. You should know by now all children grow up to ask questions and remember well scenes you think they'll soon forget, but those children don't forget. They take those memories and bury them deep in their brains, to bring them out later when they can understand. And all that I can remember tells me that the two of you are bound in ways that seem unbreakable, except by death.

My heart quickened. On the roof of Foxworth Hall, under the sun and stars, Chris and I had sworn certain vows to see us through eternity. How young and foolish to create our own traps . . .

Tears could so easily flood my eyes lately. 'Bart – how could I live without him?'

'Oh, Mother, you could! You know you could. Let him go, Mother. Give to me the kind of decent, God-fearing mother I've always needed to keep my sanity.'

'And if I can't say goodbye to Chris – what then, Bart?'

His dark head bowed. 'God help you, Mother. I won't be able to. God help me, too. Even so, I do have to think of my own eternal soul.'

I went away.

All through the night I dreamed of fire, of such terrible things I woke up, not clearly remembering anything but the fire, yet there had been something else, some dreadful remembered thing I kept shoving to the back of my mind. What? What? Unable to overcome the inexplicable fatigue I felt, I drifted back to sleep and fell again immediately into a continuing nightmare where I saw Jory's twins as Cory and Carrie, carried off to be devoured. For the second time I forced myself awake. Forced myself to get up, although my head ached badly.

I felt woozy-headed, half drunk as I set about my daily chores. At my heels the twins tagged behind, asking a thousand and one questions, in particular Deirdre. She reminded me so much of Carrie with her why? where? and whose is it? And how did it come to be his or hers or its? Jibberty-jabber, chitter-chat, on and on as Darren poked into closets, pulled open drawers, investigated envelopes, leafed through magazines and in the process ruined them for reading, making me say, 'Cory, put those down! They belong to your grandfather and he likes to read the writing even if you don't like anything but the pictures. Carrie, would you please be quiet for just five minutes? Just five?' That, of course, drew another question that wanted to know who was Cory and who was Carrie, and why was I always calling them those funny names?

Finally Toni came to relieve me of the too inquisitive children. 'Sorry, Cathy, but Jory wanted me to model for him in the garden today before all the roses die . . .'

Before all the roses die? I stared at her, then shook my head, thinking I was reading too much into ordinary words. The roses would live until a heavy freeze came, and winter was months away.

Around two in the afternoon, the telephone in my room rang. I'd just laid down to rest. It was Chris, 'Darling, I can't stop worrying about what might happen. I think your fears are getting to me. Have patience. I'll be seeing you in an hour. Are you all right?'

'Why wouldn't I be all right?'

'Just checking. I've had a bad feeling. I love you.'

'I love you, too.'

The twins were restless, not wanting to play in the sandbox, not wanting to do one thing I suggested.

'Dee-dee don't like jump rope,' said Deirdre, who couldn't pronounce her name correctly and didn't really want to. The more we tried to teach her the correct way, the more she lisped. She had Carrie's stubbornness. Just as Darren was more than willing to follow where she led, and he'd lisp when she did. And what difference did it make if a little boy his age played house?

I put the twins down for their naps. They noisily objected and didn't stop until Toni came in and read to them a story she'd promised she'd read – when I'd just read the same blasted story three times! Soon they were asleep in their pretty room with the draperies drawn. How sweet they looked, turned on their sides to face one another, just as Cory and Carrie had done.

In my own room, after checking on Jory, who was busy reading a book on how to strengthen certain lower sexual muscles, I turned to my neglected manuscript and brought it up to date. When I grew tired, distracted by the absolute silence in the house, I went to waken the twins.

They were not in their small beds!

Jory and Toni were on the terrace, both lying on their sides on the quilted exercise mat. They were embracing, kissing long and passionately. 'Sorry to interrupt,' I said, feeling ashamed I had to intrude on their privacy and ruin what had to be a wonderful experience for Jory – and for her. Where are the twins?'

'We thought they were with you,' said Jory, winking at me before he turned back to Toni. 'Run find them, Mom . . . I'm busy with today's lesson.'

I used the quickest way to reach the chapel. Through all the gardens I hurried, glancing uneasily at the woods that hid the cemetery. Tree shadows on the ground were beginning to stretch out and cross one another as I neared the chapel door. A strange scent was wafted on the warm summer breezes. Incense. I ran on, reaching the chapel quite out of breath, with my heart pounding. An organ had been installed since I was here last. I stole as quietly as possible into the chapel.

Joel was seated at the organ playing beautifully, showing that once he had been truly a professional musician with remarkable ability. Bart stood up to sing. I relaxed when I saw the twins in the front pew, looking content as they stared up at their uncle, who sang so well it almost stole my fear and gave me peace.

The hymn ended. Automatically the twins went down on their knees and placed their small palms beneath their chins. They seemed cherubs – or lambs for the slaughter.

Why was I thinking that? This was a holy place.

'And lo, though we walk through the valley of the shadow of death, we will fear no evil . . .' spoke Bart, now on his knees. 'Repeat after me, Darren, Deirdre.'

'And lo, though we walk through the valley of the shadow of death, we will fear no evil,' obeyed Deirdre, her high-pitched, small voice leading the way for Darren to follow.

'For thou art with me . . .' instructed Bart.

'For thou art with me . . .'

'Thy rod and thy staff shall comfort me.'

'Thy rod and thy staff shall comfort me.'

I stepped forward. 'Bart, what the devil are you doing? This is not Sunday, nor has anyone died.'

His bowed head raised. His dark eyes met mine and held such sorrow. 'Leave, mother, please.'

I ran to the children, who jumped up. I gathered them into my arms. 'We don't like it here,' whispered Deirdre. 'Hate here.'

Joel had risen to his feet. He stood tall and lean in the shadows, with colours from the stained glass falling on his long, gaunt face. He said not a word, just looked me up and down – scathingly.

'Go back to your rooms, Mother, please, please.'

'You have no right to teach these children fear of God. When you teach religion, Bart, you speak of God's love, not his wrath.'

'They have no fear of God, Mother. You speak of your own fear.'

I began to back away, pulling the twins with me. 'Someday you are going to understand about love, Bart. You are going to find out it doesn't come because you want it, or need it. It's yours only when you earn it. It comes to you when you least expect it, walks in the door and closes it quietly and when it's right, it stays. You don't plot to find it. Or seduce to try and make it happen. You have to deserve it, or you'll never have anyone who will stay long enough.'

His dark eyes looked bleak. He stood, towering up there; then he advanced, taking the three steps down.

'We are all leaving, Bart. That should delight you. None of us will come back to bother you again. Jory and Toni will go with us. You will have come into your own. Every room of this mammoth lonely Foxworth Hall will be all yours. If you wish, Chris will turn over the trusteeship to Joel until you are thirty-five.'

For a moment, a brief illuminating moment, fear lit up Bart's face, just as jubilance lit up Joel's watery eyes.

'Have Chris turn the trusteeship over to my attorney,' Bart said quickly.

'Yes, if that's what you want.' I smiled at Joel, whose face then turned. He shot Bart a hard look of disappointment, confirming my suspicions – he was angry because Bart would take what might have been his . . .

'By morning we will be gone, all of us,' I whispered hoarsely.

'Yes, Mother. I wish you godspeed and good luck.'

I stared at my second son, who stood three feet from me. Where had I heard that said last? Oh, oh . . . so very long ago. The tall conductor on the night train that brought us here as children. He'd stood on the steps of the sleeper train and called that back to us, and the train had sounded a mournful goodbye whistle.

It came to me as I met Bart's brooding gaze that I should speak my parting words now, in this chapel of his building, and forget about saying anything tomorrow when I was likely to cry.

He spoke first. 'Mothers always seem to run and leave the sons to suffer. Why are you deserting me?'

The tone of his throaty voice, full of pain, filled me with suffering. Still I said what I had to say. 'Because, you deserted me years ago,' I answered brokenly. 'I love you, Bart. I've always loved you, though you don't want to believe that. Chris loves you. But you don't want his love. You tell yourself each day you live that your own natural father would have been a better father – but you don't know that he would have been. He wasn't faithful to his wife, my mother – and I wasn't his first dalliance. I don't want to speak disrespectfully of a man whom I loved very much at the time, but he wasn't the same kind of man Chris is. He wouldn't have given you so much of himself.'

The sun through the windows turned Bart's face fire-red. His head moved from side to side. Tormented again. At his sides his hands clenched into tight fists. 'Don't say one word more!' he shouted. 'He's the father I want, have always wanted! Chris has given me nothing but shame and embarrassment. Get out! I'm glad you're leaving. Take your filth with you and forget I exist!'

Hours passed, and still Chris didn't show. I called the university lab. His secretary said he'd left three hours ago. 'He should have been there, Mrs Sheffield.'

Immediately thoughts of my own father came to torment me. An accident on the highway. Were we duplicating our mother's act in reverse, running away from, not to, Foxworth Hall? Tick-tock went the clocks. Thumpity-thump-thump went my heartbeats. Nursery rhymes I had to read so the twins would sleep and stop asking questions. Little Tommy Tucker, sing for your supper . . . When you wish upon a star . . . dancing in the dark . . . all our lives, dancing in the dark . . .

'Mother, please stop pacing the floor,' ordered Jory. 'You rub my nerves raw. Why this grand rush to leave? Tell me why, please say something.'

Joel and Bart strolled in to join us.

'You weren't at the dinner table, Mother. I'll tell the chef to prepare a tray.' He glanced at Toni. 'YOU can stay.'

'No, thank you, Bart. Jory has asked me to marry him.' Her chin lifted defiantly. 'He loves me in a way you never can.'

Bart turned betrayed, hurt eyes on his brother. 'You can't marry. What kind of husband can you make now?'

'The very kind I want!' cried Toni, striding to stand beside Jory's chair and putting her hand lightly on his shoulder.

'If you want money, he doesn't have one percent of what I have.'

'I wouldn't care if he had nothing,' she answered proudly, meeting squarely his dark, forbidding gaze. 'I love him as I've never loved anyone before.'

'You pity him,' stated Bart matter-of-factly.

Jory winced but said nothing. He seemed to know Toni needed to have it out with Bart.

'Once I did pity him,' she confessed honestly. 'I thought it a terrible shame such a wonderful man with so much talent had to be handicapped. Now I don't see him as handicapped. You see, Bart, all of us are handicapped in one way or another. Jory's is in the open, very visible. Yours is hidden – and sick. You are so sick, and it's pity I feel now – for you.'

Seething emotions contorted Bart's face. I glanced at Joel for some reason and saw him staring at Bart, as if commanding him to stay silent.

Twisting about, Bart barked at me, 'Why are you all gathered in this room? Why don't you go to bed? It's late.'

'We are waiting for Chris to come home.'

'There was an accident on the highway,' spoke up Joel. 'I heard the news on the radio. A man killed.' He seemed delighted to give me this news.

My heart seemed to drop a mile – another Foxworth downed by an accident?

Not Chris, not my Christopher Doll. No, not yet, not yet.

From far away I faintly heard the kitchen door open and close. The chef leaving for his apartment over the garage I thought – or maybe Chris. Hopefully I turned towards the garage. No bright blue eyes, no ready smile and arms outstretched to hold me. No one came through the door.

Minutes passed as we all stared at each other uncomfortably. My heart began to throb painfully; it was time he was home. Time enough.

Joel was staring at me, his lips cocked in a peculiarly hateful way, as if he knew more than he'd said. I turned to Jory, knelt beside his chair and allowed him to hold me close. 'I'm scared, Jory,' I sobbed. 'He should be home by now. It couldn't take him three hours even in the winter with icy roads.'

No one said anything. Not Jory, who held me tight. Not Toni. Not Bart or even Joel. The very show of all of us being together, waiting, waiting brought back only too vividly the scene of my father's thirty-sixth birthday party and the two state policemen who'd come to say he'd been killed.

I felt a scream in my throat ready to sound when I saw a white car heading up our private road, a red light spinning on the top.

Time turned backwards.

No! No! No! Over and over again, my brain screamed even as they spilled out the facts about the accident, the doctor who'd jumped out of his car to help the injured and dying victims laid on the roadside, and as he ran to cross the highway, he'd been struck by a hit-and-run driver.

They carefully, respectfully put his things on a table, just as they'd dumped my father's possessions on another table in Gladstone. This time I was staring at all the items that Chris usually carried in his pockets. All this was unreal, just another nightmare to wake up from – not my photograph in his wallet, not my Chris's wristwatch and the sapphire ring I'd given him for Christmas. Not my Christopher Doll, no, no, no.

Objects grew hazy, dim. Twilight gloom pervaded my entire being, leaving me nowhere, nowhere. The policemen shrank in size. Jory and Bart seemed so far away. Toni loomed up huge as she came to lift me to my feet. 'Cathy, I'm so sorry . . . so terribly sorry . . .'

I think she said more. But I tore from her grip and ran, ran as if all the nightmares I'd ever dreamed in my life were catching up with me. *Seek the tarnish and you shall find.*

On and on running, trying to escape the truth, running until I reached the chapel where I threw myself down in front of the pulpit and began to pray as I'd never prayed before.

'Please, God, you can't do this to me, or to Chris! There's not a better man alive than Chris . . . you must know that . . .' and then I was sobbing. For my father had been a wonderful man, and that hadn't mattered. Fate didn't choose the unloved, the derelicts, the unneeded or unwanted. Fate was a bodiless form with a cruel hand that reached out randomly, carelessly and seized up with ruthlessness.

They buried the body of my Christopher Doll, not in the Foxworth family plot, but in the cemetery where Paul, my mother, Bart's father, and Julian all lay under the earth. Not so far away was the small grave of Carrie.

Already I'd given the order to have the body of my father moved from that cold, hard, lonely ground in Gladstone, Pennsylvania so he, too, could lie with the rest of us. I thought he would like that, if he knew.

I was the last of the four Dresden dolls. Only me . . . and I didn't want to be here.

The sun was hot and bright. A day for fishing, for swimming, for playing tennis and having fun, and they put my Christopher in the ground.

I tried not to see him down there with his blue eyes closed forever. I stared at Bart, who spoke the eulogy with tears in his eyes. I heard his voice as if from a far-far distance, saying all the words he should have said when Chris was alive and he could have appreciated hearing those kind, loving words.

'It is said in the Bible,' began Bart in that beautiful, persuasive voice he could use when he wanted, 'that it is never too late to ask for forgiveness. I hope and pray this is true, for I will ask of this man who lies before me that his soul will look down from Heaven and forgive me for not being the loving, understanding son I could and should have been. This father, that I never accepted as my father, saved my life many times, and I stand here, shafted to my heart with all the guilt and shame of a wasted childhood and youth that could have made his life happier.'

His dark head bowed so the sun made his hair and his falling tears gleam. 'I love you, Christopher Sheffield Foxworth. I hope you hear me. I hope and pray you forgive me for being blind to what you were.' Tears flowed down his cheeks. His voice turned hoarse. People started to cry.

Only I had dry eyes, a dry heart.

'Doctor Christopher Sheffield denied his surname of Foxworth,' he went on when he found his voice again. 'I know now he had to. He was a physician right up to his last moment, dedicated to doing what he could to relieve human suffering, while I, as his son, would deny him the right to be my substitute father. In humiliation, in remorse, and in shame, I bow my head and say this prayer . . .'

On and on he went while I closed my ears and turned away my eyes, gone numb from grief.

Wasn't it a wonderful tribute, Mom?' asked Jory one dark day. 'I cried, couldn't help it. Bart humbled himself, Mom, and in front of that huge crowd. I've never seen him humble before. You have to give him credit for doing that.'

His dark blue eyes pleaded with me.

'Mom, you've got to cry, too. It's not right for you to just sit and stare into space. It's been two weeks now. You're not alone. You have us. Joel has flown back to that monastery to die there with that cancer he says he has. We'll never see him again. He wrote his last words, saying he didn't want to be buried on Foxworth ground. You have me, you have Toni, Bart, Cindy and your grandchildren. We love you and need you. The twins are wondering why you don't play with them. Don't shut us out. You've always bounced back after every tragedy. Come back this time. Come back to all of us – but come back mostly for Bart's sake, for if you allow yourself to grieve to death, you will destroy him.'

For Bart's sake I stayed on in Foxworth Hall, trying to fit myself into a world that didn't really need me anymore.

Nine lonely months passed. In every blue sky I saw Chris's blue eyes. In everything golden I saw the colour of his hair. I paused on the streets to stare at young boys who looked as Chris had at their ages; I stared at young men who reminded me of him when he was their age; I gazed longingly at the backs of tall, strong-looking men with blond hair going grey, wistfully hoping they'd turn and I'd see Chris smile at me again. They did turn sometimes, as if they felt the yearning hot blaze of my eyes, and I'd turn away my eyes, for they weren't him, not ever him.

I roamed the woods, the hills, feeling him beside me, just out of reach, but still beside me.

As I walked on and on alone, but for Chris's spirit, it came to me that there was a pattern in our lives, and nothing that had happened was coincidental.

In all ways possible Bart did what he could to bring me back to myself, and I smiled, forced myself to laugh, and in so doing I gave him peace and the confidence he'd always needed to give him a feeling of value.

Yet, yet, who and what was I now that Bart had found himself? That feeling of knowing the pattern grew and grew as I sat often alone in the grand elegance of Foxworth Hall.

Out of all the darkness, the anguish, the apparently hapless tragedies, and pathetic events of our lives, I finally understood. Why hadn't all of Bart's psychiatrists realized when he was young that he was testing, seeking, trying to find the role that suited him best? Through all that childhood agony, throughout his youth, he'd chiselled at his flaws ruthlessly, backing off the ugliness he believed marred his soul, steadfastly holding on to his credence that good eventually won over evil. And in his eyes, Chris and I had been evil.

Finally, at long last, Bart found his niche in the scheme of what had to be. All I had to do was turn on the TV on any Sunday morning and sometimes during midweek and I could see and hear my second son singing, preaching, acknowledged as the most mesmerizing evangelist in the world. Rapier-sharp, his words stabbed into the conscience of everyone, causing money to pour into his coffers by the millions. He used the money to spread his ministry.

Then came the surprise one Sunday morning of seeing Cindy rise and join Bart on the podium. Standing beside him, she linked her arm through his. Bart smiled proudly before he announced, 'My sister and I dedicate this song to our mother. Mother, if you are watching, you'll know exactly how much this song means not only to both of us, but to you, as well.'

Together, as brother and sister, they sang my favourite hymn . . . and a long time ago I'd given up on religion, thinking it wasn't for me when so many were bigoted, narrow-minded and cruel.

Yet, tears streaked my face . . . and I was crying. After all the months since Chris had been struck down on that highway, I was crying dry that bottomless well of tears.

Bart had hacked off the last rotten bit of Malcolm's genes and had left only the good. To create him, the paper flowers had bloomed in the dusty attic.

To create him, fires had burned houses, our mother had died, our father, too . . . just to create the leader who would turn mankind away from the road to destruction.

I switched off the TV when Bart's programme was over. His was the only one I watched. Not so far away, they were building a huge memorial honouring my Christopher.

The Christopher Sheffield Memorial Cancer Research Centre, it was to be called.

In Greenglenna, South Carolina, Bart was also the founder of a grant for struggling young lawyers, and this was called *The Bartholomew Winslow Legal Grant*.

I knew Bart was trying to return good for the evil he'd done by denying the man who'd tried his best to be his father. A hundred times I reassured him that Chris would be pleased, very pleased.

Toni had married Jory. The twins adored her. Cindy had a film contract and was a fast-rising star. It seemed strange, after living a lifetime of giving, first to my mother's twins, then to my husbands, and my children and grandchildren, not to be needed, not to have a place of my own. Now I was the odd one out.

'Mom!' Jory told me one day, 'Toni is pregnant! You don't know what that does for me. If we have a boy, he will be called Christopher. If we have a girl, she will be Catherine. Now don't you say we can't do that, for we will anyway.'

I prayed they'd have a boy like my Christopher, or my

Jory, and one day in the future, I prayed Bart would find the right woman to make him happy. And only then did I realize that Toni had been right, he was looking for a woman like me, without my weaknesses, wanting her to have only my strengths, and perhaps with me as a living model – he'd never find her.

'And Mom,' Jory had gone on during that same conversation, 'I won my first prize, in the watercolour division . . . so I'm on my way to another successful career.'

'Just as your father predicted,' I answered.

All of this was in my mind, making me vaguely happy for Jory and Toni, happy for Bart and Cindy, as I turned towards the dual winding staircase that would take me up, up.

I had heard the wind from the mountains calling me last night, telling me it was my time to go, and I woke up, knowing what to do.

Once I was in that cold dim room, without furniture or carpet or rugs, only a doll's house that wasn't as wonderful as the original, I opened the tall and narrow closet door and began my ascent up the steep and narrow stairs.

On my way to the attic.

On my way to where I'd find my Christopher, again . . .

EPILOGUE

It was Trevor who found my mother up there, sitting in the windowsill of what could have been the window of the schoolroom that she'd mentioned so often in the stories of her imprisoned life in Foxworth Hall. Her beautiful long hair was loose and flowing over her shoulders. Her eyes were open and staring glassily up at the sky.

He called to tell me the details, heavy sorrow in his voice, as I beckoned Toni closer so she could listen, too. Too bad that Bart was away on a tour around the world, for he would have flown home in a minute if he'd even guessed she needed him.

Trevor went on. 'She hadn't been feeling well for days, I could tell. She was so reflective, as if she were trying to make sense out of her life. There was that terrible sadness in her eyes, that pathetic yearning that made my heart ache to see her. I went searching to find her, and eventually I used the second set of narrow, steep stairs to the attic. I looked around. It surprised me when I saw that she must have, for some time, been decorating the attic with paper flowers . . .'

He paused as I choked up with tears, with regrets that I hadn't done more to make her feel needed and necessary. Trevor went on, a strange note in his heavy voice. 'I must tell you something strange. Your mother, sitting there in the windowsill, looked so young, so slender and frail – and her face even in death held an expression of great joy, and happiness.'

Trevor gave me other details. As if she knew she was soon to die, my mother had glued paper flowers on the attic walls, including, too, a strange-looking orange snail and a purple worm. She had written a note that was found in her hand, clutched tight in her death grip.

There's a garden in the sky, waiting there for me. It's a garden that Chris and I imagined years ago, while we lay on a hard black slate roof and stared up at the sun and the stars.

He's up there, whispering in the winds to tell me that's where the purple grass grows. They're all up there waiting for me.

So, forgive me for being tired, too tired to stay. I have lived long enough, and can say my life was full of happiness as well as sadness. Though some might not see it that way.

I love all of you, each equally. I love Darren and Deirdre and wish them good luck throughout their lives, as I wish the same for your child-to-be, Jory.

The Dollanganger Saga is over.

You'll find my last manuscript in my private vault. Do with it what you will.

It was meant to be this way. I have no place to go but there. No one needs me more than Chris does.

But please don't ever say I failed in reaching my most important goal. I may not have been the prima ballerina I set out to be. Nor was I the perfect wife or mother – but I did manage to convince one person, at last, that he did have the right father.

And it wasn't too late, Bart.

It's never too late.

Virginia Andrews
The Dollanganger Series

FLOWERS IN THE ATTIC
PETALS ON THE WIND
IF THERE BE THORNS
SEEDS OF YESTERDAY
GARDEN OF SHADOWS

When *Flowers in the Attic* was first published, it rapidly became an international publishing sensation, establishing Virginia Andrews as one of the most popular and biggest selling authors in the world.

Her spellbinding story of four children who spent days, and then years, imprisoned in an airless attic – just so that their mother could gain her inheritance – proved so irresistible that it was made into a chilling film, and was soon followed by four more bestselling books continuing the story of those loveless, forgotten children and the terrible effect their harrowing ordeal had on them and their own families . . .

Virginia Andrews
The Casteel Family Saga

HEAVEN
DARK ANGEL
FALLEN HEARTS
GATES OF PARADISE
WEB OF DREAMS

Virginia Andrews' second compelling series is the heart-breaking story of four generations of the Casteel family and their desperate fight for happiness. Again and again tragedy threatens to overwhelm them as they struggle to escape the awful shadow cast over the family by the Tattertons and their mysterious, magical home, Farthinggale Manor.